YOU'RE RIGHT NEXT DOOR

YOU'RE RIGHT NEXT DOOR

CARRIE MAGILLEN

Little Robin
PRESS

First published in Great Britain by
Little Robin Press Ltd, 2024
This paperback edition, 2024

Copyright © Carrie Magillen, 2024
carriemagillen.com

The right of Carrie Magillen to be identified as the author of this work has been asserted in accordance with the Copyright, Designs and Patents act 1988. All rights reserved. No part of this publication may be reproduced, stored in a retrieval system, or transmitted, in any form or by any means without prior written consent

A CIP catalogue record of this book is available from the British Library

e-Book ISBN: 978-1-913692-17-9
Paperback ISBN: 978-1-913692-18-6
Hardback ISBN: 978-1-913692-19-3
Audiobook ISBN: 978-1-913692-20-9

This book is a work of fiction. Names, characters and incidents are either a product of the author's imagination or are used fictitiously. Any resemblance to events or actual people living or dead is entirely coincidental

Typeset in the UK by Watchword Editorial Services
Printed and bound by Lightning Source LLC

Little Robin Press Ltd
Kemp House, 128 City Road
London EC1V 2NX
United Kingdom

Little Robin
PRESS

For Pop

My shining star, my rock, my everything

I love you to Neptune and beyond   (oops, that's Saturn!)

xxx

PROLOGUE

IF YOU'D TOLD me four months ago that I'd be lying on damp grass, clutching a bullet wound to the stomach, while next to me the love of my life lies dead from a bullet wound to the head, I'm not sure I would have believed you.

If you'd told me I'd be surrounded by three other dead bodies, I definitely wouldn't have believed you.

And if you'd said it was all because of an argument over a metre of land, I would have thought you'd lost your mind. I might have even laughed.

This is nothing to laugh about.

ONE

LAURA

Four months ago

TODAY's the day.

I'm so nervous, I might throw up.

It's my big break. The most crucial moment in my entire career. Everything I have done in my life has led up to this day: fighting with my parents to take GCSEs in music, drama, media studies and film instead of physics, chemistry and computer science. Convincing them that a university degree in scriptwriting for radio, film and television could lead to a worthwhile career. Taking an internship at the BBC, scraping by on minimum wage, and living in a tiny flat. Followed by years of rejection letters while working part-time for an audiobook producer.

Finally I've written something good enough to get me through the sturdy gates of Hardman Studios. And, once you've had a Hardman production, the doors no longer creak when they open. Or slam in your face.

Hardman has cornered the radio fiction market with productions starring the biggest names in television and film while leveraging Facebook advertising to garner an international audience of millions. Now, their radio fiction arm makes BBC Radio 4 look like Oxford Community FM. Hardman has always been a dream, not a reality.

But today I meet Chad Hardman, owner and producer of Hardman Studios. His commissioning editor liked the elevator pitch I submitted, and now I have to sell Mr Hardman himself not only on my script, but my experience in editing and sound design to bring it to life.

Yep, I am gonna throw up.

I don't realise my right knee is jiggling until a man in a crisp black shirt and tailored black trousers steps out of the lift opposite me. As he's walking past, heading through the waiting area towards the other offices on the twentieth floor, he stops in his tracks and eyes me sideways.

'Nervous?' His cat-got-the-cream smile tells me he works here and is very much at home at Hardman Studios. Unlike me.

I feign confidence, plaster on an assured smile and shake my head. Holding my shiny red presentation folder in my lap, I reach beneath it and pull my skirt over my knees, as if they're trembling from cold rather than abject terror.

He laughs. 'First time?'

I nod.

'Don't be scared. Chad Hardman may look like a wild boar, but he's actually a teddy bear. A furry old wombat.'

I laugh.

'Actually, it's better if you are nervous. It butters Chad's ego to think he terrifies the life out of everyone.'

'He does.'

The man lingers, his expression changing from humour to concern. Then he glances past me to the door of Mr Hardman's office, as if the solution to my anxiety is printed beneath the brass nameplate. But there is no solution. I have to get through this pitch, not only without throwing up, but actually sounding as if I believe in myself, believe in my play. Fuck, I do believe in this play. I just wish I were better at projecting that belief. In it, and myself.

The man says, 'You know how they say you should picture the audience naked when you're on stage?'

I nod. 'But I don't think picturing Chad Hardman naked is gonna help me.'

'Yeah, I wouldn't want to picture him naked either. But the point is to make you feel you have one up on everyone else in the room. You seem like a nice person, so I'll give you that one-up. I'll let you in on a secret that nobody knows about him. But you have to swear on your life that you won't tell a soul.'

I look left and right as if I need to make sure the corridor's empty before we exchange spy documents.

'His name isn't Chad Hardman. It's Chadwick Hardick.'

A schoolgirl laugh bursts out of me. 'Not really.'

'Honestly. And now you're the only other person at Hardman Studios who knows that. So you're sworn to secrecy. This is serious: you have to put your hand on your heart and swear. If you don't, I'll have to make you disappear – throw you down the lift shaft or something.'

'The lift shaft? Are you a writer?'

'No. Editor...'

There's a long pause. Suddenly, I realise what he's waiting for. 'Oh!' I put my hand on my heart. 'I swear on my life I will never reveal the true identity of Chadwick Hardick to a single soul.'

'Thank God for that, because I think it's a myth that you can open lift doors on to an open shaft and throw someone down it.'

'So you got me to swear on my life with an empty threat?'

'I'm a pacifist. All threats are empty where I'm concerned. Especially those involving a lift shaft and a beautiful woman.'

'Did you just say the words *shaft* and *beautiful woman* in the same sentence?'

'I did, didn't I? There must be something about you that brings out the worst in me.'

'Chadwick Hard-dick.' I start laughing again. 'Is he going to play hardball with me?'

'Probably. He is a hardass.'

'I should have worn my hardhat.'

'You seem pretty hardcore. I think you'll be fine.'

'I'll try my hardest.'

He laughs. 'I'm out.'

'Seriously? Already? You *hardly* put any effort into that at all.'

He has a charming smile that lingers after he laughs, a day or two's stubble, and warm brown eyes. His almost-black hair is so thick it stands upright despite its softness. It's styled into an organised mess that makes my fingers twitch with desire to run my hands through it. A blush lights a fire in my cheeks. It's hard to tear my eyes away from him – and the moment I hear that word in my thoughts, I smile again at our 'hard' jokes and blush even more. After a moment of silence, we both realise we're staring at each other. So he breaks the tension by asking, 'What's the pitch?'

I look down at my presentation folder.

'Ten-part radio play. *Game of Thrones* meets *Lawrence of Arabia* with a splash of *Yentl*.'

'Wow. *Yentl*? Colour me intrigued. How long is each episode?'

'Sixty minutes.'

'Double-wow. Six hundred minutes of Hardman Studios airtime. That's a big ask. Quite a coup if you pull that off. Is it any good?'

I grin. 'Best thing I've ever written.'

'Is it the only thing you've ever written?'

I give him a wry smile. 'No, but it's the longest—'

I'm interrupted by a man walking out of Chad Hardman's office clutching a folder tight to his chest. We both glance at him, trying not to stare. His mouth is turned down in a crushed pout and he's close to tears. Shuffling between me and the attractive man in black, he jiggles his shoulders as if he has to fight his way through, when the corridor is wide enough for all of us. We watch his back for a few moments then resume our conversation.

'Experience?' he asks.

I open my mouth to answer, but then I'm silenced by the sensation of eyes boring into the side of my head. I turn slowly, and the attractive man tracks my gaze down the corridor. The weepy guy has stopped ten metres away and is staring at us. We both stare back as his sorrow shifts to anger. With a storm in his eyes, the guy turns on his heels and marches away, disappearing around the corner.

'Was it something we said?' the man in black asks.

'I thought you said Chad Hardman was a teddy bear. What did he do to that poor man? I'm terrified now.'

'Honestly, he's not that bad. I wouldn't worry. Was one of us just saying something interesting?'

'You were about to grill me over my experience. Sound design and production for the BBC's *Close Encounters* adaptation that aired in February. Does that count?'

His eyes widen. 'That was brilliant.'

'You heard it?'

'Of course. Who didn't? Biggest thing on Radio 4 since *War of the Worlds*. I'm suitably impressed.'

'Thanks.'

He checks his watch and takes an involuntary step in the direction he was heading before the sight of me stopped him. 'Good luck. If *Hard*-dick takes it, I guess I'll see you around.'

'I guess.'

The man walks off and I watch him leave. I feel strangely abandoned. But then I just feel stupid and force the silly flutters down inside. Even if he was genuinely interested – as opposed to chatting up the first woman he saw in the corridor – I have no intention of getting into a relationship. This is *my* time. I have a plan and I won't let another man derail me, no matter how cute his butt is. I did that before with Shane. And the moment he got his feet in the door, he put them up. He lost his job shortly after we were married and didn't even try to get another. He didn't pay the bills, did nothing around the house, and basically expected me to pick up where his mother left off. When I finally got out of that marriage, I had no savings left and ended up in a flat even dingier than my current one. The neighbourhood was so dodgy, I was followed home three times and on the third time got dragged into an alleyway and had my handbag stolen. I was only grateful that nothing worse happened that night.

I seriously had to tighten my belt to get out of that neighbourhood. And, since then, I've been living on beans on toast to make rent. If this pitch goes well, the advance will keep me going for a few months, but it'll be the best part of a year in production. Even after it airs, it'll be a while before all the royalties come through. Two years. I'll be thirty-five by then. And only when I'm financially independent and stable will I even consider taking a risk on another man. I've watched too many friends get dragged down by losers like Shane.

There's no way that's happening to me again.

'Laura Hunter?'

I twist around in the chair. Behind me, a female assistant in a smart grey suit holds the door open. 'I'm Linda Meadows. Chad's ready for you.'

Shit. This is it.

I suck in a breath so deep I have to cough it back up. 'Excuse me. Sorry.' I grip my presentation folder too tightly, rise awkwardly to my feet, and push my skirt back down over my trembling knees.

Linda's office is large and airy, with a floor-to-ceiling picture window that looks out towards Oxford's skyline in the far distance. You can just make out the dome of the Radcliffe Camera and the weathervane on Tom Tower that touches the clouds. Resonance Tower, in the centre of Thame Square, is the headquarters of Hardman Studios. Behind the tower, there's a large industrial complex that houses sound stages, broadcasting studios, and other smaller office buildings. And surrounding the complex, a few miles out in each direction, are a number of small villages where the employees of Hardman Studios have largely taken over. From what I hear, working here means you're practically adopted by the Hardman family.

Linda sits down behind a tidy modern desk, and settles into one of those expensive ergonomic chairs in lime-green. Then she points at the door opposite. 'You can go straight in.'

I'm nailed to the spot.

Linda is still pointing at the door. After a moment or two, her lips lose the strength to maintain a fake smile and fall into a tight line. I sympathise with her impatience; she doesn't know that this meeting is the fulcrum for the rest of my life. And not stepping through those doors means not having to face the possibility of it seesawing in the wrong direction: straight down.

I glance up at the ceiling, take another deep breath and pull myself together.

'It's alright,' she says. 'He's a teddy bear.'

That description again. But I remember the miserable expression on the face of the man who only stepped out of Chad's office a few moments ago.

'Just be yourself,' she says.

Be myself. Honestly, I have no idea who that is, really. I'm a half-formed thing with a toe in this industry. Nobody knows who I am. So why would Chad Hardman take a chance on someone like me with such a major project? The attractive man in the corridor said it himself: sixty hours of Hardman Studios airtime is a big ask.

I was stupid to request this meeting. I could have pitched it to a small production company with enough clout to approach Hardman on my behalf. Instead, I've taken the risk of going it alone. Once Hardman says no, there'll be no point pitching to a middleman. It'll all be over.

And I'll never write anything this good again.

I search my mind for excuses to cancel the meeting at the last minute – I'm sick. I just got my period. I forgot another important meeting (yeah, great idea, Laura) – I can't come up with anything plausible. My mind's completely blank. I can't even remember the name of my own play.

'Miss Hunter?'

'Huh?' I glance over at Linda.

'Just picture him naked.'

A jolt of laughter breaks the glue between my shoes and the carpet. I throw the assistant a big smile in exchange for her kindness, lift my chin, take two strides, and turn the handle on the door to my future.

Chad Hardman sits behind a huge mahogany desk with a British racing green leather inlay. His wooden desk-tidy looks like an antique. Two fountain pens with two bottles of ink – black and blue – sit next to a traditional ink blotter, one of those rocking ones you roll across the paper.

Chad is old-school.

That bodes well for me. My play has all the excitement of *Game of Thrones* but it's steeped in Arabian history, myth and legend. All the things that get old-school fellows like Chadwick Hard-dick aroused. The attractive man in the corridor was right: his little secret has made me relax, smile inside.

Chad rises to his feet as I cross the carpet towards him.

'Laura Hunter,' he booms.

'Mr Hardi...' I stutter. 'Hardman. Sorry, I'm really nervous.'

His face breaks into the most satisfied smile I've ever seen, and suddenly, as if glimpsing my entire future, I know he's going to love my radio play.

TWO

GLENDA

LIFTING MY GLASSES on to my forehead, I wipe a stray tear while stacking packets of rice, pasta and udon noodles into the storage box I bought on sale in Asda three weeks ago. I bought it especially for Jason. It's his favourite colour: pale blue.

I wish he'd got the Oxford scholarship; I would have been so proud. Then he'd be staying at home instead of going all the way to Scarborough. But Oxford's focus is general computer science, and he wants to specialise in cyber security. I worry about him up there. He's a good-looking boy, so he won't be teased for his looks, but he hasn't come out of his shell yet. He's an introvert, and that will make it difficult for him to find new friends.

I don't know why he insisted on applying for the summer intake at the Scarborough campus. I didn't even know you could start university in June – I thought you had to start in September – if I had known, I wouldn't have told Jason about the lottery win until it was too late to apply. He would have been with us all summer, still working at Costa as a barista, thinking we couldn't afford to send him.

I tried to persuade him to wait – it's only nine weeks until the same course starts at Coventry University's main campus and he would have only been an hour and a half away instead of five – but he wouldn't hear of it. Anyone would think he wants to get as far away from us as quickly as possible.

That's Gerald's fault; he's so overbearing.

At least he'll have someone nearby. His friend Simon is studying drama at the University of Hull and has student digs in Malton which isn't too far away. Drama...what a waste of money. The only chance Simon has at an acting career is advertising acne cream.

I shake off my disappointment and turn around with a smile when I overhear Jason and Gerald talking in the lounge, on their way to the kitchen.

'What time is Simon picking you up?' Gerald asks.

'Nine,' Jason says.

'Pastrami sandwiches,' I hand him three in fold-over sandwich bags, one for the journey, and two to store in the fridge when he gets there. 'Are you sure I can't drive you? I'd like to drive you.'

'Leave him alone, Glenda. They can make their own way to Scarborough; they're grown men now.'

Jason had wanted to take an Uber to the station and catch the train, but Gerald wouldn't let him. Too expensive. Gerald caught me slipping Jason the cash, and told us both off for wasting money. The cheeky bugger kept it, too. That was my money. Jason didn't want us driving him there – too embarrassing – so the compromise was to drive up with Simon. It seems a waste to me. He'll have to pay half of the petrol and we could have spent those five hours in the car together.

Jason peers at the cut edges of the sandwiches. 'Sauerkraut and pickles?'

As if there was any chance I would have forgotten his favourite condiments. I nod and he stuffs them into his backpack with the bottles of kombucha I left out for him. 'Home-grown gherkins and home-made kombucha. I hope you boys know how lucky you are having a mother who feeds you right. Most boys your age are high on e-numbers.'

'Yes, Mum,' they both say in unison.

Gerald throws me a cheeky smile. 'She says boyzz, but you're the only one she really worries about. I'll be on Fray Bentos pies with Smash the moment the door closes behind you.'

'I don't think they make Smash any more, Gerald.'

'They do,' Jason says. 'Simon's mum makes it whenever I stay over. She hates cooking.'

'Really?' I'm shocked. 'You never told me that. After all the effort I go to making sure you eat right.'

Growing vegetables and raising chickens is no easy feat – smelly varmints. I make a mental note to buy rat poison and feed it to Simon's mum next time I see her. I'll mix it in with her Smash and ram it down her bloody throat. Her house has floorboards, so I can always stuff her under there.

'Glenda!' My name rattles from behind Tom's closed door. I raise my eyes at Gerald and Jason.

'Don't leave.' I point a warning finger in my son's direction and hurry into Tom's bedroom. He's propped up on his pillows, wafting the quilt and scrabbling around in its folds.

'What do you want, Dad?' I call him Dad to his face to remind him I'm his daughter. But he doesn't feel like my dad any more, so in my mind he's just Tom.

'My glasses. I can't find my glasses.' He points to the chest of drawers opposite the bed. 'Look through the top drawers; they'll be in one of those.'

'They aren't in the drawers, Dad. You never put your glasses in the dresser. I'll look in the bathroom cabinet.'

I'm heading for the en-suite when he shouts, 'No! They're in the drawer! The top bloody drawer!'

14

'You can't even read any more, Dad. By the time you've finished one paragraph, you've forgotten it and have to go back and read it again.' I should get him kids' books so he only has to look at the pictures.

Tom mumbles something under his breath that I don't bother asking him to repeat. Given that I do everything for Tom now, including all his laundry, I know exactly what's in every one of these drawers and what bloody well isn't: his bloody glasses! But I know from experience that if I don't put on a performance of searching the drawers, one by one, he'll have a hissy fit. So I do.

Tom's house used to be a bungalow. He built the second storey with a bedroom, bathroom and sitting room for himself five years ago when Gerald's company went bankrupt. We lost our house and all our savings to that stupid venture, and now I'm stuck back here, not only living with my father, but taking care of him as well.

Tom started going senile three years ago. Gerald hates me using that word, but what would he know? He doesn't know what it's like to watch your father slowly turn into a cabbage. We moved Tom down here last year after he fell down the stairs in the middle of the night looking for the bathroom. Bloody idiot.

It would have been easier on all of us if he'd broken his bloody neck.

I remember carrying this sodding dresser down from upstairs. Gerald and I almost broke our backs. I wanted to leave it in our bedroom, but Tom wouldn't have it. He's had this thing since he and Mum first got married and he struggles to part with anything she's ever so much as laid a hand on.

Tom's 'lost glasses' scenarios started last week, and this is the fourth time I've performed this shit-show. Only, this time, the far right-hand drawer sticks when I pull it open. It's Tom's man-drawer, with everything I couldn't find a sensible home for rammed inside.

I pull on the handle while rattling the drawer up and down a few times, and it inches open bit by bit. Finally, whatever was stuck gives way. The drawer flies towards me and I barely catch it before it slips off its rails. It's heavy – stuffed with used batteries, old mobile phones, and keys he doesn't need any more – so I have to quickly manoeuvre it back on to its tracks to avoid dropping it.

There's nothing obvious in the drawer itself that could have caused the jam, so I reach all the way to the back and feel around for the culprit.

My fingertips connect with paper, and I have to squash my arm between the drawer and the cabinet to get a firm grip on it.

I pull out an envelope.

Dusty and marked, it must have got creased and stuck between the top drawer and the cabinet's carcass. I unfold it. It's a letter with a fifteen-pence stamp on it, which means it's really old, more than thirty years. That's when Royal Mail started printing stamps saying just 1st or 2nd class, to overcome the problem of replacing all the stamps every time there was a postage increase.

I stare at the address and a memory comes flooding back. It was just after Mum left.

Tom never posted it.

'Glenda! My glasses!'

I stuff the letter in my skirt pocket, close the drawer and hot-foot it into the en-suite, where I find Tom's glasses in the bathroom cabinet. He always takes them off to brush his teeth and then puts them away in their hard case before going to bed. The upstairs bedroom is much bigger, with built-in wardrobes and bedside tables, so Tom had plenty of storage. He used to put his glasses in his bedside drawer before going to bed. Down here, space is tight and he confuses the dresser drawer for his bedside drawer. One sleep is all it takes for him to forget their new home in the bathroom.

'Mum!' Jason calls from the kitchen. 'Simon will be here any minute!'

I fling the glasses case into Tom's lap and, as I'm leaving the room, slide a hand up inside his quilt, feel around for his bare leg and give his weathered skin a good hard pinch.

'Ow!' Tom yelps.

It's what he deserves for stealing the last precious moments I had with Jason before he leaves for Scarborough.

Back in the kitchen, Gerald is saying, 'I never thought I'd see this day.' He obviously has a lump in his throat. 'Who'd have thought we'd win thirty grand on the lottery the day after Jase losing out on the Oxford scholarship? Someone must have been smiling down on us.'

'I bought the ticket,' I snap.

Gerald pulls me into a hug and kisses me on the forehead. 'That you did. And what a clever woman you are.' As he releases me, he disguises a sniffle by clearing his throat. 'Right! Checklist: keys, petrol money, computer, books, clothes...'

My mind wanders as he runs through the list, as if he's the one who thinks of everything. As if he's the one who makes sure Jason has all he needs. *I'm* the one who got that money for his university fees, and I'm the one who spent the last week pulling everything together at the last minute, not him. I've ironed sheets, tea towels, polo shirts and trousers. I've made sure there's nothing of Jason's left in the laundry – not even a stray sock – and I've folded and packed everything neatly. What has Gerald done? A big fat nothing, that's what.

'Have you remembered your phone charger?' I ask. That's the thing I care about the most: being able to call him whenever I need to... want to.

'Check!' Jason taps the backpack resting on the kitchen counter.

'Well,' I say, 'if you've forgotten anything, I can always drive up.'

'Mum, it's five hours. If I've forgotten anything you can stick it in the post.'

I shrug. He can say what he likes; I won't be sticking anything in the post.

A horn beeps outside.

'Right, that's it, then.' Jason puts his arms around his father.

'Did you say goodbye to Grandad?' Gerald asks.

'Of course. He was a bit out of it, though. Don't think he knew it was me.'

'It's important anyway,' Gerald says. 'Whether he recognises you or not, he's still your grandad.'

I pull Jason in close and hold on tight until he wriggles free. Then I follow him through the lounge and hall, all the way to the front door, where he gathers up his bags.

'Let me help you,' Gerald says.

'I've got it,' Jason snaps. It's not like him to snap at us, and when he realises we're both staring at him he adds, 'Must run. Simon's waiting.'

'We'd like to wave you off,' I say. 'And say hello to Simon.'

Jason checks his watch. 'Better not. We're running late. Besides, if you wave me off, I'll only cry – 'barrassing.'

'Alright, then.' I hug him again, letting go even more reluctantly this time. Then Gerald shakes his hand. I think it's the first time he's ever done that.

'Bye, then.' Jason shuffles backwards out of the door and I can't decide if he's being weird because this is as strange for him as it is for us, or if there's something more going on. 'See you in a few weeks.' And then the door slams in our faces.

Gerald and I look at each other, brows furrowed.

'Backpack!' I dash back out to the kitchen shouting behind me. 'You stop them.'

The front door creaks, but I'm half hoping Gerald won't be quick enough to prevent them driving away. If he misses them, I'll have to follow Jason up to Scarborough.

When I get to the porch, carrying his backpack, Gerald is standing in front of a red Volvo. From the back seat, Jason stares through the window, mouth turned down. I thought Simon drove a white Golf.

'Get out,' Gerald spits through his teeth.

Jason opens the door. 'Dad... it's already paid for.'

'How?'

'I saved up my pocket money.'

That must be true, I think, because Jason didn't get the money from me. What Gerald took was almost the last of it.

Gerald points an angry finger at the driver as if he's in on it somehow. 'And now you're wasting it on Ubers and a train?'

Reluctantly climbing out of the car, Jason says, 'You just won the lottery, for fuck's sake, and I can't take an Uber?'

Gerald clips him across the back of the head. 'Potty mouth! You know that money barely covers your first two years' fees and accommodation. What about books, food, mobile phone costs? I have no idea how we'll pay for year three, we'll really have to tighten our belts, and we're doing it for you! Where's Simon?'

'He's in Hull. His term's already started.'

'Get inside!'

Jason skulks around the car to the boot. As he's taking his bags out, Gerald opens the passenger-side door, leans in, and says something to the driver. A few seconds later, the car pulls away and Gerald storms up the path, pushing Jason along in front of him.

I wrap my arms around my son's shoulders and usher him back inside. I'm not angry; now we'll have another five hours together.

'Dad!' Jason pleads as Gerald slams the front door. 'I only wanted—'

'I don't care what you wanted. You never lie to me, do you understand? I didn't bring you up to be a liar. I'll drive you. We can talk about this in the car.'

'Gerald,' I say. 'Come on. It was only a little white lie.'
'Glenda!'

I hang my head. There's no point trying to talk to Gerald when he's like this. I reach for the coat rack where my jacket and handbag hang behind the door.

'You don't need to come,' Gerald says.

'What?! Of course I do.'

'No.' Gerald's firm. 'I want to have a word with my son.'

Five hours is a bloody long word. But I don't say that.

Gerald grabs his keys and wallet from the hall table, and before I even have the opportunity to protest, or even hug Jason again, they're out of the door.

When it shuts, all the air is sucked out of the hallway. Like a stone door closing on a tomb.

THREE

LAURA

In my too-tight skirt and too-high heels, I skate-walk across Hardman Studios' tiled lobby. But in my mind I'm dancing, skipping, and when I reach the revolving doors I'm Buddy the Elf spinning around between its glass wings, screaming with joy, as if I've never seen a revolving door in my life.

The dashing man in black was right; Chad Hardman is a teddy bear. A furry old wombat in a wild boar costume. After years of education and training, cutting my teeth on small projects, and months of preparation for this one, I managed to impress him. We got on like a house on fire. What's more, he loves my project; it's right up his street, just as I suspected it would be.

Does life get any better than this?

Chad is considering adapting *Game of Thrones* for radio, and thinks my project will give him insight into the viability of an action-adventure epic: whether there's a big enough audience for such a huge investment. He said, if he's happy with my final production, and he can secure the rights for a radio dramatisation of *Game of Thrones*, he wants me on that as well. It would be sensational as an audio drama. I can already hear it in my head.

I've never been this charged up, excited, happy. This is as big as it gets. My dreams are finally becoming a reality; my future is right here, paved out in front of me.

Perhaps because my mind is filled with my big, bright future, the revolving doors are smaller than I remember, and the reality of navigating them falls short of my Buddy-the-Elf imagination. Instead of running in circles screaming with joy, I have to squeeze into the tight space and totter around, grateful for the handle to keep me upright. They're motorised and move at a speed faster than I can manage in these heels, so when I burst out on to the concrete-tiled entranceway I go over on one heel and my foot slips out of my shoe.

When I stepped into the headquarters of Hardman Studios it was raining, but now the sun shines down on Thame Square, as if the grey clouds of 'if at first you don't succeed' are behind me and I will never have to fight so hard again.

Like an island diverging a river, I stand beneath the overhead vaulted glass portico, pulling my bent shoe back over my heel while people file in and out of the building. As I straighten up, the crowd disperses to reveal a woman. In a tight blue trouser suit, she strides towards me with apparently no intention of swerving. Her heels are higher than mine, but she walks in them with the grace of a tap-dancer, and with her long blonde curls bouncing around her breasts she's stunning enough to cause a pile-up. Even I can't help staring at her.

In my head, there's the crackle of an old microphone as an Underground station announcer tells everyone on the platform to make way for exiting passengers. This woman should be aware of that protocol. Instead, she steams towards me as if we're in a game of chicken. One I have no hope of winning in heels I can barely stand still in.

Just as I'm convinced she'll walk right through me — is it possible I'm actually invisible? — she stops dead a few feet ahead. Is she waiting for me to walk around her? Slowly, the woman tilts her head upwards, as if something passing overhead is caught in her peripheral vision — an aeroplane? A bird?

Her jaw falls open, her mouth so wide it's as if she's screaming, but no sound comes out. The transition in her demeanour is so sudden and bizarre, it's jarring. It crosses my mind that there's something not right about her and instinct drives me to put some distance between us as quickly as possible. Yet, at the same time, my curiosity burns. I'm like one of those YouTube prank victims who stares at an empty sky just because someone is pointing up. Only the glass portico needs cleaning, and against a too-bright sky I can only see my dirty reflection.

Taking two steps in her direction — only slightly to one side so I can skirt around her at a safe distance — I clear the vaulted portico and look up at the sky. I glimpse something black, directly overhead, but can't work out what it is.

Then I'm in the air.

Flying.

Falling backwards.

No, not falling; I don't fall. Strong arms — undoubtedly male — wrap around my waist, and when I hit the ground I'm on top of him. My body weight knocks the wind out of him and his breath whooshes through my hair, past my ear. His muscular frame is so taut, it knocks the wind out of me, too. Something sharp cuts into my back, bruises my spine. And a barrage of questions forms in my head, starting with: *what the hell do you think you're doing?* But before I have chance to open my mouth, every question is silenced by a deafening, sickening thud.

Screaming, distant and quiet, slowly builds in my ears, and I twist in the man's grip to see where it's coming from. It's the woman in the blue suit; she screams at the top of her lungs as if she's being stabbed to death, when nothing is happening to her. Eyes wide, her mouth stretches and twists as she totters backwards and lands on her backside on the concrete.

Between us lies a pile of suit fabric. Why would someone have thrown that from the roof of a twenty-floor building? But, even as I'm thinking that, a river flows towards me. Slow and blood-red.

There's a shiny shoe with a white sock inside.

There's a mangled hand with a solid gold ring on its middle finger.

It's a body.

A man.

I'm about to scream as loud as the suited woman when I'm plunged into darkness. A large hand covers my eyes and a voice, deep and soft, whispers in my ear, 'Don't look. Don't look.'

The next thing I know, the same strong arms that yanked me to the floor are beneath my armpits, hauling me to my feet. I barely keep my footing as I'm dragged backwards through the revolving doors, where I'm crushed against the man's body in the confined space. And then his arms move to my waist as he holds me upright, herds me across the marble-tiled reception. But I don't totter this time; my feet barely touch the floor. Finally, I'm pulled through a door, into a bathroom, and a lock clicks behind me.

'Are you alright?'

Gripping the counter for support, I spin around and come face-to-face with the man who told me Chad Hardman's real name. 'You?'

'Yes. It's me.' He touches his chest with his fingertips. 'Mark.'

I do the same. 'Laura.'

'Are you alright, Laura?'

Mentally, I check myself over. That sharp pain in my lower back is still there, so I run my hands around my ribs to my spine. Everything hurts, but my spine most of all. 'I think I bruised something, but I'm okay.'

'Take off your jacket. Let me look.'

I glare at him. Did he really just ask me to take off my clothes while I'm locked in a bathroom with him?

'I didn't say strip,' he says. 'I said, take off your jacket. We hit the floor pretty hard, and you said you're hurt. I just want to make sure I don't need to get you to a hospital.'

I stare at him for a moment, vacillating. My female instincts kick in. I look behind me at the dead-end wall between the stalls. Then I glance over his shoulder at the door and remember him locking it.

Stranger-danger.

Only, after our conversation upstairs, the support he gave me before facing the pitch, he already feels like a friend. He certainly doesn't look like a rapist — Jesus, Laura, what do rapists look like? — and he probably just saved me from being crushed to death by a falling body.

'Fine.' I take my jacket off, pull my shirt out from my waistband and rest my palms on the counter, bending forward so he can look.

'Where does it hurt?'

'Here.' Again, I run my hand around my ribs and locate the pain at the base of my spine. 'I think my ribs are bruised, but it really hurts here.'

Slowly, as if doing it too quickly might startle me, he lifts my shirt. Then he sucks a sharp breath between his teeth before reaching for a paper towel from the dispenser. He runs the towel under the cold tap. 'You're bleeding.'

I wince when the cold paper touches my spine.

'Sorry, I think it was my belt buckle.' He holds the towel in place and the cold numbs the pain. 'It's pretty red, bruised, but the puncture wound's small. I think you'll survive.'

As the chill of the compress takes hold, the stark contrast alerts me to a hot spot on my waist: Mark's other hand. His warm palm presses into my bare skin. The contradiction of hot and cold combined with a stranger's intimacy sends a shiver through me. He must feel it because he whispers in my ear, his words deep and soothing, 'Are you cold? Shock can do that.'

I don't know what I'm doing. I'm acting like a damsel in distress when I'm perfectly capable of holding a cold compress against my own spine. I spin around, about to tell him I'm alright now and able to take care of myself thank you very much, when our eyes lock.

He's so ridiculously attractive. Riveting. And his lips are so close to mine, I feel his breath. His eyes brim with so much warmth and concern that my protests slip away along with everything that just happened.

I shake myself out of the moment. 'I'm okay,' I whisper.

Am I really, though?

I'm not.

How can I be?

Suddenly, I'm back there, standing on the other side of the revolving doors, staring at the open mouth of the woman as she tilts her head to the sky. I picture the suited man standing on the roof twenty floors up and wonder what happened in his life to make him believe he had no other way out.

And then we're both falling.

Him forwards. Me backwards.

The inevitability of gravity.

In my mind, Mark pulls me to the ground all over again, hands gripping my waist, as they were a moment ago. And, as the light goes out of the man, Mark covers my eyes, so I won't have a body, broken on the pavement, burned into my memory for the rest of my life. Mark saved me from that.

And worse.

With two more steps, I would have been dead. Crushed by a man broken in spirit and in body. A cotton-wool heart thuds in my ears, and I totter on the spot as if I'm about to fall again. The relived memory is so vivid, I burst into tears.

Mark doesn't say anything; he just drops the compress and pulls me into a hug, wrapping his arms tightly around me. I sob tears and snot on to his shirt while gripping his arms for support, and we stay like that for so long that either of us pulling away would be more awkward than remaining like this forever.

I keep my head buried in his shoulder, my voice muffled. 'Did that really just happen?'

'Don't think about it.' Mark pulls out of the embrace and runs his thumb across my cheek to wipe away the tears.

I'm drawn into his brown eyes as if his steady gaze can hold me in the now, stop the memories of then from crashing back to steal my equilibrium. I'm as aware of the space between our lips as of the two steps between life and death outside, so close the one draws the other.

And then, as inevitable as gravity, we're kissing.

Before I can make sense of the madness, Mark slides his hands around my bare waist and kisses me with such intensity I can't breathe. I've only just met this man. Perhaps it's the residual fear of a brush with death, but it takes less than a moment of being folded inside his broad chest and muscular arms to feel more safe and secure than I ever have in my whole life.

It's too much.

I pull away.

'Sorry,' he says. 'Not sure what came over me.'

'Me neither.' I stare at my shoes on the grey tiled floor, cheeks pinking. 'I think we're both a bit overwhelmed.'

'We should get out of here. Do you have somewhere to be? I don't know about you, but I could use a stiff drink. There's a pub just across the street.'

I nod. 'Okay.'

He picks up my jacket from the counter, wraps it around my shoulders, and guides me towards the bathroom exit, one hand gently pressed into my lower back. But the moment he turns the lock and opens the door, I freeze.

Without me saying a word, Mark senses what's wrong. 'It's okay.' He takes my hand. 'We don't have to go out that way, we can go out the back.' He points down the hallway to a door at the far end.

I'm glad he knows his way around Hardman Studios, because that one tiny glimpse of blue light from the ambulance and police cars outside is enough to break the dam. And, as he leads me away in the opposite direction of the revolving doors, the tears roll again.

The pub is cosy, warm enough for me to take off my jacket. I lay it over the back of the chair before tucking my shirt back in and sitting down. The sun illuminates the little round table in an intimate nook by the window.

Mark returns from the bar gripping six shot glasses, three in each hand, with the ease of a bus-boy. Looking up, it's like seeing an old friend, even though I don't know his last name. When he sits down, I tap my chest and say, 'It's Laura Hunter, by the way.'

He nods. 'I know your name, Laura.'

'You do?'

He places a palm on his own chest then pauses as if he's about to make a confession or reveal a deep secret. 'Mark Hardman.'

My brain's a mess so it takes me a moment.

'You're kidding!'

'Chadwick Hardick the Second. Mark's my middle name. But for all the whisky in this bar, don't ever call me Chad or this relationship will end abruptly.'

'Relationship?'

Mark rolls his eyes to the ceiling then nods assuredly. 'I'd say so. We've known each other less than two hours and I've already given you solid career advice, saved your life, held you in my arms and stolen my first kiss. That's more than most men do in five dates. And I think you'd call five dates a relationship.

We're victims of fate. I think we just have to roll with it.'

I laugh. 'You're just full of lines, aren't you?'

Mark looks right at me. 'It's not a line, Laura.' And then he doesn't break eye contact until I do.

'You know, relationships that start under intense circumstances... they never last.'

'Says who? Where do you get that nonsense?'

'It's a quote from *Speed*.'

'*Speed*? The Keanu Reeves movie?'

I nod.

He laughs. 'And you get all your relationship advice from movies where buses leap fifty-foot gaps on a flat motorway?'

'Harsh but fair... No – I'm just saying we aren't behaving normally, that's all. What we're experiencing is nothing more than a coping mechanism for stress.' I down one of the whisky shots, squeeze my eyes shut and squirm under its burn. 'It's when the laughter stops that you really need to worry. Or, in our case, the stress.'

'The circumstances have nothing to do with it. I was planning on asking you out after your meeting anyway. I knew, the moment I saw you sitting outside Dad's office with those adorable trembling knees. That's why I was right behind you when you were leaving. It wasn't a coincidence.' He laughs without humour. 'Though I'd planned to pretend it was. In reality, I asked Linda to call my mobile the moment you stepped out of the pitch. I was gonna strike up a casual conversation about how it went.'

He downs one of the shots and doesn't even flinch.

'Is that right?' I'm sceptical.

'How did the pitch go, anyway?'

I smile in spite of everything.

'That well, huh?'

I nod. 'He loved it. He wants to use it to test the waters for *Game of Thrones*. And if it's successful, he wants me on that too. Scriptwriter, editor and sound design.'

'Wow... So, Dad already loves you. He's never liked any of my girlfriends. And he clearly thinks we're meant for each other; why else throw us together on such a large project?'

'What do you mean?'

He points at his chest. 'Editor and director. Dad's promised me *Game of Thrones* as well, so we'll be working side by side. Seriously, it's kismet.'

I lift my eyes to the ceiling. Kismet. Could he deliver any more lines?

'What? You don't believe in love at first sight?' He's joking, of course. But then his tone is serious, heartfelt. 'You're telling me you felt nothing in that hallway? In that bathroom back there? Because my whole world turned upside down.'

I hide a grin behind my whisky glass, holding it against my lips long enough for it to subside, then take the shot.

'You can't pretend you don't feel it too,' he goes on. 'Even with a table between us, I can still feel it. It's in the air. And I just know you hate this table as much as I do. That I'm not the only one who wants to close this gap.'

I tilt my head to one side, weighing him up, then shake it in resignation. Because he's right. All I've thought about since I sat down is crawling across this table and climbing back into that feeling I had in the corridor. And then again, briefly, in the bathroom.

I want it back so badly, it burns as warm as the whisky.

And we both know it.

But his confident swagger makes me suspect he does this all the time. Maybe not the life-saving part but engineering coincidental meetings that end with him dropping the panties of every woman who steps into his father's building with nothing more than a sideways glance.

I'm not falling for it.

This is what men do. They chase with charm. And when the chase is won, the charm switches off with the speed of a circuit-breaker.

I say, 'Whether I hate the table or not is irrelevant. I don't have time for love at first sight. And I doubt Chadwick Hardick the Second—'

'Mark Hardman.' He points to his chest again.

'—would understand what a career-defining moment today was for me. This is my entire life, the culmination of decades of rejection, small projects and hard graft. And I plan to throw everything I've got into this production – every spare second. I won't allow myself to be sidetracked by a pair of pretty eyes and a cute smile. Even if they did save my life.'

'You think I've got pretty eyes?'

'Oh, shush.'

'And a cute smile?'

I lift my eyes to the ceiling.

'Look,' he says, 'you know Chad's going to assign me as editor and director for your script as well, so we'll be working together anyway. Maybe this is your career-defining moment and love at first sight rolled into one – did you ever think of that?' He points through the window. 'My flat's just over there. And I've got a forty-year-old single malt in the cupboard desperate for a reason to be opened. I think we should celebrate your win.'

'Don't you think you should be back there finding out which of your employees just threw themselves from the roof?'

He pulls his phone out of his pocket and holds it up. 'Dad texted me, I already know. It was Donald Lovell. I didn't know him; I'd only seen him around. He's the guy who walked past us in the corridor right before your meeting, do you remember?'

'Yeah, he looked really upset.'

'He was one of our accountancy consultants. Dad found out he'd been skimming off the company and was under financial investigation. Apparently Donald had a lot of problems, personally and financially. Dad said it wasn't anything to do with Hardman. If I thought there was anything I could do, I'd be there. Right now, you're the one who needs support, and that I *can* do.'

I think about the poor man for a while, wondering what those personal pressures were that could have broken him down to the point of feeling he had no choice but to end his life. Mark's quiet too, turned in on himself, and I think he's wondering the same. We both reach for our glasses at the same time, knocking back the last shot in a salute to Donald Lovell, before slamming them on the table in perfect synchronicity.

In spite of everything, we can't help but smile at the timing.

Mark says, 'It's fate. I'm telling you. Maybe the universe dropping people out of the sky is a sign. Maybe Donald Lovell was really Cupid and he slipped from the roof while pulling back his bow.'

'How can you joke about it? That man's lying dead on the pavement. Don't you think we need a minute before jumping into …?' I stop, not knowing how to finish that sentence, not knowing what I was even going to say… Bed? A relationship?

Mark doesn't reply, and the time stretches out.

Finally, I ask, 'What?'

'Shh,' he says. 'I'm giving you a minute.'

'Dark humour in the face of tragedy aside, I can't believe how unaffected you are by this. It makes me think you're a psychopath. Are you a psychopath?'

'Do psychopaths ever answer yes to that question? Honestly, I swear I'm just as shaken up as you are. Look…' He holds out his hands and they're trembling. Neither of us speaks for a moment and then he adds, 'I can't help Donald. But at the same time, I'm not going to squander what he put in front of me. Something happened in that hallway. I felt it the moment I saw you. And something *seriously* happened in that bathroom. I've never felt like this. And if you aren't going to grab life with both hands after a brush with death, when the hell are you?'

He has a point.

FOUR

GLENDA

THE ROOF of the summerhouse in next door's garden looms over the shrubs at the back of Tom's, a blot on our landscape, and I'm locked in a staring match with it when Gerald bumbles through the front door. His coat rustles against the others on the rack and his keys jangle in the drawer, which thuds closed.

I make myself look busy, hot-footing it into the kitchen, where I put on the kettle and get two cups out of the overhead cupboard. I have to lift the door slightly to get it to close because the hinges are old and misaligned. I've never been inside Primrose Cottage, next door, but I bet Scott and Emily have a beautiful new kitchen. One of those modern shiny ones with soft-close doors.

'Did you help him get settled in?' I ask when Gerald comes through.

'No. He wouldn't let me. But I made sure he knew where his dorm was and drove him right to the door.'

'Tea?'

'Sure.' Gerald plonks himself down at the table.

I prod the teabags while the envelope I found in Tom's drawer burns a hole in my skirt pocket, branding an idea into the soft skin of my inner thigh.

'Are you alright?' Gerald asks.

I look up. 'Of course I'm alright. Why?'

'Because you've been prodding those teabags so long, the spoon should stand up on its own by now.'

'Oh.'

I look down at the dark orange liquid and wonder how I'd been lost in thought for so long. I add an extra splash of milk to take the edge off and hand a cup to Gerald before sitting down across from him.

He looks around the tidy dining area, then scans the kitchen. 'I expected to find you up to your eyeballs in one thing or another. What have you been doing all this time?'

'Nothing.'

'Nothing? That's not like you, Glenda. I think this is the first time I've ever come home and not greeted a whirling dervish. I know you're going to miss him, but you need to keep busy.'

'With what?'

'You've always said you wished you had more time for your hobbies. Now you do.'

'Gardening, knitting, watching quiz shows in the afternoon. I did those things to relax after running around after you and Jason all day. Now I have nothing to do but relax.'

'Take up something more challenging, then. Learn the piano. Learn French. You've always wanted to go to Paris.'

'You're missing the point, Gerald.'

'Well, at least I'm consistent.' He grins at me from across the table, but I don't smile back. So he adds, 'It's an opportunity, not a death sentence. There are a million more interesting things you could do... Volunteer at a charity shop...work as a classroom assistant.'

'I suppose.' Gossiping with old ladies or herding kids like mewing cats. Great plan, Gerald. 'I'll think of something.'

'And there's always the kitchen garden,' he says. 'You love that.'

I snort.

'I saw this YouTube video on vertical gardening. You could grow a lot more if you tried some of those techniques. I'll send you the link.'

'Okay.' As if my sanity can be grown from seed. What does Gerald know about sanity? About raising a child and having a purpose?

I look past him out of the window, at the roof tiles of that ugly summerhouse. The low evening sun burns the clay orange. 'It's up for sale again, you know?'

'What is?'

'Primrose Cottage. Four million.'

'Four million! Wow. Can you just imagine it?'

'No,' I reply flatly. 'Scott has all that space. He could have put that summerhouse anywhere. There was no reason to build it right on the boundary, so we have to look at it all the time. Tom put that shrub border in just after Mum left. I helped him plant it. It may be three metres high now but, if it wasn't there, it would look as if that summerhouse is in our garden, not theirs.'

'What are you going on about, Glenda? Scott built that at least a decade ago. It's never bothered you before.'

'It has, I just haven't mentioned it. In the winter, when the shrubs thin out, you can see the guttering on the back of the building. I have to look at it when I'm working in the garden.'

'First-world problems,' he says.

I glare at him.

'Why don't we take our tea into the lounge? I'll rummage through the board games in the hall cupboard and find something fun. We haven't had those out in years. Do you remember... we used to play board games with Jason all the time before he got his computer. It'll bring back memories. Cheer you up.'

I turn away and stare at the shrubs for a moment longer. 'You're right... We haven't played a good game in years.'

FIVE

LAURA

MARK CLOSES the door behind us. With schoolgirl nerves, I glance down the hall of his seventh-storey flat, attempting to get the lie of the land. Just as I did in the bathroom at Hardman Studios, I'm looking for an exit. I wonder if his windows have fire escapes, like so many American apartments.

Why don't British flats have fire escapes? Why do we have to resort to tying bedsheets together and shimmying out of the window? I guess us Brits enjoy fighting on.

I have no idea what I'm doing here.

We glance at each other for a moment, and that's all it takes for the narrow space between us to catch fire.

A split second later, I'm pinned to the wall with his mouth on mine. With our lips pressed together, tongues teasing, it crosses my mind that he's not Chad's son at all, but a random visitor to Hardman Studios who's lied through his teeth to get into my knickers. Maybe his name's really Kenny and he's the Copy Guy.

This isn't the sort of thing I do with random strangers. Ever.

Only, Mark doesn't feel like a stranger. At the pub, we talked for hours, then had an early dinner and carried on talking until, eventually, Mark looked at his watch and said, 'Have you seen the time?'

When I picked up my phone and saw it was 7.30pm, I nearly fell off my chair. The hours had flown by like minutes.

After seeing that man die like that, if it hadn't been for Mark I'd be a complete mess right now. Every piece of me would have scattered across the floor like iron filings. Instead, his magnetism swept over every part of me, scooped me up, pulled me back together. And when it came time to leave that pub, go our separate ways, I couldn't have torn those pieces of myself out of his grasp if I'd tried.

I was caught. Inseparable.

And, right now, this kiss feels too right to be wrong.

But then I've been wrong on so many occasions. I break away from him, second-guessing my decision.

'This is crazy,' I say. 'I've never done anything like this in my life.'

'Neither have I. Do you want to stop?'

I think about it for a second or two then shake my head.

'Is it me,' he asks, 'or does it feel like we've been dating for months?'

I nod. But then I feel like an idiot. Was that just another line, and I'm falling for every one hook, line, and sinker? Oh, fuck it! I just had a brush with death. And, as Mark said, if that isn't the time you grab life with both hands, I don't know what is.

He kisses me again and this time I dive right in. As the kiss deepens – shivering south – I run my hands across his back and pull at his shirt fabric, taut across his muscles. It's been a long time since Shane, and I'm aching to get Mark out of those sexy black clothes and feel his skin against mine.

In as much of a rush as I am, he yanks my blouse out of my waistband and runs his hands around my bare midriff, the sensation of his touch already familiar after the bathroom, yet so much more intense. Most men go straight for the breasts, but not Mark. He pulls me into him, wraps his arms all the way around me, and I feel safe again in his embrace.

Running my hands down to his backside, I push him into me and the seam of his trousers strains. There's too much heat, too much fabric between us, so I pull away from him and tear at the lapels of my jacket. I have to get it off, right now.

He helps me, tosses it aside, then dives straight for the top button of my shirt, sliding it out of its buttonhole with deft fingers before moving on to the next. I slip my arms between his and get to work on his buttons while we both giggle at our own madness. The second both our shirts are open, he presses himself against me, skin to skin, kissing me deeply, and we get to know each other with tongues instead of conversation. Then he drops to his knees, wraps his arms around my thighs and kisses my stomach, moving down from my belly button to the low waistband of my skirt.

I'm so wet from the proximity of his mouth that he could make love to me right now. But he takes his time, exploring the line of my waistband with his tongue while running his hands up the inside of my skirt, caressing my inner thighs.

Then he stops suddenly and stands up. I'm about to protest when he takes my hand and leads me away. 'Come on.' He pulls me down the hallway into a room at the end – his bedroom – which is all male: a low bed with a crisp gunmetal-grey quilt and matching pillowcases. A black Roman blind blocking out all the light from the street. Black furniture with a clean eggshell sheen.

He guides me to a box chair in the corner of the room – black too, with a white throw cushion – and sits me down while gently holding my fingers as if we're in a dance. I try not to think of Shane, but I can't help it; he'd have shoved me into the chair by my shoulders so hard it would have rocked on to its back legs.

Dropping to his knees again, Mark pulls me to the edge of the cushion and lifts my skirt before diving between my legs, caressing the base of my stomach while kissing me through my panties. I throw my head back and sink into the feeling.

I've never felt this way about a man before. I've never been touched this way by a man before. I'm used to men who dive straight in, all fingers and tongues, with no idea what to put where. Mark is slow, meticulous, and he's driving me mad.

Gently, he pulls the fabric of my panties aside with his teeth and kisses me softly, over and over. It's not enough. With the frustration of need, I grab his thick hair, and when I pull him against me, his tongue slides inside, stealing the last of my breath. A few moments later, I can't hold back any longer and come with a wrenching shudder.

As if that was what he was waiting for, he gets to his feet and lifts me out of the chair. Then he pulls me into him again, kissing me full and deep. I taste myself in his mouth. And his bare stomach pressed into mine makes me want him all over again.

Pulling back, I slide his belt from the loops of his trousers while he peels my shirt from my shoulders. As he lets go of my blouse, I release his belt, and they meet on the floor. Then he unzips my skirt at the side while I unbutton his waistband.

I'm about to drop to my knees, but he catches me under the arms and lifts me back up. 'Another time,' he whispers. 'I won't last. And I'm not ready for this to end.' Then he scoops me into his arms and carries me over to the bed, where he lays me down.

I inch backwards on my elbows and rest against the headboard, enjoying the view. Mark unzips his fly, lets his trousers fall to the floor and steps out of them. But when he peels off his boxers, goddamn you E.L. James, because all I can think is, *Oh, my!*

He's about to take his shirt off, but I stop him. 'Don't. I like it. You're wicked sexy in that shirt.'

'Is that so?' On his hands and knees, he crawls across the bed towards me, running teasing fingers up the inside of my thigh before slowly peeling off my panties, kissing me every inch of the way.

Tossing my panties aside, he dives between my legs again, but this time it's only a moment before his tongue is inside me and I'm moaning again. Then he licks his way up, over my stomach to my breasts. He kisses my throat, my ears, my mouth.

Hard against my thigh, he's biding his time again, driving me nuts. So I open my legs wide to let him in. But to my surprise he rolls me on to my stomach. Sliding a hand beneath me, his middle finger finds my sweet spot, and then he takes me and my breath all at once.

It isn't long before touching me inside and out at the same time is too much, and I have to stop him. 'This isn't going to work,' I pant. 'Ten more seconds of that and this will all be over.' I push him on to his back, sliding him inside me as I straddle him.

But that only lasts a few moments before he presses his palms into my thighs, forces me to sit still, and echoes my line. 'This isn't going to work either. Ten more seconds of *that* and *this* will all be over. Especially with this view.' He stares at my breasts for a moment before picking me up and rolling me on to my back. He's not that broad or muscular, yet he lifts me as if I weigh nothing at all, and seriously, I'm no skinny girl.

Kissing me with a teasing tongue while running his fingers through my hair, he doesn't move. But it's driving me insane, and I can't take it any longer.

'Please,' I say. 'For God's sake, please.'

In control of himself now, he moves inside me until I come a second time, with a moan so unrestrained that every occupant in the building must hear me. And it's only then that Mark finally lets go.

Lying on our backs, we twist our fingers together in a playful kind of thumb war. Slowly my brain unscrambles and, far too soon, my thoughts spin. Blue lights. Black fabric. White socks. A gold ring.

A river of blood.

I try to push Donald Lovell out of my mind, but something keeps pressing at the edges. A question. Something that doesn't make sense.

I let go of Mark's hand and prop myself up on my elbows. 'How did you know...? Earlier, I mean. How did you know a body would fall out of the sky? You were behind me, and even I didn't know.'

He stares at his lonely fingers, lost in his own thoughts. And all the time he's thinking, I am, too. I imagine the view from Mark's perspective. I'd only taken two steps out into the open, caught barely a glimpse of black fabric in the sky. So, from behind me, Mark wouldn't have been able to see a thing. How did he know? Is it possible he had something to do with Donald's death? How else could he have known Donald was going to jump?

Finally, my question sinks in. Mark gives a double-take and turns on to his side, resting his head on his elbow so he can look at me properly. 'Well...' The word comes out more like a huh? 'The woman in the blue suit in front of you. She was screaming. She was looking up at the sky and screaming. Jesus, it was so gut-wrenching, I can still hear it.'

'No. That's not right. She did scream, but not until afterwards. Not until he hit the ground. You'd already pulled me out of the way by then, so how did you know? You couldn't have known. All you would have seen is a woman looking up at the sky. She could have been looking at anything: an aeroplane, a bird. That's what I thought she was looking at.'

'Sure, she screamed when he hit the ground, after I'd pulled you out of the way, but she was screaming well before that. Don't you remember?'

I don't.

I think back to that moment again, picture the beautiful woman with her silent, gaping jaw. Am I remembering it wrong? Maybe I am. Maybe she was screaming.

We're silent for a while, then Mark asks, 'So, what's *the plan*, then?'

'Now? Do you want me to go?'

He laughs. 'No, don't be silly. I meant before. All that stuff you said about having a plan and no man with pretty eyes and a cheeky smile was going to derail it. What's *the plan*? And why would I derail it?'

'It's just...I don't want to get in a relationship with anyone. Not yet. Not while this project is going on, and even then, not until I have financial independence. Until I can support myself, comfortably.'

'That's just silly.'

'Excuse me?'

'Sorry. I just mean you talk as if life should be linear. As if you have to wait for one thing to finish before you can start something else. You won't get much done going about life in that way. It'll pass you by. Besides, this is a major project; it'll be stressful. Having fun in the down-time is really important.'

'And you're suggesting you could be that fun?'

He gives me a wicked smile but when he speaks, he's serious. 'Not just fun. I know we just met, but I'd like to see you again. A lot. Surely one or two dates aren't against the rules?'

'Well, they start out as dates, and then before you know it you're in a relationship.'

'And...?'

I suck in a breath, wondering whether I really want to get into this, now, with a relative stranger. But I guess, since I have no intention of taking this any further, he deserves to know why. 'It's just... I was married before. It didn't last long. Ended badly. And I'm not ready to get into another relationship, serious or otherwise.'

I tell him about Shane, about how I came out of the marriage with nothing and had to start all over again. I tell him about the dodgy neighbourhood I ended up living in, about being attacked on the way home. 'That's why this project is so important to me. And why I won't get into another relationship until I can support myself. I need my independence, and I refuse to put myself in that situation ever again.'

Mark doesn't try to argue. He just pulls me into him, holds me tight, runs his fingers through my hair. But, for me, the memories of how difficult everything was after Shane have flooded back. Much as I like Mark, I can't stay here any longer. I'm not doing this. Not with anyone. Shane was the same when I first met him, all charm and possibility; I'm not falling for it again.

I pull myself out of his arms and fetch my panties from the floor.

When he realises I'm getting dressed and not just going to the bathroom, he says, 'You're leaving?'

'Yes, I'm going home. I'll sleep better there.'

'Wow. I'm not sure how I feel about that. What if I'd got up right after coming inside you and started putting on my trousers...'

He has a point, but I'm determined not to change my mind. It's been such a lovely afternoon, and I don't want to spoil it by getting all serious, so I tease him instead. 'Oh, come on, needy girl, you've had half an hour of cuddles at least. Most men can't wait for the woman to leave. Basically they're just fighting to keep their eyes open.'

'Is that right?'

'Unless they're the possessive type. Are you going to lock me in the wardrobe, so I can't leave for work in the morning?'

He shrugs. 'I might. I've never experienced love at first sight. Who knows what I'm capable of.'

'Oh, shush with all the love at first sight. I'm not falling for it. I told you, we aren't getting into a relationship.'

'If you say so.'

I pull on my shirt and put all my focus into doing up the buttons, so I don't have to look at him. I know if I do, he'll weaken my resolve. That cheeky smile. Those warm eyes. That broad chest with its line of dark hair running down the centre, tapering off at his belly, then starting again lower down leading to... For fuck's sake, Laura! Pull yourself together. You're not doing this and that's final!

'You free Saturday?' he asks.

I look up. 'That's tomorrow.'

'Too soon? I can play hard to get if you like?'

I shake my head and laugh.

'Seven?' he says. 'Same pub?'

I let out an exasperated breath. 'Fine.'

Good job, Laura. So much for resolve.

SIX

GLENDA

'HEY, HONEY.' Fresh from his morning shower, Gerald steps into the lounge and catches me staring out of the window. The terracotta roof tiles of the summerhouse have been staring back at me for the past hour, looming over the thicket hedge. Quickly, I fold the unopened envelope and stuff it in my pocket.

He comes up behind me, wraps his arms around me. 'Are you alright? You've been out of sorts since Jason left.'

'I'm fine.' I brighten my voice. 'Speaking of Jason, he said he'd left some books behind. I thought we could drive up at the weekend.'

'Glenda...' Gerald lets go of me and turns to the dining table to organise the contents of his briefcase, which are always in order.

He knows it's a white lie. Although Jason almost got away with his jaunt to Scarborough on the train, Gerald can usually spot white lies from a mile off. It's a skill he picked up as a child: gauging whether his mother really was going to the off-licence instead of the bakery; whether the bottle he'd found hidden in the linen cupboard really was the last one in the house. It's the bigger lies Gerald struggles with.

The life-altering lies.

Perhaps it's because they are life-altering that he fails to see them. His subconscious turns a blind eye to true deception.

'Leave him alone,' he says. 'He's settling in, finding his way around campus, making friends. The last thing he needs is his mother breathing down his neck less than a week after starting.'

Gerald didn't go to university. It bothers him. He thinks if his mother hadn't swallowed all the child support, he would have been able to go. That he would have been so much more than the man he's become. He doesn't realise that an education wouldn't have made a blind bit of difference. He'd still be a sheep, just a better-educated one.

I didn't go to university either, but I wasn't interested in a career. I've always believed that men bring home the bacon and women take care of the children. I did my part, raised a smart kid who's on his way to a great career in cyber security. Gerald should have done his part too. Instead, he blew everything we had by starting a company that had no chance of success with a sheep at the helm.

When I was growing up here in Clay Norton, Gerald had seemed a catch. At fifteen, he'd come to live with an aunt, and being from outside the village made him more interesting than the boys I'd grown up with. I guess I was too young to know any better. I shouldn't have let those first kisses at sixteen turn into marriage at twenty-one. By the time he was twenty-eight, he was working for Lämsä Life – the same life assurance company he works for now – and, back then, twenty-five grand seemed like a fortune. Gerald was a catch. If he hadn't left to start that stupid company, he'd be a manager by now. Instead, he's back in the same position, earning the same salary. He's lucky they took him back at all.

Gerald's a compliance officer for Lämsä. One of those jobs that, when he tells people what he does for a living, they reply, 'Oh, right,' and swiftly change the subject. They don't ask about it, don't want the details of his day-to-day responsibilities, because the job title itself is a beacon of boredom. His job description should come with a warning that says: *Beware! Reading this will make you want to gouge out your eyeballs with a fork.*

I usually jump in and say, 'He makes sure the company follows government rules and internal guidelines,' so Gerald's poor victims don't have to suffer ten minutes – or more – of eyeball-gouging.

After thirty-five years of the same routine, while most of us would be going to work without eyeballs, Gerald's still happy as Larry. He gets up every morning, puts on his cheap suit, picks up his briefcase and leaves the house with that same benign smile.

And there it is now: that smile.

It's that hard-on for routine that keeps him inside his little box; he never pushes against the walls. Because he went back, grovelling on his knees for his old job, he's been passed over so many times that men half his age are on twice what he earns. He won't even fight for a pay rise to match inflation. So, every year, our lives get that little bit harder, that little bit worse.

Well, he won't keep me in a box.

It's thanks to me that Jason won't end up like Gerald.

I say, 'Bryan should never have got that promotion. It was yours.'

'What?' He looks up from his briefcase.

'I said, Bryan—'

'No, I heard you, I just wondered where it came from.'

I realise then that I've been down a thought rabbit hole and the last thing I did was lie to him about Jason. Bryan came out of the blue. 'Oh, it just plays on my mind sometimes, that's all.'

'Can't you let that go, Glenda? You know why Bryan got the job: he exceeded all of his objectives and got a five-star performance review. I got three stars because I met mine and do the job I'm asked to do – perfectly well, apparently.'

'Yes, but length of service should count for something. You only took a year out and, all told, it's thirty-five.'

'If managers were chosen based on length of service, Arthur would have got the job. And then he would have retired three years later. If I'd wanted that promotion, I would have needed to put in the same overtime Bryan did. I wouldn't have been there to help Jason study for his exams and it would have meant time away from him and you. You know how he struggled with revision, and if he'd failed his A-levels no lottery win would have got him into university. I like to think I did my bit to get him there.'

'He barely scraped in,' I mutter.

'Glenda...' His tone is soothing. He comes over and puts his arms around me again, speaking over my shoulder. 'We have a fantastic kid who's gone off to university...food on the table. We have everything we need. We're the lucky ones.'

'I know. I guess I just...'

'What?'

'Nothing.'

'It doesn't sound like nothing to me. What's going on?'

'It's the injustice of it, that's all. It keeps playing on my mind. Like that summerhouse out there.' I point at the clay roof tiles. 'I've always wondered why Tom never objected to planning over that.'

'Huh? You're not going on about that again, are you?'

'It's practically in our garden.'

'Your dad didn't care, so why should you? It's his house, not ours. We're lucky to be here. And besides, you said yourself you can only see it when the shrubs thin out in winter. You don't spend much time in the garden then anyway.'

'I might if I didn't have to look at that monstrosity.'

'Now you're just being silly.'

'I'm not. The house will be ours when Tom goes. What if we want to sell it? It'll affect the value of the property. All that space. Scott could have easily built it two metres further into his garden and it wouldn't have made a difference to him. Tom should've put a stop to it.'

'Glenda, for heaven's sake. That building never entered your worried head until Jason left. You're just looking for something to complain about, to occupy your thoughts. Boredom is the hobgoblin of idle minds.'

'I think you're mixing your metaphors, Gerald.' I wriggle out of his arms. 'You're going to be late.'

'Oh, gosh!' He bobs away from me as if driving to that mind-numbing office is a trip to the circus. I picture myself arriving at Lämsä to do Gerald's job and banging my head on his desk until I lose consciousness.

I'm sure Gerald suspects that if we'd met later in life – in our thirties, perhaps – I wouldn't have given him the time of day. But I've loved him in my own way, even though he's aged before his time; his hair is already white, receding far back on his forehead. Once, I bought him a pack of that Just for Men hair dye with the Tesco shop, but he never used it. I even tore out an article from the dentist's copy of *Women's Health* that outlined a procedure where they take hair follicles from the back of your head and stick them on the front. But Gerald just laughed and said, 'What do I need that for? I've already got you.'

Got me.

Like a guppy on a fishhook.

I don't have to turn around to know that Gerald is gathering up his leather briefcase, jacket and newspaper. Once he's picked them all up, he'll put them down again to search for his glasses. His briefcase thuds the kitchen table and, without turning away from the window, I say, 'They're on the Welsh dresser.'

Gerald kisses me on the cheek. Quickly. Perfunctorily. 'See you tonight.'

Then he leaves me cold, staring into next door's garden.

Those burnt-orange roof tiles stare right back.

SEVEN

GERALD

'Jason's settling in really well,' I say. 'He's got over the first two weeks – apparently they're always the hardest – and he's made a couple of friends.'

Tom doesn't reply, he just spoons tomato soup into his mouth, half of which dribbles down his chin on to the napkin I tucked into his collared T-shirt. I don't know why Glenda insists on buying him T-shirts with collars. Given how much time he spends sleeping these days, he'd be much more comfortable without them. Glenda says, just because his mind is slipping, it doesn't mean his propriety should as well. He always wore collared shirts before and, in Glenda's mind, this is the next best thing.

'Glenda is keeping your kitchen garden up,' I say. 'She made the soup from the tomatoes in your garden.'

'Hate it,' Tom says, mid-swallow.

'You don't like the soup?'

'No! The garden.'

'You don't! You've always loved your garden.'

I try not to disagree with Tom, but sometimes it comes out without thinking. I have to remind myself that even though his memory isn't reliable any more, that's not what's important. Whatever he believes in this moment is what really matters. Because it's true for him right now – even if it won't be tomorrow – and you wouldn't question the sincerity of a friend under normal circumstances.

Tom says, 'Not me. Her. Don't know what she's doing in it.'

'All sorts! She's found a real taste for it lately.' Tom probably just remembers Glenda finding it boring as a child. 'It keeps her busy, and she needs things to distract her now Jason's gone. Besides, we all benefit from it. Organic veggies don't come cheap.'

Tom snorts, then mutters something under his breath while eating another mouthful of soup. I don't ask him to repeat it. He's not in a good mood today, and whatever he said probably wasn't nice – I think I caught the words 'bitch' and 'dying' in there somewhere – he won't have meant it.

Tom's a great guy; he's always been kind to me. The best father-in-law anyone could wish for. I never forget who he is, even on his really bad days – worse even than this – when he lashes out with a quick punch or a kick. He's not as strong as he used to be, so they don't hurt that much. I wouldn't have wanted to take a punch from Tom in his forties or fifties. After decades of turning over soil in that kitchen garden, he was built like a brick shithouse.

'Shall I read "Cathedral" again while you eat your soup? We've finished the rest of *Where I'm Calling From* and that was your favourite story in the book. Do you remember how much it made you laugh?'

Tom slams his spoon down on the over-bed table. It clatters so hard against the rim of the bowl, it almost breaks it. 'No! Fuck off!'

With a deep sigh, I heave myself out of the chair. 'Your wish is my command, Tom.' I roll the bedside table away and pick up the red-stained bowl with a puddle of soup unfinished in the bottom. As I'm walking away, I can't resist sticking a finger in and licking it. At the foot of the bed, I turn back to Tom. 'She's a genius, your daughter. You've got to hand it to her: it tastes just like Heinz.'

Tom huffs something under his breath. Then he flips on his side, turns his back to me and crosses his arms over his chest.

'I'll let you rest.' I tap his foot a few times to let him know I care about him, even when he has got the grumps.

When I come through to the kitchen-diner, yet again Glenda is staring out of the window with an envelope in her hand.

It's been two weeks since Jason left, and she's spent most of it lost in thought. I think she's just figuring things out, adjusting, deciding what to do with her future now it's child-free. I think she watched the vertical gardening video I recommended, and she's making plans to implement that. I hope she plants more tomatoes; I do love that soup.

We still call it 'Tom's kitchen garden' but, since he built the extension for us, it's a lot smaller than it used to be, with just a few raised beds. It seems funny to call it a kitchen garden now; it's more of a vegetable patch. Tom used to grow everything from cornichons to cucamelons, but poor Glenda only has room for the basics.

I know she doesn't think it's ideal to be back living in her childhood home, but it was incredibly kind of Tom to build the extension after my company went bust. And it's wonderful to be back in Clay Norton again; it's such a lovely village to live in. We couldn't have afforded it when I was running my company, let alone on how little I get paid by Lämsä. I don't know where we'd be without Tom. It's such a shame he was hit so hard by that second wave of Covid. I think it accelerated his disease; he went downhill rapidly after that.

I shake off the memories of better times and wrap my arms around Glenda. 'What are you doing?'

She jumps out of her skin and quickly stuffs the envelope in her pocket, clunking my ribs with her elbow.

'Sorry, I didn't mean to startle you.' I readjust my hold on her and slide my hand down to her pocket. 'What's that?'

She slaps my hand. 'Nothing. And you didn't startle me. I was just trying to decide whether to plant comfrey over winter.'

'It's a bit early for that, isn't it? There's still plenty of time left for vegetables. What about some more tomatoes?'

She doesn't answer.

'What's going on, Glenda? You're so distracted. Does it have something to do with what you're hiding in your pocket?'

'I'm not hiding anything. It's nothing.'

'It's obviously not nothing. Why won't you show it to me?'

'Because it's mine. It's private.'

'We don't keep secrets, Glenda. If you don't show me the letter, I'll think the worst. I'll start to imagine you have a lover or something.'

'Don't be silly, Gerald. It's a surprise. For your birthday. Now stop going on about it or you're going to ruin it.'

Now I feel guilty. 'Ooh, I like surprises.' I give her a squeeze. 'I like your tomato soup too. Are you going to plant more tomatoes?'

'Gerald...' She ignores my question. 'If someone stole a penny from you, would you do something about it? Call the police, I mean? If you knew beyond any shadow of a doubt they'd taken it, and you could prove it?'

'What *are* you talking about, Glenda? A penny?'

'I mean, it's the principle of the thing, isn't it? Not the money. If they're okay with stealing a penny from you, they'd happily steal a pound, right? And if that's okay, where does it stop?'

'In for a penny, in for a pound,' I say, cheerily.

She turns around then, wriggles out of my arms. 'I'm serious. You're the one who's always banging on about principles...right and wrong...about how white lies are still lies, and about being truthful no matter what it costs you. So, you'd call the police, right?'

I laugh. '101 maybe. But not 999.' Then, since this conversation is going way over my head, I change the subject. 'I've given Tom his tea. What are we having?'

'Fray Bentos pie and Smash.'

'Sense of humour still intact, then.' And that makes me feel better, worry less about her. I hug her again, squeeze her gently. She'll be okay. It's not that long before Jason's summer holidays and he'll be home until mid-September. She just needs time to adjust, find something to get her teeth into.

EIGHT

LAURA

Two months later

When Finn belts out a cacophony of barks for the hundredth time today, I raise my eyes to the ceiling and fight the urge to scream. Another bloody delivery driver! But then the front door closes and I realise it's Mark. He's home early.

Leaping to my feet, I dash into the hallway and let out the rant that's been building throughout the day. 'Arghhh! How do you live like this? How can you work from here?'

I promised myself I wouldn't get involved with anyone until I had all my ducks in a row, and there I went, shacking up with a man a month after meeting him. Sure enough, it's only taken another month for my work to start suffering for it. What the hell was I thinking? That's the problem; I wasn't thinking. I let Vajayjay do all the thinking for me, and she's still doing it, with a wink and sideways smile. And damn her all to hell, because the past two months have been so much fun, I don't want it to end. Yet, at the same time, arghhh! I can't stay here!

Mark laughs, throwing his keys on the sideboard. 'I don't, mostly. I use the studio at the office.' Finn has rushed to the door to greet him and he musses his head. I swear, in just eight short weeks, Finn has fallen for Mark as much as I have. Sometimes I think he loves him more than me. Traitor. It's Mark's thick hair and stubble, that's what it is. Finn's confused. He thinks Mark is another Weimaraner.

'I should never have let my flat go,' I say. 'It was a mistake.'

Mark stops fussing Finn and rushes over to pull me into his arms. 'No, no, don't say that. It was crazy you paying rent when you were here every night. And you're so much closer to the office now. We'll make it work.'

As usual, Finn's head is pressed into Mark's thigh, and, having followed him to my side, he tries to muscle his way between us. Mark pats his head. 'I'll get the flat soundproofed if that's what it takes to keep you here.'

With a dog's head wedged between us, Mark squeezes me tight, but I keep my arms by my sides. I flop my forehead on to his shoulder as if the frustration of the day can leach out through my skin, soak into the fabric of his shirt and evaporate.

'Oh, dear.' He rocks my stiff body from side to side. 'This is serious. I think you're suffering from an acute case of plankitis. And there's only one cure for that.'

'If you say you need to take me into the bedroom and give me an internal, I'll...'

'You'll what?'

'I don't know. I'm too pissed off to think of anything funny. So I guess I'll just scream.'

'Actually, screaming is one of the side effects of the antidote for plankitis. Apparently, patients tend to scream, *Oh, God, Mark! Yes! Yes! Yes!*'

'Mark specifically? Not John, Jeremy...James?'

'No, just Mark. The contra-indications are very specific. It's a powerful treatment, but we'll have to risk the side effects. They say plankitis can lead to timberosis, and that can be deadly. Just a quick check with my endocavity probe and then—'

'I thought you diagnosed timberosis with a lumbar puncture.'

'Har har.'

I pull out of his arms. 'I'm serious, Mark. I can't work here.'

'But you said you loved my studio. That it makes yours look like something from ToysRUs. And Finn loves it here, don't you, buddy?' He bends down and ruffles my boy's velvet, liver-brown ears.

'I do love your studio. And of course it blows my piece of crap out of the water. But what difference does it make, if I don't get to use it because of constant interruptions? It might as well be Abbey Road for all the time I get to spend in there. If it's not the postman, it's FedEx. If it's not FedEx, it's Amazon or UPS. And if it's not a delivery company it's one of your neighbours coming to pick up their package. And every one of them has figured out I work from home and can be used as a parcel drop-off service. Look at this...' I pick up the box on the sideboard. 'They're actually putting us in their delivery instructions.'

Mark reads the label that says, *If out, leave at Flat 20.*

'Finn's barking his head off fifty times a day, and I'm up and down like a yoyo. And it's you, too. Do you have to order *everything* online?'

'I've sorted that. Everything's coming to the office now.'

That douses my flames, and I take a breath, but it's not enough. 'It doesn't matter,' I say. 'I'll still be taking in parcels for the entire building, with the neighbours ringing the doorbell every ten minutes to pick them up.'

I'm exaggerating, but it might as well be accurate. This project means so much to me, and I know I'm not doing it justice. There's no way this is my finest work; it's mediocre at best. I can't stay here.

Mark gets it, I know he does. And I love that we do the same job, because so few people grasp how damaging interruptions are to the creative process; nobody understands the effort it takes to silence your thinking mind. There's a long and winding path to creative fertile ground – you get so lost many times along the way – and every interruption, no matter how small, puts you back at the head of the path.

Creating a radio play is like daydreaming a movie in your head. You start the scene with no idea of what's coming next, what's going to happen, or how it will end. And when you hit on that spark of an idea – that perfect obstacle that will inject conflict and palpable fear in your characters – tension thrums inside you with exhilarating intensity. You've nailed it and you know it. You actually experience the emotions you've created, the gut-punch of a scene's crescendo that leaves you wrung out, cheeks burning and tears falling. And then comes the joy of knowing your listener will experience those same emotions. You've corralled the scene in your mind, each beautiful nuance a firefly in your imagination, and you're just about to write it all down when the entire scene dies with the tone-deaf squawk of the doorbell.

It's gone.

You fight to get it back, but what you cobble together is the dead corpse of the original. Your scene is Frankenstein's monster. It walks, it talks, but it doesn't function like the original breathing, spirited idea.

And you're bereft from its loss.

It wouldn't be so bad if the parcel were for you: a reminder not to buy anything online because you'll pay for that purchase in more ways than one. But it's always for someone else. It's Stan from Royal Mail asking if you can take in another parcel for Madge from Flat 10 because she's at the post office – as she always is on a Tuesday, paying her TV licence weekly by cheque. And instead of withdrawing cash for her Thursday morning shop at the same time, she'll walk into town on Wednesday for that, and I'll get her parcels for both those days as well.

I've tried to help her. I offered to set up her bills by direct debit, open a credit card for her shopping, but she won't listen to me. It's all cheques and cash. Jesus, I can't remember the last time I wrote a cheque; I don't think I even have a cheque book any more. But not Madge. Three times a week, she's gone all morning when her post arrives. And on those same three days, she's squawking my doorbell in the afternoon to collect them.

I suggested Stan leave them in a safe place for her, but there are no safe places in these hallways. Madge thinks someone will steal them if Stan leaves them under the lobby stairs, so Mark offered to install a lockbox down there, but she wouldn't have that either.

I know why she does things this way. She's lonely. And this routine fills her days with people to talk to. She has family – a sister with two daughters – but they're too wrapped up in their own lives to care about Madge. It breaks my heart that the most important people in her life are a neighbour she barely knows and the assistant at the post office counter. But Hardman Studios aren't paying me to entertain lonely, sweet old ladies in the middle of the afternoon, and if I don't meet the deadline on this project they'll hand it to a different editor and sound designer. They own it now, so they can do that. Chad Hardman has taken a chance on me, and I can't blow it.

'It's not just you,' I say. 'Madge kept me on the doorstep for almost an hour this afternoon.'

Mark pulls me back into his arms and kisses me on top of the head before running his hands through my hair, massaging out the tension.

'You have to tell her. Let her know you're on a strict deadline and you have to get back to work. I know what she's like but talking over the top of her while slowly closing the door in her face has always worked for me.'

I let out a despondent laugh that gets buried in the folds of his shirt. 'I couldn't do that. I'd spend the next hour feeling guilty for hurting her feelings, and then I'd get no work done because I was worried about her. Besides, I've heard her. She's completely different with you.' I do an impression of Madge. '*Heavens, Mark! I'm absolutely mortified to have disturbed you. I didn't know you were working from home today, I was hoping Laura would answer the door.* Then she vaporises.'

He laughs because he knows it's true.

'If you're a woman at home during the day, you're either a mother, up the duff, or a kept woman. It never crosses anyone's mind you might have a full-time job. And Madge has been retired so long she's forgotten what one is. She thinks the most important thing I have to do each day is wash your fucking underpants.'

'And iron them. You do iron them, right?'

I thump his chest playfully. 'It's not just Madge; everyone treats us differently. We both work here sometimes but there's this assumption that you have a job and I don't. Or, if I do, yours must be far more important than mine.'

'Well, I am the big Hardman cheese.'

'Oh, come on, they'd respect you no matter what you did.'

'Because I have a penis.'

'Exactly. Whereas I have a vagina. An echo chamber for mindless chatter.'

'Come on.' He takes my hand and leads me into the kitchen. 'You need a drink.'

He lifts me up on to the counter then goes to the fridge while I rant some more. 'You know, there are twenty flats in this building.' I count the delivery companies off on my fingers. 'Royal Mail, FedEx, Amazon, Yodel, DPD. They've all figured out that Laura in Flat 20 works from home. That's five delivery companies, twenty flats, a hundred parcel drop-offs and another hundred collections. You do the maths. It's an interruption every two bloody minutes!'

Mark hops up on the counter next to me. 'A slight exaggeration, but I get the picture.'

We're silent for a moment, then he adds, 'You actually sat down today and did those sums, didn't you?'

I smile: guilty as charged. 'I know I'm exaggerating, but you know what it takes to do this job. Even if it were an interruption every half-hour, it would still be impossible. If I have to stay in this flat one more day, I'll go completely off my rocker.'

'Hmm... we can't have that. I prefer my women sane.'

I look directly at him, serious now. 'I don't *want* to leave. The last two months have been a lot of fun. But I have to find my own place, rent another flat.'

He stares down the hollow neck of his beer bottle, turning it around a few times. I place a hand on his knee to reassure him this has nothing to do with how I feel about him. Then a broad grin spreads across his face.

'What?'

He jumps down from the counter. 'I just have to make a quick call.'

Moments later, Mark is talking quietly in the hallway, pacing up and down. I have no idea who he's talking to; the only words I catch are, 'Yes, I know we said next weekend, but if it's okay?' And, 'Brilliant. Yes, half an hour. Thank them for me.'

Then he comes back in the kitchen with an even bigger grin than the one he left with. 'Beer down, shoes on,' he says. 'We're going for a drive.'

NINE

LAURA

'What are we doing out here?'

'I told you. It's a surprise. I was going to give it to you at the weekend, but I managed to bring it forward.'

Mark drives along the familiar lane towards Clay Norton, a picturesque village on the outskirts of Oxford. It's the closest village to Hardman Studios that has any charm, so a lot of Hardman employees live here. It's almost a company town, as Bournville was to Cadbury. Over the past two months, whenever we've both been in the office on the same day, it's been our go-to place to wind down after work. I have to go in once or twice a week for project meetings, so we come here a lot. It's such a beautiful village that we've even come out here a few times on the weekends to walk Finn. There's a river path that ends at the pub, so we stop for lunch and a beer.

'Are you buying me dinner at the Dewdrop Inn? Is that the surprise?'

'No.'

'The Devil's Punchbowl, then?'

'Nope.'

I wait for him to explain but he refuses. So I test his resolve by trying to bore the information out of him with my eyeballs. Not a word. Not a goddamn word. And he's still wearing that broad grin he's had since I told him I was moving out. I can't believe he's happy about that, because he's done everything in his power to alleviate the interruptions for me, like having all his deliveries sent to the office. He's clearly up to something. And not being in on the joke is driving me nuts. I usually like surprises, but it's been the shittiest day of all time and I'm not in the mood for pranks.

'What then?' I can't disguise my impatience and he's clearly enjoying it.

'You understand the concept of a surprise, right?'

'I do. But you know I don't like them.'

'You liar! You love surprises!'

'Alright, I love them. But not today. Today, I loathe them.'

'Well, you'll just have to run with it.'

'You leave me no choice. I'll have to tickle it out of you.' I wiggle my fingers in the air.

'You could try, but I'll crash the car. And I give you my word that this surprise is better than the emergency room.'

I squirm in my seat.

Mark glances over at me. 'You really can't stand it, can you? You're such a control freak.'

We're heading for the Devil's Punchbowl, and we never eat there – the food's not as good as at the Dewdrop – so I assume he's taking me there for drinks. But then he brings the car to a sudden stop about a hundred yards before the pub car park and pulls into a wide gravel drive.

At the end of the drive sits a quirky cottage with a wood-stained picket fence. Either side of its enclosed entranceway grow yew trees shaped into lollipops. Its tiled, undulating roof has carved eaves, and, set back beneath an awning, there's a heavy oak front door.

'Mark...' I glare across the car at him. 'You should have told me we were visiting friends. Given me a chance to get changed and charge my social batteries. At the very least, you could have plied me with a few more beers. I'm not exactly on good form today. I'm going to make a shit first impression.'

He just grins even wider.

'Oh, for fuck's sake, just tell me what you're up to.'

'Come on.'

He opens the driver's side door and his feet crunch gravel. Reluctantly, I follow suit. After my day, I'm in no mood for polite conversation or laborious attempts at witty banter with Mark's friends. Don't get me wrong, the ones I've met so far have been really nice. But they're always posh and rich. And this is Clay Norton; property here is in demand and commands a premium. The cottage might be modest, but whoever lives here is definitely both.

Mark opens the gate and rings the doorbell while I stand back a little way, tugging at my T-shirt, wishing I weren't wearing ripped jeans.

A genial man opens the door. 'You must be Mark.'

I look from Mark to the man, confused; whatever their relationship is, they aren't friends. They clearly haven't met before.

'This is Laura, my girlfriend.'

The man shakes my hand. 'Scott. Come in.'

'Sorry about the last-minute change of plan,' Mark says. 'I hope it wasn't too much trouble. Something came up.'

'No, it's fine,' Scott says. 'Actually frees us up for the weekend.'

We step into a long hallway that belies the modesty of the front of the property. The ceiling rises over two metres, with a lilac chandelier hanging from the centre. Its glass columns shimmer in the light of a Velux window that takes up one third of the huge ceiling. There's a log burning stove in the hallway, set in an inglenook fireplace with a stone mantelpiece. Who has a fire in the hallway?

I'm about to elbow Mark in the ribs and ask him what on earth we're doing here when Scott says, 'This is the hall...obviously. And in here is the smaller of the sitting rooms. It used to be a bungalow, and this was a bedroom. But we added the second floor.'

What? This is property-selling talk. I glare at Mark, wanting to ask why we're wasting this poor man's time by viewing a house that's far too big for the two of us and clearly far too expensive. But Mark refuses to look directly at me; he just nods politely as Scott takes us from room to room, pointing out various features. There's a long dining room, big enough to seat twelve people, and at the far end there's an adorable snug with patio doors that look out on to a narrow courtyard garden. A moment later, we're in a downstairs bedroom as big as a five-star hotel suite with its own adjoining bathroom. I assume this is the master bedroom until Scott says, 'This is the main guest room. The master's upstairs, obviously.'

We go from room to expansive room where everything is perfectly appointed with vintage furniture, luxurious rugs, and heavy drapes. The kitchen has an enormous island in its centre and a huge range cooker which Scott says is staying because it's too heavy to move.

Eventually, we make our way upstairs to the master, which has two walk-in wardrobes, a fireplace and, right in front of that, a roll-top bath. By the time we've covered the majority of the cottage, I realise that if they abandoned me in any one room I'd struggle to find my way back to the front door. It's like the Tardis: from the driveway, you would have no idea of the scale of the house behind.

Clearly wanting to save the best for last, Scott finally shows us into the main lounge, which, despite its size, is cosy and inviting. Oriental rugs divide the large room into two separate areas, with another huge inglenook fireplace between them. On one side there's a coffee table surrounded by high-backed chairs for entertaining, and on the other, sumptuous leather couches surround a footstool and a wall-mounted widescreen television.

'It's beautiful.' The words slip out without effort, because it really is.

'If there's anything you'd like us to leave,' Scott says, 'we're happy to discuss it.'

'Everything,' I joke. And he laughs.

'Come on.' He opens the lounge patio doors. 'This is the best part.'

'I'm not sure it could get any better,' I say. But when Scott steps aside, my breath catches. Stretching out before us is a landscaped garden on two split levels, like something from a stately home. On the top level is a balconied patio with white pillars overlooking a border of shrubs and flowers. And on the lower level, there's a wide lawn with a fountain in the middle.

We follow Scott down the bullnose stone steps towards the fountain and, as we cross the lawn, I notice a soaring monkey puzzle tree in the far corner of the garden. Then Scott points to his right and I follow his gaze. Tucked away in a tall shrub hedge is an enchanting building with carved eaves and a balustrade surrounding a decked patio.

'That's the summerhouse,' he says.

I glance sideways at Mark and he winks at me. Suddenly, I realise why he's brought us to see this particular house. Not because it's in Clay Norton – our favourite village outside of the city and close to Hardman's headquarters – and not because it's the most beautiful cottage either of us has probably ever seen, but because of something far more crucial and important to me: that summerhouse. It would make the perfect garden studio.

Absolute peace.

Zero interruptions.

This is all for me. Mark's doing this for me.

Scott stops at the fountain and ceremoniously – as if he's never seen his own house before – spins around, opening his arms as an instruction for us to do the same.

We spin.

'Oh, my God!' The words slip out of me at the breathtaking view of the cottage from this perspective.

'Beautiful, isn't it?' Scott says. 'This is the true front of the house. From the driveway, you wouldn't know.'

The house has the dimensions of a stately home but the charm of a small cottage with an orange, clay-tiled roof that slopes around three dormer windows on the second floor. The chimneys are topped with Victorian clay pots, and the patio doors we just stepped through have white columns either side. On a second balcony above the patio, there's a quaint table and chair set beneath a sunshade, and I imagine Mark and myself sitting there in the evening sun.

I almost burst into tears.

And it's not really the house – I mean, yes, of course the cottage is insanely beautiful – it's everything else. Everything I went through before meeting Mark. Coming to terms with having to end my marriage to Shane. Traipsing from rented flat to rented flat in the dingiest parts of town. Fighting for space between a tiny kitchenette, a pull-out sofa-bed and my mixing desk. Struggling to make ends meet, constantly plagued by the pressure to give up my dream and get a 'proper job'.

At first, Mark's flat was a haven. Not only did I have the perfect guy, I had the perfect home. I had room to move, work, breathe. A proper studio. Now he's brought me here I feel like an ungrateful arse for complaining about it.

I listen for a moment.

Silence.

I'm so overcome by Mark's disproportionate response to my petty complaints that I have no idea what to say to him, so I keep as silent as my surroundings. Is he really prepared to go this far just to give me a peaceful environment to work in?

Surely he realises how excessive this is. Surely he isn't under the impression that I *need* all of this. It's far too much.

Mark is more than enough.

I knew that already, but this is a stark reminder. And seeing this place – Mark's idea of what it would take to make me happy – fills me with remorse. My outburst seems infantile in the face of this. In reality, all I need is a new pair of headphones, ones with better noise cancelling and – of course – to stop answering the door. After all, how can I expect other people to be respectful of my work time if I then disrespect it by responding to these constant interruptions? If I didn't answer the door, the delivery drivers would soon learn that I'm not at home to take parcels. And eventually the neighbours wouldn't use Mark's flat in their delivery instructions. The doorbell would ring less and less each day and, eventually, Finn would have nothing to bark at.

It'll take a little time, a little patience, that's all.

I'm annoyed with myself that it's taken this much excess for me to appreciate how much I already have. But then I steal a glance at the summerhouse and picture myself working in there. All that space. It's bigger than my last flat. I imagine myself throwing open the doors on a day like this and hearing only birdsong. Even in my wildest dreams of earning enough from my radio scripts to support myself and maybe buy a small house instead of a flat, I never imagined anything like this. I wouldn't even be able to afford a tenth of this cottage. It feels wrong to be falling in love with it. Wanting it feels hedonistic.

Scott interrupts my thoughts. 'I'll leave you here to chat. The gardens surround the cottage on all sides, so feel free to take a walk around. That gate down the side there will take you round the back.'

'Thanks,' Mark says.

He sits down on the fountain's edge and I join him, dipping my hand in the water. The chill is a welcome relief against the afternoon sun and reminds me to keep a cold grip on reality.

Yet, at the same time, I'm curious. Who wouldn't be? So I say, 'Go on then, how much is it?'

'Four million.'

I laugh, and the stress of the day finally leaves me.

'It's perfect, isn't it?' He glances over at the summerhouse.

'Yes, it's perfect.' I get to my feet and hold out a hand for him. 'Come on pipe-dream-boy, let's go to the pub.'

Mark doesn't move. 'You don't like it?' He's confused. 'You don't want it?'

I laugh again, only this time it's more of a snort. 'It's not a case of not liking it or not wanting it. It's a case of it being ten times above my pay grade. I get why you brought me here; you're right, I was being a drama queen. And all this excess has made me realise that. Point taken. Let's stop wasting Scott's time and go to the pub.'

'*I'm* not wasting his time.'

'Mark...'

I have no idea what to say. He's serious. He actually wants to buy this place. But I can't let him do that, not for me. I would lose my autonomy to eternal gratitude, be forever in his debt for doing so much – too much – for me. I don't want our relationship to begin on such uneven footing. When I insisted on giving him what I was already paying in rent towards his flat, I knew he didn't need the money, but it wasn't about that. I felt as if I was making a meaningful contribution. I can't do that here.

'Come on, let's go.'

'No. Not till you explain. This place is perfect. Do you know how rarely places come up for sale here? Especially places like this. Look at that studio.' He points at the summerhouse. 'It's perfect for you. And I heard what you said back there. You asked Scott if he would leave everything as it is. You love this house, I know you do. You just won't admit it.'

'I admit it, alright? I love this place. So what? I can't afford it.'

'But *I* can.'

'Mark...don't you get it? Living at your flat is different. I've always felt it was temporary until we bought a place together. This place feels permanent. And even if we were at the right time in our relationship to buy a house together, I'd still want it to be fifty-fifty.'

He hangs his head, shakes it. 'This is so silly. The moment I got the notification that this house had come up for sale, I knew I was going to buy it, just from the particulars. It's exactly what I've always wanted: a cottage just like this one, right here in Clay Norton. But you're saying that, even though *I* can afford it, I'm not allowed my dream house because *you* haven't got two million pounds. That's madness.'

He's right. If this is his dream house, he should be allowed to buy it. And I know everything he's saying makes perfect sense. But it's not who I am. I've always been the breadwinner, in my marriage, and since the divorce. I can't reconcile the idea of resigning that role. I wouldn't recognise myself if I didn't need to do that any more.

I say, 'I just...just...don't want to feel like a kept woman.'

'Kept woman – pfft – what is this, 1940? Pay me rent, then. Give me the same rent you insisted on paying towards my flat. You can keep saving and, if things don't work out between us, you can still get your own place like you planned.'

'Oh, come on, Mark, be serious. At least my rent makes a noticeable difference to the utility bills on your flat. If I paid the same towards this place it probably wouldn't even cover the gas bill.'

'You could eat beans on toast for a year, then you could cover the water rates as well.'

I smile. 'You're not as funny as you think you are.'

'Why are we even talking about you paying half, anyway? Who cares who pays what as long as we have what we need and we're both happy?'

'So, I *am* to be your kept woman?' I wink at him to let him know I'm not entirely serious, but no matter which way I turn this, it goes against my grain. It's all too much and it's all too soon. 'I'm not doing it, Mark. I love the house but we're not buying it. I don't want it.'

He shakes his head at me again, hanging it in that way he does. 'Laura, Laura... why do you have to hold on to everything so tightly? I know you had this fixed plan in your mind, but plans change. Why can't you let someone be there for you once in a while, do something nice for you? Why can't you let me do this one little thing for you?'

'You aren't asking if you can help carry my shopping bags in from the car, you're asking if you can buy a four-million-pound house to make my work days a little easier. It's not exactly one little thing.'

Feeling my resolve slipping, I fold my arms across my chest and Mark gets up. He tugs at them, tries to unfold them, while I put up a fake pretence of refusing to budge.

'Look, this isn't just for you,' he says, 'or even for us. It's a sensible investment. Property prices are going up and up. And you know what Clay Norton's like: nothing comes up for sale here unless some old granny dies. I'll make half a million on this in six months. You'll be doing me a favour.'

'How? You don't need *me* to buy this place.'

'I do... If you refuse to live here with me, I won't buy it, because I need to live wherever you are. So if you say no to this place, you'll have cost me half a million. What's that, forty years' rent?'

Now it's my turn to shake my head at him. 'You're so annoying sometimes.'

'Why? Because I'm always right?'

A laugh bursts out of me.

'So...' he says. 'We're buying it, then?'

I unfold my arms. He's making far too much sense and I feel myself wilting in submission.

'I don't know. I guess, now you put it like that. Maybe.'

'Good, because I already did.'

'What??'

'I put an offer in two days ago as soon as it went on the market, got them to take it off, so we didn't lose it.'

'Mark!!'

He backs away from me. 'Are you mad at me? I mean, like, really really mad?'

I take a few steps in his direction and as soon as I get close enough to grab him, he runs. Before we know it, I'm chasing him around Scott's fountain and we're both laughing.

As we're following Scott to the front door, I turn in the direction of movement in my peripheral vision. A woman in a white trouser suit, naturally beautiful, striking, floats down the stairs. When she catches sight of me and Mark, she stops in her tracks. Then she peers at us, surreptitiously, as if she thought we'd already left and has been caught out.

'That's Emily,' Scott says. 'My wife.'

The prolonged glance they exchange is so uncomfortable I have to look away. But then I remember my manners and stride across the hall towards her, holding up my hand to the banister rail. 'I'm Laura,' I say. 'And this is Mark, my boyfriend.'

Emily scoops up a red Pomeranian that's struggling to negotiate the steps with its too-short legs and tucks it beneath one arm before taking my hand. Her handshake is so limp, I'm convinced my grip will snap her fragile fingers, and I'm grateful when she lets go. But she doesn't say *nice to meet you*, or anything like that. She doesn't say a word. She barely manages a smile. Instead, she just turns on her heel and climbs back up the stairs, still carrying the dog.

'Well, I hope you liked the cottage, Laura.' Scott pulls back the front door latch.

'I did,' I stare up at Emily's disappearing figure. 'Very much.'

'Well, as I told Mark, the last sale fell through just days before exchange, but they've agreed to share the searches and surveys with the next buyer. So, if you want to use their estate agent and solicitor, conveyancing will sail through in a few weeks. Our purchase went ahead regardless, so we can move out whenever you like.'

'That's great,' Mark says. 'We'll get the ball rolling.'

TEN

GLENDA

'WHAT ARE you doing!?' Gerald shouts as he strides across the garden.

'Look.' I point beyond the shrub border past the back of Scott's summerhouse. 'Look what he's done! Tom didn't notice because the shrubs were so overgrown. But the boundary fence is gone.'

'What boundary fence? I don't remember there ever being a fence back there.'

'It was behind the shrubs. Scott must have taken it down when he built that *thing*.' I stab a finger at the eyesore. 'I know this garden like the back of my hand, and when I was a kid the fence was all the way back there. They've stolen half Tom's garden!'

Gerald looks around at the mess I've made. The bushes were so thick, so tall, that their cut branches and leaves now cover every raised bed in the vegetable garden and half the lawn as well. But I don't care.

He runs his hand over his forehead, across his bald patch, and finally finds what little hair remains at the back. 'What have you done, Glenda? You've said over and over that you hate having to look at the back of that summerhouse – its ugly gutters – and now you've cut down all the shrubs that hid it from view! Why would you raze it all to the ground?'

'Because! With the shrub border in place it doesn't look like Scott did anything wrong. But he's trespassed into our garden! I sent them a letter this morning telling them they had to tear that thing down, move it back into their own garden, or we'll be taking legal action.'

'You've sent them a letter...already? You don't think you should have discussed that with me first?'

'You were busy, Gerald.'

'I'm never *that* busy, Glenda. You could have called me at work to discuss it. We can't afford legal action.'

'They don't know that.' I turn back to the bushes, pruning saw in hand, and carve through another stem, tossing it behind me before tackling the next.

'Your vegetable garden!' Gerald pulls a huge branch off of one of the raised beds. 'You've crushed all your plants, even the tomatoes. You've ruined everything.'

'Sod the vegetables! This is more important. How dare they take advantage of my father in this way? If he wasn't loop the loop, he'd be doing exactly this.'

Gerald mutters something but all I catch is '...loop the bloody loop.'

I stop carving, turn around, and point the pruning saw at him. 'What did you say?'

'Nothing.' Gerald climbs over the mess to get closer to the boundary. 'Are you sure about this? Where do you think the boundary is?'

'Back there!' I point to an imaginary line in Scott's garden.

Gerald walks along what's left of the border, along the back of the summerhouse, kicking the ground and moving leaves about with his feet. 'I don't see the remains of any posts. There's no evidence of an old fence. How can you be sure where it was?'

'I told you. I know this garden like the back of my hand. And when I was a kid, Tom put the fence in and planted the shrubs in front of it. The fence rotted because it was behind the bushes and he couldn't maintain it. But it was back there. Scott must have removed what was left of it when he built the summerhouse. By the time you count its eaves and gutters, that thing is over a metre inside our garden!'

Gerald looks from left to right along the boundary, clearly trying to imagine what it would have looked like all those years ago, so he can form a mental image to assess. 'It doesn't make sense,' he says. 'Why would Tom put a fence all the way back there and then plant a shrub border this far away from it? He wouldn't have left a big gap like that.'

'You don't understand. Look at this.' I point to one of the cut branches. 'That's cherry laurel.' Then I point to the others in turn. 'That's Japanese rose...white poplar...and those are snowberries. There's a reason they're called *garden thugs*, Gerald: they can take over half your garden. All Scott had to do was take the fence down and keep cutting back his side of the shrubs to open up more and more of the land. And Tom wouldn't have known what he was doing back there; he wouldn't have realised the bushes were migrating this way.'

Gerald isn't convinced. 'But...even if Scott did do that, why would Tom replace his original kitchen garden for this small row of raised beds? And why put them out here instead of back there?'

'Because he couldn't handle the big vegetable plot any more. And when he first put these beds in, he left plenty of room to move around behind them. There's no room any more, thanks to Scott.'

'But...a metre, Glenda? Is that really worth getting so upset over? It's nothing. Such a small amount of land must be practically worthless.'

'It's not the money, it's the principle! He has all that land.' I wave my pruning saw at his garden. 'He had no reason – no right – to steal from my father who has so little. You said yourself you would go to court over a penny—'

'I didn't say exactly that—'

'Well, this is a lot more than a penny, Gerald. And if we let him get away with this, what will he take next? He's just pushing his luck.'

'But Scott is selling, isn't he?'

'Exactly... which is why we need to raise this now. He won't be able to sell the house with a boundary dispute on it. The buyers won't be able to get a lender. That's why I had to get the letter out straight away.'

'I'm not sure this is a good idea, Glenda. Boundary disputes are stressful, they get out of hand. People lose their houses in legal fees. Your dad could lose his house over this. I'm not sure that's a risk I'm willing to take over a metre of land that nobody's missed for years.'

'It's not *your* risk to take, is it?' I huff, puff and saw through another branch.

'No, and it's not yours either. Have you spoken to Tom about this? What does he say?'

Another three-metre-tall branch crashes to the ground, and Gerald has to step out of the way to avoid being hit by it. I stop for breath. 'I'm keeping Tom out of it. The stress will be too much for him, even if he could understand what was going on. I have power of attorney over his property and financial affairs, so I can deal with it on his behalf.'

'Power of attorney? When did you do that? *How* did you do that? Tom doesn't have capacity to sign an LPA.'

'Online. Months ago. Tom was having a good day and Jean across the way witnessed it. She's known Dad for years, but she hasn't seen him for ages, so she didn't realise how bad he was.'

'Christ. Is that even legal? How much did it cost?'

'A hundred and twenty pounds.'

'That's probably more than the land is worth! Why didn't you just ask Scott for the money? He would have paid us for the land. What's a hundred and twenty pounds to Scott?!'

With only a few stems left to cut, I start sawing again. 'You're not listening, Gerald. I just told you, it's not about the money, it's the principle. We deserve compensation.'

'Compensation?! How much did you ask for?'

Gerald rarely raises his voice. I look at his pink, appalled face and pause. 'Ten grand.'

'Ten grand!? He's not going to give us ten grand!'

'He will if he wants to sell his house.'

Gerald stands there in silence while I saw through the last of the stems. And, when the final branch falls to the ground, I stand back and take it in. Just as I suspected: with all the shrubs down, it looks as though the summerhouse is sitting right in our back garden. It may look pretty from the front with its wooden veranda and balustrade, but from behind it's just boards and guttering. And the building is so huge, it's a monstrosity. And it's right here. In our garden. On our land. Why should we have to look at it?

'There,' I say. 'Now it's clear as day. Everyone can see what he's done.'

Gerald grabs a long branch by its stem and lifts it off the tomatoes. All the plants are flat, crushed beneath the weight of the shrubs, their stalks snapped. Dejected, he drags the bush across the lawn towards the side of the house. 'Come on, let's clean up the mess.'

Wait till I get the money. He won't be sad then.

ELEVEN

LAURA

I FLINCH AT the squeeze of a hand on my shoulder and spin around from Mark's mixing desk to find him standing there. Finn's face is pressed into his thigh, begging for attention. He didn't bark, which is odd; Mark must have crept in quietly.

'You're home early.'

I get to my feet and plant a kiss full on his lips, draping my arms over his shoulders. If he's come home early for a good reason, I'm on board with that! I could do with a little stress relief after my day. Ignoring the doorbell, pretending you're not home and waiting for the person to leave while Finn barks his head off is as much of a disturbance as actually answering the door.

Finn muscles his face between our legs as usual. He thinks he owns all the cuddles in this house. I don't know whose attention he's craving, but I'm pretty sure it's not mine. Mark is downcast, so I guess he hasn't come home for the reason I'd hoped. I flop back into his chair. 'Is everything alright?'

'You got your wish,' he says.

'What wish?'

'We can't buy the house. Apparently there's a boundary dispute on it. Five days after I put the offer in and the estate agent marked the cottage as sold, the neighbour slapped Scott with a boundary dispute. He got the letter this morning.'

'That seems like awfully convenient timing. What are they claiming?'

'That he built the summerhouse part-way inside their garden. They're demanding he tear it down—'

'My studio!?'

'Yeah, or pay them thirty-five grand.'

'Thirty-five grand! How much land is he supposed to have stolen?'

'A one-metre strip.'

'A metre of garden can't be worth thirty-five grand, surely?'

'Of course not. It's probably worth no more than a few hundred. But if we want to buy the house and Scott wants to sell, we either have to move the summerhouse or pay them.'

Thirty-five grand may not be a lot of money to Mark but that's my entire nest egg. He gestures for me to get up so he can sit down, and then he pulls me on to his lap.

'What's Scott going to do?' I ask.

'He offered them five thousand to make it go away. It's more than ten times the value of the land, but he knows how these things can go.'

'And?'

'They rejected it outright, insisted on thirty-five.'

'That's ridiculous. How can they justify such a figure?'

'I know,' Mark says, 'it's insane. They've just pulled that number out of a hat. It has nothing to do with the value of the land or any losses to either property in terms of value. And Scott refuses to pay them a penny more. He said he hasn't trespassed on their land, they don't have any evidence, and he thinks they're just using the sale as leverage for extortion.'

'Well, he's right, thirty-five grand *is* extortion. So what happens now?'

'Nothing. We can't buy a house with a boundary dispute on it, and Scott can't sell. So that's the end of it.'

I shift around on his lap and run my fingers through his hair. 'Are you okay?'

He shrugs. Clearly he's not.

'You really loved it, didn't you?'

He nods with childlike enthusiasm. 'I could just see us there. You...me...Finn.' Finn has his chin on Mark's knee, no doubt leaving a wet patch of drool on his trousers, and Mark rubs his head. 'I pictured myself coming home and finding you out in the studio, relaxed and happy.'

'I am happy.' I say the words, but it's a struggle to conceal the disappointment in my tone.

'You're not. You said you had to find another place.'

I did say that, and, now that we can't have the cottage, I don't know how to respond. Working here is almost impossible, but I don't want to leave either. Even more so now I know the lengths Mark is prepared to go to, to make me happy.

He says, 'I know you didn't want the house—'

'I never said that.'

'Yes, you did. You said, "We're not buying it. I don't want it."'

'I didn't say exactly that...'

I think I did say exactly that, but it wasn't true. I loved the house. I was just scared of what it would do to our relationship, how I would cope with feeling forever in his debt. For me, the house was a pipe-dream anyway, so losing it feels not unlike waking up. But it was a reality for Mark, and now I feel bad for him.

'It's not that I didn't want the house...I just... I guess a tiny part of me is relieved. This – us – is all moving so fast as it is. I never imagined meeting anyone...I mean, I didn't *plan* on meeting anyone, let alone moving in with them so quickly. And I probably would have felt like your kept woman at Primrose Cottage. So maybe this is fate. Things sometimes happen for a reason. Maybe we weren't *meant* to have that house. Maybe it wasn't supposed to happen right now and in a few years, when I'm settled in my career, we can buy a place together, equally...' I finally run out of steam and look at him. '*What?*'

He shakes his head at me in exasperation. 'You do want it, don't you? You want it just as much as I do. Admit it: you're as disappointed as I am.'

An image of the cottage pops into my head, its beautiful garden and summerhouse, and suddenly I'm smiling; I can't help it. I let out a small laugh. That whole speech about fate was really just to make Mark feel better but, alongside the tiny part of me that's relieved, there's another part of me – a bigger part – that feels cheated.

'Okay, I admit it. I am disappointed. I don't think I realised just how much I wanted the house until you said we couldn't have it.'

'Oh! You're one of *those* types.' Mark puts on a girly voice. '*I don't want you as my boyfriend but nobody else can have you either.*'

'Don't be silly. Of course I'm not like that. If we didn't want the house I'd be happy for someone else to have it as long as they loved it as much as we do. It's not that – it's the principle of the thing. Who are these neighbours anyway? And how can they have this much control over our lives? Surely, it should be our decision whether we buy the house, not theirs? Besides, it's all your fault. You took me to the most beautiful cottage in Oxford and then expected me not to fall in love with it.'

'No, I took you to the most beautiful cottage in Oxford *knowing* you would fall in love with it, and then I'd have you in my grasp!' He wraps his arms around mine, trapping them by my sides. 'Ha ha ha!'

I glance at him sideways.

'That was my *evil plan* laugh, by the way.'

'Yeah, I got that. Don't give up the day job.'

He's serious again. 'What are we gonna do? We could pay them.'

'By *we*, you mean you.'

'Yes, I mean *I* could pay them. It's only thirty-five grand.'

I shake my head in despair at his lack of any concept of how the other half lives. Even with the project advance, that's my entire year's income – in a good year.

I think about it for a moment, about how much I love the house and how far I might be prepared to go to get it, and then I say, 'But...I think Scott's right. They *are* using the sale as leverage, and that's essentially blackmail. There's a reason you don't pay blackmailers. If we give them thirty-five grand, what's to stop them coming back for more? What if they come up with another scheme to extort even more from us after we've moved in?'

'So...what, then? We lose the house? This is Clay Norton. And that property is unique. We won't get another chance like this any time soon. Maybe not ever.'

I hardly want to suggest what I'm about to, because it's his money, but...

'What if you just bought the house anyway?'

'Honey, how rich do you think I am? I mean, yes, I'm not exactly strapped for cash, but I don't have four million just sitting around in bank accounts. I'll need a mortgage. And I won't get one for a property with a boundary dispute lodged against it.'

'Daddy won't lend it to you? With interest, of course.'

'Ha! Dad's never lent me a penny in my life. I asked him for fifty quid when I was at university once and he flat-out refused.' He impersonates his father. '*Men need to learn to stand on their own two feet, son!*'

'So, that's it, then?'

'I guess so.'

This is what I wanted all along, right? Not to be a kept woman, not to feel forever beholden to Mark for what he'd done for me. It *is* what I wanted. Isn't it?

What I actually feel is sick with regret.

TWELVE

LAURA

'MARK!' I run into the studio where he's been working on the second pass of edits – the first three episodes – since he came home. My new noise-cancelling headphones keep glitching, so I'm concerned parts of the sound aren't right. I'm glad he's editing it; I need that second pair of ears and I trust him not to make changes for the sake of it.

'This is really great,' he says. 'The two main characters particularly – where did you find these women?'

'They're fabulous, aren't they? They do a lot of takes, which is a lot for me to edit, but they're both perfectionists, so they don't stop until they've got every line just right. They're really throwing themselves into their performances, don't you think?'

'Yes. But it's not just them; you'd never know this was recorded in a sound booth. The sound effects are incredible. They're so real, I feel like I'm actually there. I'm blown away, honestly. You're a bloody marvel, woman. Dad's gonna love this!'

'Thanks... Hang on, you're not just blowing smoke up my ass because you're having sex with me, are you?'

He bobs his head from side to side. 'We-ell...'

I glare at him.

'Don't be stupid, of course not. If I thought there was anything wrong with it I'd be stepping in to help out or putting Steve Banks on the job. You don't need me!'

'Steve Banks! That sleazeball? You wouldn't dare. Did I tell you he emailed to ask if I needed help with the project? He said he'd heard I was "behind schedule".'

Mark laughs derisively. 'I'm not at all surprised. He's chomping at the bit to get in on this.'

'Why?'

'Because he knows Dad's lined you up for *Game of Thrones*. And anyone involved in this production will also get first dibs on that.'

'I might have known it was nothing to do with me or my little project.'

'Hmm. Although I wouldn't write Steve off altogether. He might be a sleazeball but he's a bloody brilliant sleazeball. You know he did those *Top Gun* spin-offs, don't you? The sound effects were phenomenal. After that and *War of the Worlds*, listeners were finally comparing radio to film. And Steve's a big name in the industry. It wouldn't do you any harm to have his name next to yours on this project. Plus, the deadline's already tight—'

'I'll stop you right there. This is *my* baby. You know what Steve's like; he'll get one foot in the door and completely take over. Suddenly, all my ideas will be dismissed, and his name will be front and centre. Nobody will even know I wrote it.'

'Alright...but—'

'No buts. Anyway, that's not why I came in here. I think I've found a solution for the cottage.'

'Seriously?'

I nod.

'You mean you really want this?'

I'm still not entirely sure whether I do or not, whether fate is waving warning flags. But since Mark told me yesterday that we'd lost the house I haven't been able to stop thinking about it. It's as if the neighbours have stuck a knife in my ribs, and I won't settle until I pull it out.

I say, 'Whether I want the house or not isn't really relevant. The point is, *you* want it. And if this is blackmail, the idea that those fuckwits should get away with taking it from you really pisses me off. If it's not extortion – if it's a genuine boundary dispute and Scott has stolen their land – we'll give it back. Move the summerhouse. Problem solved.'

'Sounds fair enough. But how do we make sure it's all sewn up and legal?'

'With a boundary agreement. Both we and the neighbours sign it and lodge it with the Land Registry. I found this chartered land surveyor with this incredible website on boundary disputes. So, I emailed him, and he came back with a surveyor in our area. I spoke to her, and she suggested what's called ADR: Alternative Dispute Resolution. So, I spoke to the estate agent, and she called Scott and the neighbours. Apparently the neighbours want a solution as much as we do, so they've all agreed to meet the surveyor on Monday afternoon. She'll assess the boundary and put forward a solution that suits everyone. I'm going along, so I can hear both sides of the story and find out if they have a real case.'

'You're a genius,' he says. 'But what about the project?'

'It's only an afternoon out. I'd spend that long handing over one of Madge's parcels.'

'Fair point. So...we still have a chance, then?'

'We still have a chance.'

THIRTEEN

GERALD

'Honey, I'm home!' I call from the hallway. That always gets a little smile from Glenda, and she could do with a few of those these days. Especially since Jason took that summer job with CyberStroke in Scarborough instead of coming home. I should probably come up with something funnier after saying it for twenty-odd years, but Jason used to love it too. Hearing me call from the hallway would be the highlight of both our days, and he'd come toddling out to greet me, chubby arms aloft, nappy-clad bottom bouncing.

I miss those days. He was our little miracle. There was no IVF back then. Almost twenty years we'd been trying for a baby before we finally gave up. Then, two years later, Glenda fell pregnant. Jason was the most adorable baby. Our miniature Michelin man with arms and legs that looked as if they'd been tied too tightly with string at two-inch intervals. I loved him so much it hurt. I knew that as he grew up he'd lose interest in his old man, but even as a teenager he perked up whenever I came home. I might not have been the most successful wage-earner, but I made up for that by being the best father I could. I think Glenda would give me that much.

I wish he'd come home for the summer. Perhaps if he'd been here for the past five weeks, Glenda wouldn't have taken her anger out on that hedge. She's acting as if she's the only one who's been upset since Jason called in July to say he wasn't coming home. As if she's the only one who's missing him. If she would just give him enough space to breathe and be his own man, he might want to be with us as much as we want to be with him.

The smile I was hoping would greet me isn't there. Glenda is sitting at the dining table, staring at her laptop. I drop my newspaper and briefcase on the opposite side.

'What are you up to?'

While I wait for an answer that doesn't come, I glance over her head out of the window at Scott's summerhouse. Now that it looks as if it's sitting in our garden, you can't exactly *not* stare at it. Glenda knows what she's doing — she's a smart woman — and I know taking the shrub border down was for a good cause; it's just, now I have a permanent reminder of this boundary dispute, and it's not what I want to think about after a long day at the office.

Glenda says, 'Scott's buyers have instructed a chartered land surveyor. She's coming here to meet both parties, review the evidence, and suggest a settlement.'

I perk up. 'That's good news. We don't want this stringing out for months, or reaching the point where we need legal advice. The only people who win these things are the lawyers, and we can't afford to be lining their pockets. This is good. You'll prove this encroachment, Scott will settle out of court, and this whole thing will be over before it starts. Then we can grow our hedge back.'

I skirt around the table, about to kiss her on the forehead, when she glances up at me with a troubled expression and quickly closes her laptop.

'What?'

'Nothing,' she says. 'Scott thought he could make it go away by making some paltry offer, but I turned it down.'

'How paltry?'

'Five hundred.'

'Five hundred pounds isn't paltry, Glenda! It's probably more than the land is worth. Have you looked into the price of garden land per metre?'

'No, because it's irrelevant. I told you before, it's not just about the land or having to look at the back of that eyesore. This is about principles. As soon as the chartered land surveyor sees all my evidence, she'll tell Scott and his buyers what it costs to go to court. That'll give them pause for thought. Some of these cases I've been researching have run into hundreds of thousands of pounds. When they realise that, they'll see that ten is a good deal. She's coming Monday afternoon, so I have to be prepared.'

I lean over the table and study two sets of title deed plans Glenda has printed off. There are more sheets of paper beneath, so I slide them aside to reveal several photographs of Tom's garden when Rosie – Glenda's mother – was still here.

'Where did you find these?' I look at the photographs one by one.

'In the loft.'

There's a photograph of Rosie standing in front of a fence. She really was a beautiful woman. Troubled, fragile, but beautiful. I ask, 'So, that's the fence Scott removed?'

'Yes.' Glenda looks up at me expectantly. 'Look how much further back it was.'

The picture was taken before Tom started growing vegetables in the garden. Back then, he and Rosie had an allotment on the outskirts of town. Tom was really popular down there; the committee even kept him on after he gave up his plot because he had so much knowledge and willingly shared it with everyone. I tilt my head to one side and look at the photograph again. 'You can't really tell. There's just the lawn and the fence; there aren't any landmarks to go by.'

'Well, believe me, it was a lot further back. And look at this.' She slides one of the title deed plans in front of me, the one for Primrose Cottage.

'Where did you get that?'

'Off the Land Registry website. Look at—'

'How much did that cost?'

'Nothing! Fifteen pounds.'

I run my hands over my forehead until my fingers sink into the hair on the back of my head. When I run my fingers over my head these days, it takes longer and longer to reach those white tufts. And I suspect this boundary dispute is going to significantly increase that distance.

'Glenda, you aren't spending a fortune on this, are you? It's money we don't have. With Jason's university fees and taking care of your dad—'

'For Christ's sake, Gerald, it's fifteen pounds. It's not going to break the bank. Look!'

I lean over the plan, palms down on the table, while Glenda uses her forefinger like a laser pointer in a pre-prepared presentation. 'This line is the boundary between our properties. This is Primrose Cottage – you know they have that snug at the end of the dining room?'

'No. How would I know that? I've never been in there. How do *you* know they have a snug?'

She points to another sheet of paper on the other side of her laptop.

'I downloaded the property details from Rightmove. Anyway, that's their snug. The wall is the boundary line, see? That's where the old fence used to be.'

'Right in front of their patio doors?'

'No, don't be silly, Gerald. I mean that's the boundary before Scott bought the property. Do you remember Oliver and Nancy Huntington-Whitney?'

'Vaguely.' They were the owners before Scott, but we didn't know them. Nancy sold the property after Oliver died.

'Oliver extended Primrose Cottage in the '90s. And he extended right up to the fence line.'

'How do you know?'

'I remember Tom complaining about it, saying the extension was too close.'

I look at the property details and point to Oliver's extension. 'But if the snug wall is the boundary, Oliver wouldn't have been allowed to install patio doors and windows. The council wouldn't have approved them.'

'It didn't have patio doors and windows when Oliver built it! Scott put those in later, when he laid the patio. I checked the council website and there's no planning application. Which means he put them in without permission.'

'Well, if Scott contravened planning regulations, why didn't Tom complain at the time? Get the council involved?'

'You know what Tom's like.'

'Why do you insist on calling him Tom? You used to call him Dad.'

'Never mind that. Anyway, that's where the boundary is. In line with the snug wall. And the summerhouse oversteps that by at least a metre. Probably more.'

'If you say so. You know these houses better than I do.'

'I do. Wait till the surveyor sees these title plans and photographs. Scott will have to move that eyesore and we'll get our garden back. Either that, or we'll get ten grand in compensation. Compensation we deserve.'

We really could use that money. The lottery win covered Jason's fees and his accommodation and expenses for the first two years. But, after that, things will get tight.

'What time is this thing with the surveyor?' I ask. 'I've got a meeting in the morning, but I can come home early.'

'No, Gerald, there's no need.'

'Of course there's a need. We have to show a united front.'

'Well you can't, it's on Monday morning. You'll be in your meeting, and work is more important.'

'I thought you said she was coming in the afternoon?'

'No, I said Monday morning.'

'Bugger. Can't you change it?'

'No. The surveyor is apparently very busy. She's squeezing us in as it is. And you said yourself you didn't want this thing dragging on.'

I mumble an agreement, but I don't like it. I know Glenda can handle herself — she's much better at these things than I am — but I would have liked to hear what this surveyor had to say first-hand. I've had enough of this conversation now, though.

'I'll get changed. And then do you fancy a walk across to the pub?'

'Sure.'

I leave the room and, as I'm climbing the stairs, hear Glenda on her mobile. Pausing halfway up, I try to listen in, but all I hear is 'Monday morning. Yes,' and, 'Ten o'clock.' The room goes quiet then, so I climb the rest of the stairs.

Although I don't like confrontations, Glenda appears to have this in hand, and it could be a good thing. Not just for the money, but for her. It's given Glenda a new purpose, so that's something.

I guess.

FOURTEEN

LAURA

I WAIT FOR MARK in the pub opposite Hardman Studios, the same pub he took me to on the fateful day we met. After being in Clay Norton with the chartered land surveyor this morning – seeing Primrose Cottage again and revelling in its peace and quiet – I can't face going home to Mark's flat just yet. I called him on the way back into the city and suggested we meet for a late lunch to talk about the meeting.

He bounds in with a spring in his step, and when he realises I've already bought him a pint he slips out of his jacket and sits down. 'Ooh, thanks.'

He's wearing the same black shirt I removed the day we met and the memory pinkens my cheeks. I wish he hadn't worn that today; I can't concentrate when he's in that shirt. Especially when he combines it with those tight black trousers, tan belt and shoes. I reach behind me and stroke my spine, feeling the memory etched into my skin: his buckle left a tiny scar when I fell on top of, and in love with, him.

'So...' He takes a swig of his pint. 'How did it go?'

I put on my most serious sad face.

'What? We can't buy the house? Is Scott taking it off the market?'

Unable to keep it up any longer, I burst out, 'It's ours! The chartered land surveyor said the title deed plans can't be used to define the boundary unless they have accompanying measurements and that, without them, the neighbours don't have enough evidence. Given the financial risks of taking this to court, she advised them to sign a boundary agreement.'

'What? And they agreed? Just like that?'

'Not exactly. I offered to pay the surveyor's fees in full, the legal expenses of lodging the agreement with the Land Registry and the costs of putting up a new fence – I hope that's okay? I thought we should offer something in return for them dropping the dispute. The chartered land surveyor did the site survey then and there. She's going to send it to your solicitor. But I shook hands with the neighbour – a gentlemen's agreement – so, it's official.'

'No way!' He shakes a fist at me for pretending it all went wrong. 'You!!! How could you do that to me?'

I pick up my pint. 'Here's to our new home.'

'Our new home.'

We chink glasses and barely contain our smiles enough to take a sip.

'I have been thinking, though,' I say.

'Oh, God.'

'No...nothing bad. Nothing *really* bad, anyway. I'm just thinking... I mean, I've already made up my mind about this...' I pause, hoping it comes out right. 'If this project doesn't pan out and my career ends up in the toilet, I need you to promise you'll sell the cottage – take your half-million profit, or whatever – and we'll live somewhere we can both afford. At least somewhere I'll feel like I'm a contributor. Deal?'

'If that's what you really want, then of course – deal. Buuut ...something tells me that once you've lived at Primrose Cottage for a few months I'll have to drag you out of there, fingernails clawing the floorboards.'

'No,' I say firmly. 'I'd never ruin those beautiful floorboards.'

He laughs. 'It doesn't matter anyway. I've finished the final edit on the first three episodes, and your play is gonna be a smash. It blows *War of the Worlds* out of the water, and if you carry on in that vein there's no way you won't make sound design on *Game of Thrones*. Probably scriptwriter as well.'

'We'll see. Episodes four to six have been a struggle with those headphones still playing up. Maybe you can use them for your edit and see if they give you any problems?'

'Sure. They're brand new though, you just bought them, so if there's a problem why don't you just send them back?'

'I can't consistently replicate the issue. It's so frustrating. I'm getting worried about the deadline now.'

'It'll be fine. Now this is all sorted out with the house, we'll be in in no time and you can work in complete peace. So...what are they like, these new neighbours of ours? What are their names?'

'Glenda and Gerald Skinner.'

'Seriously? There's a couple named Glenda and Gerald?'

'Mmm. There really is!'

'Old and boring, then?'

I have to think about that. How would you describe Glenda Skinner? That's a difficult one. I say, 'Well, I only met her, not the husband. But no, not really. She's difficult to age. She could be ten years older than me, but she could be twenty as well. She's really strait-laced – on the surface, anyway – but I wouldn't describe her as boring. She was...weird, actually. Really weird.'

'Weird how?'

Unable to put my finger on it, I screw up my face, searching for the right description. 'It was more of a feeling... It's difficult to describe.'

'Do you think she'll turn out to be one of those nightmare neighbours?'

'I don't think so. She looks too prim to do anything socially unacceptable. Plus, I don't think she's very bright. Gosh, that sounds mean, doesn't it? I'm not saying that to be cruel, she might be very well educated, but she doesn't appear to grasp basic concepts.'

'What do you mean?'

'Well, she showed the chartered land surveyor her evidence, and all she had were these old photographs of a fence and our title deed plans. But the photographs don't identify the fence's location or who owned it. All they prove is that, decades ago, there used to be a fence between the properties...somewhere. And the plans have a big red warning on them from the Land Registry stating they don't match actual measurements on the ground – that they can't be scaled up. The surveyor explained to Glenda that a one-millimetre line on the plan equates to over a metre on the ground, but she still kept insisting the snug was the boundary. The surveyor explained it to her three times, in three different ways, but Glenda couldn't grasp it. She couldn't understand that the boundary line on paper running along the snug wall equated to a strip of land more than twice the width of what she was arguing over.'

'Sounds like she didn't want to grasp it. But, either way, stupid doesn't necessarily mean weird.'

'No, it wasn't that. When the surveyor explained that she would lose if she went to court with so little evidence, and it would be in her best interests to sign a boundary agreement, she shook hands with me. Obviously, I was over the moon. So, I said to her, "It looks like we're going to be neighbours, then." At which point, she put her hand on my knee and said, "I think best friends, don't you?" Honestly, it freaked me out.'

'She was probably just being nice.'

'It wasn't so much *what* she said, it was the *way* she said it. It was really creepy.'

'*It* was creepy or *she* was creepy?'

'*She* was creepy.'

'In appearance?'

'No... I mean, yes... But it was the whole package.' I draw an air-circle around an imaginary Glenda. 'She dresses like a 1940s housewife. Stiff wool skirt and high-neck blouse with ruffles around the collar. And she had on those tights that older women wear: thick, beige. But it's her eyes, mostly – they're the strangest brown, almost gold – and she peers at you with them through these huge glasses. As if you're an insect in a jar. And they're as old-fashioned as she is, like Vera Duckworth from *Coronation Street*.'

'You'd better watch out, she sounds just my type.'

I laugh, but then Glenda is back in my head. 'She has a weird smile too, a trout pout.'

'She doesn't sound like the type of person who'd have plastic surgery.'

'No, I think it's naturally like that!'

'So, basically, we'll be living next door to an ugly fish who wears Vera Duckworth glasses and Nora Batty tights?'

'Yep. Only, she's not ugly, she's strangely attractive. Not beautiful, but stunning. Stunning and completely bizarre. God, she's difficult to pin down with words. You'll just have to meet her to see what I mean. It's as if the person you're looking at isn't really her. As if Glenda Skinner is... well... a skin suit – ironically, and for want of a better description, something she wears to cloak the person underneath. I'm not explaining myself very well.'

'Well, as long as the fish can sign her name, that's all we care about.' Mark's phone pings, and he glances at the header of an incoming email on the front screen. I catch the name of his solicitor, Angela Shaw. 'Speaking of which, it looks like Angela's already drawn up the boundary agreement ready for when the plan arrives, and she's sent through the contracts for exchange.'

'Wow! She doesn't waste any time.'

'There's a reason she's my solicitor.'

While I wait for Mark to skim the email, I take a sip of beer and, as I put my glass down, movement near the bar catches my eye. A man gets up from a table, takes the strap of a leather satchel from the back of his chair and swings it over his shoulder. Then he gathers a pile of folders, straightens the bundle and presses it to his chest before turning around.

There's nothing unusual about his actions, yet for some reason I can't look away. There's a fluidity and grace to his movements that are cinematic. It's as if I've been cast back in time, and I'm playing an extra on a black and white movie set. Only, it's not the film that's shot in black and white: real life is black and white. He's the only thing in colour, the star of the show, and all eyes are on him.

Mark pulls my attention away from the stranger.

'It's done.'

'What is?'

'I've signed the contract. So has Scott, Angela says. We're ready to exchange.'

'What? How? What about the boundary agreement?'

'I've signed that too – Angela uses e-signatures for all these things. She says she can lodge the boundary agreement at any time. She said a gentlemen's agreement from the Skinners was enough to get things moving.'

'Oh, my God! We're really doing this!' We chink glasses. 'I'm so excited but I confess, I wish we had nicer neighbours.'

'If they turn out to be really odd, we'll just keep to ourselves, stay on our side of the proverbial fence. They're far enough away not to bother us if we don't want to socialise with them.'

'Yes, it's a relief the houses aren't right on top of each other. Speaking of fences—'

The man from the bar walks towards us, heading for the door. As if my eyes are connected to him by an invisible string,

I can't stop myself from staring. And when he looks back at me with the most unusual eyes I've ever seen, liquid grey, my heart dances in my chest and my mouth falls open.

Mark follows my gaze and spins around in his chair to see what's caught my attention. Then he leaps to his feet and darts over to the man. For the briefest second, I think Mark has read my thoughts and is springing to action in a fit of jealousy. But he throws his arms around the man.

'Saeed!'

'Mark.'

I stare at them as they hug each other warmly, their arms wrapped tightly around each other. When they release, they shake hands, holding on to each other for a time that would make anyone but the best of friends uncomfortable. Their interaction, although not out of the ordinary, is mesmerising, magnetic. I feel strangely alone on the outside of it.

'I am very happy to see you,' Saeed says. 'What are you doing in Oxford?'

'I've been here for years, mate.' Mark points across the road to his office. 'Hardman Studios. That's me and Dad.'

'Hard-*man*,' Saeed's eyebrows draw together forming a deep crease in his olive-brown skin.

'Yeah, that was Dad. He thought we needed a bit of a name change.'

'I never put two and two together,' Saeed says. 'If I had, I would have come to see you. I have missed you, old friend.'

Mark looks over at me then. 'This is my girlfriend, Laura.'

I look up and smile. 'It's nice to meet you.'

In one fluid motion, Saeed moves towards me, puts his folders down on the table and, when I hold out my hand for him to shake, he takes it in both of his, saying, 'It is nice to meet you too, Laura.'

Every hair on my body stands up and quivers.

Then he lets go of my hand.

'Stay,' Mark says. 'Have a drink with us.'

'I would love to, but I have a client in fifteen minutes. I have to get back to the office.' He unclips the front of his satchel, takes a business card out of a small front pocket and hands it to Mark. 'Call me. Meet up next week?'

'Next week, sure.' Mark throws his arms around Saeed again. 'Oh, man, it's so good to see you.'

'You too, my friend.'

They shake hands again then part ways and, as Saeed leaves the pub, my eyes track his departure. Once caught on Saeed, his presence keeps me snagged by a fish hook that's tied to his line.

Mark sits down with a wry smile. 'Don't even think about it.'

'What?'

'I know what you're thinking. It's what all women think.'

'And all men, by the looks of it. Could you *be* more in love?' I swoon. '*Oh, Saeed, it's so good to see you. Stay. Have a drink with us.*'

'Shut up.' Mark laughs.

'You're blushing!'

'I am not.'

'How do you know each other?'

'Our parents are old friends, and we were best mates until...eighteen, twenty...something like that. But then his parents moved back to India, and Saeed went up north to study. Edinburgh, I think, I don't remember. We lost touch.'

'He seems nice.'

'I told you, don't even think about it.'

'Oh, don't worry. He's not as nice as you. You have a cuter butt.'

'You were checking out his butt?'

'Oh, shush.'

'What were you about to say before Saeed showed up? You said *speaking of fences*...'

'Oh, yeah. I was saying we have to get that fence up as soon as possible. The whole reason she's been able to bring this dispute in the first place is because there's no fence between the properties. I don't know what happened to the old one; maybe it rotted away and the owners before Scott never got around to replacing it. He said he never bothered because a shrub hedge on their side already separated the gardens.'

'I remember it. It grows behind the summerhouse.'

'Not any more. Glenda has razed it to the ground – her own shrubs – to open up the two gardens on to each other.'

'Why on earth would she do that?' he asks.

'To make it look like the summerhouse is in their garden. You should see it now. You can see right into their place from ours.'

'Alright, a new fence is top of the list when we move in, then. In fact, I'll book an installer to coincide with that. We'll need it for Finn anyway; we can't have him wandering into the neighbours' garden. Especially if they're as weird as you say they are.'

'That's a good point. I didn't even think of that.'

'There's a reason they say good fences make good neighbours.'

I lift my glass again. 'I'll drink to that.'

FIFTEEN

GLENDA

'She seemed nice,' I tell Gerald. 'Interesting. A little too... feminine for my taste, girlish, but not in a vacant way. She's quite fascinating, actually. Clever. She's written this epic drama for Hardman Studios which she's now producing. She's a sound engineer too, puts all the special effects in the background to make it realistic. She could be famous one day.'

'Impressive,' Gerald says. 'And what does he do? Something equally impressive, no doubt, if they can afford that house.'

'What does *he* do? I just told you, Gerald. Don't you listen to anything I say? Put that newspaper down! Mark is a radio producer as well. His father is Chad Hardman.'

'*The* Chad Hardman?' He folds the newspaper in half and drops it on the carpet beneath his armchair.

'Yes, the very one.'

'You mean we'll be living next door to Chad Hardman's son?'

I nod.

'Imagine rubbing up against people like that.'

'I know. I think she liked me, too. I think we're going to become fast friends.'

'Not if we're in a neighbour dispute.'

Gerald is right. And I realised that the moment I found out who she was. So, I decided to let it go and shake hands. Sure, we could use the money, but Jason's college fees and accommodation are covered for now, and I'll get my hands on what we need for his third year. I always find ways.

I can just see myself going around to the Hardmans' for afternoon tea, sitting out in the garden with Laura. Half the employees of Hardman Studios live in this village; they'll be so envious that we're friends with Mark.

Finally, after all these years, I'll be invited into Primrose Cottage.

When I was a child, I used to picture what it looked like inside. Of course, that was in the days before house details were plastered all over the internet and you could have a nose; I know what it looks like now. But the Huntington-Whitneys had very little to do with us. Tom always tipped his cap at Mr Huntington-Whitney – sycophant – even gave him some advice on his roses once when they had black-spot. But we weren't on a first-name basis, and they weren't very neighbourly towards me or Mum.

Everything will change now; I'll know Primrose Cottage like the back of my hand. Laura works from home and plans to set up her studio in the summerhouse, so she'll be there all day. It'll practically be my second home. I imagine the next time I run into Cynthia in the village, *Oh, yes, we were round Mark and Laura's just last night and Chad and Portia joined us for dinner. Salmon en croute with caviar. They're such interesting people. They produce radio dramas, you know?*

I don't actually know Mrs Hardman's first name, but I imagine she's called something well-to-do like Portia, or Prunella, some beautiful name like that.

Mark and Laura aren't married yet, but they will be. And of course, as neighbours, we'll be invited to the wedding. I'll need a new dress, a hat – of course – and a matching handbag and shoes. I'm not sure where I'll get the money for those now, but I'll find a way, I always do. I don't know why he had to go and do such a stupid thing; everything was perfect. Maybe I should start saving now; who knows how long it will be till the wedding? I could squirrel away some of the shopping money.

I glance out of the window. The stubs of shrub border are already sprouting leaves. Nature is a force you can't hold back. Laura agreed to pay for a new fence along with everything else, but I won't let the hedge grow any higher than that. Then, we can chat over the top of it whenever I see her in the garden.

'Did you hear me?' Gerald asks. 'You say I don't listen, but you're just as bad! I said, we won't be friends if we're embroiled in a boundary dispute.'

'That's all sorted now, Gerald. We reached an agreement and shook hands on it.'

'Really? Oh, that's marvellous! What did the chartered land surveyor—'

The doorbell rings.

Gerald and I stare at each other. We aren't expecting visitors. It's too late for the postman, and we aren't anticipating parcels either. He heaves himself out of the armchair and I follow him to the door. But Gerald doesn't even need to open it for both of us to know who's standing there. The silhouettes are enough.

We glance at each other, wondering whether we can get away with not answering, but they'll have seen our silhouettes just as we've seen theirs. It's too late. The mottled glass blurs their edges and distorts their forms into dark aberrations. But Gerald will have to open the door for the horror to really begin.

I suppose a visit from his mother is overdue.

She almost made it to the end of the month without her benefits running out. I swear when she looks at Gerald she doesn't see a person, she sees a little bag of white powder. While I beam with pride at my own son, Sherry grins at hers because his wallet oozes with the stench of her fags and booze.

I don't feel sorry for Gerald often; there's rarely a need. He's content with his simple life and keeps a smile on his face despite all the knock-backs. He's a dog that wags its tail even after you've whacked it with a rolled-up newspaper. But once a month, when I stand in this hallway and watch his face fall at the sight of those shapes behind the glass, my heart breaks for him. Just a little.

He twists the handle.

And something twists in me.

I march towards the door. 'Step aside, Gerald!' And the moment it swings open, I sucker-punch Sherry so hard in the mouth, her teeth hit the back of her throat. Arms flailing, she hits the porch like a sack of potatoes, choking on shards of amalgam...

'Come in,' Gerald says.

'Hello, Glenda,' Sherry sneers. 'You're looking pale, dearie.'

'Hello, Sherry. Nice to see you, too.'

Ricky, Gerald's twenty-something stepbrother, files in behind Sherry, and it's only then that Gerald and I see who else she's brought in tow.

'No,' Gerald says. 'Not him. He's not coming in.'

Liam, Sherry's latest husband, stands in the doorway with sick-looking skin, dilated pupils and cracked lips.

Sherry says, 'Oh, come on, Gerry. Don't be a douche. Let him in.'

'No.' Gerald slams the door in Liam's face, and I swell with pride.

Sherry tries to fight her way past Gerald, back to the door, but he blocks her way. 'That was rude, Gerry!'

'It's Gerald, Mother.'

'For the thousandth time,' I mutter under my breath.

Her husband being abandoned on the doorstep doesn't stop Sherry inviting herself into the lounge, followed close at heel by Ricky, who – as always – is tastefully dressed in a wife-beater with a string of gold chains and a baseball cap. The boy couldn't be more of a cliché if he tried.

Sherry plonks herself down in Gerald's armchair, spreading her legs just wide enough for me to see the gusset of her knickers beneath her cheap cotton dress. I make a mental note to add plastic chair covers to my shopping list. Her hooded eyes are black with too much mascara, and her hair is pulled into a high ponytail that's so tight I think she's trying to give herself a facelift. Two inches of grey hair grows out from her brassy home-dye job, and this is Sherry on a good day.

Gerald never fitted in with his family. He was the black sheep, thank God – an introverted boy who sat on the periphery watching the Skinner family's living hell play out like something on Jeremy Kyle. Eventually, he realised what his life would turn into if he didn't exit the shit-show and moved in with his aunt. That's when he finally started working hard. He left school with good enough grades to get into college but the rest of his family mocked him for that. Who needs grades, or a job? That's what Social Services are for, right? It would never occur to someone like Sherry that's she's stealing from people who genuinely need Social Services. Anyway, some children mimic their parents and some rebel, and Gerald rebelled with so much determination, you'd struggle to believe Sherry is his mother. Or that Ray – who's now in prison – is his father. He's as different from them as butterflies are from blobfish.

His straightforward, steadfast honesty made Gerald a trusted colleague and employee, so he slowly but inevitably moved up the career ladder. That was, until he set out on his own and started that foolish business. After he went back to Lämsä, I thought he would keep climbing. It never occurred to me that his steadfast honesty would end up being the thing that held him back in his career. Gerald has no idea how to be the meat in the sandwich; he can't tell those middle-management white lies: *I would've given you a bigger raise if it were up to me... No, I'm not aware of any layoffs ahead.*

Gerald shook off the trailer-trash accent and learned to communicate in polite society, but the damage Sherry did with her constant lying left a scar that never healed. We pay for that every day. Gerald's aversion to white lies has meant struggling to meet bills, to save for Jason's education, or to provide a better life for us. If it wasn't for me...

I hate Sherry.

I hate her so much, it's physical: blood-coursing, heart-pounding, fist-clenching revulsion. The woman – if you can call her that – wouldn't know polite society if it punched her in the face. I picture her sitting across the table from Chad and Portia Hardman, the Christmas turkey and trimmings between them.

Chuck us the roasties, wouldya, Portia? Ooh wot are these?

They're parsnips, Sherry. Goodness gracious me, have you never seen a parsnip?

Nahhhh.

I shut my eyes to black out the carnage.

Ricky throws himself on to the sofa, splaying across it with his feet up, while Gerald and I stand and face our execution by firing squad. Sherry says, 'You didn't need to leave Liam on the doorstep like that.'

Gerald's response is flat but firm. 'I'm not having a child-molester in my house.'

'Child-molester, what bollocks! She looked eighteen. And that wuz years ago. It weren't 'is fault.'

'What do you want, Sherry?'

'Mum,' she says. 'I ain't Sherry, I'm Mum.'

'What do you want?'

She twists her lips into a rotten-tooth smile, 'I need another loan, Gerry.'

I say, 'If you're going to ask him for money, Sherry, at least have the courtesy to call him by his name. It's Gerald.'

''E's my son. I'll call 'im what I like!'

'Jesus.'

''E ain't gonna 'elp ya,' she laughs. ''E ain't never 'elped me! But you will, wontcha, Gerry?'

'I can't.' Gerald stands up straight. 'Not this time. I was passed over for promotion again. Anything we manage to save at the end of the month is for Jason's final year of university. I don't have anything to give you, Sherry.'

'Mum!' She stabs her chest. 'You have to. It's different this time. I... I owe it.'

'To who?' Gerald asks.

'Troy Cullen.'

'Troy Cullen?!'

I have no idea who Troy Cullen is, but Gerald sounds scared. 'How much?'

'It's not what you fink, Gerry. It weren't for drugs or anyfink like that. Ricky borrered 'is car and it got stolen. Now Troy says we 'ave to pay him back.'

'Did he report it to the police?'

'Well...'

'Of course he didn't. It was probably stolen to begin with. How much?'

'Just over six.'

'Hundred?'

'Don't be stupid, Gerry. Thousand.'

'Get out.' Gerald speaks so quietly I question whether I heard him correctly. Then he says it again, louder. '*Get out.*'

A smile breaks across my lips and I stand as tall as him.

Sherry doesn't speak, but she doesn't move either.

So I say, 'You heard him, Sherry. Get out. We aren't giving you any more drug money.'

She gets to her feet. 'Come on, Ricky. I think we've outstayed our welcome.' She pauses as she walks past us and pats Gerald on the cheek. 'You'll fink about it, wontcha, Gerry? And, after you've fought about it, you'll come round wiv the money.'

A few moments later, the front door slams. Gerald slumps into his armchair, then leans forward on his elbows and buries his head in his hands, fingertips in his white tufts.

'You won't, will you, Gerald?'

'I'll have to. They'll break her legs. And that'll only cover the interest.'

SIXTEEN

GLENDA

In some ways I feel sorry for Laura.

Insomuch as you can feel sorry for a bright, young thing who's probably got everything she ever wanted from the moment she fell gracefully out of her mother's womb. She's so dainty and pliable, I bet her mother didn't even break a sweat. My mother screamed bloody murder for two days until they finally cut me out.

It's obvious she's marrying Mark for money. She said herself they'd only been together a few months, and she's already living in his flat. She would have seen him around Hardman Studios and set her laser sights on him the moment she found out he was Chad Hardman's son. What chance did Mark have once she'd used the same wily charms she used on me? I'll admit, she had me captivated – briefly – when I met her with the chartered land surveyor.

If they can afford Primrose Cottage, they can buy any house they like. And if they love it as much as Laura made out, they'll do the right thing.

I tear the labels from three tins, screw them into tight, unrecognisable balls, and decant the contents into a Tupperware box, ready for tonight's dinner.

For a moment there I almost toyed with the idea of actually using Tom's kitchen garden. Of harvesting the vegetables instead of letting them go over and burying them under the soil. I thought that tending it wouldn't seem such a mind-numbing chore if Laura were chatting away on the other side of the fence. Good neighbours becoming fast friends.

But it's not as if Laura would have been handing money over the fence, helping us with Jason's fees. Sherry's visit yesterday was a stark reminder of who we are, where we come from, and the man I married. He's such a sap, such a sucker, that he'll pay Sherry's debts no matter what I say and leave us living on next to nothing. I'm damned if I'm doing that. Sherry got my priorities back in check.

The money I kept back for myself is almost gone. Soon I'll have to ask Gerald for more, and he won't pay for food when there's a perfectly good kitchen garden sitting idle outside. He certainly wouldn't let me carry on wasting money on seeds; Tom always collected and stored them, constantly harping on about them as an endless supply of free food, and now Gerald's fixated on it, too.

Of course, Gerald doesn't have the first clue what a challenge it is to plan meals around what's ripe, or what a monumental pain in the arse it is to harvest seeds. Mashing fruit and washing off the flesh before letting seeds dry out in the airing cupboard. And don't get me started on saving lettuce and carrot seeds. Waiting for them to bolt, drying out the flower heads, and separating the seeds from the chaff. To hell with all that! Just to save a few pounds? It's so much quicker to decant the shop-bought ones into seed envelopes and label them. What Gerald doesn't know won't hurt him.

I pop the Heinz tomato soup in the fridge, wash my hands, dry them on a tea towel, and pick up my mobile.

Laura's bright tones tinkle down the phone while she tells me the chartered land surveyor has drawn up the plan, and her solicitor has drawn up the boundary agreement for me to sign as Tom's power of attorney.

'You should have it tomorrow,' she says.

'No.'

'I'm sorry, what did you say?'

'I said, no. I won't sign it.'

'But...' she stammers. 'You agreed. You shook hands; it's binding. That's a gentlemen's agreement. And we've paid a thousand pounds for the survey, more for the solicitor. You can't pull out now.'

'I can.' My voice is hard.

'Glenda...' I do love how she says my name, softly, yet with the absolute precision of her privileged lineage. 'You know what Primrose Cottage means to us. If you renege on this deal, we'll lose it. It's our dream home.'

'Well,' I say, matter-of-factly, 'if you want your dream home, you'll have to pay us thirty-five thousand pounds.'

She's breathless.

'Thirty-five... this is crazy... Glenda, the surveyor told you you don't have a case. You don't have any evidence. And, even if you did, the land isn't worth anything like that. It's worth no more than a few hundred pounds.'

'I know my father's garden. You don't. I'll get the evidence.'

'Glenda, please, I'm begging you. Don't do this.'

I don't speak.

'That's it?' she asks. 'You aren't going to say anything else? Can't we talk about this? Get the land surveyor back for another meeting?'

I don't speak.

'I'll pay for it, Glenda. She can explain it all to you again.'

I don't speak.

'Okay, what if we paid you the five thousand pounds Scott offered you? Along with all of the other costs as well?

115

The chartered land surveyor's fees, the solicitor's fees, Land Registry, the fence, everything?'

'I said thirty-five thousand.'

Laura hangs up.

'Who was that?' Gerald steps into the lounge just as the call ends.

'Laura. The new neighbour. She just reneged on the boundary agreement.'

'What?'

'She said they won't pay us for the land.'

'I thought it was all sorted?'

'So did I. I thought we'd reached an agreement. We even shook hands.'

'What was the agreement? What did you negotiate?'

Fortunately I never got around to telling Gerald yesterday about the deal we struck, because Sherry showed up. Much as I hate that woman, she may have saved my bacon with her loathsome visit.

'Ten thousand,' I say. 'That's what the chartered land surveyor felt was fair: the value of the land itself plus the devaluation of Tom's property from losing a whole strip of garden.'

Gerald's face falls. 'We really could have used that money,' he says. 'That would have paid Sherry's debts. Now, I'll have to dip into the savings for Jason's second year, and heaven only knows how we'll pay for the third. I'll have to take out a loan, and we'll really have to tighten our belts to make those repayments.'

'I know.' I put a reassuring hand on his cheek. 'But don't worry, I'm not giving up just yet. If they're decent people, they'll come around. They'll do what's right. They'll have to if they want the house.'

'That's such a shame. I didn't want things to start out this way with our new neighbours. I'd hoped we might get along.'

'I don't think that will happen now. But if we can sort it

out quickly, perhaps they'll realise we're just asking for what's fair. They won't hold that against us, surely.'

'Ten thousand doesn't seem like it would be a lot of money to them,' he says. 'You'd think they would have paid it if the chartered land surveyor felt it was a fair valuation.'

'Greed, Gerald. The greedy rich.'

'So what happens now?'

'We let them stew for a bit.'

SEVENTEEN

LAURA

MARK COMES home late and finds me soaking in his tub with a huge glass of wine on the tile surround. Finn's curled up on the floor by the radiator. His tail wags when Mark comes in, but he doesn't get up. Not this time. He knows something's wrong.

I spent the first three hours after putting the phone down on Glenda trying to think of a solution. I spent the next pacing the floor of Mark's lounge. And the last staring at the four walls of this bathroom.

Since we saw Primrose Cottage I've been ignoring the door, but it hasn't been working. The delivery guys just knock harder and longer, and Finn gets so worked up, it takes more time to get over the interruption than it would to quickly answer the door and accept the parcels. Then, this morning, Madge was banging so frantically on the door, calling my name, that I ended up answering because I was worried about her. It turned out her fridge had stopped working because she had it plugged into an extension cable with half a dozen other appliances and had blown the fuse. By the time I'd sorted out an arrangement of extensions, plugged into different sockets so they weren't all drawing off the same one, two hours had passed.

I should be working on my project now, but my brain won't stop churning. Any creative person will tell you that your Muse and your Monkey Mind share the same lodgings. Your Monkey Mind creates mental chaos by feverishly prattling on about every one of your problems, while acting out every imaginary scenario that's bound to make them worse. And your Muse... well, she's far too polite to say anything until he shuts up. So, instead of listening to my story come alive with exhilarating dialogue and special effects, I've listened to five hours of monkey chatter while imagining Glenda Skinner's trout-like smile.

I want to smash her face in.

Mark says, 'Bubble bath? Wine? That solemn face...? This can't be good.'

I look up at him but don't say anything.

He's serious then. 'Are you alright?'

I'm not prone to bursting into tears, but it happens anyway.

Mark gets down on his knees, hooks an arm over the tub, and takes my hand. 'Laura, what's happened?'

'We've lost the house. Glenda pulled out of the agreement.'

'But... she can't. She shook on it. We've signed the contracts.'

'She can, and she has.'

Mark lets go of my hand, slides on to his backside and lifts his knees up to rest his elbows on them.

I say, 'It could take ages to find another house. And if there's a chain, it could be months before we move. I've tried to figure a way out of this but there isn't one. I have to go, Mark. I can't stay here. I need to get out of the city, rent somewhere quiet.' I tell him about my day, about Madge and her refrigerator, and the constant disruptions in spite of my attempts to ignore the door.

'We'll rent somewhere together, then.'

'I've looked at everything within commutable distance for you. Either there's no room for a studio or they don't take dogs. I was lucky to find my last place and they only let me bring Finn because it was so tiny, nobody else wanted it. It'd sat empty for months. We'd have to live so far out of the city, we'll barely see each other with you commuting. You'll be exhausted. Here, you're ten minutes' walk from the office. You have your beautiful studio. It makes no sense for you to leave. It'll just be temporary, until we find another house.'

Another house.

Now I've seen Primrose Cottage, the words 'another house' bubble like acid in my stomach. I know I thought it was a crazy idea at first, Mark buying such an excessive place, but once we'd made the decision I'd begun planning out what would go where, and the closer we'd come to having it, the more attached I'd got to it. It's got its hooks into me, and now it won't let go. It wasn't just bricks and mortar; it felt like home the moment we stepped through the door. Even though the cottage is huge, and the rooms are big, it felt small, cosy, warm. It's so perfect for us. I *saw* us there. Happy. It's as if we already own it, and now it's being stolen from us.

I bite back the tears, try to be strong. 'I'm going to stay at Mum's until I can find another place to rent,' I say. 'She has an annexe I can work in. I've got a removal company coming the day after tomorrow to take my studio out of storage and transport it to hers. I'll pack the rest of my stuff tomorrow and head there in the afternoon to get organised.'

'Cambridge? That's two and a half hours away.'

'It'll just be until I can find somewhere closer.'

'Don't. Please. I don't want you to go.'

'We can Zoom and stuff. But I can't afford any more days like today. If I'm going to make the deadline, I have to focus, get back on track. I'll be working all hours just to catch up anyway.'

'You care about this project more than me?'

'Of course I don't. But it's my job, and this project could change my life.'

'I thought I was going to do that.'

'You have. As I said, this is just temporary. Once I'm back on track, we can start searching for places to live or rent together. But I don't have the time right now. I can't be taking days out left and right to go to viewings. This way, I'll be up and running in a few days.'

'How could she do this to us? Over a bloody metre of land?'

We're quiet for a while, both lost in our own thoughts. Then, more out of desperation than anything else, I say, 'What if Scott really did build the summerhouse part-way into their garden? You said we should consider paying them. What if they're telling the truth, and somebody else pays them? They'll be living in our house for the sake of thirty-five grand.' The moment the words leave my lips, the sour churning in my stomach tells me I'm just wishing it were true while not believing it for a moment. Glenda doesn't want the summerhouse moved; if she did, she would have objected to it years ago. She wants money. But a buyer with questionable scruples, who isn't concerned about right and wrong, could snap up Primrose Cottage.

'You said she didn't have any evidence.'

'She doesn't. Just stories about what the garden used to look like when she was a child, and a couple of photographs that don't prove anything.'

'But you believe her now?'

'No.' I shake my head vehemently. 'I know she's lying. Now I've met her, seen her lack of evidence, and had the chartered land surveyor come down entirely on our side, I know Glenda Skinner has fabricated this entire dispute. It's not about land; it's about money. And even if we did move the summerhouse, they'd find some other way of getting paid. You should have heard her on the phone. She was a completely different woman from the one I met with the surveyor. I was speaking to the woman beneath the polite charade. I told her what the house means to us – that it's our dream home – and she was ice-cold. She said, if we wanted the house, we'd have to give her thirty-five grand. It's extortion. I don't doubt it for a second.'

'So, for argument's sake, we pay them... move in. How do you think you'll feel about the house after that?'

'Sick to my stomach. Every time I ran into her, I'd know she extorted money from us. I don't think I could live with myself.'

'Me neither. Fucking bitch. I've never struck a person in my whole life, but I want to wring her fucking neck.'

We're quiet again. There's nothing else to say.

Suddenly, Mark leaps to his feet. I think he's about to walk out and actually go to Glenda's house to wring her neck. But instead, he climbs into the bath, fully clothed in his suit, belt and shoes.

'What are you doing?' I laugh.

'If this is my last night with you, I'm not wasting one more minute of it. I need you in my arms.'

He settles down behind me in the tub, and I press my bare back into his chest as he wraps himself around me. The left front panel of his jacket floats up beside me but the right panel sinks. I plunge my hand inside and pull out his mobile phone. We both burst out laughing.

'I didn't want to talk to anyone but you, anyway,' he says.

'It'll dry.' I lean over the side and drop it on the bathmat.

We sit like that until the water turns lukewarm, Mark running a hand up and down my belly while scooping water over me. 'Do you really have to go?'

I nod. 'I don't want to.'

'There has to be a way out of this. The Land Registry holds the title deeds; surely it's their responsibility to say where our boundary is?'

'*Hold* is the operative word. It's up to homeowners to define and maintain their boundaries. Like so many places in old villages like Clay Norton, Primrose Cottage and Oleander House are both so old that they used to be tied properties; they were owned by a four-hundred-acre farm. And when the farmer sold them off in the '50s, the transfer deeds were lost. The original transfer isn't online. I even called the Land Registry and begged them to check their archives, but they have no copy. They said compulsory registration was still being phased in back then, so a lot of documents are missing. Which means, we can't prove, historically, where the boundary was. If we could, we could shut Glenda down.'

'The police, then. You said she doesn't have any evidence, and this is extortion. That's a criminal offence, right? So let's get the police involved. She'll back off then.'

Mark is thinking of every solution I've already exhausted. And I feel for him, because, now, he's experiencing the disappointment I felt being stymied at every turn. I sigh.

'I spoke to them, too. I called 101 for advice. They said the Crown Prosecution Service won't bring a case for extortion. They said, all Glenda has to say is that she *believes* the land belongs to her. Then any attempt to demand money from us is appropriate given that belief. They said boundary disputes are civil matters the police don't get involved in. So, the only option left is to take Glenda to court, and that could take a year at least. And yes, I called a boundary solicitor for advice as well. If you can believe it, he said we should pay them. He said it would be the cheapest, least stressful way out of the problem.'

'You aren't serious?'

'I am. I couldn't believe it either.'

'This is insane. You're saying someone can literally walk on to your property, say *That's mine!* and there's nobody to stop them? No laws. Nobody to help you? And the legal advice is to pay them?'

'It's crazy, right? But it's true. There's no concept of stealing land in British law. If she broke in here and stole your thirty-five-grand mixing desk, the CPS would do everything for you. They'd charge her with theft, and you'd go to court as the victim. But if someone steals half your garden the police won't do anything. The crook only has to mutter two words: *boundary dispute*. Then it's not a criminal offence. The victim has to take their own perpetrator to court and prove that what's been stolen belongs to them. And if the judge gets out of bed on the wrong side and the victim loses, they pay their perpetrator's legal fees along with their own. People lose their houses over this shit.'

Mark takes his hand off my belly and worries his forehead with it; he's right where I was five hours ago.

'Sorry you've had such a shit day,' he says. 'After a whole morning of interruptions, you must have spent the other half on the phone.'

'Not really. The calls didn't take that long, I wasted the rest of the afternoon reeling over them. I couldn't focus; I just kept trying to come up with solutions. We were *this close*.' I pinch my fingers together. 'Angela still thinks we're exchanging contracts tomorrow morning. I didn't have the heart to make that phone call. I still keep thinking there must be a way out of this.'

'I'll have to call her first thing. I'll call the estate agent, too, get her to tell Scott what's happened. Unless Glenda has called him, he won't have a clue. Shit, I mean, this is bad enough for us, but think of Scott and Emily. They've already had one sale fall through, and they've already bought somewhere else. Now they're stuck with two properties and they won't be able to sell unless they pay the Skinners. Can you imagine it, being the victim of extortion, forced to pay your blackmailer just so you can sell your house, and the police won't do anything about it?'

Mark's right: I was so wrapped up in my own disappointment, I'd forgotten about Scott and Emily. 'God, it makes me spitting mad. She's actually going to pull this off. Thirty-five grand.'

I imagine Glenda doing a victory lap around her garden. It makes me want to smash her face into one of those raised vegetable beds. The thought of Mark making those calls tomorrow, putting an end to our dream, makes me feel sick. Somebody has to stop that woman.

I say, 'I'll call Angela and the estate agent.'

'You have a big day tomorrow.'

'It's fine, I want to run through everything I've tried with Angela, make sure I haven't missed anything. And I need to speak to the estate agent anyway, chat about what we'd be looking for in other potential properties.'

'I guess, as you said, things happen for a reason,' Mark says. 'But I won't lie – I don't think I've ever been this disappointed by anything in my life.'

'Me neither. I'm heartbroken.'

He kisses me on the cheek, and I twist around in the bath to kiss him back. Knowing this will be our last night together for a while, I peel back his jacket, anxious to get him out of those wet clothes. A few moments later, my breasts are pressed against his naked chest. And with my arms wrapped around his back, clinging tight while he's inside me, we rock back and forth in the water.

And, when it's over, Mark kisses me so deeply, it feels like goodbye.

EIGHTEEN

LAURA

PERCHED ON the edge of the sofa, I check the clock in the top-right corner of my laptop. I've been checking it every sixty seconds, waiting for 09:00 to appear and the solicitor's office to open. Mark keeps flitting in and out, making trips between his studio and the kitchen. Coffee. Coffee and toast. More coffee. He isn't going in to the office today; he's doing any urgent tasks from home so he can spend time with me before I leave for Mum's this afternoon.

08:57.

Mark comes in again, on the phone this time. 'I'm not in today, Ben, but I'll get on that now.' He goes through to the kitchen, I'm not sure what for this time. Then he comes out again. My foot twitches, my knee bouncing the laptop up and down. 'Yes... No... Yes, I loved her audition. She's perfect. Sign her up. Yes, tomorrow, for the meeting.' He winks at me, then goes out again. His studio door closes softly, and I wonder how long it will be before he makes another trip. I bite the edge of my thumb where a hangnail has formed.

08:59.

Music floats out from beneath the closed door of his studio. He's started the final edit of episode four of *Malikbay*. He's like me: he'll get immersed in the work, lost in time...

12:17.

I stare at my laptop. I haven't moved from the spot, haven't packed a thing.

The studio door opens and Mark comes out, headphones draped around his neck. I don't know how he can use those Bluetooth ones. Too much trouble. They disconnect when you move away from the computer, and then I can never get them reconnected again. Or they connect to my mobile phone instead of the computer and I have to fanny about trying to force them to switch over.

I'm expecting him to go into the kitchen for another snack – he snacks a lot while he works – but instead he flops down on the sofa next to me, practically horizontal.

'What did Angela say?' His voice is tinged with sadness, the unpalatable leftovers from the news Glenda force-fed us yesterday.

'Nothing.'

'Nothing? She must have said something.'

'I didn't call her.'

He sits up straight. 'What do you mean, you didn't call her?'

'I mean...' My voice breaks, and I clear my throat. 'I didn't call her. Or the estate agent.'

Mark checks his watch. 'It's gone twelve. You said you'd call at nine.'

'I know.'

'Quick, call her now, we might still make it.' He leaps to his feet. 'Where's your phone?'

I shrug.

He scans the sofa cushions, the coffee table, and when he can't find my phone he heads for his studio. 'I'll call her.'

'It's too late,' I say to his back. 'She emailed half an hour ago to say congratulations. We've exchanged contracts.'

He turns around slowly. 'Laura... What the fuck have you done?'

I shrug again. I consider telling him I forgot to call Angela, or that I tried several times and couldn't get through. But I don't want to lie to him.

'I couldn't do it, Mark. That woman! I couldn't let her steal our dream from us. Then I realised how stupid I was being and picked up the phone, but Angela's email came through while I was on hold... I suppose we have to buy it now.'

'No. *I* have to buy it now.'

I hang my head. 'I'm sorry, Mark.'

'You didn't even want the house and now you've exchanged contracts without telling me? Without telling Angela? She might have had an idea how to fix this.'

'There was no fix.'

'Jesus, Laura, you're impossible! Nobody can help you, can they? You have to do everything yourself. You didn't think I should have a say in whether I spent four million pounds on a house with a boundary dispute?!' He runs his hands through his hair, starts pacing. 'Four hundred thousand. The deposit was four hundred thousand. If we pull out now, I'll lose almost half a million pounds. What the fuck is wrong with you? What were you thinking? Were you thinking at all?'

'Of course. I'm not stupid.' I leap to my feet, reach out to him. I don't deserve it, but I want him to take me in his arms and comfort me. But although he stops pacing, he won't release the tight grip he has on his hair. That beautiful, thick hair. I was running my fingers through it only last night. And, when it came down to it, I couldn't leave him. I just couldn't. 'Mark... Mark, listen.' I grab his elbows and pull his arms down. Reluctantly, he lets go of his hair and flops his arms to his sides in exasperation. 'Please...let me explain. Will you sit down and listen, just for a minute?'

He perches on the sofa's edge, his back stiff. 'I'm listening.'

'Okay, so... Scott built the summerhouse ten years ago and he submitted the planning application for it a year before the build. The Skinners didn't raise any objections then. Why? Why wait over a decade to bring a boundary dispute against Scott?'

'We *know* the answer to that.' He can't help sounding exasperated, and I get it, really I do. 'The sale. It was their leverage.'

'Exactly. Just five days after you put the offer in, when the estate agent marked the property as sold, suddenly Scott has a boundary dispute. We said back then that the timing was too convenient.'

'This isn't news, Laura. We know it's extortion; it doesn't change anything.'

'No, but you're missing the point. They have no evidence. The surveyor told them that if they went to court on the basis of what they have, they would lose.'

'So?'

'So, they can't take *us* to court. If they lost, they'd have to pay the legal fees on both sides, and that could cost them their home. I saw their house that day at the surveyor's meeting. They don't have money to burn.'

Mark relaxes a little, leans forward, rests his forearms on his knees. 'So, if they can't afford to lose, they'll never risk going to court.'

'Exactly. We move in, we put up a fence. They can't take it down because it'll be on our property, and if they tear it down we'll call the police. They might not get involved in boundary disputes, but property damage is a crime. Nobody will help the Skinners any more than they would help us. The Land Registry, the CPS, the police – nobody will get involved in their fabricated dispute. They'll be powerless. They can demand their thirty-five thousand till they're blue in the face, but once we're in, we have no reason to pay them. No conveyancing, no leverage.'

He thinks about it for a moment, weighing up my plan, then slowly nods before saying, 'There's just one problem. Angela could lose her licence for not informing the mortgage company that there's a boundary dispute on the property. And, if they find out, we could lose the mortgage, then the house.'

'She didn't know. And neither did we.'

'But...we did...the phone call, yesterday. Glenda will be able to prove you knew.'

'Only if she recorded it. And I called her out of the blue. She wouldn't have known who was calling. She gave me her number during the meeting, so I could call her when the boundary agreement was on its way, but I didn't give her mine. So unless she had the wherewithal to quickly start a recording app in the middle of our conversation, she has no proof of what we talked about. It could have been anything; I could have been checking her details for the agreement. I called the estate agent at midday and asked her to email Glenda and tell her the agreement was on its way. Glenda will reply saying she isn't signing, and that'll be the only evidence she pulled out – it'll come *after* exchange. Angela will be covered; we'll be covered. Glenda could try to cause trouble, but we'll just deny it. I'll say she said nothing of the sort, and it'll be my word against hers.'

'You're an evil genius.'

The relief that Mark's okay with this, that he understands why I've done it, comes out in one long breath.

But then he says, 'But what if you're wrong?'

'I'm not wrong.' I take the seat next to him. 'I promise you, once we've moved in, this'll all go away.'

He sits there for a minute not saying a word, not even turning to look at me. So I stare at the side of his head, watching the cogs whirring though the dark hole of his ear canal. Finally, he turns to look at me. 'You're not leaving?'

I grin. 'I'm not leaving.'

He throws his arms around me and holds me so tight, my neck cricks up at the ceiling. It's hard to talk in this position but I manage five words. 'And you own Primrose Cottage.'

'*We* own it,' he says, joy and relief cracking his voice. 'And you're not leaving. You're so fucking smart – I would never have thought of it. Thank God you didn't call Angela.'

I thank God, too, that Angela's email came through when it did. Because now, Glenda Skinner…you'll finally realise who you're up against.

NINETEEN

GLENDA

IT FEELS LIKE forever since Jason left for university. The days crawl by. It's only a week since I reneged on the boundary agreement but even that feels like a month. But Thursday is almost here. Gerald has taken some time off and we're driving up to Scarborough tomorrow afternoon to spend a long weekend with Jason. I've packed him a food parcel, and all that remains is to get a few tiger loaves from the village shop. They're his favourite, and he can freeze two of them. I bet he's lost weight since leaving home. No doubt he's been living on packet noodles and takeout burgers. Or, if Simon's mum has anything to do with it, Fray Bentos pies and Smash.

As I walk past Primrose Cottage, I smile broadly just in case Scott or Emily happen to be looking out of the window. They must know that if they lose Laura and Mark they'll never be able to sell that place. They'll be stuck there. I glare at their front door as if my thoughts will penetrate the wood and seep into their expensive home: *give us the money, and this will all go away.*

Either they will cave, or their buyers will. It's like watching a game of chicken where the only person who wins is me. Will it be Scott and Emily who swerve and end up paying us, or will it be Mark and Laura? My money's on Laura; she practically begged me over the phone—

'Glenda!'

I collide with Cynthia.

'Not looking where you were going,' she chides.

'No.' I don't apologise.

Cynthia's an interior designer. She always looks the same, and yet I've never seen her wearing the same outfit twice. Her wardrobe is a homogeny of flowing knitwear. Before she leaves the house in the morning, I imagine she sketches herself into a fashion croquis on one of those A3 drawing pads that artists use. I see her testing out various ensembles in beige. Always beige.

I bet her sketches are skinnier than she is.

Cynthia's tall; she looks down when she speaks, talks through her nose. She reminds me of a schoolteacher I hated as a child.

'What's it like being back in Clay Norton after all those years?' she asks. 'Where are you living again?'

She knows exactly where I live, we've been here for five fucking years. 'Tom's. We came back to take care of him.'

'That must be cramped with so many of you—'

'Jason's at university. So there's just the three of us.'

She ignores the interruption. 'But at least you'll get the house when he goes. I mean, your sister can't expect you to split it with her if you're living there, can she? That wouldn't be reasonable.'

'We built an extension for Tom out of the profits from our old house, so no, probably not.' That's not strictly true. There were no profits from our old house; Gerald remortgaged that to the hilt to start his business, and we lost it all. Tom paid for the extension, and it was initially for us not for him. But

Cynthia doesn't need to know that. 'He has his own room at the back with an en-suite.'

'Really? Goodness, there can't be much of a garden left after extending. It was small as it was.'

'We're not keen gardeners, so we don't miss it.'

'Tom always was. Didn't he grow roses...and fruit and vegetables?'

'He can't get around like he used to.'

'You need a place like Primrose Cottage, Glenda.' She nods in its direction. 'Do you remember Anne Huntington-Whitney?'

I grit my teeth and force a smile. 'Of course.'

'You were so obsessed with her when you were little, do you remember? So desperate to be friends, always dying to be invited to parties at Primrose Cottage, so you could play in their garden. But her mother never thought you were good enough for little Anne, did she? Her prim, perfect daughter. What a snob Nancy Huntington-Whitney was. I never agreed with the way they treated you.'

Cynthia says that now – she's said it before, many times – but when we were kids she was always invited to Anne's parties, and she used to lord it over me. She thought the way Mrs Huntington-Whitney treated me and my mother was a hoot.

I reach into my handbag. Thanks to incredible forethought on my part, I stashed my chef's knife in there just before I left the house. I had a feeling I might run into Cynthia and it's always handy for occasions like this. I rummage around until my palm makes contact with the handle, which I grip tightly as I pull it out. With all the force I can muster, I stab Cynthia straight in the eye. The blade plunges all the way through the socket – so satisfying – into her mushy, vacant brain...

'Did you hear?' she says. 'Scott and Emily are leaving tomorrow. Such a shame. There's a new couple moving in.'

I don't respond because I'm distracted by the knife handle bobbing up and down in rhythm with the cadence of her speech. That, and the blood and eye goop running down her left cheek...

'They aren't leaving after all,' I say. 'Their sale fell through.'

'What? No...that's not right. Emily told me herself. They're definitely leaving tomorrow morning. The new couple move in in the afternoon.'

My heart thrums and I narrow my eyes at Cynthia. 'A young couple?'

'Yes. And clearly upwardly mobile, since they can afford Primrose Cottage. They probably work at Hardman's like everyone else in this village.' She waves a hand around as if the residents of Clay Norton are beneath her. 'But they must be very high up in the company. It sold for four million, you know? They were here yesterday with some contractor, by the looks of it. I guess they're having work done right away. The woman's very pretty. Polite. We only had a brief chat, but I think we'll be great friends. She's my type of person, if you know what I mean?'

So Laura is Cynthia's type, is she? Young and upwardly mobile. Not like me and Gerald: old before our time and downwardly mobile, having to live with my father because we can't afford a house of our own, let alone a nursing home for Tom. Not without sacrificing all of my inheritance. We can't even afford one of those places that stinks of piss because the staff are too busy abusing the patients to wipe their squishy old butts.

'They're not that young,' I say. 'She's been married before.'

'Really? How do you know?'

'I've met her, too. We had a long chat.'

We didn't have a long chat. I Googled Laura and nosed through the General Register Office to find out as much as I could about her. You never know what might prove useful about a person.

'Oh, so this is her second marriage—'

'They're not married.'

Again, Cynthia ignores the interruption. 'Second-chance romances. I just love those, don't you? That *Second Bite of the Apple* by Madison Stackhouse left such an impact on me.' She makes a sound like a mini orgasm – the only kind she's ever had, I imagine – while I reach into my handbag again. After a quick forage around, I pull out a hardback copy of *Second Bite of the Apple* and, holding it in both hands like a baseball bat, slug Cynthia round the face with it. Blood spurts from her nose; droplets fly through the air in slow motion and splash across the pavement. Her perfectly powdered cheeks wobble back and forth from the force of the blow, and pink spit flies from her lipsticked mouth to blend with the blood on the tarmac. It could be a Jackson Pollock.

Tarmac? Or is it asphalt? I never have known the difference...

'Well,' I say, 'best be getting on.' And I walk off before she has the opportunity to be an even bigger cunt than she already is.

TWENTY

LAURA

MARK COMES into the lounge carrying a handful of papers, when he should be carrying packing boxes. He signed up for the heavy work – getting the right cartons into the right rooms – while I volunteered to unpack and organise everything into its rightful place. Only he catches me red-handed, opening the patio doors to the garden, with a small box under my arm, my headphones resting on top.

'I see what you're up to.'

I glance down at the package I'm carrying, marked 'Audio Cables', then at the others in the hallway marked 'Kitchen'.

'What? It was in the way, I kept tripping over it.' My cheeks flush.

'That little box was in the way? I've seen you sneaking in and out of there all morning. How come I get to lug around all the boring, heavy stuff while you have fun in your new studio?'

'It's not fun, it's my job. I need to make sure everything's set up and working, so I can start early tomorrow.'

'How is it?'

During the past week, between exchange and completion, Scott and Emily were kind enough to allow access to the summerhouse so that Mark could have it kitted out with a state-of-the-art recording studio. He wanted me to be up and running as soon as we moved in. Most of the equipment is overkill for my needs, but with the sound booth I'll be able to produce everything from audiobooks to radio plays. Just being in the studio makes me feel like a seasoned professional.

'Ridiculous,' I say. 'Completely excessive. And I love it.' I lean over and kiss him. 'Thank you.'

'You're welcome.'

'Speaking of getting things working, did you get a chance to check these headphones?' I lift them off the box under my arm and wave them at him. 'I did a quick test in the studio and I'm getting every other word. I don't know if it's the headphones, the cable or the console.'

'No, I got so caught up with the move. I thought you were going to return them anyway?'

'I was, but then they started working again.'

'Well, the console's brand new, so it's not likely to be that. It must be the cable. Have you tried them with your iPhone?'

I pick up the cable and wave the quarter-inch headphone jack at him.

'Ahh... yes. That's not gonna work, is it? I don't know why you don't go Bluetooth.'

'I'm old-school.'

'Luddite. Those headphones are shit anyway. I'll get you a new pair.'

'Don't you think you've done enough? If it's not the cable, I'll get these repaired.'

'Let me treat you,' he says. 'There's no point fixing something that was bad to begin with. Besides, a repair'll take time. Time you don't have. If you don't like Bluetooth, I'll ask the team what they use. They've been through dozens over the years. They know which ones to steer clear of.'

'Ah, yes, the team...' I say through gritted teeth.

'What?'

'Steve Banks called again. This time, to tell me the deadline's been pulled forward a week, and to ask again if I was sure I didn't need any help.'

'Why the change? I haven't heard anything about schedule alterations.'

'I wouldn't be surprised if he's persuaded Chad that he should give it a final edit and implement any changes he sees fit. I don't know why he can't keep his nose out of my project and focus on his own.'

'I told you why. He wants in on it to set himself up for bigger things. And I think he feels threatened by you. Rightly so. He wants to know just how threatened he should be before it airs. I'm not surprised he's desperate to hear it. And man, will he feel intimidated after he does!'

'He's just trying to get his name on it somewhere.' I don't tell Mark that this deadline change has me seriously worried, and I was already up against it. 'I promise I'll unpack the kettle, tea bags and coffee machine ready for the morning. But can we leave the rest of the boring stuff till the weekend? You've bought me all those new toys; you can't expect me not to play with them.'

'You're so naughty.' He leans over the box in my arms and kisses me. When he pulls away, I remember the papers he's been holding this whole time.

'Anyway, you're not carrying boring boxes either. What's that?'

'Just the post.' He flips through the envelopes one by one. 'Most of it's for Scott. He said he'd set up a redirect, but I guess these fell through the net before it activated.'

My face falls. It's silly, I know, but I wanted to be the first one to walk down the driveway and collect the post. Primrose Cottage has a cute mailbox by the roadside. It's such an American thing to do: walk to the mailbox at the end of your drive. It even has one of those red flags to let you know there's something inside. It's so quaint and romantic. Not like having your letters shoved through a hole in the door to land on a dirty doormat.

'I just saw the neighbours,' Mark says. 'I see what you mean about Glenda. She's seriously creepy.'

'I know, but stunning too, right?'

'Striking is perhaps a better word. The way she looked at me. It was like coming face-to-face with...' He thinks about it for a moment. 'A psycho android serial killer dressed as a puritanical 1940s housewife.'

I laugh. 'Yep, that about covers it.'

'Well, I think we're safe for tonight at least. Their car was loaded up with cases; they must be going away.'

'That's good. With the fence going in tomorrow, it's best they're not here to make a fuss. Have you seen what she's done back there? It's a mess. And with our gardens opening right on to each other, I'm having to keep Finn tied up so he can't—'

'Speaking of making a fuss...' Mark has opened one of the envelopes and is scanning the letter inside.

'What is it?'

'It's from *her*.'

'Glenda? What does it say?'

Mark reads the letter aloud. '*OFFICIAL NOTICE. To: The Owners of Primrose Cottage, Orchard Lane, Clay Norton, Oxford, OX55 5NG.*'

I put down the box I was carrying and lean over the letter. 'Is it from a solicitor?'

'No. It's signed *Glenda Skinner, Lasting Power of Attorney for Thomas McBain.*'

I tilt the letter in his hands so I can read it, too. 'Why would she address us like that? She knows our names.'

Mark reads the rest, emphasising every word Glenda has capitalised. '*NOW, you are hereby served 30 days' notice that your implied right to Oleander House's land is removed.*

And NOW you are hereby served 30 days' notice to remove structures from the curtilage of Oleander House, Orchard Lane, Clay Norton, Oxford, OX55 5NG. Please refer to Title Deeds HP32450 and HP34897 and Planning Application 23/00465/ FUL identifying the boundary between Oleander House and Primrose Cottage. AND FURTHER TAKE NOTICE that, after this 30-day period, the owner of Oleander House will make an application to Magistrates' Court for a disposal order. If a disposal order is not granted, Oleander House will undertake the removal of all structures and may recover from you the reasonable expenses incurred in undertaking this task. Glenda Skinner, Lasting Power of Attorney for Thomas McBain.'

It takes a few seconds for the letter to sink in. 'What the hell?'

Mark screws it into a ball.

'What are you doing?'

'It's not real,' he says. 'It's meaningless. It's not from a solicitor, it's just a letter she's written herself. No doubt from some template she downloaded off the internet. She's trying to make it sound official, but it's not a legal letter.'

I take the ball of paper from him and unscrew it. 'We should keep it, though. As evidence. Just in case.'

'Just in case what? In case it escalates? You said once her leverage was removed this would all go away.'

I swallow and force a smile. I did say that. And I genuinely thought it would. Now I'm scared I was wrong. But I don't want to admit that to Mark; it's his money on the line, not mine. I say, 'What's she gonna do? Tear down the summerhouse? We'll call the police if she tries anything. Besides, the fence goes up tomorrow, and that will be the end of it.'

TWENTY-ONE

GLENDA

'GERALD! Gerald!'

Huffing and puffing, he lugs the suitcases in from the car. They bang against the hall table so hard that even from the kitchen-diner the noise shakes my already rattled bones. When the front door closes, I call him again. 'Gerald!'

'Let me get in the door, Glenda.'

'Come in here!'

He rustles into the room, still wearing his scruffy raincoat. 'What?'

I don't say anything, I just stare out of the window, waiting for him to see for himself.

'What the...?'

'They had no right!' I step away from the glass, unable to look at the fence for a moment longer. 'Cowards! He saw us leaving. They waited for us to go away and then put that fence in the moment our backs were turned.'

'You would have thought they'd have the courtesy to speak to us first, ask us if we were okay with the design, given that we have to look at the back of it. And they owe us money. That chartered land surveyor said we were in the right, didn't she? So they've put it in the wrong place without paying us?'

'Yes.'

'And they've seen the proof? You showed *them* your evidence as well as the surveyor?'

'Yes.'

'Well, then, this is outrageous!'

'You're right, Gerald. It's absolutely outrageous. Ten grand is nothing to them, and yet still they'd rather steal than pay it. They have no sense of accountability to anyone. This is why they're rich in the first place. It's just typical of people with money: they're too used to getting everything they want the moment they click their fingers. And you're going to be reminded of that, every time you look out of that window.'

Ouch. Given Gerald's upbringing, that's got to sting.

When Gerald was a teenager, his whole school knew his mother was a drug addict and an alcoholic. Sometimes she drove him to school while off her head, or didn't take him at all. He'd have to walk three miles and show up late and tired. He never had lunch money, wore a second-hand uniform, and had holes in his shoes. One of the teachers took pity on Gerald, encouraged him to move in with his aunt and helped him through his exams so he could get a bursary for the City of Oxford College and a business diploma. And Gerald's well aware that if it weren't for his aunt and that teacher he probably would have ended up like Ricky: on drugs and in and out of youth detention centres.

But being the poor boy on a bursary meant he was bullied by the rich kids. Most people make lifelong friends at college, but not Gerald. He kept his head down, got the grades he needed and then an internship at Lämsä. He didn't have the smarts to get into Oxford University and be a doctor or a lawyer like most of his peers but, given the shit he'd dragged himself out of, Lämsä was a big deal for Gerald.

And being pushed around by rich kids is one of his primary triggers.

I glance over to see if I've had an impact. Yep! Before, he was angry; now he's steaming mad. He's fixed on the fence with a steely glare, his right eye pulsing with its own little heartbeat.

I pile it on. 'I can't believe they're taking advantage of my poor father like this. He's in no fit state to fight these people. And they know we don't own the house. That *Laura*...' I say her name as if it's a disease '...saw his name on the deeds during the meeting with the surveyor. They're counting on the fact that a man of his age, in his condition, won't be able to do anything to stop them.'

'How are *we* supposed to stop them?' Gerald asks. 'Should we call the police? Report them for trespassing?'

'The police won't do anything. They'll say it's a civil matter.'

'What, then? We can't afford a solicitor.'

'No, we can't. So what choice have we got? We'll have to deal with this ourselves, take matters into our own hands.'

He thinks about that for a minute. 'You're right! We won't be bullied like this.' Then he storms out of the kitchen-diner towards the back door.

'What are you doing?' I call after him.

'You'll see.'

I watch through the window as Gerald marches across the lawn, fists clenched, arms pumping by his sides. At first, all he does is pop his head over the fence and look into the neighbours' garden. But then he grabs the capping rail and rocks it back and forth. I'm expecting – hoping – the force will ripple along its full length and show just how flimsy it is. But the fence hardly budges. It's sturdy, well made. It would take a tractor or a car to run that thing down, not a little man like Gerald.

He stares at the fence for a moment longer, scratching the hair on the back of his head. Then he runs a hand down the side of one of the panels. In a split second of excitement I think he's going to kick it down.

But he doesn't. He walks away.

Typical!

My palm slams against the glass to stop him, push him back, force him to stay there and be a man for once in his life. I turn away from the window and glower at the back door, waiting for it to open. I rehearse a desperate spiel in my head that will get Gerald even more riled up than he was before.

Only the door doesn't open. He doesn't come back inside.

Hang on... what's that? It sounds like a drill, coming from the garden.

I spin back to the window. Gerald's marched back to the fence, battery-powered drill in hand. But his chubby body inside that old raincoat obscures whatever he's doing. Is he drilling holes in the fence?

He swings from side to side, moving down the fence post, drilling as he goes. Then moves to the next panel, and the next, each time starting at the top and working his way to the bottom.

He's not drilling. He's unscrewing!

I laugh out loud, I can't help it. He's actually taking it down!

After pocketing all the screws, Gerald slides each fence panel out of its retaining post and, one by one, lays them in next door's garden beside their summerhouse. Within twenty minutes, they're all down.

He doesn't stop there, though. After a trip back to the garage, he uses the screws in his pocket to attach a wooden jig to one of the fence posts. Then, a moment later, he's pumping away at the car jack like a man possessed.

Inch by inch, the first post ratchets out of the ground and finally topples over. Gerald unscrews his jig, attaches it to the next post, and starts pumping again.

I clap my hands.

I didn't think he had it in him.

Go Gerald! You fucking marvellous man.

TWENTY-TWO

LAURA

THE NEW Bluetooth headphones Mark bought me are a dream; their depth and clarity make my project sound better than I could have imagined. He keeps joking that I've finally moved into this century, and he has a point, but the Bluetooth on these headphones is in a different league from anything I've owned. I slipped them over my ears two hours ago with every intention of starting episode seven, only I can't focus. I've been sitting here for two whole hours, getting nowhere.

All I can think about is the fence.

Steve Banks called again this morning asking why they hadn't received the audio files for episodes four to six. With the adjusted deadline they should have been in by now, but Mark's still finishing the final edit. I used the house move as an excuse for the delay. Once again, he offered his assistance. He even offered to come and work with me here. As if! His oily soliciting turned my stomach, and I ended up cutting off the call a little more abruptly than I should have. Whether

I like Steve or not, if this project is a success, I'm probably going to have to work with him in the future. I shiver at the thought.

Concentrate, Laura! Concentrate!

The moment I visualise my characters in action, imagine the accompanying music and sound, Glenda strides on to my stage. I try to evict her from the set by closing my eyes and shaking my head, but she won't piss off.

I've never hated anyone in my life. Especially someone I don't even know. But just the thought of her – the vision of her that's morphed in my head every day since meeting her; those bulbous eyes and trout-puckered lips – makes me want to pick up one of those fence posts and beat her to death with it.

I know the hatred I have for Glenda is exaggerated by the burden of guilt I endure for landing us in this situation, but it doesn't stop the malice. In my head, it's as if she made an unspoken promise that once we'd removed her leverage she would give up her extortion racket and leave us in peace. I'd reassured myself that I'd live content in the knowledge that I made the right decision. That Primrose Cottage was our happy ending, and every moment from this point forward would be a re-enactment of some romantic comedy finale.

I was stupid, of course. Glenda Skinner made no such promise.

And I'm not as smart as I like to think I am.

There's a reason romances end abruptly after the climax and resolution. Nobody wants to watch the carnage of real life that follows. Real life that starts when people like Glenda begin a new scene, one you would never have written into your own story. Was it Sartre who said 'hell is other people'?

We called the police about the fence, but they can't do anything. No surprise there. They said they couldn't charge Gerald with property damage on the basis of a few screw holes in some fence posts. And, since he didn't steal the fence, it's not a crime. They said the Skinners were entitled to remove someone else's belongings from their land, provided they returned them to the owner. Mark pointed out that it's our land and therefore they were trespassing, which *is* a crime. It didn't make any difference.

I'm not oblivious to the fact that, when you make these accusations out loud, our complaints to the police sound ridiculous. Arrest that man! He put holes in my fence posts and stepped two feet into my garden! Jail him for life! Of course the police have better things to do than arrest people over trifling misdemeanours. And that's how they see these boundary disputes: both parties equally guilty of wasting police time over a petty squabble. What they can't possibly understand is the stress. The mental anguish Glenda has subjected us to with her attempts to steal our dream, blackmail us for thirty-five thousand pounds, harass us with threatening letters and finally tear down our fence, which was expensive to install in the first place.

Mark's put up temporary barrier fencing – they kind they use on building sites, bright orange and plastic – just to keep Finn in the garden. Stretched out behind the summerhouse from the monkey puzzle tree to the snug wall, it looks hideous. But it serves the Skinners right since they have to look at it, too.

Shake it off, Laura! Forget about the bitch next door. Think good thoughts. This studio is a dream come true and so is Primrose Cottage.

I dive into the unfinished scene.

I enjoy sound design, special effects, but what I really love is editing dialogue for audio drama. Choosing the best takes, being surprised at the intuition of the actors, who almost always grasp the intent of a scene without any direction. When it's a really talented actor, speaking dialogue with all the passion and precision you dreamed up when you wrote it, it's an indescribable thrill to hear your imagination come to life in sound.

I'm blending in a pick-up Jodie re-recorded for me over the weekend, laughing to myself while she reads my notes aloud into her mic. She's giggling because I've pointed out that she's taken two words from the script – tenacious and persistent – and blended them into pernacious. 'I seem to have made up a word,' she laughs into her mic. Then, she says, 'tenacious and persistent' over and over a few times to get the sentence straight in her head. Finally, she takes a few deep breaths, throws herself into character and records the pick-up saying 'pernacious' exactly as she did before. 'I've done it again,' she giggles, while I laugh too.

There's a sudden snap.

I stop laughing.

It takes me a second to realise it wasn't on the recording. It came from inside the studio. And whatever made the sound was loud enough for me to hear through noise-cancelling headphones. I slide them off my ears and leave them draped around my neck. Spinning around in my office chair, I search the garden left and right for the source of the sound.

There's nobody out there.

Staring straight ahead through the closed patio doors, I listen for the noise again. Everything is still. Apart from the boundary between us and the Skinners, the garden is completely surrounded by a tall privet hedge; nobody can get in from the front.

I take my headphones off, lay them on the desk, and slowly get to my feet. Cautiously, I move towards the cabin's left wall and peer through the window. Something flies at my face, something small and round. Forgetting the glass is there, I flinch, shut my eyes and lift my hand to protect myself. The same loud snap resonates through the summerhouse, even louder this time without my headphones.

When I open my eyes, there's a crushed-ice mark in the middle of the glass surrounded by a spider's web of blue fissures.

My breath catches.

It takes a moment to process what happened.

But the moment I do, I'm running.

I throw back the bi-fold doors so quickly I lose my grip on the handles, and they crash into the wall. But I don't stop to make sure they aren't broken. Rounding the corner of the summerhouse, I expect to run into Glenda or Gerald, but come to a sudden stop when there's nobody there.

Hands on hips, I glare into the Skinners' garden, daring Glenda to show her face. My ears and cheeks burn as if I'm being taunted, laughed at, and my skin crawls with the sensation of someone watching me from the shadows. But no face appears. There's no rustling of bushes, no sound except the tweeting of birds.

Convinced that if I turn my back on the orange plastic fence I'll get a stone in the back of my head, I keep my eyes on their garden as I retreat. Glancing around one last time to make sure nobody's there, I kneel down by the flower border beneath the summerhouse window. There are two pale orange stones, one slightly smaller than the other, resting on top of the woodchip mulch. I pick them up and bounce them up and down on my palm before looking behind me again, then back at the window. The chip in the glass is a stain on my beautiful summerhouse, as if they've opened a crack in my life that won't heal.

'Go fuck yourselves!' I shout, loud enough to be heard halfway up the street. Then I storm into the cottage still carrying the stones.

'Aren't you going to say anything?'

Mark looks at me, eyes wide, and laughs without humour. 'Honestly, I don't know what to say. They're behaving like children. She must be fifty-something and she's throwing stones?'

'We should call the police again.'

'They won't do anything.'

'I get why they couldn't do anything about the fence. But they have to do something about this.' I hold out the stones, as if they carry the weight of my argument. 'It's property damage.'

'They're hardly going to send out two squad cars to investigate a chip in a window.'

'I'm calling them.'

'It's a waste of time, babe.'

'Not 999. I'm calling 101. I don't expect them to do anything, but I want it on record. Then, if they pull another stunt like this, the police will know there's been an ongoing history of property damage.'

Mark opens his mouth, about to disagree, but then he closes it again and says, 'You're probably right. We should have it on record. Just in case they do something even more stupid.'

I head for the door, pulling my mobile from the back pocket of my jeans, then turn back to Mark. 'Steve called again chasing the episodes. Have you finished the edit? Can we get the files off?'

'Yeahhh.' He draws the word out. 'About that…'

'It's not good?'

'Oh, no, it's good. Brilliant actually. It's just a little…'

He doesn't want to hurt my feelings.

'Don't pull any punches. I don't have the time.'

'The levels are a little out of balance. The dialogue's way too loud. It drowns out the music and sound effects. I think you need to take it down a few notches. The first three episodes were perfect but these are different. It doesn't flow when you transition between episodes three and four; the change is stark.'

He said, 'just a little', then used phrases like 'way too', and 'stark'.

I say, 'That doesn't sound like a little of anything. Why don't you just come out and say it's really bad?' I try not to be angry at him criticising my work. But I listened to it over and over before sending it to him, and it sounded perfect to me.

'I'm *not* going to say it's really bad, because it's not. Creatively, it's perfection. It's just the production, balancing the levels. It just needs a little work, that's all.'

That stings, because it's exactly what Steve said about me. Raising concerns about the slipping deadline, he apparently said to Mark, 'I'm not questioning her creative talent, but she doesn't have the industry experience for a production of this scale. Laura needs me.'

'See for yourself.' Mark gets out of his chair so I can sit down. He slips my headphones over my ears before leaning over my shoulder to load episodes three and four into the player back-to-back. Then he slides the playback indicator to the end of episode three and hits the space bar.

I listen for a moment. 'No. This is the one that's wrong. The dialogue is way too quiet, I'm only getting every other word.'

He lifts up one of the headphone earpieces so I can hear him. 'No. The first three episodes are perfect. It's this fourth one that's wrong. Wait for the transition and you'll hear it.'

The player transitions into the fourth episode and the dialogue is much easier to hear. 'This sounds fine to me.'

'But you obviously thought the first episodes were perfect before, otherwise you wouldn't have sent them to me. So why would you change your mind now? It must be those headphones. I thought they would be great for you – all the lads at the office use them – but I didn't consider the fact that they're probably better suited to a bigger head. You have a little noggin. The new ones will be at the store on Monday; I just have to pop into town to collect them. I'll check they're working at the shop before bringing them home.'

The day before yesterday, I told Mark I was still struggling, even with the fancy new headphones he'd chosen for me. I was just venting, I didn't expect him to fix the problem for me, but he went ahead and ordered another pair before I could stop him. They're titanium and top of the line with twin-pulse isobaric drivers. The sound engineers at Hardman don't even use those because they cost more than my car.

'I'm over the moon that you've ordered them,' I say, 'they're way too expensive – but I can't put this off till Monday. I'm seriously pushed for time. If there's a problem with episodes four to six, I need to fix them before I can carry on with on with episode seven.'

'It's getting late.' He nods at the clock. 'There's nothing you can do tonight. Let's go over it together tomorrow. And don't you worry about the police – I'll call them, tell them about the broken window. I just hope to God the Skinners don't do something even more stupid. You have enough on your plate without worrying about the idiots next door.'

TWENTY-THREE

LAURA

With the deadline looming and three episodes to tweak, the last thing I need is to waste a morning in town. But the brand-new headphones Mark bought me lasted all of three days before they started glitching as well. What is it with modern appliances? Fortunately, the shop ordered a pair for their own stock as well and they're happy to exchange them, so I don't have to wait for them to get a new set in.

I drop them on the car seat next to me, pull out of the garage and, as I'm rolling down the gravel drive, I switch the radio to media so I can listen to a playlist on my phone. Mark always switches it back to the radio and, since we take turns to walk Finn at lunchtime, it's up and down like a toilet seat.

Something catches my eye, and I slam on the brakes at the foot of the driveway. I almost run over a woman who's standing a couple of feet inside our property line, blocking my exit.

It's Glenda!

My foot twitches on the accelerator, and I have to gather my wits to stop myself mowing her down. I'm about to nudge forward, force her out of my path, when I realise it isn't her at all. The woman is dressed like Glenda – woollen skirt, blouse, tights, sensible shoes – and she has similar colouring, so it was an easy mistake to make.

I wave an apology, expecting her to move along, but the woman just stands there, staring directly at me. She's in her late sixties or seventies, with a full head of curly hair, neat but not styled. Her proprietorial stance unsettles me. And the way she looks at me, narrowed eyes and pinched lips, is the way I'd look at Glenda if she were standing there.

Putting the car in park, I press the button for the window, wind it all the way down, and lean out to ask, 'Can I help you with something?'

She shakes her head, slowly, deliberately.

I smile. 'I'm Laura Hunter,' I say, attempting to sound neighbourly in spite of the way she glares at me. 'We moved in a couple of weeks ago.'

'I know who you are,' she says.

I remember a flyer that someone from the village dropped in our mailbox last week inviting us to a social gathering in the village church after Sunday service. We were so busy settling in, we didn't go. It occurs to me that perhaps she's one of the churchgoers and we've upset the village applecart by not attending and have come across rude and unsociable.

'Mark and I work long hours,' I say. 'So we haven't had the opportunity to get to know everyone in the village yet. We'll be more sociable once we settle in. You live in Clay Norton? What's your name?'

'Over there.' She points across the road, but I can't tell which property she's referring to.

'One of the terraced cottages?' There are four in a row, opposite Oleander House, and I assume she's pointing to one of those. 'Sorry, I didn't catch your name.'

'Jean.'

'It's nice to meet you, Jean. You'll have to forgive me, though, I'm late. I have an appointment in town.' That's not true, I don't have a fixed appointment to return the headphones, but she's making me uncomfortable, and the need to escape this encounter presses on me. If it's even possible, she's creepier than Glenda. 'Perhaps we can catch up another time?'

She doesn't reply. She just stands there, staring at me with that same contemptuous expression. I give her a moment to say something, anything, and then give up. 'Okay, then. See you around.' Offering a polite wave, I wind up the window, put the car back into drive and inch towards her. For a moment I think I might actually have to nudge her out of the way with my bumper, but then at the last second, when her knees are almost touching the car, she moves aside.

As I inch out on to the road, checking left and right, I pretend she isn't still standing there. That her eyes aren't boring into the side of my head. Because, if looks could kill, this would be a car crash. And I don't know why.

'Laura?'

I look up from my pint glass. I've been procrastinating in our favourite pub across the road from the office for the past hour. I should have gone straight home after exchanging the headphones, but I needed to clear my head. What would be the point in trying to work with not only Glenda but now that weirdo Jean invading my sound stage as well?

'Saeed...?' I say his name cautiously, hoping I've remembered it right, pronounced it correctly.

'May I?' He indicates the chair opposite. 'If I am not disturbing you?'

'Of course, please.'

He sits down and lays a pile of folders on the table next to his glass of what looks like lime soda. I'm suddenly embarrassed that I'm drinking pints in the middle of the afternoon.

'Patient notes,' he says. 'It feels good to get out of the office on a day like this. I was going to sit in the garden out back, but then I noticed you in the window. I hope... I am not troubling you, am I?'

'Not at all. I'm avoiding. I have this insane deadline, and the closer it gets, the more I procrastinate.'

'You usually work from home, I understand. What brings you to town?'

'These.' I point to the headphones on the table. 'I'm on my fourth pair. They keep breaking on me. I'm starting to think we've got gremlins. The store was nice enough to change them, even though they couldn't replicate the problem. It's typical isn't it? At home they keep cutting out, but bring them to the store and they work like a charm.'

'I remember Mark saying you were producing a radio play. That sounds exciting. What is the genre, the premise? Or is it still under wraps?'

Nobody ever asks me anything about my job. It's as if the words 'radio' and 'play' cause a disconnect in people's minds. It's rare that I meet someone who realises that radio stations don't only broadcast DJs' music choices, and plays don't only happen on a theatre stage. Most of the time, people are so flummoxed by what I do for a living they just say, 'Ohhh, that's nice.'

I'm so taken aback by Saeed, I forget the premise of my own play, even though I've rehearsed the elevator pitch a hundred times.

I gather my senses. 'It's an action-adventure epic. Think *Game of Thrones* meets *Lawrence of Arabia* with a hint of *Yentl*. The main character is a woman who passes herself off as a man in an ancient city that's inspired by the Mamluk slave dynasty.'

'That sounds fascinating,' he says in a tone so deep and rich I want to cast him. '*Lawrence of Arabia* I know. But I have never heard of *Yentl* and I have not seen *Game of Thrones*. I have very little time for television. Radio I can get behind; the ability to do something productive while you listen seems a better use of one's time. You must ask Mark to tell me when your play is released. I would like to hear it.'

I stare at him for a moment, mesmerised by the exactitude of his words, the unusual precision of his pronunciation. He's even more captivating than when I first laid eyes on him. Before I met Saeed, I would have said Mark was the most handsome man I'd ever met — and he still is in the conventional sense: he's a dreamboat — but Saeed... It's hard to put your finger on what it is about him. He's not just attractive; he exudes far more than a handsome exterior. Softness. Gentility. Compassion. It's like being in the presence of a great spiritual teacher who oozes love for the whole universe from every pore. Staring into his strange grey eyes, I can't imagine him ever losing his cool, let alone his temper. And being in his company makes my heart quicken in the strangest way. Not rapid and chaotic like when you first fall in love, but with a measured swiftness that brings a heightened, yet calm, energy. It's impossible to accurately put it into words, but Saeed is thrilling. Not that I could fall in love with him — well, I could, I mean, who couldn't — but there's no doubt that my heart belongs to Mark.

'Laura?'

'Sorry, I...' I can't think of a good excuse for why I've been staring at him all this time. Probably with my mouth half open and drooling. 'Mark said you were a psychologist, with a specialism in the subconscious...sleep and dreams or something. That sounds far more fascinating than any story. It's the kind of job I'd give one of my characters — if my play wasn't set in a desert in the 1800s.'

He laughs, and it's such a hauntingly sweet sound, I want to pull out my phone and record it.

I ask, 'Can you act?'

Saeed takes a second glance at me.

'Sorry, it's just...your voice. You're perfect for radio. I'd love to cast you.'

He smiles, and my own mouth turns up. 'I am afraid not. I suspect, if you were to put a microphone in front of me and expect a performance, I would be as articulate as a circus bear.'

'I doubt that. You could just be yourself and you'd sweep listeners off their feet.'

We're silent for a moment and I stare into my glass. Then Saeed says my name again and I look up at him expectantly, wondering what he's about to say. I could honestly listen to him all day. His eyebrows, pinched together, form a deep crease at the bridge of his nose.

'Are you alright?' he asks.

Now it's my turn for a double-take. 'I'm fine. Why?'

Saeed doesn't speak for a moment. It's as if he's working out what to say and yet, at the same time, he doesn't strike me as a man who's often lost for words. I get the sense he's holding something back, that he wants to tell me something, but can't figure out how to break it to me. It crosses my mind that Mark has a secret, something Saeed thinks I should know. Something awful about his past. Or an affair. Oh, God, I hope it's not an affair.

'What?' I ask again. 'You look like you're keeping some terrible secret. If it's about Mark, you can tell me. It won't change how I feel about him.'

'It is not Mark. And I imagine the most terrible secret he has ever kept from you is that he used to cut his toenails in the kitchen. No. It is you, Laura.'

'Me?'

He nods.

'You know a secret about me?'

'Not a secret, no. You said, when I first sat down, that you were procrastinating over an insane deadline. You are under a lot of pressure.'

I nod, but it wasn't really a question.

'Then, you said you were on your fourth pair of headphones, but the store could not replicate the problem.'

'That's right; they only cut out intermittently, so...'

'And that was the same problem you had with the previous three pairs? They cut out intermittently?'

'Yes, but the first two sets were old...cheap.'

'Mark said this project, this play, it means a great deal to you and your career.'

I nod.

'And, in the midst of all that, you have just moved house.'

'That's right.'

'So you are under a lot of stress, are you not?'

'You could say that. We're actually in the middle of a boundary dispute with our new neighbours as well. It makes working almost impossible. I'm at my wits' end, to tell you the truth, and Mark bought the house partly because of me and I feel so guilty...' I stop myself before I start telling Saeed about my childhood.

'Yes, I see; it is worse than I imagined.' He pauses again. 'Laura, intense stress can manifest any number of physical symptoms, one of which is...'

There's that feeling again, the sense that he's holding back. I wait for him to finish his sentence, drop the bomb.

'...temporary hearing loss.'

I look Saeed in the eye, tilt my head in confusion.

'Laura...' He places a hand over mine on the table. 'Twice since we have been sitting here, I have asked you a question you have not answered. I suspect it happens more than you realise, but most people are too polite to say anything.'

I'm still wrapping my head around his words when he adds, 'Would you do something for me? Put my mind at rest?'

He slides a leatherbound notepad out from beneath his pile of folders, and a pen from the loop holder inside. Then he writes down a name and number. 'Will you call this man? He is a good friend, a great physician. Make an appointment as soon as you can. He works at John Radcliffe and if you give him my name he will fit you in straight away. It is probably nothing to worry about, but do not put it off. And this is my number.' He scribbles it down. 'Would you call me when you have the results? I will worry about you otherwise.'

I take the piece of paper from Saeed and stare at it, unable to process anything he's just said with the exception of three words.

Temporary hearing loss.

TWENTY-FOUR

GLENDA

'We're just going a different way this year,' Cynthia says.

'You couldn't take the trouble to come here and tell me that in person? You had to do it over the phone? I've already ordered the flyers—'

'Really? You usually leave those till the last minute. Cancel them, will you, Glenda? We're going for a fresh design this time.'

'I can't cancel them. They're being printed this morning.'

'This morning? How were you going to pay for them? You know you have to put in a kitty request before incurring expenses.'

'I was going to, but I wanted to get on top of the organisation this year and you were—'

'That's my point, Glenda. I didn't think you'd be so upset. I mean, every year you complain about having too much on your plate for the—'

'It's different this year.'

'It *is* different,' Cynthia says. 'It's going to be very different. We have Mark and Laura now and they're donating a substantial sum to the village fête. We even have enough for a marquee.'

'Just because he's donating, that doesn't mean I can't still organise it.'

'There's no need, darling. Mark has offered the services of Hardman's events co-ordinator. She may even be able to get us a famous band for the soirée. I bet Mark knows all sorts of people: Take That, Harry Styles.'

'Don't be stupid, Cynthia. Take That and Harry Styles don't play at village fêtes.'

'Maybe not. But maybe if Mark Hardman asks them to... His radio station plays their records after all.'

'How about if I work alongside Hardman's co-ordinator? After all, she doesn't know the village, and I do.'

'Hmm...I did think about that,' Cynthia says. 'But I hear relations between you, Mark and Laura are a bit... What's the word? Chilly. Didn't you tear down their garden fence or something?'

'Oh, fuck off, Cynthia.'

She squeals my name, but I only catch half of it before hanging up the phone. I scroll through my contacts for the local printer, but no matter how many times I hang up and redial, the phone just squawks a busy signal. So I grab my handbag from the kitchen counter and rush for the door.

Closing it behind me, I realise that telling Cynthia to fuck off probably wasn't the best idea. She might have paid the printer's fees out of sympathy. She won't now. And I'll be a hundred pounds out of pocket. Not only that, I'll have a thousand useless fliers lying in my garage. I had them printed with a silk finish, so maybe I could take them over to Mark and Laura's and they can wipe their asses with them.

I shuffle down the path, talking to myself in my best Cynthia accent. '*Oh, Mark has offered the services of Hardman's events co-ordinator!*' Of course he fucking has.

I stop dead when I reach my car on the drive.

From headlight to tail-light, my brand-new Ford Focus – in Fantastic Red – has a scratch along the side. As I run my finger along it, praying it's superficial and will rub out with some T-Cut, I swallow bile. The scratch is deep. All the way down to bare metal.

I suck in a sob before it has chance to escape, but when I run around the car and find a similar scratch on the other side it bursts out of me. Wailing, I give myself a good slap around the face. 'You stupid bitch, Glenda! Pull yourself together.'

I won't let the fuckwit printers, fucking Cynthia or the fuck-ass neighbours derail me. And I know this was Laura: payback for the fence.

Well, Laura, it's on! It's fucking on!

'Fuck! Fuck! Fuck!' All the parking spaces outside the printer's shop are taken, so I hang a right and speed down the Osler Road. If I skirt around the back of the hospital, I can take the Old High Street down to the Headington car park. I rap on the steering wheel as if that will make my car go faster than thirty in a thirty-mile-per-hour zone. Maybe it can also make me forget that my chances of losing one hundred pounds aren't increasing with every minute that passes.

I just keep asking myself, over and over, why?! I wouldn't be in this situation if *he* hadn't been so fucking stupid. We had it good, didn't we? Now everything's screwed up. Gerald and I will live hand-to-mouth on a paltry Lämsä salary for the rest of our lives. And nice things like clothes, handbags and this car will be out of reach.

As if thirty isn't slow enough, I enter a twenty zone. 'Fuuuuucckkk!' I don't slow down.

And then I see her.

Laura.

At least I think it's Laura. On foot, the woman turns into the road, but she has her back to me, so it's hard to tell if it's her. She came out of the hospital. I wonder why. Maybe she's sick...or pregnant...or both. I picture the scratch down the side of my car and remember coming home from Scarborough and finding her fence, practically in our garden. The brazen cheek of her. She knew the land was in dispute, yet she still went ahead and installed that fence. Surreptitiously! While we were away!

How did they even buy Primrose Cottage? Something underhand took place. I downloaded their deeds from Land Registry, and it has a mortgage on it. With NatWest. They must have concealed the boundary dispute from the bank. Mark and Laura are not straightforward people. They're not honest.

Someone should inform the bank.

I imagine Laura like Julia Roberts in *Pretty Woman*, strutting from shop to shop with Mark's credit card, buying all the nice things she wants while refusing to give us thirty-five thousand for the land. That money could fall out of one of her expensive handbags and she wouldn't even notice.

I remember being a child at Oleander House, standing on a bench, clinging to the fence, staring into Primrose Cottage's garden. Anne Huntington-Whitney and her friends would be playing with dolls, having birthday parties I wasn't invited to. I swear Mrs Huntington-Whitney thought I'd give Anne a disease.

Laura veers across the pavement, about to cross the road.

I accelerate.

The gap between us closes in seconds, and she doesn't even hear the engine. She steps out into the road just as the pedal hits the metal and my scratched Ford Focus reaches full speed. I grip the steering wheel, brace for impact, and jolt in my seat as Laura hits the bumper. She lands on the bonnet at an awkward angle, and when she bounces off my windscreen we come face to face for a second. The moment she realises who's driving the car is sheer delight, as is the shock in the whites of her eyes, the sadness in the blue-grey of her irises.

But then she disappears over the roof.

With a smile, I watch in the rear-view mirror as she tumbles across the road, arms and legs flailing. The contents of her handbag scatter, purple twenty-pound notes take wing, and Laura rolls into the ditch, where a river of blood picks up dead leaves on its journey to the nearest drain...

'Mrs Skinner...' The handsome young lad who works the till at the printer's shop greets me as I step through the door. But then his smile droops at my steamed-up glasses, my curls stuck to my forehead, my white blouse, grey at the armpits with sweat. I ran all the way from Headington car park, only to find a parking space had opened up right outside the shop. 'Your fliers are all ready for you.'

TWENTY-FIVE

LAURA

THE CRUSHED-ICE chip in the window watches me like an eye. It chastises my passivity, presses me to take action, do something about the wicked witch next door. The police were kind and understanding but said that even if *we* were convinced we knew who had broken the window, without proof they couldn't do anything about it. They suggested we put up cameras, so we'd have evidence if the neighbours caused any further property damage. Mark is ordering some that should arrive next week.

The glazier comes tomorrow, but, until then, the eye in the window chatters away, whispering in my ear: *The police won't help you. The CPS won't help you. The Land Registry won't help you. You're alone. You should take matters into your own hands.*

The new headphones aren't working any better for me than the pair I exchanged them for. Out of desperation I switched leads three times, trying to convince myself it isn't me that's broken; it's them. But I barely hear my project any more. Instead, a different production plays on repeat: chorus backing vocal one is a witch's cackle, chorus backing vocal two is a chattering eye, and layered over those tracks is Saeed's euphonic lead vocal on repeat: temporary hearing loss...temporary hearing loss.

It's become the soundtrack to my life.

Steve Banks would just love to find out about that, wouldn't he?

I'd usually take a break from work on a Sunday, spend time with Mark, but the scene loaded in my digital audio workstation should have been finished days ago, and now Steve has bypassed me altogether. Instead of calling and emailing me directly, he's pressing Mark about my abilities and commitment to the deadline. The worst part is that both Mark and I know he isn't wrong.

Mark is pushing back. For now.

I saw the physician Saeed recommended on Monday; he ran some tests and I'll get the results next week. Jodie's pernaciousness is no longer funny. I can't concentrate on anything she or the other actors are saying. I second-guess every take, change it to a different one ten minutes later, only to change it back again after another ten. I slip my headphones off my ears, lean back in my chair, and stare at the glass eye.

Mark comes in with a cup of tea.

'Thanks.' It's too hot to hold, and I put it down.

'That fence isn't gonna keep Finn in for long,' Mark says. 'I've just caught him jumping on it. He's bent it right over. If I hadn't been there, he'd have been in next door's garden.'

'I can't bear to look at it any more. Couldn't you have at least gone for green?'

'They only had bright orange. If you squint and turn your head to the side, you can pretend it's a flower border.'

He demonstrates this technique, but I don't copy him. 'It's not like Finn to want to escape,' I say. 'He usually wants to be near us.'

'Maybe it's the smell.'

'Dead bodies under the patio?'

'I think they have chickens.'

I sigh. 'That'll do it. We're going to have to put the fence back up.'

'They'll just take it down again.'

'We can't let them bully us like this. If they think they own the land, they should take the appropriate legal action. We both know they can't possibly own it. The site plan on our deeds may be too small-scale to know exactly where the boundary is, but it's completely clear that it's a straight line. The summerhouse is only a metre or so beyond the snug wall. So, for the back of the summerhouse to be in their garden they would have to own all the land right up to the snug's patio doors.'

'Surely the surveyor pointed that out to Glenda?'

'She did. But the wicked old witch just came up with a new story to explain that away. She said Oliver Huntington-Whitney extended the main property right up to the boundary, and that her father didn't complain about it at the time because it took place behind the boundary fence and his shrubs obscured the building work. She says the original snug didn't have patio doors, Scott added them later.'

'That can't be right. I looked over those architect's diagrams Scott left behind for us and the patio doors are on them.'

'So the wicked witch is lying. Shocker.'

'Not necessarily,' he says. 'I'm just playing devil's advocate but plans often change during construction when builders encounter problems. What's on the architect's diagram isn't always what ends up on the ground. Oliver Huntington-Whitney might have chosen to sacrifice the patio doors so he could build a bigger snug right up to the boundary. So those diagrams aren't conclusive.'

'Let's call Scott, then. Ask him if he put the doors in.'

'He won't tell us the truth. Installing patio doors in a wall that's right on someone's boundary, so that when you come out of them you'd be trespassing on their property, contravenes planning regulations. He could get into a lot of trouble admitting to that and not revealing it to us during the sale.'

Mark's right. My mind drifts back to Emily and her strange behaviour the day we viewed the cottage. Scott and Emily were definitely hiding something.

'There is something else, though,' Mark says. 'There's a rainwater downpipe on the snug wall that drains to a soakaway beneath the patio. That got me thinking. So I Googled building regulations, and the underground pipe connecting that to the soakaway has to be at least a metre from the building to prevent damage from downforce.'

I blink at him. 'So there's a pipe beneath the patio at least a metre from the snug wall?'

'Yes,' Mark says. 'And if you think about the logistics of that, if they own all the land right up to our patio doors, then how did the builders even lay that pipe in the '90s?'

'It's impossible. They would have been digging in the neighbours' garden on the other side of a bloody boundary fence. And not only that, with a straight boundary, they'd have to own our monkey puzzle tree as well. Since that's in line with the patio.'

'And there's even more evidence on our side,' he says. 'The foundations extend from the wall by half a metre. So if Glenda Skinner's telling the truth, her father must have sat back while concrete-pouring trucks drove over his garden to lay foundations and underground pipes.'

'And they must have been pouring that concrete right beneath the fence. The whole thing is logistically impossible.'

'I'm starting to think that woman is a complete loon.'

'You're *just starting* to think that?'

He laughs. 'No. I think it's been firmly established from the get-go. She's a fucking loon.'

'Maybe you're right. Maybe we should put the fence back up. Get the cameras installed, and if they come anywhere near the fence again, we call the police.'

'We can't keep calling the police, though. We're already starting to look like the irrational ones in all this. The police won't get involved until those wackos commit a serious crime.'

'So basically what you're saying is, we have to wait for one of them to come at us with a knife before the police will do anything.'

'You can joke,' he says, 'but those people are unstable and that scares me. They're unpredictable. We need to shut this thing down.'

'How?'

'I think we should get Angela involved. Go legal. We'll get her to write to them and explain why it's not possible for them to own the land. It'll carry weight coming from a solicitor.'

There's a sudden crash. We both glance at each other then turn to the chipped window, but there's nobody there.

'Finn!' Mark says. And we both dart for the doors.

Between the steel stakes holding it up, one panel of the plastic fence is folded over. As we run to the boundary, halfway between the summerhouse and snug wall, flashes of liver-coloured fur and white feathers dance across the Skinners' lawn. The usual birdsong and quiet hush of our sleepy village is drowned out by a cacophony of snarling and squawking.

At the orange fence, we stop dead and watch in horror as Finn charges around the neighbours' garden, feathers glued to his muzzle with blood. Two chickens already lie motionless on the grass while another, trapped by the neck between his jaws, shrieks and flaps in its bid for freedom. Finn death-shakes the chicken, drops it to the ground, and then bolts after another that's caught his eye.

Mark whistles, and I call Finn's name as we fight our way over the plastic fence, through the weeds, nettles and shrubs that have grown along the boundary over the last few weeks. By the time we get into the Skinners' garden, all the chickens are dead, and Finn has his eyes on the real prize. Because Glenda doesn't only have chickens, she has a bloody guinea pig as well. What grown woman keeps a guinea pig, for fuck's sake?! The only thing between it and certain death is a wooden-framed wire chicken run. Finn has it upturned in seconds.

Squealing loud enough to excite Finn into a frenzy, the guinea pig darts across the lawn. Despite its tiny legs, it's fast. And with his lanky legs Finn isn't as nimble. Near the house, the guinea pig makes a sharp right, an agile ninety-degree turn. Finn tries to do the same, but his legs spin out beneath him, like an inept Coyote chasing the Roadrunner. If the scene wasn't so horrific, I might actually laugh.

But Oleander House is more bricks than garden so, within seconds, the guinea pig is caught between Finn and the building. It turns and scuttles along the patio, close to the wall, while Mark and I dash across the lawn in the hope of grabbing Finn's collar and putting an end to the carnage.

Finn stops for a moment, gets low on his haunches and points his nose at his prey, planning his strike. Ahead of me, Mark is an inch from catching him, reaching out. But as Mark's fingertips touch his collar Finn side-eyes him, realises his fun and games are about to end abruptly, and ducks away just in time.

The guinea pig scuttles into the undergrowth between our gardens, only to find its escape blocked by the plastic fence. In a frantic shuffle, it pushes its way through, not realising its body is much bigger than its head and far too big for the hole.

Sensing Finn's approach and finally realising it can't get through, the guinea pig attempts to back out of the fence. Only now, its head is trapped, and the plastic has too much give for it to get any purchase. It doesn't stand a chance.

Mark and I both run, putting ourselves between Finn and the poor little mite, but Finn darts around us; he's far too quick.

I scream, 'Nooo!' as Finn snatches the guinea pig from the fence and squeezes it between his jaws while shaking it like a chew toy.

Mark grabs him by the collar, shouting, 'Drop it, Finn! Drop it!' He's about to pull the guinea pig from his jaws when I shout,

'Don't! It's half-dead already and Finn will despatch it faster than we can.'

So we just stand there and wait for the horrific squealing to stop. The time — although no more than a few seconds — is interminable.

Finally, there's silence. Finn drops the dead guinea pig.

And we turn to find Glenda and Gerald staring at us from their patio.

TWENTY-SIX

GERALD

We walked to the local shop yesterday morning to top up on groceries as usual, but Glenda forgot butter. Tom will be expecting soup for his Sunday tea tonight and even a minor alteration, like serving bread without butter, can be the difference between an evening of harmony or pandemonium. With the chickens out of their coop I didn't want to be gone too long, so we made a quick dash in the car.

Back from the shop, having pulled on to the driveway, Glenda and I open our doors at exactly the same time. We place one foot on the gravel before, assaulted by a screeching commotion, we turn to each other, eyes wide in confusion. It only takes a second for us both to realise it's coming from the back garden.

A fox!

It takes fifteen minutes to get the chickens into their coop and, knowing we'd only be gone that long, I didn't bother.

A moment of laziness.

At the front door, Glenda's scolding only makes it harder for me to get the key in the lock. 'Get on with it, Gerald! Hurry up! For goodness' sake, what are you doing?'

I only drive it home when she reaches out to snatch it from me. I run through the hall, lounge and kitchen-diner, then struggle with the key in the back door as well. My fingers tremble as the sound from the garden rasps every nerve.

Dashing down the side path, I corner the kitchen wall, and stop dead on the patio. Glenda, not expecting me to stop so suddenly, crashes into my back and almost knocks me over. Finding our balance, eyes wide and mouths agape, we take in the scene.

Like small piles of snow, our chickens lie strewn across the lawn.

There's no fox.

Mark, Laura and their ugly brown mutt are in our garden, on our side of that monstrous orange fence. Issuing from somewhere in their midst, a gut-wrenching squeal stretches out for what feels like a full minute. I beg for the sound to stop. If it's another chicken, however fast it's dying, it's not fast enough.

'Pickles!' Glenda shrieks.

It's not a chicken. Jason's guinea pig is in the dog's mouth, being shaken to death like a dirty rag.

Mark holds tight to the dog's collar and is about to rescue Pickles when Laura – who's just standing there watching, as if this is her kind of sick entertainment – says, 'Don't... He'll despatch it faster than we can.'

Then she turns to look at me.

Caught red-handed.

Glenda launches herself at Mark and Laura, so I reach out and grab her, pinning her arms by her sides as she kicks and twists to free herself. 'You BITCH!' she screams. 'You fucking cunt! I'll kill you! I'll kill you!'

'Glenda! Calm down!' I've never seen my wife so angry and upset. I swear if she got her hands on Laura she'd grab her by the hair, wrestle her to the ground, and slam her head into the grass. So I hold on tight to prevent any more bloodshed. 'Get out!' I shout at the neighbours. 'Get the fuck off our land. Haven't you taken enough from us?'

Neither Mark nor Laura move, so Glenda screams at them, 'Get out, get out, *get out!!!!*'

'Come on,' Mark says. 'We'd better go.'

'No,' Laura says. 'We need to—'

'You need to what?' Glenda spits. 'Kill something else? There's nothing fucking left! Get out!!!'

'You shouldn't have taken down the fence,' Laura says.

'Fuck you and your fucking fence!' Glenda kicks and punches in frustration at being prevented from getting to Laura.

'Come on,' Mark says again, holding the mutt by its collar with one hand and leading Laura out of the garden with the other.

'I may not look like much,' I shout after them. 'But don't let that fool you. I was a street fighter when I was a lad, and I'll take you out if you ever come on to our land again.' They don't look back. 'Do you hear me? I'll take you down!'

Only when they're out of sight does Glenda twist around in my arms and sob into my shoulder.

Pickles is still warm when I pick him up, soft and limp in my hands. His wheeks, chutters and purrs were such sweet sounds. Now all I can hear is him shrieking in agony. Pickles was nearly ten years old, and Jason's had him since he was nine. How am I going to tell him Pickles was murdered by next door's dog while we were at the shops?

I hand him to Glenda and set about picking up the dead chickens.

'He'll never forgive us,' Glenda says.

Back aching from pulling a muscle while restraining Glenda, I stand up straight, three bantams in each hand. 'He will. It wasn't our fault.'

'I don't want to tell him.'

'I'll do it.' I pile the chickens into their coop so a fox can't get to them. Knowing there's free meat available will only encourage them to return after we replace the bantams. 'Come on. Let's get a cup of tea and sit down for a bit. Then I'll make a nice wooden box for Pickles and we can bury him tomorrow. Give him to me, love.'

Glenda gives him back to me.

'I'll put him in the shed for now,' I say. 'It's cool in there. Go on, you go inside. Put the kettle on. Everything's better after a cup of tea.'

Glenda's eyes bore into the back of my head as I walk towards the shed with Pickles in my arms, and I have no doubt what's going through hers, because I'm wondering the same thing.

How to pay Laura Hunter back for this.

TWENTY-SEVEN

LAURA

Numb, zombie-like, I follow Mark through the patio doors into the lounge and, unable to stand any longer, almost fall on to the sofa. Finn jumps up, but I take his collar and pull him back down to the floor. His muzzle is covered in blood, and he has a self-satisfied smile.

I can't look at him.

I sit there, knees trembling, hands shaking, while Mark pours me a whisky from the drinks cabinet.

'What the hell just happened?' I burst into tears.

'Hey, hey.' Mark puts the tumblers down on the coffee table, sits next to me and pulls me into his arms. 'It wasn't our fault. We put the fence up to keep Finn in the garden, and they took it down. That's on them, not us.'

I shiver. 'Oh, God, that sound. That shrieking won't stop ringing in my ears.'

'Mine too.'

We're silent for a while, then Mark says, 'Why did you stop me when I tried to save their guinea pig?'

'It was for its own sake, honestly. Standing in their garden, watching Finn shake it like that, brought back a memory of when he was a puppy. We were out walking with my friend and her Vizsla. We disturbed a squirrel in the undergrowth, and when it ran for the nearest tree my friend's Vizsla chased it down. It managed to catch the squirrel by its tail and pull it down the tree trunk. It was exactly the same as what just happened with Finn. While the Vizsla death-shook the squirrel, my friend and I ran to its rescue. She grabbed her dog by the collar, while I prised open his jaws and made him drop it. It was the worst decision we could have made. The squirrel was only half-dead, and we just stood there while it died slowly, in agony. God, the sound...it was just like that guinea-pig. I can still hear it now. It went on and on. She picked up a tree branch with the intention of putting it out of its misery, but neither of us had the strength to beat an animal to death. So we just stood over it, crying, saying, "You do it... I can't... You do it... I can't." Until the poor thing finally died on its own. That's why I stopped you. I didn't want that happening again, that poor guinea pig suffering while we figured out how to put it out of its misery. It was better that Finn did the job quickly.'

'I figured,' he says. 'It was the right decision. To be honest, I'm not sure I could have killed it either. Not that I would have made you do it, of course, but I'm glad you stopped me. I think beating a guinea pig to death would have stayed with me for a very long time.'

'But I think Glenda thinks we set Finn on the guinea pig. I think she mistook what I said about despatching it...the look on her face. I need to go round there and explain.'

I get to my feet, but Mark pulls me down again. 'Are you crazy? You can't go round there.'

'We can't leave it like this. We have to explain what happened. We at least have to compensate them for their losses.'

'Let's give them a day to cool off, then I'll go round there while Gerald's at work. I don't fancy taking on an angry ex-street-fighter.'

'Do you think that's true? He really doesn't look the type.'

'With those two, nothing would surprise me.'

TWENTY-EIGHT

GLENDA

THE DOORBELL RINGS as I'm rinsing blood off my marigolds.

Struggling to get them off in a hurry, I splash pink water on my blouse. 'Shit!' Tottering down the hallway, I brush down my skirt, as if straightening that will make up for my dishevelled hair and blood-spattered blouse.

There's a man at the door – a shape I don't recognise through the mottled glass – a delivery driver, probably. Though we aren't expecting any parcels. More likely a local councillor or a Jehovah's Witness. I hope it's a Jehovah's Witness, I like to watch their faces when I tell them I'm a Satanist. If they stick around after that, I fetch my copy of *Satan Wants You* from the hallway drawer and offer it to them. It's just a history book about Satan-worship in sixth-century Persia, but they never stay long enough to realise that.

Gerald doesn't think it's funny.

As I pass the hall mirror, I quickly check my reflection. Sweat glints on my forehead and dank curls stick to it. My cheeks are flushed from all the exertion, and my lipstick has worn off. I look out of sorts, with colour in all the wrong places. I puff up my hair, plump my lips, shake off the past two hours, and open the door.

'Mark!' I take a step back and look behind me.

'It's alright,' he says. 'Please...I'm not here to cause trouble. I've come to apologise.'

'*Apologise!?*' The word bursts out.

'Yes. For Finn. For your chickens...and your guinea pig. We're really sorry.'

I check behind me again; the lounge door is open, and Mark can see right through to the kitchen-diner. I try to compose myself.

'He's a Weimaraner. A hunter. It's not his fault, not really. It was what he was bred to do. It's why we put the fence up so quickly.'

'In the wrong place.'

'I'm not here to discuss that,' he says. 'We're looking into it.'

'There's no *looking into it*. I've lived here my whole life. I know these gardens. I know the boundary, and you've overstepped it. Pay us thirty-five thousand pounds and you can put your fence back up.'

'That's not why I'm here,' he says again. 'We can talk about that another time. I've just come to say sorry and explain. What Laura said about despatching your guinea pig...she didn't mean what you think she meant. It was already half dead, and she didn't want it to suffer. That's why she told me to leave it. She knew Finn would put it out of its misery faster than we could. She's really sorry. We both are.'

I glance behind me again, not sure what to do. I can't focus on what he's saying. All I can think about is all the blood in the kitchen.

'Anyway,' he says, 'we wanted to give you this.' He holds out an envelope.

Reluctantly, I take it from him. It's thick, padded with soft folded paper. 'What is it?'

'A thousand pounds.'

'A grand?!' I stare at the envelope wanting to open it and see what that much money looks like in notes. I want to run upstairs with it, jump up and down on the bed, throw it into the air like confetti and bathe in it, just like they do in the movies.

'I know that doesn't cover it. The trauma. It won't bring your pets back. But we wanted to foot the costs of replacing them and give you something extra to say how sorry we are.'

I can get six bantams and a guinea pig for fifty quid. The rest? A nice dress maybe. Leather shoes. A designer handbag that will make Cynthia choke. Only the service is due on the car, and Gerald will insist we use it to pay for that.

If I tell him.

'Please accept our apology,' Mark says. 'And the boundary thing, we'll sort that out too. We've just got off on the wrong foot, that's all. We really hope we can move on from this. Start again as friendly neighbours.'

I look at him properly then. The antithesis of Gerald. Thick dark hair instead of thin and white. Brown eyes that sparkle with vitality rather than colourless with the clouds of age. High cheekbones instead of sagging jowls. Tanned skin instead of sallow grey.

And money.

Mark has so much money, he stuffs it into envelopes and gives it away.

I reach out to touch the arm of the sleek black shirt straining against his form, smooth as silk. I think it's the real thing; it lacks the cheap sheen of imitation fabric. I can't imagine Mark ever wears shirts made from flannel cotton check, two sizes too big.

It's not like I haven't seen Mark before. I have. Briefly. I've caught snatches of him as he's driven past the house or put out the bins. And I'd be lying if I said it hadn't crossed my mind how lucky Laura is. But I've never been this close to him. He's slimmer than he first appears, taller, broader across the shoulders. But it's not his frame, his handsome face, or that luxurious dark hair.

It's his straight back, wide shoulders and open posture.

It's the way he makes eye contact with that assured smile. It's his energy. It sucks everything out of the air between us, replacing it with tingling static. It's his presence. His magnetism.

It draws you in.

I can barely breathe.

My mouth falls open slightly, my breath warm, a quiver between my legs.

Suddenly, his mouth is on mine, his tongue exploring. One hand finds my breast while the other wraps around me, grabbing my backside, fingers digging into my woollen skirt, desperate and probing.

Then his hands are in my hair, tugging my curls, pulling my head back so he can kiss me harder, deeper. One hand slides up my skirt, trails up my inner thigh, finds and stirs that quiver in my panties.

We stagger backwards through the hallway. My heel knocks the bottom stair, and I fall backwards but he catches me, holds my full weight in his arms for a moment before lowering me on to the staircase. Then he drops to his knees.

Wrenching my blouse from my waistband, he rips it open and the buttons clink against the wall. His face is between my breasts as his fingers tear at the cups of my bra, the straps straining at my shoulder blades. My nipple is in his mouth.

'Fuck me,' I moan.

'Not yet.'

He lifts my skirt over his head and dives between my legs, kissing the fabric of my tights and panties before tugging them down to find bare skin. I slam one hand against the wall and grip the staircase spindle with the other when his tongue plunges inside me. I cry out, 'Christ... Oh, my Christ.'

A few intoxicating moments later, he's tearing open his shirt to reveal a sliver of dark hair that descends between ripples of pecs and abs to his waistband. I reach out, desperate to run my fingers through it. Sliding a hand down his stomach, beneath his waistband, my fingers connect with him, rock-hard. I massage him with one hand, unzipping his pants with the other, while he cranks his belt.

The foot of the stairs is a tangle of black silk and wool tweed. Mark is inside me. His powerful hands grip my wrists and pin them to the treads. The carpet burns my spine with each thrust, the force of him driving me upwards, higher and closer to oblivion, one delectable stair at a time.

The sensation is so fierce, I'm delirious as I cry out, 'I'm coming!' My shout resonates across the landing above me and drifts through the open front door below me. In the street, Cynthia — who hasn't had a good fuck in so long, it's probably healed over — watches Mark's delicious ass as he pummels me into next week.

When he pulls out, he drops to his knees again. 'Take me.' And I do. I take him in my mouth, tasting myself while he groans on the brink of satisfaction.

I open my eyes, and Gerald is standing at the front door, watching us.

I don't stop.

Eyes on Gerald, I keep going until Mark comes in my throat, bent over double as he clings to the banister. When he pulls out, I wipe the corners of my lips with my index finger and slide that into my mouth, sucking it clean...

'Gerald,' I say flatly.

'What's *he* doing here?'

'Mark came to pay us for the chickens.' I pull at the front of my skirt as if the pulsing between my legs is visible beneath the tweed.

Raincoat rustling, Gerald barges past us through the front door. 'That's something, I suppose.' But he doesn't stop to say hello; he just storms along the hallway and disappears into the lounge.

Before closing the door on Mark, I tip my glasses forward on my nose, wipe the corners of my mouth again and say, 'Thank you. I'm very much obliged.'

TWENTY-NINE

LAURA

'How did it go?' I've been hiding out in the summerhouse while Mark went next door.

'Pretty well, I think. Gerald came back while I was there, and he didn't punch me in the kidneys so that was something.'

I don't know why, but I'm not really interested in Gerald, I'm only interested in her. I know he says he was a street-fighter when he was a lad, but I just can't picture that. There's not even a shadow of a strapping young man in him. I try to imagine Gerald, stripped bare except for a pair of shorts and black fingerless gloves, dancing back and forth while punching the air. But all I see is an old man with wobbly breasts, skin drooping over the waistband, and a butt that won't hold up his shorts. Gerald is a bland but gentle old soul. At least that's how I see him.

Glenda frightens me.

'And her?' I ask.

'She was really fucking weird. I felt like Clarice Starling facing Hannibal Lecter. The way she looked at me through those huge glasses. I was half expecting her to suck her teeth then eat my liver with some fava beans and a nice Chianti.'

I laugh. 'I know, right? That's what makes her so weird. Those tweed outfits and cropped hair that's curled as tightly as she is don't match the vibe she gives off. It's like...' I can't think of the words to describe it.

'Like she sweats malice through her pores, instead of water.'

Mark's description is so bang on, I shiver, shaking my shoulders. 'Brrr...she gives me the chills.'

'Hannibal Lectweed.'

'Tweed Bundy.' We're both laughing now.

'Well,' Mark says, 'she seemed happy about the money. I think that's appeased her, for now, at least.'

'Good, because I could do with getting her out of my head so I can focus.'

'How are you getting on?'

'Slow going, but I'm getting there.' I don't tell Mark the truth: that every hour has felt like ten minutes, yet I've been fighting my way through revisions for that many hours, every scene like pulling teeth. I glance at the clock in the corner of my screen. It's gone six already and I didn't even realise. I take it back; it's actually twelve hours of tooth-pulling. 'Jesus, where did the time go?'

'Let's call it a night, open a bottle of wine. Finish it tomorrow and I'll go over it. You're probably just tired. You've done far too much today. You aren't taking enough breaks.' He kisses me on the lips, lingering for a moment. 'I'm starting to worry about you.'

I slide my headphones on to my shoulders and tilt my head on to the headrest. 'Do that again.'

He kisses me again, longer this time. 'At least at the flat Madge forced you to take a break now and then. Since we moved here I haven't even seen you eat lunch.'

'You're right. I'm tired and hungry. I'm hangry.'

He slides the headphones off my neck, takes my hand and lifts me out of the chair. 'I'm taking charge of you. I'm the boss, remember? And the boss says it's time to go home.'

Mark leads me to the bi-fold doors, switches off the lights and locks the studio behind us. Then he takes my hand again, hooks my arm around his, and leads me across the lawn.

When we get to the lounge patio doors, I turn around and call Finn inside. He's nowhere to be seen. But it's been a hot day, and if my studio's too warm he'll head for the bushes where it's cool.

'Finn!' Mark calls, louder.

Finn always comes when he's called, just in case there's a treat to be had.

I traipse across the lawn, checking his favourite spots under the bushes, but there's no sign of him. 'Where is he?'

'I thought he was in the studio with you. He must be in the house.'

We go inside, calling his name, and then separate, searching the house room by room. It's not like Finn to skulk off on his own for too long. Back at my flat he was by my side 24/7, but since I met Mark – especially since we moved here – he's divided his attention between us. I love that he adores Mark; dogs know people, and Finn's trust makes me trust, too. Yet, at the same time, I still get these silly pangs of jealousy. I want my dog back.

'Finn!' I call into the spare bedroom.

Mark comes down the stairs. 'He's not up there.'

We head back into the lounge, out the patio doors, and into the garden, calling his name.

'Where is he?' I whine.

'Maybe he slipped through the hedge.'

'I'll check out front. Can you make sure we didn't shut him in my studio by accident?'

'Sure.'

I run back into the house and through the hall. If Finn did slip through the hedge, I can't see him going anywhere. It would scare him to be too far away from us. No doubt he'll be sitting by the front gate waiting to be let back in.

Throwing open the front door, I almost trip over a bundle on the doorstep.

Then I scream.

THIRTY

LAURA

'Mark! Mark!!!! No, no, no, no!!!!'

Finn lies on his side, eyes closed, one ear drooped across the doormat, the other folded back on itself. Both front and back legs are stretched out stiff and straight, and he's covered from head to toe in blood.

I drop to my knees and shake him, 'Finn!? Finn!!!'

He doesn't move.

So I shake him even harder, screaming now, 'Please! Please! Please! No, Finn! No, no. Wake up, Finn! Wake up!'

Mark comes running up behind me. 'Oh, Jesus Christ!' He bends down next to me and shakes Finn too, calling his name over and over.

'He's dead! He's dead!' I sob. Mark throws his arms around me, and I bury my head in his shoulder, grabbing at his shirt as I wail and cry. We stay there on the doorstep for what feels like hours until my convulsive sobbing subsides.

Then Mark takes my face in his hands and kisses my tears. 'I'm so sorry, baby, I'm so sorry.' He holds me for a while longer until my feet are numb from sitting in the same place for too long. 'Come on...' he says. 'Let's get him inside.'

Mark helps me to my feet, makes sure I can stand upright, then scoops Finn into his arms, shutting the front door with his back. I follow them into the kitchen where he drops to his knees and lays Finn on his dog bed before pulling me into his arms again. All three of us are covered in Finn's blood. It's all over our clothes, in our hair, on our cheeks.

So much blood.

I rock back and forth in Mark's arms. 'She did this. You know she did this.'

'We'll have it on camera. If it was Glenda, we'll have caught her putting Finn's body on the doorstep. We'll go to the police tomorrow. She won't get away with this.'

'I'll kill her.' And this time, it's no joke. I really mean it. 'I'll fucking kill her.'

Wrapped in each other's arms, we sit on the kitchen floor in silence, our backs against the cabinets until it's pitch black outside, until we're shivering from the cold tiles, numb physically and emotionally. And when we finally separate, it's only because we have no choice but to pick ourselves up and carry on.

Mark helps me to my feet, but I barely manage a step before my legs give way and he has to hold me up.

'You're freezing.' He pulls me back into his arms, presses his warm body into mine and holds me like that until feeling returns to my legs, the numbness giving way to pins and needles.

Pressing my face into his shoulder, the tears and Finn's blood now dry on my cheeks, I hold on to Mark, unwilling to let go this time. I can't let go of this liminal moment because doing that will mean moving forward into a life that doesn't have Finn in it. After eight years of feeling his soft muzzle pressed against my thigh, I will feel nothing.

No longer will my shadow have four legs and a tail.

'This was my fault.' I choke out the words into the fabric of Mark's shirt. 'We should never have bought this house. I knew she was a fucking psycho that first day I met her. I suspected she would cause trouble, and still I pushed us into buying this place. And all because I had to stand up to her, fight for what I thought should be ours. Now Finn's dead because of me.'

Mark squeezes me tighter. 'Don't say that. You couldn't have known. Who would do a thing like this? What kind of woman—'

Something pushes our thighs apart, squeezes between us, and we both look down.

'FINN!!' We drop to our knees, calling his name in unison. Then we both run our hands over his bloody fur, checking for injuries.

'He's alive!' I throw my arms around his neck. 'He's fine. He's alive.'

Finn sinks to the floor, lies on his side and, as if nothing is wrong, rolls on to his back begging for a tummy rub. I oblige, laughing and sobbing at the same time.

'What the fuck just happened?' Mark examines Finn's body again, checking every inch for a puncture wound. 'He was dead. And where the hell did all this blood come from? Do you think he killed something?'

'No,' I say. 'That doesn't make sense. He was unconscious, dumped on the doorstep like that. I think Glenda must have drugged him, covered him in blood to make it look like he was dead. It's payback...for the chickens and the guinea pig.'

'She's sick! Who would do a thing like that? Torture people like this?'

'She would,' I spit out the words.

After cleaning Finn up in the bath in our bedroom, we empty out the pink water, clean out the tub and refill it. Then we strip off our bloody clothes and climb in together while Finn rubs himself dry on the bathmat.

Facing each other, my legs draped over Mark's and wrapped around him, he sponges the blood from my face and hair, while I check Finn every few seconds until he finally falls asleep, exhausted.

'Maybe this will be the end of it now,' Mark says. 'Finn killed her pets; she made us pay for it.'

I shake my head, vehemently. 'She won't stop. Not until she gets her money.'

'Maybe you're right – I don't know. When I went round there to apologise, she said if we wanted the fence back up we had to pay her the thirty-five grand.'

'And if we don't? What if this was just a warning, and next time she really will kill him?'

'We have to call the police...again.'

I can't bear to look at any more blood, so I take the sponge from Mark and wipe his face and hair. 'We've tried the police. You know they won't help. Even if we show them footage from the front door camera, she'll just say she found him like that and dropped him home.'

'We need it on record though. If Glenda keeps this up, we might have some chance at a harassment charge. But I think you're right. It was a warning. And we'd be stupid to assume that she won't take it even further next time. Kill Finn.'

'I can't bear the thought of anything happening to him. But I won't be able to live with myself if we pay that woman after what she's done. And even if we did, we know what she's capable of now. What's to stop her demanding more money after we've paid her? Once she knows how much Finn is worth to us, she could keep using him as a bargaining chip. We can't give in to blackmail. We have to think of another way out of this. You must know people... Someone who'll threaten her maybe, get her to back off, permanently?'

'Threaten her? Jesus, Laura!'

'I'm not suggesting we hire someone to break her kneecaps. Just someone who'll frighten her the way she frightened us tonight.'

'You think she won't retaliate? You think this won't escalate? No,' he says flatly. 'We've got to do this properly, through the proper channels, put an end to this legally.'

'The proper legal channel is a determined boundary with the Land Registry. But if we submit an application for one and the Skinners object—'

'Which is inevitable.'

'—then it goes straight to court. And from what I've read, judges look down on anyone involved in a boundary dispute, even victims like us defending ourselves from extortion. They won't even award the winner legal costs above fifty or sixty per cent because, apparently, they shouldn't be going to court in the first place. To them, this is a petty squabble that should be resolved amicably through mediation.'

'But how do you mediate with a blackmailing psychopath?'

'Exactly. We're in a no-win situation. We either pay our blackmailer thirty-five grand or pay legal fees that could run to a hundred grand. No wonder people take matters into their own hands. What else are they supposed to do?'

'I'm not hiring goons to threaten our bloody neighbours, Laura. We need help; solid legal advice. For Christ's sake, why is accepting help so difficult for you? Why do you have to do everything yourself?'

'Because, as I've said a thousand times, nobody else will help us. And the courts will let us down too, right after the lawyers have bled us dry. If you want something done, you have to do it yourself. You can't rely on other people.'

'You can rely on me. You know that, right?'

I nod, then twist around in the water to rest my back against Mark's chest. I need to think this through. That bitch won't get away with what she put us through tonight. The only thing evil needs to triumph is for good men to stand by and do nothing. And they have no idea who they've taken on.

Glenda Skinner will rue the day she tried to blackmail Laura Hunter.

THIRTY-ONE

GLENDA

'I'M JUST SAYING there are alternatives, that's all.' I help Gerald into his raincoat. 'Take your hat. It's pouring.'

'Alternatives. What alternatives? Are you suggesting I sit back while Troy Cullen breaks my mother's legs?'

'Well...' I draw the word out.

'Glenda!'

'He probably won't go through with it. These types are all mouth and no trousers. Then we'll have paid out six grand for no reason. And that's if Sherry's even telling the truth; you know what a liar she is. Maybe she's not in debt at all and you're just funding her drug habit for the next six months.'

'Sherry is a liar but she's not lying about this. I called an old friend who knows Troy, got him to look into it for me. And I know Troy by reputation; he's done a lot more than break a few legs. He will go through with it, and afterwards, he'll still expect payment in full. Her debt will keep getting bigger and bigger, and he'll keep coming back till he kills her. That's how loan sharks work; they aren't all mouth and no trousers. If people weren't terrified of them, they'd never get paid by the likes of Sherry.'

I've never met this Troy, but I picture him and his thugs beating Sherry to death.

I smile.

Gerald grabs his keys and wallet from the hall table, together with an envelope stuffed with six grand. Two hundred of it came out of the chicken money from Mark and the rest came out of Jason's second-year university fees. He doesn't need to know how much Mark really paid us. He thought two hundred was more than generous and it's not like it'll make a real difference to the money we need. What Gerald doesn't know won't hurt him, and he'll believe the handbag is as fake as the rest of them.

I have another thought and my smile falls. 'How are you going to put that money back?'

'We'll tighten our belts. I'll get an evening job if I have to.' Gerald opens the door, fingers trembling on the latch.

'So, you pay this time. What about next time?'

'I'm going to see Sherry after I see Troy. I'm cutting her off. If she ever comes to our house again, I won't open the door. I'll call the bloody police on her if I have to. I'm done.'

Gerald shuffles down the garden path to the car and I watch him go. He's never stood up to Sherry before and I'm not sure I buy it. Gerald's weak, pathetic. But something's different: there's a decisiveness, a finality to his tone that I've never heard before. Maybe Sherry has gone too far this time. Maybe she's finally broken him. Maybe he really will finally stand up to her.

Go Gerald!

I make the most of a break in the rain by trimming the hedge by the roadside. Gerald keeps saying he'll buy one of those battery-powered hedge-trimmers, but just when we think we can afford it, something always comes up. Something like Sherry. So I have to stay on top of it with garden shears. I don't mind, not really. Hedge-trimmers are noisy, and I find the shears therapeutic. I imagine each protruding stem is Sherry's neck.

Snip snip.

I glance up as a car drives past, and my heart thuds excitedly at the flash of sage green.

Laura's car.

It's an unusual colour; there's nothing else like it in the village, so I know it's her. Unless the scrumptious Mark is driving it, but I don't think he does.

Tyres screech.

The whine of a reverse.

And then Laura's getting out of the driver's side, marching towards me. I smile, still going about my business with the shears, as if we're neighbours chatting over a fence.

'You!' She points a finger at me as she approaches. I doubt she'd be quite so bold if there weren't a hedge between us.

I raise my eyebrows at her and smile again.

'I'm warning you,' she says, but I only half listen.

The thing about Laura is, she's so feminine – like Cynthia – that it's difficult to take her seriously. Not just because I'm taller and... well... not fatter exactly, but big-boned and wider, but because I feel almost masculine next to her. Powerful. Like I could just... snip snip.

She raises her voice with her petticoat threats, and I try not to laugh. She should have sent Mark round; it would have had more impact. Only for different reasons. I smile at that delicious thought.

'Look at me,' she shrieks. 'Look at me when I'm talking to you. Do you think this is funny, you crazy fuck?'

She's getting annoying now, ruining my peaceful afternoon. And I have enough on my mind, like Gerald having to face a loan shark mobster who breaks people's kneecaps if they don't pay their interest.

'We gave you the money for the chickens. We said we were sorry. What you did... I swear to God, if you ever go near Finn again, I'll kill you. Do you hear me, you fucking lunatic? I'll kill you!'

Her screeching is so annoying, a burning rises up inside me. It bounces between my ribs like a pinball, past my thudding heart and down my arms to my fingertips. My hands lift the shears, open them either side of Laura's neck, and snip snip...

As she's storming back to her car, I call after her, 'I never touched your ugly mutt!' and then, on the other side of the road, I catch sight of Jean's head. Her mess of grey hair bobs over the wall like one of those Kilroy drawings we used to do on our schoolbooks. I want to say *Wot no privacy?* But instead I smile, wave, and say, 'Hello, Jean!'

She sort of waves back. Sort of.

Jean's such an oddball. No wonder her son killed himself. If I had to live with her, I'd kill myself, too. But I'm grateful for the nosy parker today. Her timing is perfect; she overheard Laura threatening to kill me.

It's time for a change of clothes.

Gerald has those steel-capped boots and those gardening trousers with the Kevlar knee pads.

Those'll do nicely.

THIRTY-TWO

LAURA

As soon as I'm free of the hospital's no mobile phone area, I'm dialling Saeed's number.

If my parents were still alive I'd be speaking to my mother, but in their absence there is only Mark. He's the only family I have apart from Finn. I know my first instinct should be to call him, but something stops me. Weakness perhaps. Perhaps not wanting him to worry. Perhaps because telling him would make it real.

And this can't be real.

I'm not ready for Mark to see me at such a low point, and I know his first response – his knee-jerk reaction – will be to try to fix everything. Fix me. That will mean involving Steve Banks and taking over my project. I'm not going to let that happen. Not until I have no other choice. I'll tell Mark about the results when I absolutely have to, when I know for sure, not one second before.

Saeed tells me, in his melted-chocolate tones, that he has a cancellation and to come straight over, so that's what I do. I run to my car and drive to his office as fast as I can.

Sitting across from him on an oxblood leather couch, I tell him the results, what the doctor said.

'It won't sink in,' I say. 'This is the kind of thing that happens to other people.'

'And it will be permanent?' Saeed asks gently.

'He said it was hard to know at this point. That it was good I hadn't left it too long – thanks to you – but that the window to treat this kind of hearing loss closes between two and four weeks after onset. Before that, the prognosis is reasonable – about fifty per cent recover some or all of their hearing. He's given me a prescription for corticosteroids – for three weeks – and wants me to start them straight away. But if they don't work…'

I can't finish the sentence.

Saeed finishes it for me. 'It will be irreversible.'

I nod, swallow tears. 'It's been a month already, at least. And it isn't getting better. He was kind, sympathetic, but, even though he wouldn't say it outright, I don't think he's holding out much hope for me. When I had the tests, I never imagined for a moment it would be permanent. I thought that was something that would only happen to me in old age, or if I had an accident.'

'Conductive hearing loss,' Saeed says, 'such as an obstruction or damage to the outer or middle ear that prevents sound being conducted to the inner ear – that can be temporary or permanent depending on the cause. But sensorineural hearing loss is permanent, unless it is caught early and the cause is removed.'

I look down at my hands, make fists, press my fingernails into my palms. I register the pain. Then I close my eyes, press my lips tightly together and breathe in the scent of Saeed's office: leather and tobacco. I need to feel all my senses together, all at once, in case one is gone tomorrow.

'Your tests all came back negative: you have no bacterial infection, no physical damage. Which means – as I suspected when we met in the pub – that the most likely cause is stress. If that is the root cause, you need to remove it, Laura.'

'That's easier said than done. And it makes no sense to me how stress can cause hearing loss. Who doesn't have stress in their life? Why aren't people going deaf all over the country?'

'It depends on the individual. Stress produces adrenaline in all of us, but an overproduction can dramatically reduce or even stop blood flow to the inner ear. Translating sound into electrical impulses that the brain interprets is a delicate task. The inner ear has tiny sensory hairs that perform this work, and they depend on good circulation. When they become damaged, or die, they can no longer send messages to the brain.'

I choke back a sob, desperate not to cry in front of someone I hardly know. But then he gets up from his desk, picks up a box of tissues, and comes to sit opposite me. His kindness is all it takes for it to pour out. 'Sorry. It's just... this is my career, my life.'

'I am so sorry, Laura. I hoped it would be better news.'

Saeed waits for me to cry it out, waits for me to speak. He doesn't say what my mother would have said: *everything will be okay, honey, the steroids will work and you'll be just fine*. Which isn't what I need to hear, because, if it's going to happen, I need to prepare myself emotionally, physically, mentally. And sticking my head in the sand pretending this isn't real won't solve anything. He doesn't leap into Mark mode either: jumping on to any tool, process or action he can implement to fix the problem before even letting me catch a breath. Allow the news of a very different future from the one I envisaged to sink in.

I say, 'I feel like I need to choose between my life, and my ability to hear. If I continue with my career, the stress it brings could cost me my hearing. But, if that happens, my career is over anyway. And if I stay at Primrose Cottage, the stress of the boundary dispute could take it from me. It's the perfect home, the perfect place to work, and I don't want to leave. But if I stay and lose my hearing I'll have no choice but to leave anyway. I can't stay there with Mark, unable to contribute financially in any way. Mark doesn't need me to work, but it'll be so difficult to do another job when I've given up on my dreams. I'll make us both unhappy. I see no way out. No matter what I choose, I lose. This play with Hardman Studios was a dream come true for me. If I can't hear, my life is over.'

'You are looking a long way down a very long road, Laura. From where you stand, you cannot see the left and right turns you may encounter on the path, the choices and opportunities that could open up for you. That is a normal response to a situation like yours, of course. As human beings, we feel the need to process, mentally, every worst-case scenario we might face on any journey. But the truth is, they are not real. They are no more real than your dreams. What has passed cannot be altered, and what is to come cannot be known. All you have, all you can experience, is right here in this single moment. And, right now, you still have your hearing. Right now, you know you may or may not have that forever. But that is all you can know. So, all you need to consider is what you can do right now, in this moment, with the information and tools you have to hand.'

I think about that for a moment. What can I do? 'Reduce stress as much as possible,' I say, slowly. 'Take the steroids. Maybe accept help with my project to minimise the pressure that's putting on me. But — if I admit now that I can't cope, they'll take it, give the production to someone else. If I can *just* finish it before I lose my hearing, get it out there — hopefully to good reviews, to know it was a success — I think maybe I'll be able to face losing my dream, knowing I achieved something, left something behind. But if someone else takes it from me now, it won't be my work. I won't know if it was my contribution or theirs that led to the success. All these years I've been working towards this moment. I can't fall at the last hurdle.'

'I understand, why you feel that way. But these dreams, they do not last. The euphoria you experience from achieving this goal will quickly dissipate. And your ability to hear is a very high price for that.'

I'm not sure I agree, so I don't reply.

Saeed asks, 'Have you ever bought something very expensive: a dress, a pair of shoes, a new handbag perhaps?'

'I'm not much of a shopper. Expensive headphones are more my style. Although Mark bought those for me.'

'Of course. I should have remembered that, from our chance encounter in the pub. That works just as well. So tell me... after getting your expensive headphones, how long does the pleasure last? How long before they are just another item on the long list of things you own?'

'A month,' I guess. 'Six at most?'

'That is how long the euphoria will last from achieving this dream that, right now, seems so desperately important to you. More important than your hearing. What then? What happens after that?'

I shrug.

'The most unhappy people I counsel are often the most successful. Because they are forever seeking themselves, their happiness, in places where it cannot be found. And, when they have achieved every objective they set for themselves and the euphoria has yet again worn off, they are left bereft. So they find another dream, another goal, until there are no dreams left to dream, no goals left to reach. Happiness is *inside you*. And it can only be experienced in this very moment. It cannot be found by reimagining the past or dreaming of some potential future that, inevitably, will not match up to your visions.'

'I don't know how to do that: how to be happy now, knowing what's to come. How do you do that?'

'Get out of your own head. Silence the voice that chatters in your mind, reminding you of the past while worrying about your future. That voice is only interested in should-haves – things that cannot be changed – and could-haves – imagining every possible pitfall you may never encounter. Ask yourself this: what problem do you have right here, right now, sitting in my office?'

'I don't know...I guess I don't have any problems right now. But I'm not sure I can silence the voice in my head. It's constant. And it's not something I control, it's just there. Isn't that the same for everyone?'

'For most people, yes. Will you try something for me?'

I nod.

'Focus on my door and imagine there is nothing but darkness beyond.'

Saeed's door is still slightly ajar from when I barged into his office half an hour earlier on the brink of tears. There's a reception desk and seating area beyond, but there's no one out there. His receptionist is out for the afternoon and the clients' sofa's empty.

I picture the room in total darkness, the gap between the door and its frame a black square.

'Now,' Saeed says, 'imagine that your next thought is going to walk through that door. What is it? What does it say?'

I stare at the black square. Nothing comes through the door. The voice in my head that usually chatters away about Glenda, Steve Banks, my project and whether it will make a success or failure of my career is silenced, gone. In the quiet, all I hear is my heart thudding softly against my ribs. I sense the tingling warmth of my being inside the shell of my body and that's all there is. No voice in my head, no fears or doubts, no past or future, no worries or problems.

There is only this moment.

Everything in it, everything on this side of Saeed's door, is vibrant and alive. Time slows, and the single minute I spend looking at that nothingness feels like ten. Suddenly, I'm aware of how much time I spend trapped inside my head. How much of my life I waste re-living a past I can't change or pre-living a future I can't know. Perhaps for the first time in my life, I'm right here, right now.

Then Steve Banks walks through the door, complaining that I don't have the experience to handle a production of this size. He's closely followed by Glenda, shouting about how I've stolen her father's land. I shake my head as if it's a coin jar I can rattle them out of.

Saeed reads my mind. 'It is okay that the voice comes back. The point is to recognise that it exists, and learn to silence it as often as possible. The overwhelming majority of stress we experience as humans is not from the problems themselves that we encounter, but from the time we spend inside our own heads worrying about them. We ruminate over challenges long before and long after the moment when we actually have to deal with them. You will reduce your stress levels significantly if you can learn to silence that voice. Practise, every day, watching a door for the thoughts that come through. When they do, be mindful of them. Silence them and try again.'

'And if I still lose my hearing? What then? What will I do with the rest of my life, stare at an open door?'

He smiles and it's so warm, so magnetising, that I mimic him in spite of everything.

'I am no radio producer,' he says. 'But I would imagine that the hardest part of your job is coming up with the story, envisaging the characters, their personalities and dialogue. And during the production, it is to bring each moment to life, orchestrate the sounds that will create a visual scene in the head of your listener?'

I nod. Saeed is right, the story itself is the hardest part.

'The script you can still write, whether you can hear or not.

The tone of a conversation, you can describe to a voice artist. And the sound effects, you need only relay to a production assistant. You will need help, that is true, but you will still be able to do your job.'

I hadn't thought of that. I hadn't thought that there could still be a way to do my job without being able to hear. Radio is only sound. But just because I can't hear it, that doesn't mean I can't create it.

'It is often the case,' he says, 'that when one sense is lost the others are heightened. You may find that, *after* hearing loss, in the peace of pure silence, your ability to imagine and recreate a living scene is far superior. Getting someone to implement your vision in sound is mere mechanics. Creativity is your talent, Laura, and that will never be lost.'

I stare at him, trying to take this in, and Saeed checks his watch. 'I am sorry, I have a client. It would not be ethical for me to treat you, since you are a friend, but I would be happy to come to your house in the evenings, after my final client, and teach you more techniques for coping with the stress you are under. Let me know if you would like me to do that.'

He gets to his feet, and I crane my neck to look up at him in the cramped space between us.

'I would,' I say. 'Thank you.' And whether it's appropriate or not, I don't care – I throw my arms around him and hold him tight for a long time. I'm glad I'm not his client, since this wouldn't be okay if I were, and right now Saeed is holding me up in more ways than one. His calling me a friend filled me with a familial warmth I haven't felt since my parents were alive, and his friendship already means more to me, in three brief meetings, than any I have had since they died.

At the door, I turn and wave goodbye before stepping out into the reception area. Expecting the empty room that greeted me on my arrival, I'm surprised to find a young girl sitting on the sofa, presumably waiting for her appointment. She's striking, with shoulder-length, multi-coloured hair in pastel tones. The girl has the strangest smile, self-satisfied, and I wonder what problems she faces at fifteen or sixteen, since she can be no older. Her air of confidence fills the small room to its corners until it's hard to breathe in her presence. I wonder what the voices in *her* head say about her past and her future.

Or whether, at such a young age, she's in such meticulous control of her own mind that nobody talks at all.

THIRTY-THREE

LAURA

It was so good to see Saeed. Just being in his company, I felt calm for that too-brief time. And I want to go back to his office, where the whole world disappears while you listen to his velvet-soft tones and revel in the enchantment of his proximity. I imagine that, for all his clients, an hour is never enough. The time is too short before you have to return to real life and drive away from him.

Now, with my prescription sitting on the passenger seat like a hitchhiker I regret picking up, my hands tremble on the wheel. I love Mark – I can't believe how hard I've fallen for him – but the more I think about everything that's happened since I met him, the more I remember how peaceful my life was before.

I stop myself right there. I'm doing it again: re-living the past and worrying about a future that isn't real. I picture Saeed's office door and silence the voice that's telling me how awful everything will be when I lose my hearing. I try to keep the open door black and empty, but it doesn't last. Inevitably, someone barges in.

Glenda.

She's the only other thing that crowds my thoughts.

I've never confronted anyone like that in my life, but God, it felt great. She deserved it. Not that it'll do any good. Glenda is Teflon. She didn't even get angry or try to defend herself, she just stood there clipping the hedge with that fish-smile.

The closer I get to home, the more she gets under my skin. *Ugly mutt.* Finn is the most beautiful dog in the world – sleek, elegant, intelligent. I don't know how Glenda has the audacity to deny what she did. I hope I never run into her again; I'm not sure what I'm capable of doing to that woman. She'd better stay out of my way. I hope I never even catch another glimpse of her. I wish she'd move. I wish she'd get hit by a bus. I wish...

'Jesus Christ!'

I swerve but it's too late. There's a loud shriek as a body bounces off my bonnet and hits my windscreen. I slam on the brakes, the car skids a little, then stops dead. My chest slams into the seatbelt, then the momentum of the emergency stop throws me backwards as the body rolls off the car on to the road.

Gripping the steering wheel, I heave in breaths, too terrified to move, too terrified to get out of the car and discover I've killed someone. As long as I stay in here, that won't have happened.

I stare out of the windscreen, waiting for the person to get up. An eternity passes. They don't. Whoever I've hit is obviously badly hurt.

I can't sit here and do nothing. Whatever I've done, I have to face it.

I snatch my phone out of my handbag and call 999.

'The ambulance has been dispatched, ma'am, but I need you to get out of your car and go and check on the person.'

I burst into tears. 'I'm too scared. What if they're dead?'

'They might not be, and they may need your help,' she says. 'Just follow my instructions, okay?'

I nod.

'Are you still there, ma'am?'

'Yes... Yes, I'll do what you say.'

'Make sure the road is clear in both directions, then exit your vehicle.'

My hands shake so badly I can barely grip the door handle, but somehow I manage to get out. I tiptoe around the car, delaying the inevitable for as long as possible. As I round the bumper, a hefty pair of garden boots appears, bulky trousers, a black hard-shell jacket with peeling reflective tape around the midriff and sleeves.

'I hit a man,' I say.

But then, the man on the tarmac rolls on to his back.

'Glenda!'

'You know the person?' the operator asks.

'Yes, she's my neighbour. She was trimming her hedge; she must have been out in the road. I didn't see her.'

'Call her name,' the operator says. 'If she doesn't respond, gently shake her shoulders.'

'Glenda!' I shout in her ear and shake her. 'Glenda? She's not responding.'

'Stay calm.'

'Okay... okay.'

'Very carefully tilt her head back and make sure her airway is clear. Put your cheek close to her mouth and, while you feel for her breaths, watch for rise and fall in her chest.'

There's no sign that Glenda is breathing. Tears roll down my cheeks, and I wail, grabbing my hair as if that might hold me steady, 'She's not breathing. I've killed her. Oh, my God, I've killed her.'

'Stay calm,' the responder says again. 'The ambulance is on its way. Is there an AED nearby?'

'I don't know what that is!'

'Is there a shop, a petrol station, anything like that?'

'No, there's nothing nearby. Should I give her mouth-to-mouth?'

'No. But you're going to have to do chest compressions, alright?'

'I don't know how to do that!'

'I'll talk you through it. I want you to put me on speaker and keep the phone next to you.'

'Okay.'

'Now, interlink your fingers and place both hands in the centre of her chest. Push down firmly, then release. Push at a regular rate, and don't stop until the ambulance arrives.'

'Okay. Okay.' I press the speaker button on the phone, lay it down on the road beside me, interlink my fingers, and hover over Glenda's chest.

I pause, too scared to touch her. What if I get it wrong? What if I make it worse? What if Gerald sues me?

Come on, Laura! Come on! I pull myself together and remember you're supposed to do chest compressions to the beat of 'Staying Alive'. Only, instead of remembering the chorus, my mind conjures John Travolta sauntering down a Brooklyn street carrying a tin of paint while singing the intro. And you can tell by the way he uses his walk that the rhythm's all wrong, and John Travolta doesn't even sing that bloody song. Fuck, fuck, fuck!

Keep it together, Laura!

Tentatively, I put my hands in the centre of Glenda's jacket. I'm just about to press down when a gasp escapes her lips.

'She's breathing!' I shout at the phone. 'She's breathing.'

'That's good,' the operator says. 'Roll her on to her side and use her arms and legs to support her body. Then very gently tip her head back to make sure her airway stays clear. Watch her closely for rise and fall in the chest. And if she stops breathing again, roll her on to her back and restart compressions, alright? I'm going to stay on the phone until the ambulance arrives.'

'Okay.' I roll Glenda into the recovery position as sirens wail in the distance. 'They're coming,' I shout at the phone. 'They're coming.' And then I sit back on the tarmac, wrap my arms around my knees, and watch Glenda's chest as it rises and falls.

THIRTY-FOUR

LAURA

'Where have you been? I was worried sick—' Mark's mouth falls open when he clocks the police officer standing behind me. 'What's happened? Are you alright?'

'She's fine,' the police officer says. 'Just a bit shaken up, that's all. I'll leave you with your husband, but you'll need to come to the station tomorrow with your ID. Okay?'

'Thanks, officer.'

'No problem. You're going to be okay?'

I nod, and trudge into the hall. Mark mumbles something to the officer before closing the door and chasing after me. Finn tries to jump up, get a cuddle from me, and I'd usually respond by sitting down on the floor and letting him hop into my lap. But I just pat him instead. 'Not now, Finn.'

Mark ushers me into the lounge. 'Can I get you something? Sit down.'

'Whisky. I need a bloody stiff drink. I just ran Glenda over with my car.'

'You what?! What the f—'

'Drink first, expletives after.'

When he hands me a tumbler and sits down next to me, I blurt out the whole story in a rush. I'm so physically and emotionally drained, I just want it over with.

I say, 'I thought it was Gerald at first; she was wearing his clothes. His wellies, those gardening trousers he wears, and that black jacket. It was only when she rolled over that I realised it was her. Fuck, Mark, she's going to press charges. She said I swerved across the road to hit her. The only reason I haven't been arrested already is because she isn't hurt. She put on a bloody good show, though—'

'What do you mean, a bloody good show?'

'One minute she was out cold on the road, but the second I go to start chest compressions she suddenly starts breathing.'

'Let me get this straight. You run into Glenda, threaten to kill her in front of a witness, and two hours later she's dressed in Gerald's clothes on the bonnet of your car?'

I nod.

'That's awfully convenient. What was she wearing when you first saw her?'

'I'm not sure. She was behind the hedge. But she definitely didn't have his jacket on. A blouse, I think. One of her usual ones.' I picture Glenda holding those shears. 'Yeah, I distinctly remember the frills around her neck.'

'And by the time you come back, she's wearing Gerald's jacket? That stiff one with the reflective bands, that he wears when he's working outside?'

I nod. 'And his boots and trousers. Those ones with the knee pads.'

'I bet those boots have steel caps. Protective gear. To make sure she didn't get hurt. How fast were you going?'

'Really slow. You know what that corner's like. It's so narrow, and you can't see oncoming cars until they're right on top of you.'

'And Glenda would know that; she's lived here half her life, right?'

'I guess.'

'So she ran inside, got changed, and then waited out there all that time, pretending to trim her hedge until you got back.' He shakes his head, laughs caustically. 'You have to give it to that crazy bitch, she's got balls, jumping out in front of your car.'

'Shit, though, none of that crossed my mind at the time. It really shook me up. I honestly thought I'd killed her.'

'You'd have done the world a favour.' He sighs. 'I'll go with you to the station tomorrow. We'll tell the police what she's been putting us through. They'll have a record of the calls we've already made to them. She isn't hurt. And as soon as they find out she changed into protective gear they'll drop this, I'm sure. But maybe stay out of her way, okay? That woman's a bloody loose cannon.'

I take a gulp of whisky and press my forefinger and thumb into my eyes. 'It's getting worse. I'm starting to think we should sell up and get the hell out of here.'

'Until we solve the boundary issue, we're stuck here. Unless we can find a four-million-pound cash buyer who isn't worried about living next door to a lunatic bitch from hell. We'll sort it out. In fact, *I'll* sort it out. You get back to work, focus on your project. And for once, let someone do something for you, okay?'

I nod, reluctantly. 'What are you gonna do?'

'Call Angela. We're going legal on their asses.'

'Won't she just say the same thing as the other boundary solicitor I spoke to? That the cheapest and least stressful way out of this is to pay them?'

'Not Angela. She's all about right and wrong, not the easy way out. She'll know what to do.'

THIRTY-FIVE

GERALD

'I THOUGHT you'd left ages ago.' Glenda limps through the lounge wearing her neck brace.

I look up from the letter on the dining table. 'I was on my way out when the post arrived. Do you still need that thing? You weren't wearing it yesterday when I got back from playing golf.'

'I told you, it itches. I just needed a break from it.'

'If you're wearing it in case the insurance investigator drops by unannounced, I think they only do that in the movies. I'm sure they'll call first to organise the interview.'

'Oh, what would you know, Gerald?'

I shrug.

Last week, I rushed out of work when the police called to say an ambulance had taken Glenda to hospital. I had visions of her on a gurney in a full-body cast, one of her legs slung up in the air. As it happened, by the time I got to John Radcliffe she'd already been discharged, and all I had to do was drive her home.

At the time, I was livid. If it had been Mark driving, instead of Laura, I might have gone round there and shown him the business end of my meat hooks. But I could hardly get into a fist fight with a woman and Glenda was fine, so I eventually simmered down.

In some respects, Laura might have done us a favour. If the insurance pays out, it'll not only replace what I borrowed from Jason's university savings to pay Sherry's debts, it'll cover his third year as well. On the other hand, I'm beginning to wonder if these potential payouts are worth all the stress. Since Jason left for university, our lives have completely changed. They used to be quiet and peaceful; the worst thing we ever had to deal with was one of Tom's bad turns, and those never lasted long. Now, Pickles is dead. All our chickens are dead. The crazy bitch next door has tried to kill Glenda with her car. We're in a boundary dispute, and now an insurance investigation.

Glenda hounds the police every day, insisting they bring dangerous driving charges against Laura. Apparently she threatened to kill Glenda only two hours before, and when she saw her standing by the roadside she actually swerved to hit her. Jean saw the whole thing from across the street, but told the police that, although she overheard Laura's threats, she didn't see her car swerve. Tom has a soft spot for her, but Jean has always seemed a touch odd to me. But lately, she really hasn't been herself. She's even more jittery than usual, and a little...vacant. I suppose it's to be expected. She's probably too scared to go up against Mark and Laura; it seems to me that the whole village has been sucking up to them since they offered to donate so much to the village fête.

'I'm just popping to the shop,' Glenda says.

'Are you sure you're up to it? I can go on my way home from work.'

'No, I need to keep moving or I'll seize up completely.' Glenda groans in pain as she makes a meal of leaning over the table to reach for her keys. For the first few days I was helping her with these little tasks, but I stopped when I noticed she struggled with minor things like this yet didn't have a problem dashing for her mobile when it rang.

As she bends over, her handbag swings around from behind her back and the strap slips off her shoulder. She catches it before it falls without so much as a wince. The bag has Marc Jacobs stamped on the front and I immediately think of Mark next door. Mark Hardman, Marc Jacobs – either one could be a high-end fashion designer. It looks like real leather, expensive.

'What's that? Another new bag?'

'No, I've had this one ages.'

Is that true? I don't remember seeing it before. I almost query it again it, but Glenda knows better than to lie to me. I'm not sure why she needs so many bags and shoes, but I guess it's typical of women in general. And at least she gets hers from the market instead of buying the real thing. Right now, with everything going on, I don't have the energy to take her to task on small purchases, explain how they add up.

Glenda points to the unfolded letter on the table. 'What's that?'

'It's from Mark's solicitor. They're inviting us to take part in the RICS Neighbour Dispute Service.'

'Why did you open it?'

I'm taken aback. 'It was addressed to both of us. I can't open my own post?'

'Of course you can, Gerald. I just don't like you stressing yourself out with this when I'm happy dealing with it.'

'Well, I didn't know who it was from until I opened it, did I?'

'Give it to me. I'll take care of it.'

'I haven't finished reading it yet.' I scan the first page. 'I don't understand why they're inviting us into this Neighbour Dispute Service now. Not when they reneged on that Alternative Dispute Resolution thingy you did with them.

Okay, this seems more official – it's all handled by the Royal Institute of Chartered Surveyors – but it's still just another review of our evidence. Why would a second chartered land surveyor reach a different conclusion from the first one?'

'I don't know, Gerald. Who knows what goes through the minds of lunatics?'

'Hmm... well, it doesn't make sense to me. If Mark and Laura want to put an end to this by taking it legal, why not pay us what the chartered land surveyor recommended? It would be cheaper than lawyers, surely? Even half would put us back on track, and we'd be happy with that. So I don't understand what the problem is.'

Glenda folds her arms and taps her foot waiting for me to finish reading the letter.

I get to the end where the costs for the service are all laid out. 'Two hundred and forty pounds just to appoint the surveyor? Two thousand, six hundred and forty pounds for all three stages? And we're expected to pay half? We can't afford this, Glenda. The land can't be worth more than five hundred pounds, surely. This is utter madness; what are they thinking?'

'Gerald!'

I sit upright. I can't remember the last time Glenda snapped at me like that.

Her voice softens. 'Give me the letter. I said I'd deal with this, and I will. You don't need to worry yourself with it. Plus... look at the time, you're going to be late for work.'

I glance up at the clock, spring to my feet and hand the letter to Glenda. I stab a finger at it. 'We aren't doing that. I'll go and see Mark after work and negotiate a cheaper solution. They wouldn't pay ten thousand and that's fair enough. I was shocked the surveyor arrived at that figure anyway. It'll cost them far less to give us the value of the land – say, five hundred pounds – and then nobody has to fork out these ridiculous RICS fees. They'll be paying this Angela Shaw a fortune on top, so if I can push it to the cost of this NDS service, two thousand, six hundred pounds, it'll be happy days for all of us.'

I scan the table and kitchen counter for my wallet, then pat down my pockets.

'You left it on the hall table,' Glenda says.

'Oh, right! Thanks.' I organise the contents of my briefcase, shut the lid, and head through the lounge, stopping at the door when Glenda calls after me.

'I'll speak to them, Gerald. I think it'll be better coming from me. It's my father's land after all.'

'Alright, but this ends now. Tell them they can put their bloody fence up. We'll get a new batch of chickens as soon as we can afford it. And maybe we can start repairing our relationship with them. You know I can't stand conflict, Glenda.'

'I know, Gerald. I know.'

THIRTY-SIX

LAURA

'ARE YOU OKAY?' Mark puts his boxers, socks and wash bag into his travel case. 'You seem quiet.'

'I... I have...'

I'm about to tell him about the hospital, the tests, the steroids, seeing Saeed last week. I should have told him as soon as I got home – I know that – but I kept putting it off, and now I can't, not when he's going away tomorrow. It's too long a conversation, one for another day. And, once I've told him, it will no doubt end in him getting Steve Banks on board. I'm not ready for that, not when I've only been on the steroids a week and there's still a chance they'll work.

'I'm fine. Just tired.' I flop back on the bed, stifle tears.

'I can cancel it, send someone else.'

'No, it's important. You need to go.'

Mark has a meeting with a fiction podcast company in Cornwall. They're ahead of the game with a loyal fanbase, and Chad wants to expand Hardman Studios into that burgeoning field, buy them out. I don't want him to go away, not right now. But when it comes to schmoozing successful entrepreneurs into selling their business there's nobody better than Mark. When he first told me about it, I was really excited. Producing mini-series for fiction podcasts might have opened up a whole new avenue for me as well.

Only, now, I'm wondering if I'll have a career at all in two weeks.

Mark zips up his suit carrier and comes to lie down next to me. Propping himself up on his elbow and resting his head on his hand, he says, 'Is it the neighbours? Are they playing on your mind?'

'Always.'

'Angela said Glenda emailed agreeing to the RICS process, so she replied straight away with the official paperwork for Glenda to print off and sign. And she's advised them to get their own solicitor. She said that, outside of court, this is as serious as it gets. So unless they want to waste tens of thousands in legal fees they'll follow the process and take the advice of the chartered land surveyor seriously. It's different this time. Formal. Legal.'

'Let's hope.' But when I say that, I'm not really thinking about the Neighbour Dispute Service. I'm thinking about returning to the hospital after this course of steroids and getting the worst possible news.

If I tell him, he won't leave. And what good will it do if he stays? It won't stop it happening. All he'll have done is miss a golden opportunity for Hardman, and I can't let him do that. I swallow down the tears before they can well up.

'We have all the proof we need now,' he says. 'We just need to convince them of that, and this will be over.'

'You really think Glenda will listen to this second chartered land surveyor any more than she listened to the first one?'

Mark thinks about that for a minute. 'Not her. She won't listen to anyone. It's like a vendetta to her. She'll fight to the death, even though she knows she's wrong. It's Gerald I'm banking on. He seems like a reasonable man. He'll listen to sense, I'm sure.'

I roll on to my side, turn my back to him, then grab his hand and hook his arm over my stomach. At least this way he can't see my face, can't witness me falling to pieces right in front of him. With my backside pressed into him, tension swells in his body, his muscles tighten. I know what he's thinking, but it's the last thing on my mind right now. And if I did make love to him, emotion would get the better of me, and I'd end up a weeping, hot mess.

I sit up. 'I'm so tired. I think I'll run a bath.' And when I get up from the bed I deliberately don't look at him.

'Shall I join you?'

'If you like.' I lean over the tub and turn on the tap.

'Are you sure you're okay?'

I run a hand under the water, pretending it's taking a long time to reach the right temperature. 'I'm fine, honestly, it's just been a long day.'

Unbuttoning his shirt, he says, 'You know, I've been trying to make sense of the fuckwits next door, trying to figure out why they would risk their father's house in a legal battle. I mean, why blackmail us for thirty-five grand when they could end up losing three times that in an adverse costs order? Then, I remembered something Angela said when I called her last week to set up this RICS thing. She asked me the strangest question.'

'Mmm?' I don't look up from the running tap.

'She asked what car Glenda drives.'

That does make me look up. 'What an odd question. Why?'

'I know, weird, right? I couldn't remember on the spot and didn't think much of it at the time, but when I asked her why she wanted to know, she said because it's always bored housewives who drive Vauxhall Corsas that bring boundary disputes.'

'That's a little harsh on Corsa-driving housewives. And Glenda drives a Ford Focus.'

'You're missing the point. She's saying people do this out of boredom. It's not the money, or the land. Apparently there was a huge surge in boundary disputes during Covid, because people had nothing better to do with their time. They were just bored.'

He adds something else, but I don't catch it over the running tap.

'Sorry, what?'

'Powder.'

I turn off the tap. 'Sorry, I still didn't hear you. Did you say powder?'

'I said, it's part boredom, part power. Didn't you say – ages ago when you first met her – that she's on a ton of committees and stuff?'

'Yeah, I found her name on all sorts of things: allotment committee websites, petitions to various city council departments, letters to newspaper editors. She's always complaining about something: too few road crossings, inadequate signs, banning dogs from green spaces—'

'Exactly... power. Women like Glenda, who sacrificed their careers for their children—'

'And probably resented them for it.'

'Probably. I mean, didn't you say her son left for university recently?'

'Yeah, a few months ago.' I found Glenda on Facebook; her profile isn't private. She'd posted about her son, Jason, moving to Scarborough. 'He's gone off to study security something or other. Something to do with computers.'

'Well, that explains it, then – why she left it so long to object to the summerhouse. I'd put my money on empty-nest syndrome. And this boundary dispute is just her way of filling that hole.'

'That's what she said.'

Mark laughs at the reference to *The Office*, then slides into the water with me. We slot ourselves together as usual, face to face, my legs over his. I'm not really in the mood for humour, but I'm also too tired for an analysis of Glenda Skinner's motivations. I blame her for the stress that will potentially cost me my hearing and don't care what her reasons are. I almost wish Angela hadn't asked Mark about the bloody car, but I get why he needs to make sense of it. It's what you do when you're in the midst of something like this: try to figure out why anyone would behave this way, ruin someone's life over a metre of land. However, discussing the neighbours relieves the pressure I'm fighting to blurt out what happened at the hospital last week, so I humour him. 'It isn't only women bringing boundary disputes, though, surely? There must be plenty of bored men out there seeking power.'

'Of course. Angela was just generalising from her own experience and it got me thinking. Take Gerald, for example. By going into the office every day, he has power, a role. When he comes home and bigs up all the things he got done that day, while she washed his underpants, you can imagine how that would make any woman feel. But for a woman like Glenda... it's a bomb just waiting to go off.'

'Do you think she looks down on Gerald? Needs to feel she's the one in control, the one with all the power?'

'I do. But now, she's lost her job, so to speak. Before, we thought the timing was all about the sale, leverage—'

'But she doesn't have that any more.'

'Exactly,' he says. 'And yet she's still pressing on without it. Which means, she could just as easily have tortured Scott and Emily over it, years ago, when the summerhouse was first built. But she didn't. The sale wasn't Glenda's tipping point; it was her son.'

'You're saying she's essentially been made redundant? She hasn't even made it to sixty without being quietly and unceremoniously dismissed from the organisation she's slaved for for nearly twenty years. No gold watch. Not even a thank you—'

'Yes... and no new employer would take her on. Her skills are two decades out of date, and she probably feels too old to start retraining now. So Glenda, who thrives on power and respect, has suddenly been stripped of all of it.'

'That's true – she is on the older side to have a son just going off to university. She must be close to sixty, which would put her in her forties when she had him. It is late in life to be starting a whole new career. So, in the absence of that, I guess this boundary dispute is her new vocation.'

'Yes,' Mark says, 'and a worthy one at that. Defending her father's land from common thieves! It's far more rewarding than raising kids or going into an office every day, shuffling paperwork.'

'Christ, I hope you're wrong. Because if you aren't, she really *will* fight us to the death.'

'No,' he says. '*We* aren't fighting any more. Angela is. In her letter to Glenda, she forbade them from making contact with us directly in any form. All communication goes through her from this point. As far as I'm concerned, Angela is CEO of this situation. We just do what she says, when she says, and detach ourselves from this emotionally. Glenda may be having the time of her life, but we're going to treat this like a mundane job.'

'That sounds like a really good idea. And maybe, if we don't fuel her excitement, she'll eventually get bored and find something more interesting to do.'

'One can hope.'

I say, 'She probably has Gerald and half the village convinced that Scott stole that land from her father, and we're the bastards refusing to pay. You can guarantee she won't reveal any of our evidence to anyone – the tree, the underground drainage, the foundations – and they won't be interested enough to ask. People love for things to be black and white.'

'True. Maybe even Gerald doesn't know the fine details. He'll just be relieved Glenda is handling it, finally has something to occupy her empty mind, and something remotely interesting to say when he gets home from work with a splitting headache.'

I picture Glenda with that self-satisfied smile, and think Angela and Mark are right. That *is* what this is all about. Maybe not power over us – I doubt she cares much about us at all. But by making out she's fighting the good fight – protecting a defenceless old man against evil – that's power in the company of others: her husband, her grown-up child, her friends, her peers. No doubt she's loving every second of this.

We silently process our thoughts, until Mark says something that twists my gut. 'She's probably a psychopath.'

'I'll check the doors and windows are locked before I take a shower.' I'm only half joking.

'I don't mean in the Norman Bates sense of the word. I mean a functioning psychopath. She lacks the switches most of us are fitted with that prevent us from terrorising another human being this way: guilt, remorse, empathy.'

'What if this vocation is so important to her, she'll do anything to keep it going? If she is a functioning psychopath, as you say, she's capable of anything. I'm scared, Mark. What if we win this thing and she's so angry about it she does something to one of us? Look at what she did to Finn.'

'She won't.'

'How can you be so sure?'

'Well, firstly, incarceration would strip her of her deepest desire: power. And secondly, she needs us. Without us, there is no neighbour dispute.'

'She doesn't need Finn, though. What if she throws poisoned meat over the fence or something?'

'We'll keep an eye on him when he's out in the garden. Maybe do the rounds a few times a day, check the boundary and make sure there's nothing suspicious on the ground.'

I spin around and rest against him. I'm tired of talking, tired of listening, both of which take too much energy right now. But everything Mark has said plays on a loop in my mind. Because, if he's right, Glenda won't want this to end. No RICS Neighbour Dispute Service will make her stop. And their tight finances won't prevent her going to court either. She'll testify on her own behalf. She wouldn't want a barrister taking away all her fun. Imagine the power surge she'd get from defending herself in a courtroom. Even if she loses, she'll appeal, over and over.

Glenda Skinner won't ever stop.

THIRTY-SEVEN

LAURA

'DID YOU hear me, Laura?'

I look in the dressing table mirror at Mark's reflection. I didn't even hear him come into the bedroom. A moment of panic sets in. How long has he been standing there? How long was he talking to me before I even heard a sound?

'Sorry. I was off in Cloud Cuckoo Land. What did you say?'

His concerned expression tells me he's been standing there for a while. 'I asked if you were okay.'

Instead of watching the open bedroom door and focusing on the next thought that walks through it – as Saeed taught me – I've been staring in the mirror for God only knows how long. I can't stop my mind. I know I'm not helping myself by stressing over everything that's happened, or might happen, but it's not as easy when Saeed's not here to talk me down. My hearing gets a little worse every day. I know it's only been eight days, but they should have started working by now. How long will it be before it's completely gone? What will be the last sound I ever hear? Probably one of Finn's farts. If it is, I hope it's one of those high-pitched ones he does when he's sleeping. At least, then, my final sound will be something I can laugh about.

It seems ages since I laughed at anything.

Mark's leaving in an hour and instead of spending the morning with me he's been on the phone trying – and failing – to fend off first Steve Banks, then his dad. I know dropping a grenade then running for the door wasn't his intention, it's just bad timing, but it still feels like that.

I say, 'Of course I'm not okay. Would you be okay with having your baby taken from you? Something you've worked on for as long as I've worked on this?'

'Steve's not taking it from you, he's just providing assistance. You need help, Laura.'

'I can do it. I just need more time. A few extra days to catch up. A week at most. I'll work through the bloody night if I have to.'

'You're already pushing too hard, and it's scheduled to air. You had to redo the last three episodes entirely because you were off your game. This whole thing – ' he points out the window at Oleander House ' – is throwing you off.'

I want to tell him I'm not *off my game*. I want to tell him about the hospital. But there's still two weeks of the course left, still a chance the steroids will start working. And, if I tell him I'm going deaf, he'll hand my project over to Steve completely.

'I can *do it*!' I slam my palm on the dressing table, but the frustration isn't aimed at Mark. I know he's done all he could to stop Steve's involvement, to allow me to keep my baby to myself.

'Come here.' He takes my hand and pulls me away from the dressing table, hugging me then kissing me on the forehead. 'Sit down.' He plonks himself down on the bed and drags me with him. Then he pulls my hand into his lap and squeezes it. 'Listen. I know you're disappointed. But we couldn't have predicted this. You genuinely believed Glenda would back off once we had the house. You couldn't have known what we'd be up against, what an impact she'd have on our lives, on your work. But it's happened. And now we have no choice but to roll with the punches.'

'And the punches just keep rolling in.'

Yet again, I'm not only thinking about the project, but the results too. It's impossible to focus creatively when your mind is split in three: Glenda, the loss of my hearing, the loss of my project. The worst thing is, I know Mark's right. If I accept Steve's help, we'll make the deadline no problem. By taking that pressure off my shoulders, it may even improve the symptoms with my hearing. But I never imagined anyone else working on my play. It's *my* vision. *My* creation. And Steve will steamroll over it.

My shoulders slump. 'It's just not what I wanted, what I dreamed of. Now, nobody will even notice my name buried beneath his.'

'I won't let that happen,' Mark says firmly. 'It's *your* story. And you've done the bulk of the sound design and production. I'll make sure your name is in lights, and his is in a tiny font.'

'Four-point Comic Sans?'

'Papyrus.'

I laugh, something that's so rare these days, it feels odd.

Mark knows how many times I've watched Ryan Gosling's *Saturday Night Live* 'Papyrus' sketch. I defy any writer not to find that hilarious. Those tiny observations – the attention he pays to who I am and what makes me tick – are why I love Mark so much. We haven't been together that long, but he knows me.

'Look,' he says, 'the fact that Steve Banks wants his name on this project at all speaks volumes. He read your script and he didn't just love it, he's haunted by it. I haven't seen him this obsessed by a project since the *Top Gun* spin-offs. Don't you get it? Steve won't put his name to anything he doesn't believe will be an absolute smash. You know Hardman uses radio fiction to test the water for film. Steve must think it's going in that direction. And whether you like the guy or not, he knows his stuff. He's the Spielberg of radio production. His name on the project will drive ratings.'

I flop on to my back, close my eyes and groan.

Mark says, 'You can refuse. Autonomy is in your contract. But I'm begging you to accept help. Nobody in the industry has any idea who Laura Hunter is – not yet – not even after *Close Encounters*; you were buried under too many names. But not this time. I swear to you, I'll write the credits myself.'

I sit up on my elbows, 'What will they say?'

'They'll say...' Mark impersonates Hardman's best voiceover actor '...Malikbay *was written by Laura Hunter. It was directed by Mark Hardman. The executive producer was Steve Banks. Editing and sound design was by Laura Hunter.* His name'll be lost in the weeds, not yours.'

'You promise?'

'On my life.'

I flop down again, put a hand over my eyes, as if this decision can be found in darkness.

'I'm begging you, Laura, please say yes. This isn't just about the deadline. *I* believe in you. Even without Steve, one way or another I know you'll finish this. You'll work through the night, somehow find your mojo in all that exhaustion, and it will be perfect. But what good is perfection if nobody discovers you, nobody listens to it? Steve isn't just a great producer, he's a creative marketer with a huge social following. He bullies the marketing team into doing things his way, and he doesn't stop until his shows are number one. That's why he's so successful. You don't have that influence at Hardman and you're far too nice to bully anyone. And what if you say no so many times that Steve feels snubbed, loses interest and moves on to another project? If things get even worse with the fuckwits next door and you have no choice but to accept help? What then? You'll end up with some B-roll producer who'll still want his name at the top. Wouldn't it be better to accept Steve's help now? Wouldn't it be better to give your baby the best possible start in the world instead of being a stubborn single mum?'

I manage a smile. 'Did you just call me stubborn?'

He flops down next to me. 'Never. Rarely. Occasionally.'

I laugh.

'This could skyrocket you. Chad's set a meeting next Friday to discuss Steve's involvement. Say yes.'

'Alright.'

'What?'

'I said, alright.'

'No, I heard you. I just can't believe it. The self-reliant Laura Hunter has just accepted help.'

I prod him in the ribs.

THIRTY-EIGHT

GLENDA

GERALD WAS wrong about the insurance company, the investigator did arrive without warning, but I never answer the door without my neck brace. I'm not stupid. The interview went swimmingly. The man was very sympathetic and, I think, found me quite charming. He even made the tea because he felt sorry for me limping around the house. It was a relief to get that over with, so I don't have to wear that itchy contraption any more, but it'll all have been worth it once it pays out.

And I can always tell Gerald the payout was smaller than expected.

That Angela Shaw chased me for the RICS Neighbour Dispute Agreement yesterday and I told her it was on its way when it wasn't. I only completed the application form this morning. I dated it, but I didn't sign it. I pop the envelope in the postbox knowing the last collection is at 4:45pm and I've missed it by over an hour. Now it won't get picked up till tomorrow – and I put a second-class stamp on it.

If they think I'm paying to prove my father's land is my father's land, they can go play in traffic. There are millions of boundary disputes in the UK every year; RICS will take weeks – even months – to get back to us, and by then Mark and Laura will have paid up.

I'll make sure of it.

When I come back from the postbox, I confess I'm surprised to find Laura standing on my doorstep, banging on the door. Gerald must be in the shower, getting ready for darts at the Devil's Punchbowl. I'm surprised he hasn't heard her.

Laura should have more sense now the Crown Prosecution Service has agreed to press charges for dangerous driving. I could add harassment to the mix. I convinced Jean to change her mind about Laura's car swerving with a choice titbit she didn't want the village to know about her son.

'What are you doing here, Laura?'

She spins around.

'Have you come to threaten me again? Run me down with your car again?'

She points a finger at me. 'I know what you did. The police were just at my house questioning me about the accident; they're pressing charges! I know you staged it. I told them what you did.'

I barge past her and put my key in the lock. 'I don't know what you're talking about.' Opening the door, I step inside and turn to look at her, wondering if she has the balls to get up in my face. She doesn't, which is telling. She has no idea what I'm capable of and she's gutless, afraid. She stinks of fear. As she should.

'You went inside and changed, didn't you? Put on all that protective clothing before jumping in front of my car. How did you get Jean to change her story? Did you threaten her?'

I casually slide my hands into my pockets and lean on the door frame.

'Laura, I think the only person making threats here is you. I'm the victim, remember?'

'Victim! Don't play innocent with me, Glenda Skinner. You know exactly what I'm talking about. If you don't get the police to drop these charges I'll—'

'You'll what?' I pull my mobile from my skirt pocket. 'Hold on, because I'd like to get this on tape. Can you say that again, nice and loud for the recording? If I don't get the police to drop the charges you'll do what to me, Laura?' I open the Voice Memo app, tap the big red circle and hold the phone up to her face.

She glares at me.

'I'm sorry, I can't quite hear you. Weren't you just threatening me again?' I press the phone closer to her face.

She doesn't speak, she just scowls, nostrils flaring, anger puffing out in clouds. I snap out a laugh and pocket my phone. 'Oh, Laura, are you trying to intimidate me? You are funny.'

'You think this is funny?'

I stand upright, take a step closer, tower over her. 'I love how people like you – so privileged, so used to getting everything you want – morph into frustrated children when you don't get your own way. Look at you, clenching your little fists and stamping your little feet. And you *are* a child in this neighbourhood. I've lived here my whole life, and I know how things are. You're in the wrong, not us.' I reach around the door to the hall table and snap up the present I've been saving for her. 'You should take a look at this. I got this just for you.'

She snatches the envelope from me then waves it like a stick. 'I know what you're doing. And I know why you're doing it. This is fun for you, isn't it? Taking down our fence, throwing stones through our windows, drugging Finn—'

'Finn...? Finn...? Oh, your mutt.' The mention of her dog alerts me to a distant howl, something the mutt does when he's left alone, which means Mark isn't home. That's unusual for

6pm on a Thursday. And now I come to think of it, I haven't seen his car since yesterday lunchtime.

Laura's alone.

I cup a hand to my ear and listen to the howling. 'He sounds fine to me...in fact he seems a little distressed that you're over here threatening me, instead of back home where you should be. Why don't you run along?'

'I swear, if you go near him again—'

'If I go near him? I think, once again, you're confused as to who the victim is here. Your mutt is fine and yet, thanks to you, all *my* animals are dead. You've moved into your big swanky house – or your boyfriend's big swanky house, I should say – thinking you can use your money and power to intimidate poor people like us. Well, you don't intimidate me.'

She snorts; it's quite adorable. 'You actually believe you're the victim here. You're insane.'

'Now, now, I don't think calling people insane is PC these days, is it?' I take another step closer to the threshold and loom over her. 'I think you're supposed to use words like *unpredictable, reckless, fearless.*'

She takes a step back.

'This is starting to look like harassment, Laura. I think it's time I called the police again, don't you?' I take out my phone once more. 'Let's see. What would they be interested to know? Well, for a start, that your boyfriend handed me an envelope of cash to pay me off for stealing my father's land.'

'That was for—'

I talk over the top of her. 'You reported us to the police when all we did was return a fence you erected in our garden. You vandalised my brand-new car. Killed all our livestock. Twice accused me of poisoning your dog. Threatened to kill me. Ran me over with your car. And now you're back here threatening me again. Whose sanity do you think the police will question when they hear all of that? Who do you think they'll believe is the real victim?'

She visibly shrinks.

Upstairs, the hiss of the shower stops, and the pipes clunk. It won't be long before Gerald's out of the bathroom.

With a little less bluster, Laura says, 'This stops now. While we're waiting for the results from the RICS process, we're going to put that fence back up and you're going to leave us alone.'

'If you put that fence up, I'll take it back down. The only way that fence is staying up is if you pay us what we're owed.'

'We won't be blackmailed, Glenda. We'll never give you that money.' She points through Tom's house to the back garden. 'That land is worth five hundred pounds at most. Scott offered you ten times its worth, and you turned it down. This is extortion. And what's more, I know you don't own it. Scott left behind the architect's plans for the extension, and we have underground pipes beneath the patio that are at least a metre away from the building. That's exactly where you claim the boundary fence was. Which means the only way for you to be telling the truth is if Oliver Huntington-Whitney dug up your garden in 1993 and laid rainwater pipes straight through it! Which obviously couldn't have happened. Not only that – the boundary is a straight line, Glenda. That much at least is clear on our title deed plans. So if you own all the land right up to our snug walls, you must own our monkey puzzle tree as well. Which clearly you don't! So we know your entire story is a lie to extort money from us and we won't be paying you a fucking penny, not in a million fucking years!'

Her voice hits that annoying pitch that raises the hairs on the back of my neck. And fortunately – having finished his shower – Gerald's doing the same upstairs with my hairdryer: raising the few hairs he has on the back of his head. Bless him, he does like to fluff them up so they look thicker than they are.

But I'm running out of time here.

Laura doesn't shut up, she just keeps jabbering on. 'And even if Oliver did, by some miracle, lay underground drainage in your father's garden – on the other side of a bloody boundary fence – we still own the land. By adverse possession! That's the law, Glenda. You know it, and I know it. So this ends now! You're going to leave us the fuck alone and we're going to put the fence back up.'

She's grown a little after her speech, so I lean forward, stare down on her and speak firmly without hesitation. 'My father planted that monkey puzzle tree when I was a child. On *his* land. In *his* garden.'

She takes a small step back. 'You'll never stop, will you? No matter what anyone says, no matter what evidence we have, you'll just keep going and going, until we take you to court.'

The hairdryer stops. In a moment, Gerald will be on the landing, listening to all this.

'This conversation's over. You need to leave now, Laura.'

'I'll leave when you give me evidence of owning our tree, our pipework, our soakaway. Go on, Glenda, go and fetch that evidence. There are no easements in any title deeds to suggest our drainage is on your land. But you must have photographs from when you were a child, with the tree on your side of the fence. Go on, let's see them.'

'You should take a look in that envelope, Laura. See then if you want to press ahead with this waste-of-time-and-money RICS service.'

The upstairs toilet flushes.

'You don't have it, do you?' Laura is speaking so loudly that when the toilet stops filling up Gerald will hear every word. 'Because you don't own it. The chartered land surveyor told you you don't have a case. You don't have any evidence. So what gives you the right to demand thirty-five grand for something you don't own? That's theft. Extortion. Blackmail.'

'Be careful, Laura – those are serious accusations. I could take you to court for slander along with everything else.'

'You're stuck, Glenda. We'll never submit to extortion. We're going ahead with the Neighbour Dispute Service, and we'll take it all the way to court if we have to. Do you have any idea what you're risking? What your father's risking? Because this is *his* house, isn't it?'

The bathroom door clicks. The landing floor creaks.

'I'm not asking again. If you don't get off my father's land, this second, I'll call the police.'

'What the hell's going on?' Gerald's voice rattles as he chugs down the stairs in his dressing gown.

I turn to him, then back to Laura. 'I said you need to leave.' I point down the path. 'Leave!'

She doesn't move.

'I said, get the fuck off my father's land or I'll call the police!'

'Don't test us,' she says. 'This is no idle threat. We *will* take you to court. And you'll lose this property in an adverse costs order. Because we can prove, hands down—'

I raise a hand to my forehead, let out a distressed cry, and collapse. For good measure, I grab the crochet doily on the hall table, which brings the plant pot down on top of me.

'Glenda!' Gerald jumps the last few steps, rushes towards me and kneels down by my side. He pats my cheek, and then pulls my head into his lap. 'Glenda?! Glenda?!'

I groan to let him know I'm still alive.

'What have you done? You run her down with your car and now this? We've tried to be reasonable with you people. We never asked for any of this.'

I glance up at Gerald, beaming with pride, then roll my eyes into the back of my head, lids fluttering. 'Gerald,' I croak, 'I can't see properly. Did I hit my head?'

'Leave!' He bellows at Laura. And I don't think I've ever heard this particular Gerald before. So masculine. So frightening. 'You heard my wife. Get the fuck off our land or I really will call the police. You've got ten seconds.'

I take a peek to see if she's running away, but Laura doesn't move.

'Fuck off!' Gerald screams.

Finally Laura turns on her heels and runs down the path. And as she does, I swear a little sob escapes her lips. I try not to smile.

'Should I call an ambulance?' Gerald asks.

I struggle to sit upright then fall into his arms. 'No, just hold me. I'll be alright in a minute.'

'Come on.' He lifts me to my feet. 'Let's get you into the lounge.'

Gerald hands me a cup of tea and a plate with two chocolate biscuits. 'Eat those. They'll get your blood sugar back up. How are you feeling now?'

'Okay. Just light-headed. I didn't expect her to show up on the doorstep like that.'

'I thought you went round there on Monday, told them they could put their fence back up in exchange for what they'd pay for this RICS thing anyway.'

'I did. I spoke to Mark. He seemed reasonable; I thought it was all sorted. But then the crazy bitch showed up out of the blue. Started screaming at me on the doorstep, threatening us with legal action and accusing me of all sorts of dreadful things.'

'Like what?'

'Poisoning her dog.'

'What? What on earth is she talking about?'

'I have no idea. I never touched her dog.'

'Of course you didn't, you'd never hurt a fly, let alone a dog. Is the woman out of her mind?'

'I think she might be. I think we're dealing with some real unsavoury types here, Gerald. I think we've underestimated what those people are capable of.'

'I'll call Tony, cancel the darts.'

'No. Don't be silly. You go, I'll be fine. I'll just watch some television, rest. If I start feeling light-headed again, I promise I'll call you.'

'If you're sure? I really think I should cancel. I don't mind.'
'Honestly, Gerald, I'd rather lie here in peace and quiet, watch one of my cooking shows. You go.'

The moment the front door closes behind Gerald, I'm on my feet. I don't know who Laura thinks she is, coming round here like that, but I can't risk it happening again and Gerald getting involved. She needs to know who she's dealing with.

And I know just who to call.

THIRTY-NINE

LAURA

FIGHTING TEARS, I sink down in the tub, missing Mark. I've got so used to taking a bath together before bed, unwinding, talking about the events of the day with my legs draped over his, that the bath feels empty without him.

Under the water, I imagine this is my life.

Soundless.

The consultant said my first priority was to eliminate the source of the stress, but now I have no doubt that Mark and Angela are right about Glenda. She couldn't have made it clearer tonight that she will never let that happen. She'll systematically up her harassment until I break. And even if Mark pays her, she'll find something else to torture us over. Someone having this much fun isn't going to stop.

When I received the summons from the Magistrates' Court yesterday, and read the charges for dangerous driving, a black hole opened up beneath me. But when the police showed up on the doorstep to question me about the accident today, that hole engulfed me. It never crossed my mind that I'd get a criminal record. The thought of it makes me feel dirty, like stepping in The Bog of Eternal Stench; it'll never wash off.

That was when I snapped.

I've never thought about killing anyone, but now my daydreams are plagued with ideas of what I might do to Glenda. And they aren't fleeting thoughts. I actually see myself doing things to her in picture-perfect detail. I imagine poisoning her, the way she drugged Finn. Finding a deadly nightshade plant on a walk with him. Making jam from the berries. Buying a Victoria sponge cake from Marks & Spencer, switching out the jam, and resealing the box. Taking it round to Glenda as a peace offering while inviting myself in to talk about the possibility of paying them after all. Then I slip the Marks & Spencer receipt into her purse, so it looks like she bought it herself. While we drink tea together, she feels obliged to eat the cake. Especially now there's a chance she'll get her money. A moment later, she's on the floor, clutching at her throat, eyes bulging behind those huge glasses, white foam spewing from her trout lips. Then I simply wash up my cup, put it back in her cupboard and slip quietly away through her back door.

I push myself up from the depths and squeeze bathwater from my hair. My hands shake as if there's no blood left in my veins, only cortisol and adrenaline. I picture those tiny hairs in my ears clutching their throats, eyes bulging, white foam spewing from their lips.

When I got home from the Skinners', I called Mark. He chastised me for going over there, said Angela had told them to cease all contact with us and we had to do the same. But Glenda won't go through with the RICS Neighbour Dispute Service. I'd bet my life on it. She isn't going to lose over a thousand pounds of her scam 'winnings'. But Mark said it doesn't matter. If she refuses, we go to straight to court, it's that simple.

That simple.

But nothing about this is simple. Mark's applying rational thought to a psychopath who doesn't think rationally. But it's all we have. Without help from the Land Registry or the police, this is the best we can do to fight blackmail: drag Glenda kicking and screaming into a courtroom. And if she appeals, we go through it again. And again. And again.

Maybe in ten or twenty years it'll finally be over, and we'll put up the tallest fence we can find. I'll paint her side of it Pepto-Bismol pink and write *Glenda Skinner is a bloodsucking extortionist* across it in huge red letters. She won't be able to paint over it; the fence will be our property.

I couldn't make any sense of the contents of Glenda's envelope. It was written in old English, some schedule to an article with tithes, rods and perches that meant nothing to me. I just forwarded it to Angela. No doubt she'll say it's just more of Glenda's time-wasting nonsense. She'll do anything to confuse things and cause delays, just to keep herself out of a courtroom for as long as possible.

I sink back down in the tub, praying she'll run out of steam at some point and leave us in peace to finally start enjoying our beautiful home. Something we should have been doing from the day we moved in.

Finn barks downstairs, his cries loud and urgent.

I sit bolt upright in the tub, and water pours over the roll-top on to the floorboards. He rarely barks, unless there's someone at the front door or he's left alone. But this isn't that kind of bark. There's neither excitement nor sadness in it – it's not the thrill of receiving visitors or the howl of separation anxiety – there's only aggression. And there's only one reason Finn ever displays aggression.

Fear.

A loud bang resonates up the staircase. It's probably my imagination, but I swear it ripples the water in the tub. I leap to my feet and snag my towel from the radiator as I climb out of the bath. Barely drying myself, I grab my bathrobe from the hook on the wardrobe door and wrap it around me. Frantically tying a knot in the belt, I step into my slippers and run for the landing.

Finn barks again.

He's at the foot of the stairs, nose pointed at the front door, haunches raised, hackles up. I stare at the door too. There's no way I'm answering it at this hour with Mark away for the night.

There's another loud thump and the front door shakes.

Then another and another.

More banging comes from the back of the house, and I run down the stairs. It's coming from the utility room, as if someone is pummelling the windows. Finn's snarling, pacing back and forth, unsure which way to turn. Leaving all the lights off so nobody can see me, I dash through the hall and into the kitchen, where I switch on the outside light.

The back garden is quiet.

Empty.

Still.

Then two bangs come simultaneously. I'm not sure where from. The snug, I think, or maybe the downstairs bedroom. A series of frantic thuds resonates through the rooms and from the front door where Finn half-barks, half-howls in terror. So I run back to the hallway and turn on the porch light. It's of little comfort but, with or without the light, the door camera will catch whoever's out there; it has night vision.

Through the patterned glass of the arch-window oak door, it's still too dark to make out any shapes. The porch light is dirty, the bulb weak. The camera's light is much brighter, but its proximity sensor hasn't activated.

I can't see who's out there. Or how many of them there are.

More than one.

The silence that follows is just as terrifying as the hammering. Slowly, I back away from the door. I look left and right, through the lounge, the downstairs bathroom and then through the open door to the bedroom.

Movement at the window catches my eye.

A swift shape forms in the flash and quench of a failed cigarette lighter.

I run to the bedroom door and slam it.

I can't go outside, can't escape.

I scan the hall table behind me, the mantelpiece to my left and then, as I round the corner, the wooden chopping board in the kitchen: all the places I usually leave my mobile. We don't have a house phone – does anyone these days? – we rely on our mobiles. Of course, that means there's never a phone in a fixed place, or to hand when you're wearing a bathrobe.

My mobile could be anywhere.

Suddenly, the hammering comes from every direction at once. The front door, the utility room, the lounge, the kitchen. I stand frozen in the hallway, terrified, too scared to go into any of the rooms when the noise comes from all of them at once.

My mobile! It was in the back pocket of my jeans! I took it out and put it on the chest of drawers when I undressed to have a bath. 'Finn! Come!' I run up the stairs and Finn follows me, bounding two steps at a time close at my heel. In the bedroom, I snatch up the phone and call Mark. It only rings three times before I realise my stupidity. I shouldn't be calling Mark, I should be calling the police.

I hang up and dial 999.

Sitting on the rug by the bathtub, I hug my knees to my chest and rock back and forth while I wait for the police to arrive. By my side, Finn howls, wolflike, while the pummelling downstairs rattles the whole house along with every spindle on the banister and every one of my bones.

I gave up comforting Finn ten minutes ago; I can't even comfort myself. And, if anything, his howling is soothing, familiar.

In my head, I work out the route from the police station to here, calculate how long it will take them to arrive. I guesstimate the time it would have taken the responder to get a message to the nearest car, and how far away that car might have been when it received the call. Even further than the police station, possibly.

I've made the journey in and out of town a hundred times or more. When we lived in the city, we often drove out here to walk Finn. Since we've lived here, we've driven back into the city so many times – for drinks, dinner, the bank, post office, hairdresser – and yet, I can't remember how long it takes. I have no idea.

No memory of the journey.

No memory of anything at all.

My entire brain is consumed by the cacophony downstairs.

A collage of every horror film I've ever seen flashes in my head. Some monster of a man breaking in and finding a woman alone. Her running to the bathroom, bolting the door, knowing he'll break it down and it will inevitably end in torture, rape, death. It's all I can think about, the terror of what they'll do if these people get inside. Did I lock every door? Is there a window open somewhere?

A voice at the back of my brain says Oxford to Clay Norton is twenty minutes. And if that voice is right – and I hope to hell it isn't – twenty minutes is a lifetime when my heart is beating hard enough to break my ribs.

The next thing I picture in my mind's eye is the horror of sitting right where I am now, looking up from my knees, and finding Gerald and Glenda standing right there at the foot of the rug armed with kitchen knives. Laughing.

So I daren't look up.

I bury my eyes in the sleeves of my bathrobe and pretend none of this is happening.

Then, slowly, the sound fades...deadens...disappears. The police must have arrived. They must have chased my assailants into the darkness. The relief is so overwhelming, I dare to lift my head. But when I do, when I open my eyes, I see the strangest thing.

Finn's head is tilted upwards, nose to the ceiling, muzzle shaped into an O.

He's howling.

Silently howling.

A rock drops into the pit of my stomach and the consultant's voice echoes in my ear, *The most likely cause is stress... You need to remove the root cause.*

Finn's terrified howling wasn't the last sound I was supposed to hear. I let my head droop back into the soft sleeves of my bathrobe and sob. My heart beats against my ribs, my chest rises and falls, my lungs pant.

But none of them makes a sound.

FORTY

LAURA

I'M PERCHED on the edge of the sofa, still in my bathrobe, two police officers standing near the door of the lounge. I wish they'd sit down. One of them rubs Finn's ears and nods while the other talks; I know because his lips are moving. They're discussing sign language, and I can tell that much because the speaking officer has offered some rudimentary British signs, the ones you see most often: a fist circling his chest for sorry, a flat palm pulled from his chin for please and thank you.

That's all they have, though. They must be discussing whether they need an interpreter.

I start to say, 'I don't sign...' but I can't hear my own voice, can't even feel its vibration inside my body. I'm not confident I'm even speaking out loud. It's as if, without being able to hear them, I've forgotten the shape of words.

An uneasy terror silences me.

Finally, the speaking officer, a young man in his mid-twenties with thick blond hair, gets down on his knees in front of me and pulls a pad from his pocket. He flips through sheets of handwritten notes to a blank page and then writes:

MRS HARDMAN?

I want to say no, but words are something different now, unfamiliar. So I shake my head. He scribbles again.

YOU LIVE HERE? WHAT'S YOUR NAME?

I nod. Then I take the pad from him and write my name before handing it back to him.

CAN YOU TELL US WHAT HAPPENED?

I take the pad from him again, then pause. There's too much to write. At some point, I'll have to get used to talking without hearing myself speak. I search my memories for the sound of my voice, as if I can play it back like a recording. Taking a breath, I close my eyes, and finally speak. The consonants are much harder than the vowels, my words feel stretched out, and I have no idea how loud I am. So I use as few as possible. I tell the officer about the Skinners, the dispute, the harassment, and finally about tonight.

When I'm finished, I'm exhausted and out of breath. It's as if I've run a marathon. I dread the officer asking me any more questions, but of course, that's inevitable. When he responds, he forgets himself, speaks out loud, and I have to point to my ear to remind him I can't hear.

So he writes on the pad, IS THERE SOMEONE WE CAN CALL?

Too wrung out to say another word, I take the pen from him again and write down Mark's name and mobile.

The officer pats me reassuringly on the knee as he gets to his feet, then pulls a phone from his pocket. It's a large device, covered in thick, protective rubber. I watch as he dials Mark's number. It occurs to me that he's ten years my junior, yet he's patting my knee as if reassuring a child; would he have done that to hearing Laura? Is this my life now? Pity? Condescension? Then I chastise myself for chastising the man who's come to my rescue. He's just comforting a distressed woman.

The officer moves to the corner of the room and turns his back to me. Another odd thing to do, given that I can't hear, and his colleague has no reason not to. Habit, I guess.

Staring at the back of his jacket – at the shiny, plastic POLICE sign, blue with white text, below a line of chevrons stretched across his shoulders – I play an imaginary conversation in my head. *My girlfriend? No, she isn't deaf. You must have the wrong Laura. Are you even in the right house?*

I should've told Mark. But I thought I had more time.

I'm desperate to hear what the officer is telling Mark, but, far more than that, I'm desperate to hear what Mark is saying back. Instead, all I hear is a quiet hum from somewhere far, far in the distance. It's like a bee, trapped in the marrow cavity at the base of my spine, fighting to break through solid bone with its tiny eggshell body. I'm not sure if the hum is in my imagination or whether the sound is real; perhaps it is real and one tiny hair in my inner ear survived the carnage of blood loss.

I'm going to kill Glenda Skinner.

I'm going to take everything from her, the way she has taken everything from me.

I know it like I know my own name.

The police officer puts his phone back in his pocket and crouches down beside me again. He uses his knee as a writing table, then holds the pad up for me.

MARK ON WAY. 4 HOURS.

I imagine Mark getting out of his car, coming face to face with whoever was out there. Them beating him to death on the driveway while the police are in here with me. The movie in my head is silent. Nobody speaks. Mark doesn't scream. And the baseball bats that strike his body make no sound.

I snatch the pad and write frantically.

WHAT IF THEY'RE STILL OUT THERE?

And then the notepad passes back and forth between us in a stilted conversation I wish I had the energy and confidence to speak out loud.

WHO?

THE SKINNERS. NEIGHBOURS. OLEANDER HOUSE.

YOU SAW THEM?

NO. BUT IT WAS THEM.

OFFICERS CHECKING GROUNDS. DON'T WORRY. ANYONE WE CAN CALL? SOMEONE TO WAIT WITH YOU TILL MARK GETS HOME?

I nod, take my phone out of my bathrobe pocket, scan to the first person who comes to mind, and hand it to the policeman.

The non-speaking officer steps through the lounge door carrying a glass of water which he puts down on the coffee table in front of me. He uses a coaster, slides it towards me, and I look up and smile a thank-you. I didn't even notice him leave the room, I was too busy scribbling messages. You'd think that speaking would be easier than writing, and that drinking would be easier than speaking. But my world is topsy-turvy. I pick up the glass of water and my hand shakes so violently I have to use both to steady it before I can take a sip.

The silent officer leaves the room again and I wonder where he's going this time. To the toilet...to nose through my cupboards and drawers...to fix himself a sandwich? His wandering around my house uninvited is discomfiting, and I want to trot after him, ask him if I can help him with something. But then he comes back with another two officers in tow, and I realise he must have gone to answer the door.

My memory of the last time I heard – or will ever hear – someone knocking on my door was Glenda and her thugs. How ironic it is that Madge, constantly knocking on the door to Mark's flat, used to stress me out so much.

Now, thanks to stress, I'll never hear anyone knocking on my door again.

I will...kill Glenda.

The two new officers are clad in tactical vests over short-sleeved T-shirts. Black gear hangs from straps and pockets:

radios, keys, gloves, handcuffs, a truncheon. Do they call them truncheons these days? They're the business end of this team.

The four officers talk to each other for a while. One of the new ones keeps shaking his head. Then the speaking officer crouches down in front of me again and writes on his pad.

NOBODY OUT THERE.

I checked the camera footage when the police first arrived, but the internet was down during the whole attack. There were no connections to or from any of the cameras, no evidence. The silent officer checked the cables, and they haven't been cut. But I know it was Glenda. It can't be that hard, can it? There's probably a YouTube video somewhere on how to take out someone's internet.

The police probably think I've made it all up. A deaf woman hearing bumps in the night? The law of non-contradiction means I'm either lying about being deaf or lying about the noises.

I stare at the rug beneath the coffee table. Perhaps this whole thing is a nightmare and I'll wake up in a few minutes. I'll be in my bed with Mark beside me, him snoring softly after driving back from his meeting. There will be no dispute, no blackmail, no criminal charges, no hearing loss.

Only I don't wake up.

When I lift my eyes from the rug, there's another man in the room, talking to the blond officer. And the moment I lay eyes on his blue kurta and matching trousers I leap to my feet. It doesn't cross my mind whether it's appropriate or not, I just throw my arms around him.

Saeed holds me.

When he pulls away, I hold on for a moment longer, not ready to let go. When I finally do, he touches his lips then points to the blond policeman. I understand: he's letting me know they haven't finished their conversation. But the whole time Saeed talks to the officer, I keep hold of his hand while he looks directly at me. With his fixed gaze, it's as if Saeed's grey eyes speak to me, the soft textures of his voice filling my mind with a calm memory.

Everything is alright now. And all at once, I stop shaking.

Isn't that odd? Isn't that how the police should have made me feel? Safe? If anything, all these uniformed men, hovering around my lounge, thumbs in waistbands, makes me even more nervous. I wish they'd leave us alone.

The police officer turns the pad to another blank sheet and writes, DR SHARIF WILL STAY WITH YOU UNTIL MARK GETS HOME.

Saeed sits on the sofa opposite and Finn follows him. Usually he'd be excited around strangers, but I think the night has been too much for him, and he's drawn to Saeed's calming presence. He settles at his feet.

Saeed has brought two large writing pads and two Sharpies. It means he doesn't have to sit right next to me, or kneel down right in front of me, for me to be able to read what he has to say. I have no idea how he would know something like that. Even the police officer didn't register the inevitable discomfort of his proximity after going through an experience like tonight. Saeed appears to understand that after having my home, my safe space, violated in this way, proximity and contact need to be on my terms.

He slides a pad and Sharpie over to me before writing on his own.

CAN I GET YOU ANYTHING?

I nod, and I'm just about to speak when embarrassment takes hold. So I write WHISKY and point to the drinks cabinet in the corner.

Saeed pours us each a tumbler, a much larger one for me, and brings the glasses back to the table. Then he writes, HOW ARE YOU FEELING NOW?

SCARED. CAN'T HEAR. IT WAS SUDDEN.

Saeed reaches into a leather satchel he brought with him and pulls out a blood-pressure cuff and digital meter. He holds them up like a question.

I nod and roll up the sleeve of my bathrobe.

As he moves across the room, kneels down beside me and wraps the cuff around my arm, I watch him closely. His actions are slow and measured, as if he's afraid that any sharp movements will startle me. I'm only just beginning to realise how much we rely on sound to navigate the world around us. Saeed is – ever so slightly, barely noticeably – exaggerating his movements, so that my eyes alone can track his activity.

After taking my blood pressure, he asks to see my prescription. I retrieve it from my handbag in the hall, along with the bottle of pills the physician prescribed.

Sitting across from each other again, Saeed writes a series of conditions on his pad, then strikes them off one by one when I shake my head to confirm I don't suffer from any of them.

When he's finished, he puts the bottle of pills in front of me, turns to a clean sheet and writes, TRIPLE IT.

I shake my head.

Then he writes, TRUST ME. LONG WAY FROM PRESCRIBING LIMIT. TIME LAST TOOK?

I write, MIDDAY.

He checks his watch.

TAKE NOW.

Usually, I take three tablets once a day, so I tip the bottle over and count out nine. Then I stare at them in my palm for a while before looking up at Saeed.

I barely know him. I've only met him three times. But Mark has often talked about Saeed since that day we ran into him in the pub, told me a lot about him. And with a great deal of affection. I trust Mark. So I trust Saeed. Besides, there's something about him that would make me trust him even without Mark. Just having him in the room is soothing. And if he can help me...

I tip the pills down my throat and, with the last of the water the police officer brought for me, swallow them.

Saeed fixes his gaze on me, closes his eyes with a brief nod, then opens them with a smile.

We each sip our whisky and sit quietly for a moment. I feel as if I've taken magic mushrooms or Ecstasy, and I'm waiting for the hallucinations to start.

Saeed picks up his pad. CAN I TRY SOMETHING?

I nod.

He dives into his satchel again, and I wonder what he's going to bring out this time. A hat stand? A potted plant? A floor lamp?

He sets a metronome on the table.

I express confusion with exaggerated wrinkled eyebrows. I can't hear, so what use will a metronome be to me? I remember Mark saying Saeed specialises in the subconscious, so I assume whatever he's planning has something to do with that. But surely, to hypnotise someone, you need them to be able to hear you?

He writes, PERFECTLY SAFE. TRUST ME?

I nod. What else am I going to do with this man for the next three hours anyway?

Saeed leans over the coffee table and unclips the pendulum. As he does, the sleeves of his kurta ride up to reveal slender but muscular forearms, veins snaking beneath skin.

The sight comforts me. Beneath his gentle exterior, Saeed is clearly very strong, powerful. But, physical strength aside, his presence is so potent, it pressurises every molecule of air in the room, tight to the corners. It makes you feel fragile and secure at the same time.

If Glenda or Gerald were to show up now, I believe Saeed could strip them of all their power simply by being in their company.

The metronome is old, a wooden pyramid, a beautiful antique. Its gold pendulum over a brass tempo plaque is set at forty beats per minute. *Grave* is printed in the centre of the tempo, and I know from my music GCSE that means slowly and solemnly. Just what I need after tonight.

Saeed has come prepared with a series of instructions already printed out on sheets of paper. I realise the police must have told him I was deaf when they called. That's why he's come prepared, with his Mary Poppins satchel, able to pull out everything he needs. Everything *I* need.

Turning the pages, one at a time, Saeed instructs me to sit back, get comfortable, focus on the metronome and imagine its slow tick in my head. He tells me to relax every muscle in my body, starting at my toes, all the while counting back from fifty in time to the metronome.

I do as I'm told, focusing on each muscle group, one by one, while counting. I've never been hypnotised, never imagined it would work on me, and with typed-out instructions and no soporific voice to drift off to, it's not likely it will.

I jolt upright when my head comes into contact with the back of the sofa. For a moment there, I did almost drift off. Not into a trance or anything like that, just off to sleep. I'm so tired. It was hardly surprising it didn't work, given the circumstances.

Glancing across the coffee table, I check to see if Saeed is disappointed, but he isn't sitting there. He disappeared in a single blink. A magic trick. I look around the room for him and catch him in my peripheral vision as he steps out from behind the sofa. What was he was doing back there? Collecting dust bunnies?

He skirts around the coffee table and takes his seat again.

I point over my shoulder at the window behind me. 'What were you doing back there?'

'Just checking there was still nobody out there. How are you feeling now?'

'I'm okay. I almost drifted off for a moment there, I was so tired. Sorry... I think my mind is too logical to be hypnotised.

And you went to all that trouble, bringing the metronome and typing out...those...instruc...' My voice trails off.

Saeed smiles.

'What's going on? What did you do to me? Say something!'

'A wise old owl sat in an oak. The more he heard, the less he spoke. The less he spoke, the more he heard. Why are we not like that wise old bird?'

I laugh. 'I can hear! It's very quiet, but...something's different. When I watch your lips moving, it's as if the sight amplifies the sound. Seriously, what did you do to me?'

Saeed flourishes his hands like an illusionist. 'Magic!'

Completely lost, I just stare at him waiting for an explanation.

'Not really,' he says. 'You have been asleep for hours. The steroids kicked in, that is all.'

FORTY-ONE

LAURA

MARK FLIES into the room, falls to his knees in front of the couch and pulls me into his arms before I've even registered his presence in my peripheral vision.

Over his shoulder, Saeed is already on his feet, preparing to leave. I look him right in the eye. I don't have to say anything. The slight curve of his smile, and the shine in his grey eyes says it all; he knows how grateful I am that he came over, stayed with me until Mark got home, got me through this terrible night.

Just as Saeed is walking out of the lounge, Mark remembers himself and springs to his feet. He rushes to his friend and grabs his hand, but, instead of shaking it, he pulls him into a hug.

Saeed speaks quietly in Mark's ear, too quietly for me to hear, so I try to read his lips. I catch a few words here and there. He's telling him everything that happened here tonight.

I don't need to hear Mark's response. When he lifts his arms and runs his fingers through his hair, the seams of his shirt strain under tension, the stitches visible beneath his curled biceps. He's ready for a fight.

He's not the only one.

When the door closes on Saeed, a strange loss envelops the room. Whether I like it or not – and obviously I do – Saeed reiterated his offer to come here every night after his last client leaves. He wants to oversee my medication and conduct more guided meditation sessions like the one he did tonight.

It's thanks to Saeed that I cling to hope.

Mark sees him to the door, and when he comes back into the lounge he shouts, 'Whisky?'

I nod heartily, and he takes the tumblers from the coffee table to the drinks cabinet.

What Saeed said about the steroids kicking in while I slept wasn't the whole truth. He did hypnotise me, and slowly, while we sat in quiet contentment, the experience came back. We had a conversation that's now seared into my memory. Not only was I able to speak confidently in that state, I could hear every word, as if I were sitting in a sound booth or wearing my headphones. Echoes were deadened, our voices isolated, external noises cancelled. It was one of the most surreal experiences I've ever had.

I wonder how much of my life has slipped by. It's only when the cacophony ceases – the constant chatter of thoughts in your head that play as if on a sound loop – that, in the silence, you're able to truly experience the minutiae of the present moment. Under Saeed's direction, I was able to tap into my subconscious, focus my mind on the slightest sound, then isolate and amplify each using my memory. It was like ESP. My mind constructed the words for me. Rather than hearing them with my ears, I knew them.

The steroids are working. I just needed a higher dose. Saeed said he would speak to the doctor first thing in the morning and get my prescription changed. And if he can teach me to control my stress levels while managing my current level of hearing, I just might make it through *Malikbay*. What happens after that, who knows? One thing at a time.

Mark puts the tumblers down on the coffee table. Mine is filled to the top with whisky and the ice cubes – large enough to sink the *Titanic* – rise above the rim. He takes a seat on the sofa next to me and I twist around to face him, pulling up my feet to sit cross-legged.

He points to his ear. 'Can you hear me okay?'

I nod.

'Why didn't you tell me?'

I shrug. 'It would have made it real. I didn't want to face it. And you would have stepped in with the project.'

'I wouldn't—'

'Yes, you would. And you would have been right to. I couldn't face letting it go.'

He nods as though he gets it. 'I'm sorry I wasn't here.'

'It's okay.' Speaking still feels a little strange. 'I'm okay.'

Mark grips his tumbler, knuckles white. 'You must have been terrified.'

I nod again.

'I'll kill them,' he says.

'Not if I get there first.'

His expression flips from anger to despair. 'I'm so sorry. I should have pulled out. Lost the deposit. This wasn't worth half a million.'

I shake my head, vigorously. 'We would have regretted it, allowing them to bully us like that, take this house from us. Someone had to fight them. If it wasn't us, they would have tortured whoever bought the house – or Scott and Emily – until they got paid. And anyone with a lesser conscience would have paid them. They would have won. I don't regret standing up to them. The only thing necessary for the triumph of evil—'

'—is for good men to stand by and do nothing. You're right,' he says. 'You're absolutely fucking right.'

He sits there for a moment, and I swear I can see an oversized key sticking out of his back, turning, turning. Mark is calm, gentle; I've never seen him lose his temper. But they say the quiet ones are the worst, and I wonder what he's actually capable of, if pushed to his limits.

'Did you actually see them?'

'No.' I shake my head.

He mutters something under his breath, and it takes me a few seconds to isolate the sounds and put them together in my mind. By the time I do, he's already on his feet and halfway across the room. 'It doesn't make any difference. We know who it was.'

The moment I realise his intention, I'm on my feet chasing after him. I catch him at the lounge door, grab his arm, shake my head more vehemently this time. 'We can't prove it.'

That moment of stress, that surge of cortisol, is enough to set me back. The word 'can't' comes out twisted. I'm not sure the 'ah' resonated in my throat or any sound came out. Until tonight, I hadn't realised how little sensation there is to speech, how much we rely on our hearing to know what sounds we're making. And I think I'm shouting, making strange shapes with my mouth. Everything about talking feels as wrong as not being able to hear.

I take a breath, relax, focus on the silences. Then I speak with intention. 'They'll just deny it.'

'Don't care.' He twists out of my grip and dashes into the hall.

'Mark!'

At the front door, he spins around, holds up a hand to me, then opens the latch.

I chase after him, stopping him at the open door. Too exhausted, too out of breath to even try to speak, I shake my head, then I give him the sign for please. I'm not sure he knows it, but he gets it. I put my hands together in prayer, begging him not to go. Then I fight to get the words out. 'Please! Don't antagonise them. I can't take any more. I need you to stay with me right now.'

He doesn't say anything; we just stare at each other, fury in his eyes, pleading in mine. Eventually, he says one word, then says it again, louder. I hear the 'K' and put the rest together in my mind. He said okay.

Overcome with relief that Mark has seen sense, I swallow my fear, drag him away from the door, and close it behind us. Then I lead him upstairs with Finn in tow. In the bedroom, I empty the cold water from the tub and refill it, desperate to get warm again despite the late hour, desperate to resume the normality of our usual rituals.

Mark points at the door. 'We forgot the drinks. I'll get them.'

I catch every other syllable, but it's enough to understand him. The way he widens his mouth tells me he's shouting – at least, speaking louder than normal – but to me, if anything, he's still too quiet. He's enunciating his words, elongating them, and this tiny little voice in the back of my head says, *He's treating you as if you're learning-impaired.* I silence it. Stupid voice! Mark would never talk down to me; he's just trying to help me.

By the time he comes back upstairs, the tub is full enough to step into, and I can't wait any longer. I slip out of my robe while Mark puts our glasses on the stepladder shelf behind the bath. Then he points at the tub with a question he should know he doesn't need to ask.

'Of course. I was hoping.' Sliding into the water, I watch him undress. I need this. Normality in the midst of madness. I don't ever want to see Glenda or Gerald again, and I don't want Mark going round there either. Not yet. We need to think clearly, figure a way out of this.

Mark steps into the tub and, once we're slotted together like pieces in a puzzle that has been completed many times over, he asks, 'What are we gonna do?'

'I don't know. But it has to stop. Tonight was the last straw for me – breaking point. I think it was for you too. What they've done to us, to Finn, it's enough now. Honestly, I think if that woman pushes me any further I'll snap.'

'I feel like that too. If you hadn't held me back at the door down there... I don't know...'

'How do you *stop* people like her? This isn't normal behaviour, right? She must have some kind of mental illness?'

'I don't know. Get a restraining order, I guess, then a determined boundary.'

'That'll take time. We still have to go through pre-action protocols – she'll drag the RICS process out as long as possible – and it could be a year before we get a court date. How do we deal with them in the meantime?'

'We could try talking to them again,' he says. 'Sometimes that's all it takes.'

'I don't know if I could. Just looking at her face... I don't think I'd keep it together.'

'Me neither. Not after Finn. Not after tonight.'

'We could try ignoring them while we press on with the legal process? Stay out of their way, hope they run out of steam?'

Mark nods. 'What choice do we have?'

'Kill them?'

He laughs. 'Let's keep that option on the table.'

I knit my brows together and tilt my head, so he repeats himself more loudly. When I realise what he said, I laugh too. Then I spin around and rest my back against his chest, because talking and listening take too much energy. And I'm dog-tired.

When Mark holds out a hand to help me out of the bath, I pull away. 'I'm not an invalid.'

He recoils. 'I always help you out of the bath.'

With one foot in and one out, I stand there for a moment, realising that's true. He does always help me out of the bath. It's something I barely register. Because, before, it didn't feel like assistance, it felt like courtesy. But now...

Mark hasn't changed. I hope I don't. I hope this fight to keep my hearing doesn't put me more on guard than ever, more determined in my self-sufficiency. That's not fair on him. Am I going to turn into a person who throws civility back in people's faces, because I can't tell the difference between courtesy and being treated like an invalid?

I take his hand. 'Sorry.'

He wraps a towel around me, then one around himself. I grab his and use it to pull him in close, needing the comfort of his solid form. He holds me tight, and we stand there for a while, stealing each other's warmth. It isn't long before I feel him wanting me.

Usually, he would sneak a kiss, test the water, see if I wanted him, too. But he doesn't do that this time. He assumes the night has all been too much; he won't take anything more. Only, I feel as if something has been stolen from me – by Glenda – and in exchange I need to take something back: control.

I slide my arms over his shoulders, stand on tiptoes and kiss him full on the lips.

He doesn't hesitate for long. His tongue is in my mouth and he's pulling at our towels, as desperate for skin as I am. We make love right there on the rug and with sound drifting in and out like the sea in a shell, I'm transported to a different world.

With my other senses heightened, I connect with Mark in a way I never have before. In this moment, he's not a separate person. He's inside my mind as well as my body, as much a part of my conscious mind as my own emotions or imagination.

When it's over, there's a profound sense of loss. I want it back the moment it's gone, so I crawl into his arms, and we lie there on the rug with the towels over us like blankets.

FORTY-TWO

LAURA

The time I spent with Saeed last night, and that feeling of connection with Mark, hasn't left me. And as I wipe each coffee cup dry before placing it the cupboard, I allow myself a contented smile. Because all I have is this moment, and right now, drying cups, I don't have any problems.

I got a call from the police this morning – one of the officers who came to question me yesterday. They've dropped the dangerous driving charges after another witness came forward. Apparently Cynthia saw it all. She stopped the officers as they were leaving my house. Of course Cynthia would have known the police were here – she knows everything that goes on in the village; she must have been outside, watching the house, waiting for them to leave. News of my possible conviction had travelled around the village like wildfire – no doubt put out there by Glenda – and Cynthia gave the officers her side of the story. She confirmed that Glenda was wearing her husband's protective clothing and threw herself in front of my car.

If Glenda had been able to control her gloating, and keep her mouth shut, she would have got away with it, because *I* certainly wouldn't have told anyone in the village I was facing a criminal conviction.

The relief is overwhelming, and after getting that call I can't escape the feeling that the Skinners have done all they can do to us, that we hit a bump in the road last night, and now we're over the worst of it. We're on the downward slope and my insides are free-falling.

I picture Glenda and Gerald, and whoever they brought with them under the cover of darkness, scattering at the sound of approaching sirens. They will have seen the police cars on our driveway. And now they know we have no qualms about calling the police, surely that will give them pause for thought. They won't want to be arrested for harassment or property damage; nobody wants a criminal record.

Mark and I agreed to ignore them. We'll continue the legal process all the way to court if that's what it takes, get a determined boundary with an injunction to prevent them coming anywhere near us.

Surely they'll back off now.

They must be coming to terms with the fact that we won't ever pay them. And I can't see them risking their livelihoods or their liberty, not for thirty-five thousand pounds.

I suck in a breath and hold it. Listening. A bird chirps in the garden. Far off, a tractor drives down Orchard Lane. A light aircraft, overhead, has taken off from Oxford Airport and it's climbing. My heart beats softly behind my ribs. Saeed's suggestion that I triple my steroid intake is working. The panic of last night has subsided. And if I focus, really focus, I can hear. I just miss the occasional word or syllable. But if I keep the stress at bay, continue with the steroids, there's still a chance it will recover completely, that the damage won't be permanent.

I'm hopeful.

Mark charges through the kitchen door, out of breath. I stop wiping the cup and set it on the counter. 'What's happened?' It's not like he's been for a run; he only went to put the bins out.

'Fuck!' He spins in a circle, running a hand through his hair. When he stops turning, he stares at the floor tiles, wide-eyed, as if he's never seen them before. 'Fuck...fuck...fuck!'

'Mark! What the hell happened?'

He looks up at me, his expression guilty. 'I was just standing there, rubbish in one hand, the lid of the bin in the other, staring at their house. I couldn't stop thinking about what they did to you last night. What they put you through...it... The longer I stared at that house, the angrier I got. I was honestly thinking, if either of them came outside, I would kill them.'

'Jesus, Mark. What have you done?'

'It's alright. They didn't come out.'

I stare at him, heart beating, thanking God that neither of them did. But that doesn't explain the state he's in, so I gird myself for what's to come.

He points at his stomach, turns his hand in circles, trembling.

'This fury. It built up inside me until I couldn't breathe.' He fights for breath now. 'I saw myself, charging down Orchard Lane to their house...banging on their door...storming inside. Beating them both to a bloody pulp. The whole thing played out in my head as if I was actually doing it. I've never felt like that before. Nobody has ever made me that angry in my whole life.'

'You're really scaring me now.'

'I scared myself. I imagined myself as so calm when it was over. I just walked out of there, up Orchard Lane. Then I came in here and told you it was done. We made coffee and went on with our lives as if they never existed.'

Heart in my throat, I wait for what's coming next.

'Once I knew I was capable of it, I made up my mind to actually do it. Put an end to it all. I dropped the rubbish bag and stormed down the road to their house.'

I shake my head. 'No...no...'

'I had to stop to open their gate...' He sucks in a breath. 'I was holding on to their wall and this brick came loose in my hand, so I rocked it free. Then I threw it through the glass of their front door.'

'You...you did what?!! You threw a brick through their door?!'

Wild-eyed, a man I barely recognise nods at me, a naughty little boy who's both proud of and ashamed of his mischief.

'Did anyone see you?'

'I don't think so.'

'What about Cynthia or Jean? They're always skulking about.'

'I don't think so.'

'What the hell's wrong with you, Mark? What were you thinking?! We agreed we'd ignore them, sort this through the proper legal channels. Now we're just as bad as they are.'

'Well...I wasn't thinking.' He darts over to me and pulls me into him. Then he grabs my limp arms and wraps them around himself like a belt. Childlike, he demands to be held, but I let my arms flop to my sides. I can't comfort him for this.

He squeezes me so tight that his words strain as he speaks into the top of my head. 'I'm sorry. I'm so sorry. I couldn't think straight. I just kept picturing you here, last night, alone. Them outside. The police. You going deaf because of what they've put you through. Your life. Your career. I wanted to kill them. I was *going to* kill them.'

'Fuck, Mark. Jesus Christ!' I push him away. 'They'll retaliate. Probably against me.'

'I'm sorry.'

'What difference will *sorry* make if they come back and you're not here?'

'I won't go anywhere. I'll cancel anything that can't be done from home. I'll be here to protect you, all the time, I promise. It was my mistake, I'll make it right. I'll pay for their door.'

'You won't. You won't go anywhere near those people ever again, do you hear me? It's better they're left wondering whether it was us. If you pay for their door, they'll know it was you. We can't be the only people they've pissed off in this village. Let's hope we aren't the only bloody suspects. But I swear to God...'

He pulls me back into his arms. 'It won't happen again, I swear. I won't go near them. I won't do anything. That's it. It's over.' He kisses the top of my head again and again. 'It's over.'

FORTY-THREE

LAURA

'I'm sorry, Laura,' Chad says. 'I know you didn't sign on for a collaboration, but the deadline is upon us and you're two episodes behind. Mark told us everything that's been happening at home and frankly I'm surprised you've been able to work at all. So this is no reflection on you. In fact, I admire anyone who acknowledges when they need help. I fire the stubborn gits who take it to the wire without admitting a deadline's slipped beyond repair.'

I dip my head so that he can't see my eyes. 'Thanks.'

Steve Banks – the bloody brilliant sleazeball – smiles at me from across the conference table, lips sticking to his teeth. 'You'll still have full control. And you never know, Laura, you might enjoy it.'

I cringe.

'Look,' he says, 'I know I come across like a total dick sometimes, but don't let that fool you. I'm an alright guy, honestly.

I do listen. And I take feedback really well. If you don't agree with my creative decisions, you get the final say.'

'Can I have that in writing?'

Steve chuckles. 'If it'll make you more comfortable, I'll sign whatever you like.'

'Alright,' I say. 'Fine. We'll collaborate on the final episodes.'

Steve slaps his hands together with glee, and his eyes sparkle in a way I've never seen. He looks different then. And I see it – clearly – just how desperately he wanted me to say yes. An unexpected warmth spreads through my chest: Steve Banks – the Spielberg of radio production – wants *this* badly to work with me, to be part of my little project.

'Good decision,' Chad says. 'Displays introspection, self-awareness. I like that in an artist. Most of them are pig-headed a-holes, right Steve? So protective of their work, they lose sight of its potential. Not you, though.'

'Not me.' I squirm in my chair. 'I want *Malikbay* to be the best it can be. Nothing else matters; certainly not my own ego.'

Steve leaps to his feet and extends a hand across the table. 'I think this is the start of a beautiful friendship.'

The line's not right and it's typical Steve – cheesy – but I get to my feet, too. And the moment I take his hand, relief washes through me. It's as if someone has opened a valve in my Achilles tendon and all the stress – boiling inside me for so long – is draining out on to the conference room carpet. Mark was bang on. This is absolutely the right decision. Not only will Steve and I make the deadline easily, but there are changes I've wanted to make to the earlier episodes. During production, I've had new ideas, better ideas, but I've had to sacrifice them for the sake of time. Those edits are going to make it sing.

This is a new experience for me: letting someone in.

Steve is still vigorously shaking my hand. 'I really appreciate it.'

Then Chad booms, 'You can let go now, Steve.'

'Sorry.' Steve lets go. 'You can have that back now.'

I beam at him and for the first time, smiling at Steve, it's genuine. 'No, this is good. Us, together. I think we're gonna make this really special.'

FORTY-FOUR

LAURA

ON MY WAY OUT of Hardman Studios, I look up and remember the fateful day I met Mark, when all this began. I can't walk into or out of that building any more without looking up.

When rain starts to fall, I dash across Thame Square, regretting not bringing an umbrella or a raincoat when I knew there was a chance of rain.

The meeting was supposed to be over by four-thirty, five at the latest, but Steve had so many ideas for the final episodes – really inspiring ideas – so we kept talking and talking, spinning off each other. It shocked me. I never imagined I'd enjoy collaboration this much, I thought I'd want to get away from Steve the moment the meeting with Chad was over. But as soon he started talking about *Malikbay* – and he knows the storyline and characters inside and out – I was hooked by his thoughts and ideas. I'm more excited by my project than I've ever been, even when I wrote the first draft.

I feel awful, now, about those negative impressions I formed from our first meetings. Because he's right: he does come across like a dick when he's actually an alright guy. And it's rare to meet someone so self-aware. Any time I pushed back on his creative input, there wasn't a flicker of hurt or annoyance. As he said, he listens, takes feedback on board, and he doesn't take it personally when someone disagrees with his ideas.

We spent so long working together, the sun has gone down. The dark nights are closing in.

I couldn't get a parking space near the square, and by the time I get back to my car – which is three blocks away – I'll be soaked to the skin. I run until I'm out of breath and have no choice but to walk the rest of the way in the rain.

I'm always a little on edge in the dark, especially on quiet streets like these. I think all women are. I expect men take for granted the basic comfort of enjoying a night-time run, a stroll through a park, or a walk down an empty street after sundown.

We don't.

We keep our mobile phone in one hand, maybe pretend to be on a call, or even make one to a friend. We clasp our handbags tight to our bodies. Maybe grip our keys between our fingers like a weapon. Or even carry a can of mace or a rape alarm. I did all those things when I first left Shane and lived in that dodgy neighbourhood. Women check behind them every thirty seconds or so – just as I do now – and, if they cross paths with a man, they constantly look back to make sure he hasn't stopped or turned around to follow them.

It's nothing new. It's routine. But these days, I'm more on edge than ever. Glenda Skinner plays on a loop in my mind, and I worry, wonder, and constantly ruminate over how far they'll go to intimidate us into paying them. I can't stay in the present moment at times like this. It's all what if *this* and what if *that*.

It's a Friday evening, but there aren't many people about, probably because of the rain. When I do cross paths with anyone, I scan their features for familiarity. Glenda. Gerald. The faceless shadow at my bedroom window in the gleam of a cigarette lighter. I stare at them for too long, with too much intensity. The men smile – awkwardly or brazenly depending on their attractiveness and confidence – and the women glance down at the pavement as if making eye contact with me will put them in danger too.

Having seen a different side to Steve Banks – realising that his lecherous big teeth, twisted smile and philandering demeanour belie a more sensitive man underneath – I was on top of the world coming out of that meeting. His reputation for talent precedes him, but many people in the industry think he's got where he is from sucking up and sleeping around. It's not true. Well, I mean, he may have done those things, I don't know. But there's no question that he's a creative talent; he's interesting and interested. He drew things out of me I didn't know I was capable of. He knows how to get the best out of people, artistically. He feeds the creative brain with the kinds of questions that force you to re-think every assumption. He forces you to dive deeper into your characters and push them even closer to breaking point with a tortuous plot. I haven't felt that alive in a long time. In fact, I'm not sure I've ever felt like that, enjoyed my work so much.

I have Mark to thank. He pushed me into this collaboration. He's so insightful. He knew Steve and I would work together famously, if I could just put aside my biases about him. And, of course, my stubborn determination to do everything myself. He knew it would be good for me to – for once – allow someone else into my world and trust them with my creation.

But now, I'm no longer up in the clouds. I've gone below ground into darkness. Exhilaration has been robbed by an abandoned street, and a sickness in the pit of my stomach that churns with a voice: you're being followed.

Watched.

But, every time I look behind me, there's nobody there. I cross a main road. There are a few people, left and right, so I scan their faces, too. There are no Glendas. No Geralds.

On the other side of the road, I continue along the narrow side street to my car. I've parked on this road often – it's one of the few you can rely on to find a space because it's a bit tight and people sometimes lose their wing mirrors – but there's something different about it tonight. Something sinister. The trees that line the pavement move in the wind with a strange slowness, holding out their branches as if they're waving me away. Their leaves whisper: turn around, go back.

Go back.

I spin around and the street is still empty. Nobody has followed me down here from the main road – but, at the same time, nobody is here to help me either. I pick up my pace and glance down an alley to my left that's even darker than the street I'm on. Galvanised grey dumpsters with black lids line the walls left and right: shadowed lairs where assailants lie in wait.

Suddenly, something strikes my right arm, and I'm thrown sideways. I stumble into the alley, and my handbag slips from my shoulders as I fall to the ground. My palms scrape the gritty pavement, which strips off the skin.

Before I can struggle to my feet, I'm grabbed by the shoulders, twisted around and slammed against the wall between two dumpsters. I come face-to-face with someone and it's not the man I'm expecting, Gerald Skinner – it's a stranger I don't recognise.

A man far more frightening.

He's younger, taller and more powerful than Gerald. He's the kind of man you fear most: a man with no shame or remorse. Domination, aggression and savagery ooze from every pore. He smiles at me. Pinning me to the bricks by my wrists, he stretches my arms wide, crucifies me to the wall. I scream as loud as I can, but he silences me by pressing his lips against mine.

I gag. His breath reeks of cigarettes and ethanol. Having absorbed whatever he drank last night, his body excretes it through his pores. He takes his mouth from mine, leaves a string of spit between our lips, and whispers, 'Scream again and I'll bite them off.'

My breath comes too quickly to fill my lungs, terror sucking away what's left. I'm light-headed, dizzy. I don't scream again.

He bends low and presses himself against me, shifting me up the wall with his hips until only the tips of my toes touch the floor. Then, scraping skin, he slides my arms across the brickwork, pins them high above my head, and transfers both into one meaty palm.

Driving his free hand between our hips, crushed tightly together, he grabs my shirt and yanks the fabric up over my stomach before thrusting his hand into the waistband of my trousers with so much force, the button pops open.

'Please, please, please,' I whisper, terrified of speaking too loudly. 'Please, don't.'

He slides his fingers inside my panties and presses the middle one hard against my lips while whispering in my ear, 'Shhhh.' As if those lips express the only voice any woman has, at least, the only one a thug like him is interested in hearing. Then he pushes his finger inside me and his ragged nail catches on the folds of my dry skin.

Tears run down both cheeks, and I grit my teeth to stop from screaming.

He buries his face in my hair, takes my earlobe in his mouth, and holds me there for a moment. Then, millimetre by millimetre, his tongue slithers beneath my lobe before he spits in my ear, 'Just give them the fucking money, and this will all be over.'

His grip loosens and for a moment I think he's going to let me go. But instead he smiles again, pulls his hand out from inside my pants, and unbuttons his fly. Then he tugs down his jeans one-handed.

Too terrified to scream, I struggle in silence to free myself. But with every movement the sharp brickwork tears more skin from my arms. I'm pinned too tight to the wall to move, and my feet have no purchase on the ground. So I just sob at my impotence.

'You filthy animals!' The high-pitched shriek comes from the entrance of the alley. 'Get a room! This is a decent neighbourhood.'

The man snaps his head around, 'Fuck off, lady.'

'I won't!' she shrieks. 'I'm calling the police! This is indecent exposure!'

He lets go of my arms, stepping back from the wall, and, with everything that was holding me up removed, I collapse on to my knees.

Where the dark alley opens on to the road, the old woman is illuminated. In relief, she's vivid against the grey concrete, the light at the end of my tunnel, and my first instinct is to run to her.

But then she totters away, rummaging in her handbag, as the man strides towards her.

It takes a second to gather my wits, and then I dart out of the alley in the opposite direction from the old woman and my car. As I run, I pray he won't hurt her. But I'm too sick with fear to chase after them and defend her. I wasn't even able to defend myself.

I run through the dark streets, back in the direction of Thame Square, knowing that's something that will haunt me for the rest of my life.

Heading back for the main road, I spin around the corner and collide with Steve Banks.

FORTY-FIVE

GLENDA

GERALD COMES through from the lounge and I stuff the unopened envelope in my pocket. I'd been holding on to it – my last hope – as if gripping it tightly might will my plan for it into fruition.

'It's my birthday in two weeks,' Gerald says, taking a seat at the table, where he expects his dinner as usual. 'Then you can finally tell me the surprise you're keeping with that letter.'

I ignore him. I'll think of something for his birthday that will douse his annoying curiosity. Some evenings I get a little frustrated by this assumption that every night at eight on the dot, I'll be walking out of the kitchen, into the lounge-diner, with two plates in my hand. And that's after cooking a separate meal for Tom, whose stomach can only handle a few ingredients these days. He insists on dinner at five-thirty, otherwise he's kept awake by indigestion. Thankfully he didn't make a fuss over the tomato soup tonight – which I'd decanted into a Tupperware container in the fridge this morning – and was asleep in front of his television by seven, so Gerald and I can eat in peace.

'Put your phone down, Gerald. You know I don't like phones at the table.'

He holds up a finger. 'One second. I'm just confirming the date for the glazier and doing a quick bank transfer.' He looks tired.

I put his plate in front of him. I was going to do bangers and mash with onion gravy, but there's something in the air tonight. Despite all the setbacks, I'm feeling positive. I think all our troubles will soon be over, so I pushed the boat out and went for steak and chips.

I felt like celebrating. Jason's autumn break begins tomorrow. I called it half-term and he laughed at me, said, This isn't school, Mum. They don't call it that, it's a break between teaching blocks. He has a party tonight but then he's heading home on the train first thing in the morning. I sent him the money for the train and an Uber out of Mark's chicken fund and he's going to tell Gerald that he got a lift from Simon. I so badly wanted him home for the summer but now he's coming and we have nine whole days together. I've cleaned the house top to bottom, bought all his favourite foods and plan to spoil him rotten so he won't want to leave us on the thirty-first. Everything is coming good and soon Gerald won't look like that: worry-worn.

'The money came through from NS&I, then?' I say.

We'd invested the savings for Jason's second year in National Savings & Investments until we needed it. It takes a few days to get it back out. Gerald had to go overdrawn to pay Troy.

'Yes, and it's a relief not to have to look at that overdraft any more, and the interest.'

I grip the handle of my steak knife to stop myself blurting out that it's a relief for you, maybe, Gerald. Not for me. That was *my* money, not yours. We agreed we would never dip into it. Someone should push Sherry under a bus. And I think that someone should be me.

I ask, 'How much did you take out?'

'The whole five thousand, eight hundred.'

'You didn't have *any* money in your own account?'

'No. What with taking care of Tom and getting everything Jason needed, there was nothing left. But there's still time. I'll put it back. I've been looking for evening jobs, and I might take some gardening work at the weekends. Jason shouldn't suffer because of my bloodsucking mother. But we will have to tighten our belts a bit.'

'Maybe,' I say. 'Or maybe not. I think the Hardmans are finally realising what they're up against. I think they'll be paying us soon.'

'What makes you say that?' Gerald finally puts his phone down. 'Have you heard from Laura since she came here? Since you gave her the original transfer deeds for both properties?'

'Not directly...'

By that I mean I heard back from Troy Cullen, but I don't tell Gerald that.

'From their solicitor, then?'

I make a noise with a mouthful of food and leave him to assume it's a yes. Obviously I'm not going to mention Troy. Laura knows what I'm capable of now – the kind of people she'll face every day if she doesn't pay up. I bet she's begging Mark to pay us as we speak, just to make it stop.

I admit, I didn't think I'd have to go quite that far. And if it hadn't been for Cynthia ruining everything with my insurance claim, I might not have had to. After the police dropped the charges against Laura, the insurance company reopened their investigation. Cynthia's statement that I'd put on protective clothing and jumped in front of Laura's car was enough for them to deny the claim.

I'll make her pay for that when this is over.

I thought sending Ricky and his thug friends round to scare Laura would be enough to frighten the Hardmans into paying us, but I was wrong. Instead, we got a brick through our door. I didn't expect that of them, it seemed a bit...prosaic...vulgar. Thank God I only had to buy Ricky a few six packs, because now I'm in debt to Troy Cullen. But what choice did I have? When the insurance claim was denied, I had to escalate things.

I had to lie to Gerald about the front door. I said it was a cricket ball, some kids larking about. I couldn't have him going round there and confronting Mark. Who knows what might have come out?

I've left their solicitor hanging and chasing me over the unsigned forms for the RICS Neighbour Dispute Service. Without that, they have no choice but to take us to court. And even if they were stupid enough to waste a year of their lives doing that, it'll cost them fifty grand, maybe more. You'd have to be a few sandwiches short of a picnic to do that over a metre of land. It makes far more sense to pay us.

It's hilarious.

Honestly, I'm quite proud of myself. Who would have thought I – of all people – would come up with the perfect crime? Let's face it, how many financial scams can you think of that you won't go to jail for? I'm surprised more people aren't doing it. Literally, all you have to do is walk into your neighbour's garden and say, *I own everything, right up to the walls of your house!* And there's sweet fuck-all they can do about it. You don't need a shred of evidence – just keep insisting you own it. Keep referencing the useless title deed plans, and fabricate some story about a long-dead owner who trespassed on your land. You don't need to worry about going to jail. As long as you say you *believe* the land belongs to you, the Crown Prosecution Service won't touch you with a bargepole. Mark and Laura have called the police so many times, but they haven't done anything. Along with the Freedom of Information request I submitted to the Land Registry to force them into searching their archives for that original transfer, I sent one to the police as well. The Hardmans have accused us of all sorts of things — even tried to bolster their case by fabricating offences like breaking their summerhouse window — but the police have just held up their hands and said, *Whoa! We don't get involved in boundary disputes.*

Ha, ha! What about thirty-five-thousand-pound extortion rackets? Do you get involved in those? It's just too funny. While you go about blackmailing your neighbours for thousands of pounds, you're completely protected from criminal liability by the very people who govern the laws against blackmail and extortion.

The irony is beautiful.

What's even funnier is, the overwhelming majority of legal professionals actually encourage people to settle out of court. In other words, your victim will pay thousands of pounds to legal professionals who'll be on your side not theirs. And, if the idea of paying blackmailers turns their stomach, they'll be forced through the pre-action protocol with a chartered land surveyor whose entire *raison d'être* is to negotiate your payday. Your victim will be forced to mediate with you because, if they refuse to settle out of court, the judge won't look kindly on another trifling boundary dispute being brought into his lofty courtroom. So even if they have solid proof that they own the land, they could still end up footing not just their legal bills but yours as well, just because they refused to negotiate. They could even lose their house, and who's going to risk that?

Such fun!

All you have to do is toss a curve ball into the system, and they'll hit it right out of the park for you. Honestly, it's a master stroke. The entire legal framework is set up to help you blackmail innocent victims for thousands of pounds. All you have to do is utter two sweet, sonorous words: *boundary dispute.*

Pure genius.

'Glenda?'

'What, Gerald?' I look up from my barely touched plate and realise just how long I've been off in my own world. He's already finished his meal and now hovers over the bin holding Tom's side plate of uneaten bread crusts.

He puts the plate down on the counter, digs into the bin and pulls out a screwed-up piece of red and black paper. The label is so distinctive, he hardly has to unravel it to figure out what it is. 'What are these doing in the bin?'

Shit. Usually, I'm careful to bury the Heinz tomato soup labels under the other rubbish, but this morning I was rushing to meet Troy. I open my mouth to speak when someone bangs hard on the front door.

Still holding the label, Gerald stares at me in confusion. 'Are you expecting anyone?'

'No.' But I'm grateful. Saved by the bell.

'Who comes round in the middle of dinner without calling first?'

He drops the label back in the bin but shows no intention of moving from the spot, so I get to my feet. I point a finger at Gerald. 'You could answer the door, you know.'

'You haven't finished your dinner. Just ignore it.'

The visitor knocks again, much louder this time, and I'm only halfway down the hall when the banging turns to hammering.

'Hold your horses,' I shout. 'I'm coming.'

The latch bolt has barely cleared the frame when Mark strikes the door with his fist. It flies out of my hand, slams against the wall, and sends me tottering backwards towards the staircase.

'You!' He seizes me by my cardigan, gripping my blouse and part of my breast at the same time. 'You touch Laura again and I'll fucking kill you, do you understand?!'

I slap his hand away. 'I haven't been anywhere near her.'

He grabs me again, slams me up against the wall.

'Don't fucking lie to me, you cunt! I know you set that bastard on her.'

I try to prise Mark's hand from my clothes but he's holding on too tight, his knuckles white. He's not as sexy like this. He's taller than he seemed standing out there on the doorstep and towers over me. My hands tremble as I fight to break free. He must feel it – smell it on me, maybe – fear. I don't scare easily, but Mark's over the edge. I may have underestimated what he's capable of.

'I don't know what you're talking about.' My voice trembles too. 'Now get out. How dare you come here and physically assault me. Gerald! Call the police!'

'Assault you? You call *this* assault? He practically fucking raped her.'

'What?' My mouth falls open. 'He wasn't supposed...'

'What? Spit it out, Glenda! He wasn't supposed to rape her? What was he supposed to do? Scare the shit out of her like those other thugs you sent to our house? Terrorise her when she's all alone? What the fuck is wrong with you, you crazy fucking bitch?! I should kill you right here.'

'What's going on?' Gerald stumbles into the hall. 'Let go of my wife!'

Without letting go of me, Mark turns on Gerald. 'She's not your wife, she's a fucking monster!' He pulls me away from the wall and spins me around so I'm facing the floor. Then he grabs me by the back of my neck. 'Come on, monster. This ends now.'

'What are you doing?' I fight to prise his hand free. 'Stop it! Stop him, Gerald.'

Gerald just stands there with his mouth agape, as Mark barges past him. I stumble into the living room, through the kitchen, and when we reach the back door Mark opens it and throws me outside.

When he hauls me down the patio steps, I trip and fall face-first on to the grass. Then he picks me up by the neck again and drags me across the lawn to Tom's vegetable beds. Behind us, Gerald – finally out of his stupor – shouts, 'Let her go, Mark. We can settle this man to man.'

With Mark on my back, I can't see Gerald behind him. But I picture him with his fists up by his face, sleeves rolled to the elbow, pulling little air punches.

Pathetic.

As if he'd stand a chance against a man like Mark. Gerald thinks he's forty years younger than he is. Professional street fighter, my ass. What he means is, he used to fight his old schoolmates in the playground for money. And the only reason none of them could beat him was because they were even punier and more pathetic than he was. They found a discarded bowling trophy in a dumpster and cut off the ball, so it looked as if the man was about to swing a punch instead. Gerald scratched the name off the plate and kept it as reigning champion. It's still in the loft. Stupid little man. A real man, a man like Mark, would probably flatten him with one punch.

Mark ignores Gerald as if he's nothing but a buzzing gnat and drags me to the boundary. Now I've swallowed my fear, digested the fact that Mark isn't going to kill *me* with one punch, it's strangely arousing to be manhandled by him. I imagine him throwing me face down on to the wet grass, yanking up my skirt, pinning my wrists and fucking me right here in front of Gerald. I picture all his anger and violence spilling into me, filling me up, until we're pulling each other's hair and biting each other's lips. It makes me wet just thinking about it.

But then he pushes me away from him and I pitch forward, catching my knee on one of the raised beds as I drop to the ground.

'You tell me – ' he bears down on me, grabs me by the neck again, and points my face at his summerhouse ' – where you think this boundary is. We'll put up a fence wherever you say, and this ends now. Do you hear me, Glenda-fucking-Skinner, you crazy fucking bitch?'

'Let her go!' Gerald shouts. 'There's no need for physical violence.'

As he lets go of my neck, Mark pushes me so hard, I fall forward on to my hands. It's exhilarating. I have to hold myself back from lying down right here and rubbing myself against the grass while I imagine him fucking me from behind.

I've always wished Gerald were more of a man in the bedroom. I bought a huge dildo at a friend's hen party once. When I showed it to Gerald and suggested we give it a go, he almost passed out.

Mark turns on Gerald. 'No need for physical violence?! You send a bunch of thugs to attack our house while Laura is home alone—'

'What? I...I don't know—'

'—then you set a fucking rapist on her! What's wrong with you people? Don't fucking tell me there's no need for physical violence.'

'Now, wait a minute,' Gerald says. 'We don't know anything about this. We don't know anything about a bunch of thugs attacking your house, or anyone hurting Laura. This has nothing to do with us. My wife doesn't lie!'

'Doesn't she? *Just pay them the money and this will all go away.* That's what he said to her.'

Shit. Troy wasn't supposed to implicate us. I mean, I told him about the money, offered him ten per cent if he managed to scare her into giving it to us. But he wasn't supposed to mention it. He was just supposed to rough her up a bit, maybe steal her handbag. Leave her wondering whether it had anything to do with the boundary, but not actually know for sure.

Something in Mark's peripheral vision catches his eye, and I follow his gaze. My peat spade is sticking out of the soil in the bed where the tomatoes used to grow. I'd been turning the soil, I must have left it out in the rain. Gerald gets so annoyed when I don't put it away in the shed.

'I'll fucking kill her.' Mark storms towards the tomato bed, steps on to the wooden railway sleepers that form its edge and wrenches my spade out of the ground. Then he strides towards me, holding it aloft. I bury my face in the grass and put my hands over the back of my head to protect it.

'Mark!'

A man's voice, one I've never heard before, resonates through the dark, stopping Mark in his tracks. I risk a glance up. Laura is standing on their side of the orange fence with the man by her side. I watch their house a lot, monitor who comes and goes, but I've never seen this foreigner before. He must be a new gardener or something.

Mark appears to be as surprised by his interruption as I am. 'Saeed?'

The foreign man clambers over the plastic fence and scrambles through the overgrowth into our garden. 'Put it down, my friend.'

I spin around to face Mark, pretend pleading in my eyes. Begging isn't something I've ever done before, so it doesn't come naturally. Perhaps that's why it has no impact on him. He doesn't buy it. Mark looks right at me, the spade aloft, fury in his eyes.

And the last thing I see before closing mine is the pointed steel head bearing down on me.

FORTY-SIX

GLENDA

The rending crack of the spade splits the quiet night.

But I feel no pain.

'Mark!'

I open my eyes. It's Laura. She's followed the foreign man over the plastic fence into our garden. And the moment Mark sees her, his fury spills over again. He brings the spade down, over and over, slamming it against the railway sleeper as if it's my head.

'Stop it,' Laura says. 'She's not lying.'

With the spade still aloft, Mark's anger dissipates and his grip on the handle relaxes. Staring at his wife in disbelief, he rests the spade on his shoulder, awaiting her explanation.

I sit up and smile. It's pay day.

'Angela just called,' Laura says. 'Those really old documents Glenda gave me...they're the original transfer deeds. Angela passed them to the chartered land surveyor, and he compared the measurements with the plans he drew up for the boundary agreement. They've been telling the truth this whole time. Glenda said the monkey puzzle tree was theirs, that her father planted it when she was a little girl, and it's true, it's on their land, not ours.'

'But...' Mark drops the spade and its pointed head lodges in the soil of the tomato bed. Arms limp at his sides, completely stripped of the courage of his convictions, he's speechless.

It's delightful.

I spring to my feet, brush down my clothes, stand tall and straighten my spine. For a moment I enjoy the resignation on Mark's face. Then I clap my hands together and erupt into a frolicking jig around the garden, singing 'Money for Nothing' while little-broken-chick-Laura flies away over her ugly orange fence...

Okay, I don't really do that, but I do enjoy the look on Mark's face.

On the other side of the fence, their mutt starts whining. Unable to stand being kept away from them any longer, it starts pawing the barrier and gets its front leg stuck in the weave. Then it tries to jump the fence, bending over the metal stakes as its body crushes the plastic beneath. Unable to free its paw, it gets itself completely tangled up.

Gerald says, 'If that mutt puts one paw inside this garden again, I'll kill it.'

'I will get it.' The foreign gardener runs to the fence, untangles the dog from the mesh, and drags it back into the Hardmans' garden. Laura's fixed one of those dog parking hooks to the summerhouse, and their gardener attaches the mutt's collar to the lead dangling from it. Then he disappears around the corner of their eyesore. Rightly so, since he shouldn't have been sticking his nose in our business in the first place.

'I can't believe it,' Mark says.

'It's true.' Laura's as dejected as he is and it's a joy to watch. 'According to the surveyor, the original boundary runs from our side of the tree to the snug wall, and we're overstepping it by just over a metre. Oliver Huntington-Whitney's workshop was already right up to the boundary. And when Scott replaced it with the summerhouse, which is much bigger, he built it part-way inside their garden.'

Mark turns from Laura to us. 'If that's true, why didn't your father do something about it at the time? Why didn't he object to the summerhouse? Why didn't he report Scott to the council for putting patio doors in a boundary wall? He's responsible for this nightmare, so where is he?' At the top of his voice, Mark shouts across out garden, 'Thomas McBain! Get the fuck out here and explain yourself!'

'Leave it,' Laura says. 'I'm done. This was my fault. I shouldn't have let you buy the house. I'll pay them out of my savings. Let's go home.'

I watch them trudge back towards the orange barrier, but then Mark turns around. 'I'm not sorry. You deserve to be in jail for what you did to Laura, and we will be taking that up with the police. And whether you're telling the truth or not, you're still thieves. You should have taken the five thousand Scott offered. That's ten times what this pathetic strip of land is worth. Thirty-five thousand is daylight fucking robbery—'

'We didn't do anything to Laura,' Gerald pipes up. 'And we only ever wanted what was fair. Nobody asked you for thirty-five thousand and Scott didn't offer us five, either. You need to get your facts straight, young man.'

I spit at him, 'Shut up, Gerald!'

'What, Glenda? He's talking nonsense!' He points a finger at Mark. 'It's not Tom's fault, it's yours. If you'd just paid us a fair price in the beginning, none of this would have happened. You reneged on the Alternative Dispute Resolution. You could have given us the Neighbour Dispute Service fees, we would have accepted those. Hell, we'd have taken five hundred—'

'Shut *up*, Gerald!' Just when Laura's agreed to pay us, the stupid man is ruining everything.

Mark's temper frays again. 'If you keep talking shit, old man, you and I are gonna have words.'

'Oh, we'll have words, alright.' Gerald takes a few steps in Mark's direction.

'Come on, then,' Mark pushes his shirt sleeves up to his elbows, and he and Gerald circle each other, fists up. 'You've put us through hell and back these last months. I'm going to enjoy this.'

'*Hell and back,*' Gerald scoffs, dancing back and forth while rotating his fists, 'You're the ones who've turned our lives into a living nightmare.'

Mark takes a swing at Gerald, but he blocks it with both hands before jabbing a right hook hard into Mark's jaw. Mark staggers back, clutching his chin with shocked surprise.

I'm surprised too. I thought Mark would flatten Gerald. I guess what he lacks in brute force, he makes up for in technique. I puff up with pride.

'Alright.' Mark composes himself, stands tall. 'I thought I needed to take it easy on you, old man. Now you're gonna pay.'

FORTY-SEVEN

GERALD

'STOP THIS!' The man Mark called Saeed has clambered back over the fence into our garden. He dives between me and Mark, separating us at arm's length, then looks from him to me. He holds my gaze with such intensity that all the strength drains from my arms. I drop my fists.

He turns to Mark then, takes him by the wrists and pushes his arms down by his sides without meeting any resistance. 'Mark...my friend...this is not the solution, and you know it.'

Everything is calm, suddenly.

'Everyone is talking at cross purposes. We can resolve this amicably by getting to the truth. Starting with why that woman – ' he points at Glenda ' – is lying about the monkey puzzle tree.'

'Saeed, stop.' Laura takes his arm. 'I don't care who planted the bloody tree. The original transfer deeds prove the boundary is back there and the summerhouse oversteps it. If it's by a metre or by ten fucking centimetres, I don't care any more.'

She turns to her husband, then. 'Please, Mark, I'm begging you. Let it go. It's my savings. My decision. I'll give Glenda her thirty-five thousand. It's gone too far. Let's go home before someone gets themselves killed over a patch of grass. Come on.' She takes Mark's hand.

Laura drags Mark away, starts to lead him back towards the fence, and Saeed follows.

A wave of relief washes over me. I never did like confrontation, and never imagined I'd end up in a fist-fight with my neighbour. And Chad Hardman's son of all people.

I turn to go inside.

'Not so fast!' A voice, female, resonates across the garden, and we all turn in its direction. It came from the patio near the back door, but there's nobody standing there.

There's a rustle in the shrubs down the side of the house, and the bushes talk. 'This isn't how this ends. You don't get off that easily.' The branches move aside as something struggles to free itself, and a woman lurches on to our patio.

'Jean?' What the hell is she doing here?

By the time she extricates herself from our shrubs, her hair's a grey bird's nest and her clothes are dishevelled. Jean pulls the strap of her handbag back over her shoulder and brushes herself down as she stumbles to the end of our patio while we stand open-mouthed on the grass in front of her. Is she drunk? I've never seen Jean drunk.

Then she pulls a gun from her handbag.

It can't be real. Jean, our sweet neighbour from across the street, hiding in our bushes armed with a gun? It doesn't make any sense. But it looks real enough. It's only a handgun but it's huge, far too bulky for her small frame. Carrying it, she looks almost cartoonish.

She points it at Glenda. 'I hoped they'd kill you and I'd get to watch. Did you think I didn't know? Did you think I'd stand by while that lily-livered Laura handed over thirty-five thousand pounds after everything you stole from us?' Jean turns the gun on Laura then. 'You're pathetic!' She mimics her in a childish voice. *'I'll give Glenda her thirty-five thousand.* Now you've got your hands on Hardman money, you just hand it over like it's Monopoly. But there wasn't any Hardman money for my Donald when he needed it, was there, Mark?' Now it's his turn for a gun in the face. 'You got him caught up in that payment scheme, but when it came to paying HMRC, the Hardmans soon tightened their belts.'

I'd heard something about that. Donald was employed by Hardman via an umbrella company that paid him through some contractor loan scheme. Never needing to be paid back, these loans were a form of disguised remuneration. Tax avoidance, essentially. Despite accepting these schemes for decades, HMRC not only made them illegal but made the law retrospective. They went after decades' worth of unpaid interest on the loans and back taxes that people couldn't possibly pay. Donald had been fighting HMRC for two years, I don't remember how much he owed, but I think it was pretty big.

'It wasn't us,' Mark says. 'It was his contract firm that signed him up—' A bullet whistles past his ear and he shuts up.

'You're all responsible. Even stupid Gerald over there.'

Finally it's my turn. I've never had a gun pointed in my face and my whole body loosens; I think I'm going to soil myself. Everyone looks at me, but all I can do is shrug. I have no idea what I'm responsible for.

'Donald loved life!' she wails. 'Now my son's in his grave while you lot waste yours squabbling over a patch of grass. You don't deserve such pitiful lives, not when he's dead! I was hoping you'd all kill each other! That's what was supposed to happen!'

She spits out the words with such bile, it takes my breath away. I've never seen Jean like this; she's clearly lost her mind. Not ideal when she's got a gun.

'Jeanie?' We all turn towards Tom, who's appeared at the corner of the patio.

'Tommy.' Jean spins around.

'I thought that was you,' Tom says. 'I heard all this commotion and someone shouting my name. I was asleep. I thought I was dreaming. Then I heard your voice through the open window. Why haven't you come to see me for so long? I've missed you.'

Rarely out of bed and on his feet these days, Tom struggles along the patio towards Jean. He's doddery, bent over from spending too much time propped up against a pillow, and looks twenty years older than he is.

The sight of his aged, confused form softens Jean. 'I've been a little busy, Tommy. Donald died, you see.'

'Oh, Jeanie.' Tom shuffles a few steps closer to her. 'I'm so sorry.'

If Jean's intention was to kill Glenda, Tom probably just saved his daughter's life – maybe all our lives. Because Jean won't shoot Tom's daughter in front of him. She cares too much about him. They always had a soft spot for each other. I suspected Jean was the reason Rosie left, that they were having an affair, but nobody knew for sure, and Jean stayed with her husband until he died last year. She has no other family, so when Donald threw himself off that building it left Jean all alone.

'Donald was a good lad,' Tom says. 'Why don't you come inside? We can talk about the good ol' days?'

'Not right now, Tommy. I've got some things to do. Why don't you go inside, and I'll come and find you when I'm finished, okay?'

Tom turns back to the house, and I'm about call out his name to keep him here – the only person who might prevent Jean from doing anything stupid – when he stops. Perhaps struck by a moment of clarity, he turns back to her. 'What's going on, Jeanie? What was all the shouting about? And who are all these people in my vegetable patch?' He points to Mark, Saeed, and finally Laura. 'And why is *she* giving Glenda thirty-five thousand pounds?'

'Shut up, Tom,' Glenda says.

'You shut up, Glenda. This is still my house and I demand to know what's going on! I heard Jeanie from the kitchen. She said lily-livered Laura is giving you thirty-five thousand pounds after you'd been stealing from them. I assume you're Laura?'

Laura nods but nobody answers.

When the silence stretches to breaking, I can't stand it any longer and speak up. 'It's complicated, Tom. Mark came over because he was angry about the boundary. Then Laura came over to tell Mark that Glenda was telling the truth about the land. Then Jean showed up with a gun, threatening to shoot everyone. That's what the neighbours are doing in your vegetable patch. And him?' I point to Laura and Mark's foreign friend. 'I have no idea who he is or what he's doing here.'

'What land?' Tom asks.

I wave a hand in the general direction of the summerhouse. 'That land, back there. Oliver Huntington-Whitney's extension wall was the boundary. And when Scott put in his summerhouse he built it past that, part-way inside your garden.'

'No, he didn't.'

Glenda steps in then. 'You're confused, Dad...'

She hasn't called him 'Dad' in ages; she's placating him. I don't blame her. If we live through tonight, we'll get the money from Mark and Laura, and this will all be over. I'm not sure how they've arrived at thirty-five thousand when the chartered land surveyor only suggested ten, but we'll take it if they're prepared to pay it. I can put back the money I took from Jason's university fund and cover his third-year fees as well. Much as I love Tom, I don't really want him fucking that up.

'You get confused a lot,' Glenda is saying. 'You won't remember now, but when Mum was here, the fence used to be all the way back there. The vegetable patch was much bigger, and the monkey puzzle tree was in our garden. You planted it when I was a kid, in the '70s, don't you remember?'

Tom looks up at the tree, towering over the far corner of the summerhouse, as if he's never seen it before.

'That's the boundary,' Glenda says. 'I'm just sorting it out, that's all. Laura's agreed to pay for the land, and we're going to sign a boundary agreement. Now, all you need to do is convince Jean that this is all a big misunderstanding. That we aren't bad people. Can you do that, Dad? She's got a gun. And she's already tried to shoot one of the neighbours with it.'

Glenda speaks to Tom as though he's a toddler, which makes my blood boil.

'Why would we sign *another* boundary agreement?' Tom asks. 'And I don't remember planting any monkey puzzle tree in the '70s. I don't even like monkey puzzle trees.'

'You have no memory of the tree because someone else planted it much later.'

We all turn from Tom to Laura's strange friend, who looks back at us calmly. 'As I said before, Glenda is lying about the tree.'

'Who are you?' she asks. 'Why don't you fuck off and mind your own business? Go back to mowing their lawn or whatever you were doing before you stuck your nose in our affairs.'

Laura and the man look at each other with confusion.

'Saeed's not our gardener,' Laura says. 'He's a neuroscientist and psychologist. He runs a private practice and works at the Sleep & Circadian Neuroscience Institute in town.'

Glenda blushes, and a surge of disgust makes me ashamed that she's my wife.

'A psychologist with a penchant for monkey puzzle trees,' Saeed says. 'And you are lying about the date it was planted.

Why is that? Clearly your father did not plant the tree. And this extension you speak of, when was that built?'

'1993,' Laura says. 'We have the architect's diagrams for it.'

'Well, then, the tree was planted around the same time.'

'Oh, what the fuck would you know?' Glenda spits.

'I know because I counted the whorls,' Saeed says. 'A monkey puzzle tree grows a new layer of branches each year – a whorl – and each whorl leaves a ring around the trunk. There are twenty-eight rings. That is how old the tree is. If it had been planted in the '70s it would be close to fifteen metres by now.'

When Saeed tied Mark and Laura's dog to the summerhouse, I watched him disappear around the corner. That's presumably what he was doing: ageing the tree.

He turns to Tom then. 'Sir, may I ask, why did you just say, *another* boundary agreement? Was one already signed?'

'Yes,' Tom says. 'When Rosie left – Rosie was my wife – I didn't have the money to buy her out. So when Oliver found out I was having to sell up, he asked to buy part of the garden. He gave me twenty thousand pounds.'

'Part of the garden?' I ask. 'Tom...how much of the garden did you give him?'

'Just a strip at the back, a metre or two. It wasn't worth anything like that, of course, but I think it was just an excuse. He wanted to help a friend, and he knew I would never take charity from him. So we had the new boundary drawn up and I sent it off to the Land Registry.'

'There's no boundary agreement lodged with the Land Registry,' Laura says.

'He's confused,' Glenda says. 'Tom never sold any land.'

I frown at Glenda. There's something off about her tone, a slight tremor I've never heard before. She's right that Tom gets muddled about current events, but he remembers the past very well. If he says there was a boundary agreement between him and Oliver Huntington-Whitney, I believe him.

Jean says, 'He's not confused. I remember, Tommy. I thought you were going to have to sell up and leave. Oliver coming to your rescue sticks in my mind like it was yesterday. Did you forget to post the agreement, Tommy, dear? You never were very good at finances and paperwork.'

Tom shakes his head. 'I thought I posted it. If I forgot, I have no idea where it went.'

'I bet you know where it is, don't you?' Jean holds the gun up to Glenda's head. 'I bet you found it, realised Tom had never posted it, and figured you could use it to blackmail the neighbours. You're an old hand at screwing people over for money, aren't you, Glenda Skinner? So, how about you tell everyone where it is, and then I might not shoot you.'

'Jeanie!' Tom says. 'What are you doing? Put that gun down. I don't know what's been going on while I was asleep, but clearly everyone's lost their minds. I'll find the boundary agreement, it'll be in my room somewhere, and that'll put an end to all this silliness. Just give me a chance to look, okay? Nobody's shooting anyone over a metre of land.'

As Tom shuffles back along the patio, the penny drops.

'You don't need to go in the house, Tom,' I say slowly. 'Glenda has it in her pocket. It's been in her pocket since the day Jason left for university. The day this whole obsession with the boundary started. You keep it in your pocket so nobody will ever stumble on it by accident. Isn't that right, Glenda?'

FORTY-EIGHT

GLENDA

Since the day I found the boundary agreement at the back of Tom's drawer, it's been burning a hole in my pocket. Now it sears my skin. We were so close.

Bloody Jean. Bloody Tom.

'You bitch!' Laura screams. 'Everything you did to us! Drugging Finn. Those thugs you sent to our house! And that man...do you have *any idea* what he did to me? All so you could blackmail us for thirty-five thousand pounds! And you were lying this whole time! What the fuck is wrong with you?'

'Glenda?' Gerald asks. 'Is any of that true?'

I keep quiet.

'It's all true,' Mark says. 'Scott offered Glenda five thousand pounds for the land while the sale was going through. She refused and demanded thirty-five.'

'Thirty-five!' Gerald glares at me. 'You told me it was ten!'

'We would have paid ten!' Mark says. 'But thirty-five was extortion. And when we wouldn't be blackmailed, she began threatening us. It started small: she broke the window in the summerhouse—'

'Actually, I broke your window,' Jean says. 'And I scratched your car, Glenda. As soon as Cynthia told me about your petty squabble, I knew it wouldn't take much to get you at each other's throats. As I said, I hoped you'd all kill each other. It's what you all deserve! You especially!' Jean points the gun at me. 'I've known you since you were a nasty little girl, and I knew you'd never stop. I knew how far you'd take it. But you surprised even me. I saw that Ricky at Laura's house; I was watching.'

'My Ricky?' Gerald asks.

'Yes,' Jean says. 'That thug stepbrother of yours brought his friends to Laura's house. I saw him that night. And I saw Glenda give them beer when it was over. But wasn't hiring Troy Cullen a bit below the belt, even for you, Glenda?'

'You can't prove that,' I say. 'It's all lies, Gerald. She's crazy. You can't believe a word that woman says.'

Jean digs in her back pocket for her phone, presses a few buttons and holds up a picture of me and Troy. 'I've been following you.'

I turn to Gerald and watch the penny drop. He says, '*I think the Hardmans are finally understanding what they're up against*...that's what you said to me, isn't it? *I think they'll be paying us soon*. What have you done, Glenda? Tell me you didn't...'

I open my mouth and close it again.

Jean pockets her phone. 'It's only partly about the money, isn't it, though? That, and the stuff you buy with it – new cars, designer handbags, putting Jason through university – but mostly, it's about the anguish and suffering you put people through. You enjoy it, don't you, Glenda? It's fun for you.'

Gerald pipes up again. 'Jean, I think you need to check your facts. She may have done some of the things you say – I have no idea who's lying and who's telling the truth any more

– but Glenda won the lottery. That's how she paid Jason's university fees. And the handbags aren't real, she gets them at the local market.'

'Oh, Gerald! Are you really that naïve? A person is twice as likely to be canonised a saint than win the lottery! And what about her new car? Why didn't you question where all the money was coming from, you stupid little man? You could have stopped it. You could have saved my son!'

Gerald looks at me. 'Glenda?'

I told him I'd won the car in an online competition, but I skim over that. 'I *did* win the lottery! Somebody has to win it. Why not me?'

A bullet whistles past my ear and the gun fizzes as if it's fitted with a silencer. Jean adjusts her aim. 'You tell one more lie and I'll end you.'

I hold up my hand as if I can stop a bullet with it. 'I don't know what you think happened, Jean, but either way, you can't prove anything.'

Jean reaches into her handbag and pulls out a whole handful of envelopes, dozens and dozens of them.

'Do you know what these are, Glenda? Letters. Bank statements. After Donald killed himself, it took a while for probate to go through, but then the balance of his account was supposed to come to me. Only there was no balance. It was overdrawn. Not only that, he had taken out loans against the house and never repaid them. Donald never spent a penny on himself, so I contacted the police to find out where all the money had gone, his life savings, the loans. Whose account do you think came up time and again? And who wrote him all these love letters filled with empty promises?'

Gerald's eyes bore into me, but I keep mine on Jean.

'He called me,' she says. 'Just before he jumped. He said he'd lost the court case with HMRC and had to pay them back everything from that contractor loan scheme.' Jean turns the gun on Mark. 'A scheme your company supported. He had one last hope, didn't he? He went to your father that day and begged him for help. All that money you and your father have, and you refused. You knew about the scheme he was in! You used that umbrella company for most of your contractors.'

Mark holds up a hand to Jean in the same way I did. As if the bullet going through his palm first might mitigate the damage. It seems silly now I'm watching him do it.

'I didn't know your son personally,' Mark says, his tone amicable, diplomatic, gentle. 'And I'm sorry for what happened. I'm sorry you lost him. But it had nothing to do with me, or my father. We helped a lot of our contractors out of that mess, paid out hundreds of thousands for those who took the settlement offer from HMRC. The only reason we didn't help Donald was because he was fighting the case against them, and we needed to wait for the outcome. But then we found out that Donald wasn't just avoiding tax. A couple of months before he died, we discovered he'd been skimming from the company and—'

'You're a liar!' Jean shouts, her voice rising an octave.

'I'm not lying.' Mark holds out both hands now to placate her. 'Donald had created dozens of fake suppliers and was invoicing us for work that never took place. A colleague looked into one of those suppliers and found them registered to an abandoned office. They brought it to Dad's attention, and he organised a full financial investigation into your son. He'd stolen over fifty thousand from the company.'

Oh, Mark, Mark, Mark. You gorgeous, silly boy. You don't tell a woman her son's a thief when she's got a gun pointed at your head.

The bullet fizzes, and Mark howls. He clasps his face, blood spewing between his fingers, and totters sideways into Laura. They both go down together and Mark's head cracks on the side of Tom's tomato bed. When his hands go limp and fall from his face, Laura screams. Mark's pretty left eye is a lake of red where the bullet went straight into his brain. He lies against the railway sleepers, twisted into a strange angle, with blood oozing down his face and seeping into the grass.

That's a shame. He was nice to look at.

Laura grabs him and shakes him, screaming his name over and over.

'Get up,' Jean says, 'or you're next.'

'Jeanie...' Tom moves cautiously towards her, as if he might be next in line for a bullet. 'What are you doing, my love? Donald wouldn't have wanted this.'

Jeanie turns the gun on him. 'Back off, Tommy. I don't want to have to shoot you as well.'

Jean won't shoot Dad. And at least all Laura did was fuck Mark to get all that Hardman money, then throw in the towel and agree to hand over a ton of it to me. I fucked Jean's son for tens of thousands, so I suspect if anyone's next it's me, not Laura. Only Laura won't stop wailing.

'Get up!' Waving the gun, Jean screams so loudly that even I flinch. Only Laura isn't listening to her. Personally, if I were her and Jean had just shot my boyfriend in the face, I'd pay attention. 'Get up! Get up! Get up!'

Laura still doesn't move; she doesn't even look up from Mark's body. So Jean shoots her in the stomach, and she folds over like a sandwich bag. That shuts her up. She just sits there quietly, bent double, clutching her stomach.

Then Jean turns the gun back on me. 'Seventy-five grand. That's what he owed HMRC. But you already know that don't you, Glenda? The police checked his phone logs, got a warrant for the last calls he made, and, just before he called me, he called his girlfriend. But that's something else you already know, isn't it? The police played me that call. He begged you for help, begged you for some of the money back. And what did you do instead... when you found out the extent of his debts? Twenty years of empty promises. Twenty years of stealing from him. And the moment he needed you, you dumped him! I didn't even know Donald had a girlfriend. All those years he managed to keep you a secret from me because he was so ashamed. Because he knew I wouldn't approve of him having an affair with a married woman. And in every one of those letters, for every one of those years, you promised him you would leave Gerald as soon as Jason went off to university. It's why he gave you the money for his fees!'

Gerald is staring at me, his face a wrinkle of confusion.

'She's lying, Gerald.'

Another bullet whizzes past my ear. 'I. Don't. Lie!' Jean throws the bank statements and letters on the grass in front of Gerald. There are so many of them. All in my handwriting, all addressed to Donald.

The way Gerald looks at me then. He's never looked at me like that before. But it's far worse when he looks away. Face turned to the ground, he's lost in thought. Is he processing every lie I've ever told him? There've been so many. I wonder which he'll start with. Will he start at the bottom and run through the million white ones? Or will he start at the top with Donald and Jason, our little miracle?

The life-altering lie.

He starts at the top.

Gerald storms across the garden towards me with his fists clenched. For a moment I think he's going to punch me, but then he snatches my spade from the tomato bed and raises it above his head.

He'd never hit me. But, just in case, I take a few steps backwards and my heel crushes something soft. There's a snap, and I look down at my shoe.

I'm standing on Mark's dead fingers.

When I realise that, I step back so quickly, I trip and fall on my backside.

Spade aloft, Gerald bears down on me. I think he's actually going to do it. I think I've pushed him too far. I lift my arm to protect myself and the shaft of my spade comes crashing down on my forearm. There's a crack so loud I can't tell if it's my arm or the wooden spade handle that splintered. But then I look at the sleeve of my blouse, at the bone sticking through the fabric, the white cloth soaking red.

I scream.

Gerald takes another stride towards me, and with my one good arm I scrabble backwards across the grass. I grab one of the metal stakes holding up Mark and Laura's fence and try to use it to lift myself to my feet. Only, when that stupid mutt got caught up in it, he bent the stakes over, and my weight only pushes them to the ground.

With no purchase, I fall into the orange plastic webbing.

And then Gerald lifts the spade again.

FORTY-NINE

LAURA

Nine months later

THE MOVING VAN arrived at midday on Friday.

Burning with curiosity, I ran out of excuses to go out on to the driveway – I collected the post, put out the recycling, went back with a missed Coke can – but I didn't even catch a glimpse of the new neighbours at Oleander House. I did the same on Saturday until there was no rubbish left to take out. And there's no post on Sundays, but I checked the box yesterday anyway. We do sometimes get village fliers.

I won't rest until I know it's not another Glenda.

It's hard to believe she's gone. But it's even harder to believe that mild-mannered Gerald beat her to death with her own garden spade. If he hadn't, though, I think Jean would have shot her anyway. Whether the bullet would have killed her, who knows, but Gerald took care of the job. It turned out he came from a very violent family. I guess it was in his genes, bubbling beneath the surface for a lifetime, until Glenda's lies set it to boil.

While Gerald was beating Glenda to death, Jean turned the gun on herself. Stuck it right in her eye and pulled the trigger. Poor Tom collapsed then. A brain haemorrhage, the papers said.

It never did make sense that someone like Jean was able to get her hands on a gun. As real as it looked, and as terrified as we all were that day, it turned out to be a BB-gun with steel pellets. Still lethal if you shoot yourself in the eye at close range the way Jean did. But at a distance of a few metres they aren't deadly.

Mark lost his right eye and suffered a concussion when he hit the railway sleeper, but he's okay. He wears one of those leather eye patches and it's pretty sexy. Especially when he's in his black shirt and trousers, tan shoes and belt.

But the absolute certainty that he was dead will never leave me.

After the story hit the papers, Scott and Emily came to see us and it finally made sense why she was so strange that day we went to view Primrose Cottage. Although she was stunned at how it all turned out, she wasn't entirely surprised. Apparently Glenda had made their time at the cottage a living hell with myriad complaints about music playing too loud, or too many cars parked on the road whenever they had a party. Mowing lawns too late in the evening or too early in the morning. Basically, anything Glenda could think of to complain about.

It turned out that Scott and Emily's first buyers knew Glenda. They had an allotment in the centre of town and when Tom got sick and she took his place on the committee, she made their lives miserable. They ended up giving up a plot they'd loved and tended for a decade because Glenda had sucked all the joy out of it. So the moment they'd laid eyes on her, realised she would be their next-door neighbour, they'd pulled out of the sale.

Emily felt guilty about not telling us who we were moving next door to. She couldn't have foreseen how bad it would get, but the telltale signs were there. We meet for drinks now and then, when they're passing by the village, and they're becoming good friends.

With Glenda gone, everyone can breathe. Perhaps even Gerald has found some peace, even if it is in prison. Poor man.

I play Saeed's velvet tones in my head and – as often as I can – I try to stay in the present moment, silence the voice that replays the past.

Usually I'd walk Finn in a circle around the village, but this morning I've walked out past Oleander House and doubled back. It's paid off, because now there's a woman standing by the gate chatting to the postman. I slow down, hoping to perfectly time my passing by with the end of their conversation.

She's about my age, with close-cropped brown hair, the kind of style that needs a pretty face to pull off, and she does. A tiny head pokes out of a grey papoose wrapped tightly around her. And her earth-mother vibe – the way she touches the postman on the arm, smiling broadly – together with something warm in their exchange makes me like her instantly.

She turns slightly, clearly intent on heading back into the house, but then Charlie holds out his hand, presumably introducing himself. She says, 'I'm...' something or other that I don't catch.

Anxious to stop her from going inside, I speed up, wave and call out, 'Hi, Charlie!' But I'm smiling at her when I say it. I want her to know I'm not a neighbour from hell. Charlie waves back but then goes on his way; there are only so many conversations he can be dragged into before his post round runs late into his afternoon.

She waits for me.

A good sign.

I hurry to her gate, heart fluttering as I ravel and unravel Finn's lead around my hand. I'm not there yet – still uncomfortable with conversation – but I'm working on it. My speech and language therapist said I would quickly sort out the wheat from the chaff. True friends would prove their worth and others would dissolve into acquaintances who never had my back to begin with. They were just never tested.

He's right. It's already started happening.

I do exactly what he taught me. I sign my name as I say it, then hold out my hand for her to shake. No embarrassment, no disguises, no explanations. *My name is Laura and I'm deaf.*

He said that, before other people could accept the new me, I had to accept her first. To be as kind and patient with her as I would be with anyone else in my situation. Because most people I meet will be just as kind and patient. Anyone who isn't is ignorant and not worth the extra time and effort it takes to converse with me. Although I can read lips fairly well now, I sign not only to communicate that I'm deaf to hearing people but also for practice.

The woman doesn't take my hand.

She stares at me with that familiar expression of shock I've become accustomed to over the past nine months. At least most people usually make some attempt to conceal it. My new neighbour doesn't even try. Resignedly, I wait a second or two for her to launch into shouting and over-exaggerating her gestures as if I'm blind as well as deaf. That's what usually follows that expression of shock.

Only she doesn't do either.

She signs.

'I'm Alex.'

And then I'm the one in shock. What are the chances?

Alex speaks then, but she uses Cued Speech to help me read her lips. 'My daughter is at Montisford,' she says. 'That's why we moved here.'

Montisford is the only mainstream school within driveable distance from Oxford with a specialist deaf unit for both children and adults. It's only ten minutes from Clay Norton, and it's one of the best in the country. I often wonder if I was supposed to end up here all along.

Initially, while I was finishing *Malikbay*, I could only attend Montisford one evening a week and my progress was slow. Now *Malikbay* is finished, and I don't run myself into the ground with my work any more, I go three evenings a week. I even help out with events for the children at the weekends. It gives my life a balance I'd never realised was missing.

After Jean shot Mark, my hearing went completely, and never returned. And, with no time to adjust, I had no choice but to rely completely on Steve Banks to finish the last four episodes. I've never heard the end of my play, but I'm fine with that. From reading the reviews, nobody can tell the difference between our work. And, just as Mark promised, my name is front and centre. Steve never said a single word about the billing.

We made a connection in the conference room that day, and it's only got stronger. His passion and enthusiasm for *Malikbay* never wavered. And my losing my hearing completely, so suddenly, threw us together overnight.

But it was the attack by Troy Cullen that really cemented our bond. He'd seen me leave Hardman Studios in the dark and rain that night. He was going to offer to walk me to my car but, knowing how I felt about him at the time, he didn't want me to get the wrong idea. And let's face it, given my fierce independence back then, I probably would have said no even if I hadn't found him slimy and flirtatious. So he followed me instead. He hung back to make sure I didn't realise he was there, then lost me in a crowd of people on the main road. When he found me again, in the worst state of my life, he took care of me. He drove me home, explained everything to Mark, made sure I was okay before he left. Steve Banks turned out to be the opposite person to the one I'd taken him for.

Malikbay has been a huge success. The public really got behind my female character posing as a male warrior. They love all the challenges she faces in a violent new city. Listeners call her 'the new Lara Croft'. In fact, it's been so popular it's been commissioned for film and is due out the year after next. The *Game of Thrones* adaptation Steve and I both wanted so badly has paled into insignificance for us. Chad insisted on a second season of *Malikbay*.

I never would have thought it back then, but I think Season Two will be even better than Season One. Saeed was right about creativity being the most important part of the process and I am more creative than I was before. It's not just that I'm no longer easily distracted; there's an extraordinary depth in the silence, a rabbit hole all of its own. And what I find down there surprises even me.

Steve and I work together on developing the plot, characters, and writing the script. Then I annotate that with my ideas for the sound design. Steve peppers in his own and does all the monkey work on the mechanics of implementing them. I miss editing the dialogue, but Steve describes the actors' performances in such detail, it's as if I have actually heard it. He's even learned to use Cued Speech so it's easier for me to read his lips. Our process works like a charm. I never thought I'd hear myself think the words: I adore Steve Banks. I absolutely love working with him. He's here all the time, and so is Saeed.

Saeed is learning to sign as fast as Mark and there's a great deal of competition between them. They're like brothers. I keep trying to fix him up with friends from Montisford, but he won't have it. I think he's already in love. I think he's waiting for someone, but he won't tell me who.

He was also right about something else: the euphoria from *Malikbay*'s success didn't last. It lasted no longer than those headphones that cost as much as my car. But learning that brought with it a strange relief. Now I just enjoy the work without worrying about its potential success or failure. I know neither will stay with me for very long.

What never wears off is the euphoria from working with the children at Montisford.

I sign to Alex, 'I'm at Montisford three evenings a week. How old is your daughter?'

'Eleven,' Alex says. 'She was born deaf and has attended deaf schools up till now. But she wanted to go to a mainstream school with resource provision, so we moved here. You live in the village?'

'Right there.' I point to Primrose Cottage. 'We're neighbours.'

Alex breaks into a wide smile. 'What a relief,' she says. 'Our last neighbours were a bloody nightmare! Do you want to come in for a cuppa?'

'I'd love to. But what about Finn?'

'No problem, I love dogs. We have three, but they're out with the dog-walker right now.'

I follow her up the path and stop at her front door, bending down to take off my shoes.

She touches me lightly on the shoulder to get my attention. 'Don't worry about that,' she says. 'The dogs can't take their paws off.'

And I know right then and there that I'm going to love my neighbour.

Maggie has an impossible choice.
Stay and protect her family from the stalker in the woods?
Or return to Rose and help fight the doctors who want to
remove life support from their sister, Daisy?

There's a main at Daisy's bedside.
He says Rose can trust him.
But he's telling her disturbing things about her
new husband that can't possibly be true.

Two strangers start the clock.
It's ticking for three devoted sisters.

THREE. TWO. ONE. THE COUNTDOWN HAS BEGUN.

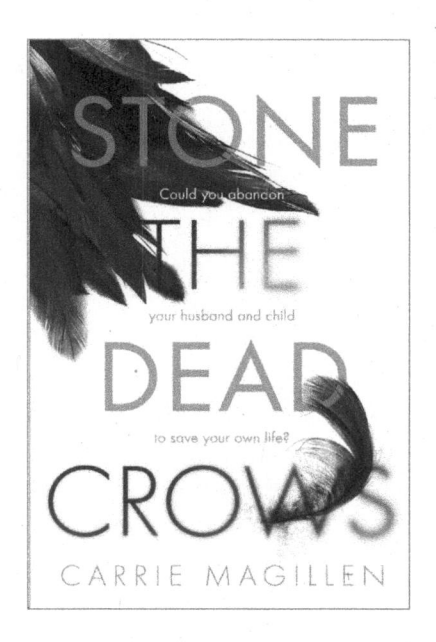

Read the first chapter of Carrie Magillen's
thrilling second novel overleaf…

ONE

MAGGIE

THERE'S SOMETHING in the trees.

I can't see it, but I can feel it. Its presence has a weight; the air is heavy with it.

We're not alone.

Ahead, the forest path climbs, narrowing on the horizon where the trees huddle, colluding in some conspiracy I'm not a part of.

The blood pulsing in my ears blocks out every other sound. And, although we're not moving, it's as if our fear propels us along the path towards its vanishing point on the skyline.

If we reach it, we'll disappear.

The trees crowd in, herding us in that direction, and I don't want to go. I'm afraid to stay. And I'm afraid to run.

A twig snaps.

I spin around, expecting to find someone standing there, but there's no one. The path is empty. And yet, instinctively, I reach behind me. My palms find Alfie's shoulders and I pull him close, making myself a wall between him and whatever's out there. He hides his face in the backs of my thighs as if he senses the danger too.

Mist clings to the trees and to my left and right, like a petrified army, their silhouetted torsos fade into the distance. The scent of damp pine, moss and resin is cloying.

It's hard to breathe.

My jeans stick to my legs, and beneath my jumper my T-shirt's damp against my spine. I don't need this wax jacket or these Gore-Tex-lined boots; I'm too hot. Light-headed. Running a hand up the back of my neck, I lift the hair beneath my wax hat and pull it away from my skin. What little breeze there is barely cools me, so I let it go and its razored ends graze my shoulders. I tuck it behind my ears which burn as though someone is talking about me.

As I scan the shadows – the dark spaces between the lichen-covered trunks – my voice trembles. 'Is someone there?'

Alfie slips his fingers, marshmallow-soft, into my hand. They're freezing. Somewhere at the back of my mind I register that his gloves are in my pocket, but I can't drag my attention from the forest. Cold hands can wait; his safety can't.

Something – someone – is out there.

Not only can I feel him, I can still hear him. His breath comes thick and fast, rasping. It drowns out the heartbeat in my ears. His eyes are fixed on me, I know it. They travel up and down my body, clawing like fingernails that leave red marks in my white skin.

This is private land. There are no public footpaths and I've never seen a soul trespassing here. But, because it's privately owned, it's not as well maintained as the local country parks and nature reserves. The trees are closely packed, the undergrowth dense with rotting leaves and fallen branches. The air is musty and dank, starved of sunlight by the crowded canopy.

Another twig snaps and I spin again. Gripping Alfie's hand, I take a few steps backwards in the direction of home, and his soft flesh squirms against my palm. I'm squeezing him too tightly. But I can't let go. Left and right, right and left, my eyes sweep the empty wood for the slightest movement between the trees.

Nothing.

But still it breathes.

He breathes.

I take another few steps away but I don't run. I'm afraid to turn my back on whoever is out there.

'Cairo!' I shout her name into the canopy and the crows take flight. She disappeared between the trees ten minutes ago when she caught sight of a deer. 'Cairo, come!'

She won't come.

Cairo's a Blenheim Cavalier King Charles spaniel, chestnut-red and white, quiet and fragile. She spends most of her life sleeping on a large pillow by the wood-burner in the cabin. But if she catches sight of prey, even ten times her size, that fragility evaporates. She bolts into the trees, disappears in a flash, and stays on the hunt for hours. She's her own mistress, responds to commands when she feels like it, and doles out affection on her own terms. She's more cat than dog.

I whistle but the sound doesn't carry. In my mind's eye, my silver dog-whistle, on its leather lanyard, swings from a hook on the storeroom door back at the cabin. Luc always laughs at me. With his melodic intonation (a tinge of the French Loire Valley where he lived till he was five), every T and S ringing with a sherbet-sweet-and-sour tone, he says cooling hot soup isn't whistling. Then, with two fingers in his mouth, he'll whistle loud enough to hurt my ears.

I wish he were here now.

The breathing gets louder, draws closer, as if the stranger's lips are pressed to my ears. Then, like a crackling fire, dead leaves crunch underfoot. The sound comes from the trees to our right.

Finally, I turn and run.

The stranger's breath rasps in my ears as I drag Alfie along behind me. Heavy exhalations chase us down the narrow woodland path, but I can no longer tell if it's coming from the trees or my own lungs. Fear clouds my judgement and I swear I hear my name on the wind, trapped in bubbles of sound, caught in his breath.

Alfie can't keep up. And when his little legs trip and stumble, forcing me to grip his hand even tighter, I'm convinced his wrist will snap. So, still running, I scoop him up and stagger a few paces, balancing him on my hip until I find my rhythm again. I'm out of shape, carrying the last stubborn pounds of pregnancy fat along with the child who put it there. And tears of anger sting my eyes at my inability to get him out of danger any faster when I've had more than enough time to get fit again.

Ahead of us, the trees break and, finding a burst of energy from deep inside, I sprint for the lake. I can just make it out in the distance. When we finally stumble into the clearing it's as if the stranger's stale breath reaches out for us: a disembodied smoke-grey hand, determined to pull us back into the forest's darkness. Twisting to look behind, I stumble and fall to my knees.

The path between the trees is empty. The wood is still, the breathing silenced.

There's nobody there.

Alfie squirms in my arms, desperate to be set free, and I don't have the energy to fight him. So, reluctantly, I release my wriggling child, who breaks free of my embrace and runs for the lake, his clumsy wellington boots crunching the gravel. As if nothing has happened, he points to the still water and says, 'Stones, Mumma, stones,' with his eighteen-month-old lisp that sounds as if he's blowing bubbles.

And suddenly I feel stupid. I stare back down the path, searching for the slightest movement, but there's nothing there.

'Stones, Mumma!'

'Not now, sweetie.' I catch up with him and take his hand again. 'Let's go and say hi to Daddy.'

Alfie yanks his hand away and totters sulkily along the lakeshore towards the cabin.

I follow.

And all the way, I check behind me.

TWO

ROSE

FINGERS GRASPING the door handle, I pause at the unexpected sight. The open integral blind in the door's small, square window reveals a strange man looming over Daisy. He's dressed in a black shirt with a mandarin collar, and is clearly not a doctor.

Tenderly, almost lovingly, he brushes her red curls back from her face, and although I can't hear a sound through the door I know he's talking to her because his lips are moving.

He leans further forward and his shirt falls open slightly; the four contrasting red buttons that end beneath his breastbone are just for show. He has dark chest hair, a salt and pepper close-cropped beard, and salt and pepper hair. He's strikingly handsome but not in a conventional way: soft around the edges, with a kind face.

I've never seen him before.

Who is he?

Nobody talks to my sister but me.

All right, that's not strictly true. Zesiro, one of the hospital porters, and Dionne, the catering assistant for this floor – they speak to Daisy. But they're different. They're special. They're born of that rare breed of humans who genuinely, deeply care about other people. Even people they don't know. But they don't have long conversations with her like this, they just utter a few words of encouragement.

Nobody *really talks* to Daisy but me.

My sister makes people uncomfortable.

Because she doesn't talk back.

So who is this man? What could he possibly have to say to her that's taking so long? And why isn't *he* uncomfortable?

There are two things I know about my sister: she doesn't have any friends left; and there's no way on God's earth she would have formed a romantic attachment before ending up in here.

I'm about to throw the door open when he brushes back her hair again, his evident affection stopping me. I pause – I don't want to deprive Daisy of this rare moment. Her bed faces the door but slightly off to the left, so I lean sideways to get a better view, my nose almost pressed to the cool glass. A tug of longing, as if I'm outside peering in on a warm room, pulls at the base of my ribs. But then my phone pings in my handbag, a text message alert, and I duck as if I've been caught snooping through someone's kitchen window. I back away, keeping my head low. Once I know I can't be seen, I pretend I wasn't spying and stride towards the door, opening it as if I have no idea anyone's in there.

The door's squeaking swoosh startles the man and he stands bolt upright, turning towards me. I guess he didn't hear my phone after all.

'Can I help you with something?'

The undertone of hostility wasn't intentional and I almost apologise for it. It's all those wires and tubes, stuck on Daisy with adhesive pads or pinned into her with needles:

they bring out a fierce protective side of me that I didn't know existed.

As the man comes out from behind her bed, I glance down at his shirt. It almost reaches his knees. Beneath it, he's wearing matching black cotton trousers and sturdy leather sandals. It's far too early in the year for sandals.

'I am Dr Sharif.' He holds out his hand for me to shake. But I don't take it; my mind is still reeling. Who is he? And what's he doing in Daisy's room? She's been stuck in that bed for three years and I've never seen this man – or any man for that matter – visit her before.

But then I register he said he was a doctor. He must be off duty.

Across his outstretched forearm, exposed to the elbow by the rolled-up sleeves of his shirt, thick veins charm their way over taut muscles. He has a slim but strong frame. Prominent biceps and pectoral muscles strain the seams of his thin cotton shirt. And he has a conspicuous Adam's apple.

When my eyes finally meet his, my presence of mind returns; I have no idea how much time has passed. But, in spite of my rudeness, he's still holding out his hand for me to shake, almost laughing at the discomfort.

'Sorry...' I take the hand. 'Sorry. I'm Rose.'

Although he's clearly very strong, his grip is surprisingly gentle, his skin soft. 'Of course! Rose. Daisy's younger sister. She spoke of you often. You were very close, I understand. I seem to recall her saying you were not just sisters but best friends as well.'

And the moment I hear the precision in his words, the lyrical, almost Dickensian phrasing, all the pennies drop. He *is* a doctor, but not of medicine.

My mind's eye drifts back three years. It fixes on the clean lines of Daisy's lips as this man's name trips from them. In Daisy's pruned and serious tone, his name has rung in my ears dozens of times.

When she was still with us.

When she was still conscious.

When her life was so horribly grave.

Her description of the fine-looking Indian man who pronounced every word in full comes back to me. I remember her laughing about it with affection – and she rarely laughed back then. Back then, this man was the only thing keeping her together.

'Saeed,' I say. 'Saeed Sharif. Daisy's therapist.'

'Psychologist. You must have a good memory for names.'

'She talked about you a lot.'

My phone pings in my handbag, reminding me of the unopened text message. And, realising he hasn't let go of my hand, Saeed says, 'Oh! I am sorry. You can have that back now.'

I don't have to look in the mirror to know there's an orb of red in each cheek. So I brush my hair back, lift my face and pretend I'm standing in the snow, a cool breeze blowing over my face. It works almost every time to stop the perpetual cycle of a chronic blush: blushing because you're embarrassed and then embarrassed by the blushing. It doesn't help that I have pale pink lips, ice-blonde hair and baby-powder skin; I wear my emotions like clown paint. But over the years I have learned to manage my condition.

Dr Sharif points at Daisy. 'They say the stimulation of both sound and touch are helpful... I hope you do not mind—?'

'No, of course not.' He's worried he's overstepped the therapist's line by touching Daisy, but I'm grateful he's doing everything he can. We both look at her then and I say, 'She stopped breathing on Monday. They've been keeping her on the ventilator while they run tests.'

'I know,' he says. 'I am sorry. I went to see Dr Anderson when I arrived. He told me that Daisy's condition has worsened.'

He picks up her chart, hanging from the foot of her bed, and runs a finger down the page, nodding as he reads. Clearly the chart makes sense to him when, to me, it's written in an alien language. Of course, he could be showing off, trying to impress me with his intelligence by pretending he understands it. But he doesn't strike me as the type of man who would do something like that. He seems grounded, comfortable in his own skin, certain of himself but not conceited.

'You're a proper doctor?'

He looks up at me with a broad smile.

'Sorry...' I add. Beneath concealer, my cheeks burn, my heart flutters, and my hands tremble as if I've committed some unforgivable sin for which I'm to be sent to the scaffold. 'You know what I mean.'

When he nods, a disproportionate relief washes over me, as if he's exonerated me. What *is* that? I've always been a shy and flighty sort of person – like a robin – not afraid of people but cautious and careful – yet these days I'm on eggshells all the time. Self-conscious about everything I say and do. Is it Daisy? The overwhelming emotion of being here?

I wish I were more like her: bold and self-assured. But I'm not. And stupidity is a self-fulfilling prophecy: walking on eggshells at the thought of something stupid coming out of my mouth always makes something stupid come out of my mouth.

Yet Dr Sharif doesn't seem to mind. He says, 'I *was* a proper doctor. In a previous life. A neurosurgeon. I switched to psychology and neuroscience three years into my speciality training.'

'Why?' I blush again, unprovoked, and do the exercises – snow and cool breezes – while trying to keep my mind on the conversation.

'I prefer the mystery of the mind over its biology.'

'I see. I think I would too. I wouldn't want to be cutting up brains. It's icky.'

He laughs.

'Daisy's chart makes sense to you, then?' I ask.

'It does. And I believe this is only a temporary glitch. They will perform a tracheotomy if she needs the breathing tube for too long – it is easier to maintain – but I suspect, when they remove the tube, she will breathe on her own again. There are no changes to her MRI or CT. And in fact her EEG shows an increase in brain activity, not a decrease.'

He looks more closely at the chart and then flips the pages back and forth, cross-referencing something that makes his eyebrows draw together and a deep crease form between them.

'What's wrong?'

He stares at the chart.

'Dr Sharif?'

He glances up at me, then back at the chart again. 'Oh. Nothing. Just...um...'

'Just?'

'Nothing.' He smiles. 'There is nothing to worry about here. It is all good.' He hangs the chart back on the end of the bed.

'That's a relief. I was so worried when she stopped breathing. I don't know what I'd do without Daisy.' I move to the bed and straighten her blankets even though they're straight already; it's not as if she tosses and turns.

After a moment of uneasy silence, I fill the void by saying, 'You're not at all what I imagined. Daisy never said you were so...'

Eggshells cut the soles of my feet. I'm doing it again: speaking before my brain is in gear and having to check myself before the rest of the sentence falls out. And now I have no idea how to finish it without sounding like a silly schoolgirl. I'm not sure it *is* Daisy making me feel this way. And I don't think it's Dr Sharif either. On the contrary, I feel calm in his company – calmer than I've felt around anyone in a very long time. At the same time, it's as though he's altered the chemical balance of the air in the room and I can't quite catch my breath.

'So...*Indian?*' he rescues me with a boyish smile.

'Yes,' I lie. 'She never said you were from India.'

'Rajasthan.' He moves to stand on the opposite side of Daisy's bed, his movement intentional. As if he senses my need for protection, for a barrier between me and the strange man I've never met. 'Although I have been in England most of my life.'

'I've never been. To Rajasthan, I mean. Of course I've been to England!' I fiddle with the blankets again, face burning at my own idiocy, then add, 'I've never even seen pictures. But I've always thought it sounded romantic.'

'It is. The Water Palace, the Palace of Winds, Mehrangarh. You should go some time.'

I laugh. The idea of Nathan taking me anywhere like India seems absurd. Paris is more his style. Monaco. Vienna. 'One day. Maybe.' Then I ask, 'So what brings you to the hospital? Why have you come to see Daisy?'

'I come every week. Usually on a Friday – her regular lunchtime appointment – but a patient no longer needs this slot, and it is easier to visit Daisy on my way home. So for the last few weeks I have come on a Thursday afternoon.'

'Committed, or cured?' Oh, God. What kind of question is that?

'Cured, actually. It turned out there was nothing wrong with her. At least, nothing a radical exorcism could not cure.'

'You perform exorcisms too?'

'Sometimes.' He laughs. 'Metaphorically.'

'Of course...metaphorically...I didn't imagine...' I pick up one of Daisy's ginger curls and twirl it around my finger, mesmerised by its orange-peel vibrancy and shine. My mind races and time stretches until I finally blurt out the question that's been plaguing my mind for three years.

'Do you think she did it on purpose?'

'What?'

'Took sleeping pills and underdosed on her insulin?'

My question hangs in the air for a moment, then Saeed says, 'I am sorry, Rose. I have no idea. It came as a shock to me too. I saw her just two days before she was admitted and observed no suicidal tendencies. On the contrary, she was very much at peace. I cannot say much, obviously, but she said she had found happiness again. That makes me think it was a mistake. If she had wanted to kill herself she would have taken the whole bottle of pills and no insulin at all. Perhaps she had not calibrated her glucometer for some time and the pills were because she was having trouble sleeping.'

I reach out and touch his arm. 'I can't tell you what a comfort it is to hear you say that. All these years, I've wondered whether it was my fault, whether she was crying out for help and I just didn't hear it.'

'It is not your fault. Do not even think it. When she first came to me, she was broken. I remember the day she first walked into my office: I thought she was ill. Physically, I mean. She was so pale, so fragile. But after a year of sessions she was finding her way again. If she did do this to herself and either one of us could have seen it coming, it should have been me, not you. I *have* to believe it was an accident. If I thought...'

His voice trails off and I understand why he can't say the words. The guilt is too much. And now I know what he's doing here, why he comes to see her every week even though, now, he's the only one doing the talking...

Sly Trap for a Fox

**Could you murder in cold blood
to save the life of a stranger?**

Diane is trapped in her apartment. Four years ago,
a near-fatal car crash left her with crippling agoraphobia.

But when another car goes over the embankment at
Cruickshank's Fell, she suspects her own brush with death
was no accident. Unless Diane confronts her fears and
escapes before it's too late, the next woman will die.

How far will she go to save the life of a stranger?

How far would you go?
Find out by downloading your **FREE** e-book from
carriemagillen.com

Available now!

GRIPPING audiobooks for
When He's Not Here and *Stone the Dead Crows*

SLY
Could you murder in cold blood
TRAP
FOR A
to save the life of a stranger?
FOX
CARRIE MAGILLEN
WHEN
Six seconds
HE'S
Pick one
NOT
Your husband or your child
HERE
CARRIE MAGILLEN
STONE
THE
DEAD
One secret
CROWS
CARRIE MAGILLEN
YOU'R
RIGH
NEXT
DOOR
CARRIE MAGILL

ACKNOWLEDGEMENTS

FIRST AND ALWAYS to you, reader, for buying and reading this book. Without you, it's a heart with no beat. A special thank you to everyone who read the others in the series, left wonderful reviews (yes, I read every single one), and propelled them up the charts. And an extra special thanks to those who wrote to say they loved them and hounded me for more: this one's for you.

Heartfelt thanks and best wishes to Carly Weyers and Sarah Tubert at *What the Deaf?* Although the story ends by the time Laura has lost her hearing, your open honesty and candid discussions really helped to write those moments and, since it's impossible to truly fathom your world without living in it, I can only hope I did them justice.

Although this novel is a work of fiction and all the characters and events are products of my imagination, the legal and emotional truths expressed in this book are absolutely real. In the UK, it's not fiction that your neighbour can simply walk on to your property, claim they own it, and attempt to extort money from you without the police or Crown Prosecution Service lifting a finger to stop them. It's not fiction that solicitors will advise you to pay your extortionists, nor that you could lose your house in legal bills attempting to prove you own your own land. It's not fiction that it's the perfect crime with no jail time where the victim is forced to pay. If you live in the UK and don't have precise measurements in your deeds, but you do get on with your neighbours, for all that is good and true, I urge you to sign a boundary agreement with them specifying the extent of each property in clear and certain terms. You could save every owner who comes after you the agony of a boundary dispute.

And, with that in mind, I'd like to dedicate this novel to every reader who has ever had neighbours whose life's mission it was to make theirs a living hell. I feel your pain.

On a lighter note, I'd like to thank my phenomenal editor, Linda McQueen. Not only is she incredibly talented, she's also a sparkling human being and, after four years of working together, one of my closest friends as well. So that's a real plus for me! I love you, wonderful lady. You've pulled up a chair and made yourself at home in my heart.

Thank you again, Charley Chapman, for your meticulous proofreading and attention to detail. I can't wait for the next one because it's always a joy. As I always say, all errors are mine; the lovely Linda and Charley don't make mistakes, they just do their best to catch them.

To Mark Read, my gifted designer, who keeps coming up with beautiful covers while indulging my pernickety tweaks! You have a heart of gold, the patience of an angel, and an eye for haunting beauty. Sunflowers next year!

To the phenomenal Douglas Kean for your support with the audiobooks and passing the torch so generously in retirement. I'm so lucky to have found such a talented producer whose company is an absolute joy.

For my husband, Darrell, who continues to support me through this rollercoaster writing life and who, despite not liking fiction, reads my books anyway!

For my best friend, Ayeesha Menon, for all our wonderful walks in the woods where we hammer out plots and gossip about our characters as if they're real people. For reading my drafts, being honest when I screw up, and for being one of the most beautiful people I have the fortune to know.

Thank you to my wonderful writers' group, without whom I wouldn't be where I am. To Luke, for talking through plots until it gets dark in Australia and to Shady, Elisa, Madelaine and Tilly for reading drafts and buoying me up on the choppy seas of the writing life. Thank heaven I chose Wollongong over Melbourne; I'd be lost without you all.

Thank you, Mavis, for making me feel like a writer the first day I stepped into your classroom and for every day since when you've championed me as if I'm Stephen King instead of Carrie Magillen!

To Stephen and Darren for keeping me upright while making me laugh until I fall down (nothing to do with too many beers in Cambridge, obviously).

To Teresa and Stella for being my best friends and biggest (totally biased) fans. I love you girls to the moon and back.

And, as always, for Nick. My angel-sister, my beautiful girl. I know you're looking down on me, kicking me up the ass every time I procrastinate! I miss you every day.

On a final note: Laura's radio play, *Malikbay*, is a nod to *Tumanbay* by John Scott Dryden and Mike Walker. It's far and away my favourite radio drama, a fiction podcast on an epic scale where, as Laura says of her own work, *Game of Thrones* meets *Lawrence of Arabia*. If you enjoy listening to fiction, or have never heard a radio drama before, head over to Spotify, Audible or BBC Sounds and pick this up. You won't regret it.

CARRIE MAGILLEN spent fifteen years as a computer engineer working for IBM and Sun Microsystems, all the while with a yellowing copy of *Plot* by Ansen Dibell on her bookshelf. She left IT in 2006 and studied creative writing at Webster University in the Netherlands, Wollongong University in Australia, and Winchester University in England. She lives in Hampshire with her husband and two American cocker spaniels.

Her debut novel, *When He's Not Here*, was a No.1 bestseller in 2020, and her sophomore novel, *Stone the Dead Crows*, was a Silver Falchion Finalist for Best Thriller. You can download Carrie's free novella, *Sly Trap for a Fox*, from her website. *You're Right Next Door* is her fourth novel.

Carrie loves hearing from readers and you can reach her via her website:

carriemagillen.com